Saving Wishes

by GJ Walker-Smith

Saving Wishes
Print Edition

© 2013 GJ Walker-Smith

Cover by Scarlett Rugers
http://www.scarlettrugers.com

Contact the author:
gjwalkersmith@gmail.com
https://www.facebook.com/gjwalkersmith

Dedication

To my wonderful husband who has supported and loved me forever. I'd go anywhere with you.

To the three best sons a mother could spend wishes on. I love you very much.

Kisses and gratitude to, Sherry. If not for you, I would've painted it yellow years ago. Thank you for encouraging me to continue.

Beaucoup d'amour pour Marie, ma belle amie. The story you told me about meeting your Adam in Bath will stay with me forever. Thank you for inspiring me.

Special love to my Fairy Godsister, Jane. You told me I was an author. You taught me to believe in myself. You also taught me that it ain't no party without a bus.

Table Of Contents

1. Close Calls

Alex, my brother, sometimes calls me wicked. Sometimes I am.

I blame it on the fact that I've been bored for the majority of the seventeen years of my life. Growing up in a small town does that to you.

Pipers Cove sits at the base of sweeping cliffs that take a vicious bite into the southwestern coastline of Tasmania. Next stop south, Antarctica. To an eccentric artist, antique dealer or hermit it would seem like heaven on earth, but I am none of those things, nor have I ever aspired to be. I am the girl who has always been desperate to get the hell out of there.

Spending another Saturday morning hanging out with my best friend while she worked her shift at my brother's café was shaping up to be just as boring as it had been the week before. I could feel the wickedness kicking in.

"We could take the money from the register and make a run for it," I suggested, pacing the café. "We could be in Melbourne by morning." I was met with a disapproving glare. I wondered for a moment if she thought I was serious. Perhaps I was.

Nicole Lawson, my best friend since kindergarten, was my true partner in crime – even if she did draw the line at being my accomplice in a robbery. We were unlikely friends. Straight down the line, back and white with zero tolerance for any shades of grey summed her up perfectly. I felt scattered and indecisive by comparison. My grandiose ideas were fleeting, mainly because of her uncanny knack of talking sense into me. Nicole was the responsible one. She'd held her part-time job in Alex's café since we were fourteen. It wasn't always a boring gig, especially in the summer months when the tourist season kicked in.

Our sleepy little coffee shop was located at the edge of town, opposite a car park with killer views across the Cove. Tourists seeking a great photo opportunity and quality coffee make it a popular place, if only for a few months each year. Alex was very savvy, catering to their every need. Besides decent coffee, he also stocked newspapers, magazines, stationery and other bits and pieces that negated the need for them to shop anywhere else. Retirees in their campervans made up the majority of the visitors, but occasionally we met young, broke backpackers who were living the life I yearned for. Hearing stories of their travels was like a window to the outside world.

Winter was much slower. Cold June days were downright oppressive.

I stared across the road through the salt-hazed windows. The car park was practically deserted, and would remain that way for months.

"Are you sure I can't change your mind?" I asked, sighing heavily.

"Escaping will have to wait," replied Nicole, checking her reflection in the back of a spoon and fluffing up her platinum blonde hair. "We have a wedding to go to today, remember?"

How could I forget? It had been the main topic of conversation around town for weeks. Attending her sister's wedding was a torturous prospect. Technically I'd be gate crashing. I hadn't been invited. My role was purely as moral support for my best friend, the chief bridesmaid.

Nicole's sister, Joanna, was a poster child for small town folk. Standard procedure for a small town girl is leaving high school and getting a mundane job while waiting for Prince Charming to arrive and sweep her off her feet. Joanna's prince was a fisherman called Max. Joanna was barely twenty-one. I needed to believe there was more to life than that.

"All the more reason to make a run for it," I muttered.

"Where are you running to this time, Charli?" Alex asked, barging through the back door with an armload of newspapers.

"Melbourne. The last flight out is at ten." My brother didn't look anywhere near as horrified as he should have. "I was going to steal the money from the till to fund it."

"Nice plan."

"She's not going to bail today," Nicole reassured him. "She's coming to the wedding reception with me."

I groaned. "You should be the one going, Alex. You were actually invited."

"Can't. I'm allergic to weddings."

Nicole giggled as if he'd told the world's funniest joke. Her shameless crush on my brother had been obvious for years. The only person who seemed oblivious was Alex, and for that I was grateful. He would never have coped. Nicole's crush was wrong on a million levels – the first being the fact that my brother was thirty-four.

The rain belted down solidly for the next half hour. I took my familiar stance near the front window, waiting for a break so I could head home.

"Just make a run for it," advised Nicole.

"With or without the money?" Tired of waiting, I grabbed my raincoat from under the counter and draped it over my head. "I'll see you later."

Leaving her there hardly seemed fair. Alex had given her the day off but she'd turned up anyway, promising her mother she'd be home in plenty of time to get ready for the ceremony at three. I wasn't sure if it was a ploy to steal a few more pointless hours with Alex or if she was just escaping the mayhem of her house. Her place always seemed to be bursting at the seams with people, and the noise her little brothers made without even trying was deafening. Today would be worse.

Our house was always quiet.

I stood at the edge of the road waiting to cross. The rain stabbed at me, forcing me to pull my coat so far forward I could barely see. After a quick glance left and right, I clumsily ran across, making it just before a black car peeled into the car park. It missed me by inches. What I didn't escape was a deluge of water as it ploughed through the puddle in front of me.

Shocked, drenched and seething, I watched as the driver practically leapt out of the car and ran towards me.

"I'm so sorry! I didn't see you there. Are you hurt?" he yelled, compensating for the noise of the rain and the distance between us.

"What the hell is wrong with you?" I fumed. "How could you drive that fast in this weather? Of all the stupid things to do!"

By the time I finished my rant he was in front of me. "You're absolutely right," he agreed. "I have no excuse."

His shoulders were hunched forward, in an attempt to keep the rain from his face. The stance wasn't very successful. His blue shirt was saturated and sticking to his skin. His beautiful black Audi was obviously toasty and warm – he wore no coat. His eyes, expectant and full of concern, nearly pinned me to the ground.

"You need to learn to slow down," I added.

"You're absolutely right."

Agreeing with me made arguing somewhat difficult. So did the smile across his face as he did it.

"I'm not hurt," I conceded.

Water streamed down his dark hair. "I'm glad."

He spoke with a strong American accent. I struggled to remember the last American I'd met, but was fairly sure they wouldn't have been driving anything as sleek as the lethal Audi.

There wasn't a reason to keep him standing in the rain. "I have to go."

"Here, let me help you to your car."

"I think I can find it," I replied. The only two cars there were his and mine, and there was no chance of confusing the two. My old Toyota hatchback had dents and scratches all over the once white paintwork, but I loved it anyway. It provided a little step towards the freedom I so desperately craved.

"Okay, then." He made no effort to race back to the comfort of his car.

I walked slowly. It was impossible to get any wetter. Perhaps he thought the same, which is why he stood there until I reached my car.

"My name is Adam," he called, as I jammed the key into the lock of my car door.

"Fine."

"I am sorry."

He was persistent. I tried to think of something smart or witty to say and failed miserably.

"It's fine."

The car door squeaked as I wrenched it open.

"You never told me your name."

"You never asked me," I replied, thrilled that my sense of wit was improving.

2. The Beautifuls

Our gravel driveway turned into a treacherous maze of potholes every time it rained. Thankfully, the house was in better shape than the driveway. The small weatherboard cottage stood at the back of the elevated five-acre property, offering glimpses of the Cove from the front rooms. Truthfully, I liked the view more than the cottage.

Touching only one of the three steps on my way up to the veranda, I headed to my room.

It was the smallest of the three bedrooms, and that explained the constant clutter. I never spent much time in there, probably because I'd never needed to. Alex and I lived alone, which meant I pretty much had peace and privacy no matter what room I was in.

Prepping for a wedding that I had no interest in attending wasn't thrilling, and the outfit I'd chosen reflected my lack of enthusiasm. I stared into the full-length mirror on the back of my bedroom door. The long black skirt and white blouse were reminiscent of something a waitress at a cheap restaurant would wear. I considered changing, and was still raking through the tragic selection in my wardrobe when I heard Nicole's car.

I met her at the door.

"I have so much to tell you!" She battled to contain herself as she bolted up the front steps, making no concession for the long length of the pretty bridesmaid's dress she was wearing. Nicole got excited over anything she considered newsworthy. It was one of the things I liked most about her. I was wickedly hoping to hear that the wedding had been called off. Drama like that didn't come around often.

I ushered her inside and followed her down the hallway to my room.

"Well? Tell me," I demanded, closing the bedroom door like we needed the privacy.

Nicole sat on the edge of my bed, sighing like she needed more time to piece it all together.

"Just after you left the shop, a guy came in. He had the cutest accent, American I think. He was gorgeous, not like anyone around here... unless you count Al–"

My hands flew over my ears. "Don't say Alex."

"Alex *is* hot. Ask anyone."

"Get back to your mystery man," I ordered, trying to scrub her last comment from my memory.

Nicole wagged her finger at me. "Don't play innocent. I know you saw him."

"I ran into him in the car park," I admitted, impressed by my private joke.

"He came in wanting directions." She grinned smugly. "I was only too happy to help."

"I'll bet you were," I replied dryly.

"He asked about you, too."

My smirk died immediately. I sat on the bed, inexplicably winding a lock of hair around my fingers. "What did he ask?" Even to my own ears I sounded desperate for information.

"He said he'd just met a girl in the car park and wondered if I knew her. I asked him what she looked like." Nicole spoke slowly, drawing out the tale. My glare prompted her along. "He said she was pretty, blonde and about so high," she said, indicating my height with her hand. According to her re-enactment, I was three feet tall.

"What did you tell him?"

"I asked him if she was mouthy, unpredictable and wearing a blue raincoat."

I folded my arms across my chest. Except for the height estimation, her description of me was pretty fair.

"So where did he want directions to?"

"Spinnaker Road." She shrugged her shoulders. "I guess he's visiting someone in town."

"Well, I'm sure he was grateful."

Giving him directions was a service to the community. If Adam had been left to find it himself, every pedestrian in town would've been in mortal danger.

"I didn't give him directions to Spinnaker Road. There are eleven streets in this town, for crying out loud. He would've found it eventually. I gave him directions to my house."

"Slick, Nicole."

"I thought so. I told him if he wanted to see you again, you'd be at the reception this afternoon."

I took a moment to process this. Maybe he thought he'd hurt me. I could think of no other reason why he'd ask about me. I could think of even fewer reasons why a stranger would show up at a wedding reception.

"He won't show," I declared.

"We'll see." Smoothing down the front of her dress with both hands, she began studying her reflection in the mirror. Her grape coloured satin dress gathered under her bust, and a long skirt skimmed her body. Nicole's hair colour changed from one day to the next and I wasn't sure that I liked the current platinum blonde look, but it looked pretty coiffed in an elegant bun. I suddenly felt bad for not putting more effort into my outfit.

"I should change," I muttered.

She abandoned the mirror and, enthusiastically threw open the wardrobe, a woman on a mission.

"How about this?"

The sage green dress she was waving at me still had the tags on it. We'd picked it up in Hobart months earlier. The sales assistant claimed it was vintage. The fifty dollar price tag made me doubt her, but I didn't care. It was a cute summer dress – summer being the operative word. I had no idea how I was supposed to pull it off in the middle of June. It was also cut a little too low for me, which explained why it had a permanent home in the back of my wardrobe.

"It's a bit revealing, don't you think?"

"No. It's impressive." She carefully slipped it off the hanger and launched it at me, not so carefully. I dragged my shirt over my head, dropped my skirt to the floor and manoeuvred my way into the dress. I tore off the tags and stood in front of the mirror, fussing with the neckline while Nicole fussed with my hair.

Being the daughter of hairdresser meant she was supposed to possess natural talent when it came to styling hair. She didn't. Five minutes of pulling and twisting resulted in nothing more cutting edge than the blonde ponytail I'd started with. Reaching for the brush on my dresser, I dragged out the elastic and tried neatening it up.

"Okay. You're done," she announced after a few seconds. Patience had never been her strong suit. "You've got a party to crash."

The rain had dulled to a drizzle by the time we arrived at the Lawson's house. The line of cars stretching down the street convinced me that Nicole wasn't exaggerating when she'd told me everyone in town (except Alex and his wedding allergies) would be there.

Being such a small town, there were no reception centres or fancy golf clubs to accommodate large parties. Christenings, weddings, wakes and everything in between were held at the host's house. Joanna Lawson's wedding reception was supposed to be a quaint garden party in her family's yard, but the rain had put a dampener on things, so to speak. The lawn was scattered with vacant white plastic tables and chairs, and sodden pink decorations hung limply from the row of lemon trees near the fence. I felt bad for the bride. It looked like a disaster zone.

The house didn't seem to have fared much better. It was overloaded with guests and there was nothing quaint about it. I could hear the music thumping from the car. Staying put seemed much more favourable than going inside.

Nicole unbuckled her seatbelt. "Are we going to sit here all day?" She angled the rear vision mirror in her direction, checking her reflection while she waited for my reply.

"Could we?"

Nicole threw open the car door and stepped out on to the lawn, surprisingly gracefully considering the ridiculously high heels she was wearing.

"Get out," she ordered.

My exit wasn't as polished and I nearly stumbled on the verge. We hadn't even made it to the front steps before her mother bombarded us.

"Nicole! Where have you been?" she barked. "We've been waiting to take photos. Carol Lawson's hands were planted firmly on her chubby hips. Her skin-tight mauve dress clung to every pudgy curve on her body. The silver belt around her waist was pulled in two notches too tight. I wondered if she could breathe but the way she was ranting at Nicole confirmed that she could. "This is your sister's day. Remember that." She pointed her finger as if she was hexing us.

"How could I forget?" asked Nicole.

"And you, Charlotte." She said my name as if it was a swear word.

"Yes, Mrs Lawson?" I spoke sweetly. The last thing I wanted to experience was the wrath of Carol. I'd been there before and it wasn't pretty.

"Make sure you're on your best behaviour," she warned.

Charlotte Blake, chief troublemaker. I wasn't hearing it for the first time. At least I knew where I stood with Carol. She always let me know exactly how she felt. She was one of the most genuine people I knew on the inside, and yet every part of her appearance was fake – gaudy bleached hair, long acrylic nails and a fake tan in a strange shade of orange. The woman was a walking contradiction.

I crossed my heart. "Best behaviour. I promise."

I doubt she believed me, but she let us on to the porch anyway.

The music was so loud that I could feel it pulsing through my feet as I walked inside. Nicole shrugged off her coat and tried to hang it on the crowded wooden hatstand in the hallway. Already overloaded, the extra weight was too much and sent it toppling towards her.

Moving quickly, she caught it.

"Hang your coat before it falls again," she yelled, fighting to be heard over the music, still holding the stand upright. One more coat would have signalled the end.

Someone turned the music down and I was relieved not to have to scream my reply.

"I'll keep my coat on." I didn't want to take it off. The neckline on my dress felt positively obscene at that point.

"Last chance," she warned, preparing to let go.

I shook my head. "I'm good."

Nicole released her grip, and we watched as the mound of coats began to fall.

Adam was walking out of the lounge room just as it fell. He stumbled as the pile of coats blindsided him.

"Oh, my God. I'm so sorry!" gasped Nicole, reaching for the hatstand with both hands.

Adam slung the armful of coats he'd managed to catch back on the stand. "No harm done," he replied.

He looked different – calmer maybe. His hair, no longer soaked by the rain, was a lighter shade of brown than I remembered, but his eyes remained dangerously bright.

Nicole extended her hand. "I'm glad you came. It's Adam, right?" she asked, sounding falsely unsure.

I looked to the floor to hide my smirk. Her play at innocence was ridiculous.

Adam shook her hand. "That's right. Thank you for the invitation. It's shaping up to be quite a party." Noticing my expression, he laughed. "Aren't you having fun?"

I didn't want to answer, and received a reprieve when Carol bustled through the door.

"The photographer's still waiting, Nicole. Get outside, now!" Her mother brushed past her, shoving into the lounge room to round up other wayward members of the bridal party.

I could tell that Nicole was mortified. The colour of her cheeks now matched her lipstick. She excused herself from the conversation and for a split second, I considered reaching out and dragging her back.

My eyes darted in every direction but Adam's. He said nothing until I turned and walked out the same door I'd come in only a few minutes earlier.

"Are you leaving so soon?" he asked, following me out.

The rain had stopped but the cold air felt thick. A few small groups were gathered along the veranda, chatting, laughing and sipping drinks from dodgy plastic cups. I was glad that we weren't the only ones out there.

He put his hands in his pockets. "I hope you decide to stay, just a little longer."

"Why?"

"Because I don't know anyone else here."

"You don't know me either."

"Well, that's not entirely true. We met earlier today. That has to count for something."

"You nearly mashed me with your car." I grinned. "I'm not sure it counts for anything."

"Maybe we could start again." He held out a hand. "Hi, I'm Adam."

"Charli," I replied, ignoring the warmth that tingled up my arm as I took his hand.

"Short for Charlotte?"

"Only when I'm in trouble."

"I imagine that's quite often."

I pulled my hand away, embarrassed that he'd drawn that conclusion so quickly. "Why would you think that?"

Adam leaned forward, reducing the gap between us to inches. "I just think you show a little spark."

I looked at him through narrowed eyes. "Are you always this forward?"

He grinned. "I'm from New York. We have a reputation for being pushy."

"So why are you here?"

He shrugged. "I've always wanted to see Australia."

His generic answer held no conviction. I knew there was more to it.

"People who want to see Australia usually visit the Sydney Harbour Bridge or the Great Barrier Reef. The south coast of Tasmania will shoot any dreams you had of a sunny Australian holiday down in flames."

"I like it so far," he said, smiling. I concentrated on not reading too far between the lines. "Besides, I have family here."

I was pretty confident that I knew everyone in town. Possibilities ran through my head.

"Who?"

"My cousin. Gabrielle Décarie." I gritted my teeth and forced a smile, but my strain must have been obvious. "Do you know her?"

I did know her. Mademoiselle Décarie taught French at high school. I detested French, and I was quite sure she detested me because of it.

Getting away with anything underhanded at school was tricky. There was no such thing as scheduled parent and teacher meetings. All discussions involving late assignments, poor grades and ditched classes were held across the counter of our café. Poor Alex cringed whenever a teacher walked through the door. Gabrielle Décarie was no exception to the rule, and it didn't help that Alex was a bumbling fool in her presence. She was an exquisitely beautiful woman with coppery hair and porcelain skin. It was easy to see how he'd fallen under her invisible spell.

"Mademoiselle Décarie is my French teacher. She's also French. You're American. How does that work?" I wickedly wanted to hear that she wasn't French at all and the accent was a sham.

Adam took his hands out of his pockets and folded his arms. "My father is French. We moved to the states when I was a child. Gabrielle is always telling me how nice it is here. I thought I'd check it out for myself."

It was a long way to come for a big fat nothing.

"So how long are you in town for, Adam Décarie?" The exaggerated spin I put on his surname sounded ridiculous. I made a mental note never to attempt it again.

"I don't have to be home for a couple of months."

"Running a girl down with your car is the most excitement you can hope for here. You'll be clawing the walls in a week, desperate to get out of town," I teased.

"Have you always lived here?" he asked.

"Always."

I wanted to tell him that Nicole and I planned to leave as soon as we were done with school. I wasn't one of those boring small town girls, and it pained me to think that Adam might think I was. I shouldn't have cared what he thought. I didn't know this boy from, well, Adam.

Turning my back to him, I leaned on the lattice railing, looking into the garden, enjoying the cool air on my face. He moved beside me, resting his elbows on the railing.

"You could be my tour guide," he suggested.

I couldn't help smiling. "Do you have a spare five minutes?" That's all it would take. There were only so many views of the ocean or ancient trees I could show him before he'd lose interest.

"Like I said, I have a couple of months. Would you show me around?"

"Why do I get the impression you're not going to take no for an answer?"

"Because I'm a pushy American with plenty of time on his hands. So what do you say?"

I opened my mouth to refuse when two of my least favourite people, Jasmine and Lily Tate, tottered along the veranda, making a beeline straight for us. I'd been avoiding them since kindergarten and had become quite good at it, but now I was caught.

Both sisters were almost pretty. Lily was seventeen and possessed the knack of dressing like a cheap stripper. She also had the misfortune of being as dumb as a box of rocks. Jasmine, more intelligent and twice as catty, managed to tone it down a little bit but her pushed-up boobs still spilled over everything she wore. Her signature heavy makeup made her look much older than her nineteen years. Generally speaking, they were an all round hot mess.

"Charli!" Lily screeched, running at me in her red stilettos. She threw her arms around me, trapping my hands tightly at my sides. "Aren't you going to introduce us to your new friend?" she purred, her eyes firmly fixed on Adam. Jasmine stood so close to him that he was jammed against the railing.

"This is Adam Décarie," I said.

"Who are you here with? I haven't seen you around here before. I never forget a face, especially one like yours," Jasmine gushed, squeezing against him. She linked her arm through his, staking her territory.

Adam looked at me, silently pleading for rescue. I gave it my best shot.

"Adam's French, Jasmine. His English is not very good," I improvised.

Jasmine dropped her bottom lip and patted his arm. It was as if I'd just told them he was suffering from a terminal illness.

"Are you enjoying your holiday?" asked Lily. She spoke slowly and loudly, managing to make "holiday" a four-syllable word.

I smirked, doing all I could not to laugh. "He's French, not deaf."

Adam covered his mouth with the hand Jasmine was not squeezing the life out of and coughed. I wasn't sure if he was covering a laugh or if being choked by their perfume.

"Are you staying with Miss Décarie?" asked Jasmine, still talking as if he was mentally impaired.

"Yes he is," I answered for him.

Lily leaned forward, glancing at her sister. Their prey remained firmly sandwiched between them. "We could show him around, like, a tour de Pipers," she suggested. Her French accent was worse than mine, something I didn't think was possible.

"Fantastic," I encouraged.

"Can you tell him we'll pick him up from Miss Décarie's at ten?" Jasmine asked, momentarily turning her attention to me. Perhaps she didn't know that I'd ditched every second French class for the past two years.

"Adam." I spoke slowly and waved my arms. "You have a date tomorrow, at ten." I held ten fingers in the air for effect.

Lily clapped as if I'd conquered the language barrier.

"Fabulous! Well, we'll see you tomorrow," said Jasmine, poking her bright pink fingernail into his chest with every word spoken.

"Très bien," replied Adam, muttering his first words since the ambush.

"What did he say?" quizzed Jasmine.

"He said he's looking forward to it." I smirked.

As soon as their date was set, the sisters released their grip. Adam sidled next to me, perhaps hopeful that I would protect him.

Lily pulled at the hem of her stretchy skirt, which was riding up. Jasmine flicked her hair off her shoulder. Adam coughed again. Definitely the perfume. The girls walked away, their clicking heels acting as a warning system for the next man they set their sights on.

Adam waited until they were out of earshot. "You realise what this means, don't you, Charlotte?" he murmured.

"It means you have a hot date with the Beautifuls tomorrow," I replied, ignoring the fact that he'd just called me by my horrid full name.

"The Beautifuls? Is that what you call them?"

"That's what we've always called them."

You have a strange perception of beauty, Charli."

I felt the need to clarify. "They think they're gorgeous and that's the point. The Beautifuls – it's just who they are."

"So if they're beautiful, what does that make you?"

I wasn't expecting the question. Adam waited, not watching me.

———

"Big trouble," I announced, flashing my wickedest grin.

The corner of his mouth lifted just enough to reveal the dimple on his right cheek. "Really?"

"*Huge* trouble," I warned, throwing back my head and drawing out the words.

"I'll consider myself warned," he chuckled. "Right, what time am I picking you up tomorrow?"

"You have plans," I reminded him.

He shuddered. "I'm not planning on being anywhere near Gabrielle's house when those girls show up. You got me into this – so you have to save me from them."

Earlier that morning I'd been desperate for an escape. And I wasn't too dumb to realise that Adam might have been it.

"Trouble, remember?" I pointed at myself.

"Do you need me to sign a disclaimer or something? I'll do it, you know."

I blushed. "That won't be necessary."

"Great. It's a date then."

3. Games

The first thing I did when I woke was check my phone for messages, certain that Adam would have hunted down my number and called to cancel, but there were no I-just-realised-you're-a-nutcase texts waiting for me. I pulled the covers back up to my chin. The morning was cold but the sun glaring through the window made me hopeful that the rain would stay away.

I contemplated getting up and cleaning my room to pass some time. The floor was scattered with the rejected outfits from the day before, including the obscenely low-cut dress that I swore would never see the light of day again. I opted for breakfast instead.

Alex was already up, reading yesterday's newspaper while he ate. I sat down and he slid a box of cereal and a carton of milk towards me.

"I thought you were never going to get out of bed."

The blistering look I gave him was wasted. "It's seven o'clock." I huffed.

"I know. The day is practically over."

He was serious. Alex's day started at the crack of dawn, because he was a slave to the sea. Surfing was his bliss, and rain, hail or shine, his morning started at the beach as if he had no choice in life. I wasn't quite as dedicated, but couldn't deny my affinity to the ocean either. The difference was, I wouldn't curl up and die if I missed a morning or two in the water.

"What were the waves like this morning?"

"A bunch of chop, actually."

"I didn't miss much then," I replied smugly.

"You got lucky, that's all. How would you feel if you'd slept through the best waves in the southern hemisphere this morning? You would have spent the rest of your youth hearing nothing but the legend of how I mastered the waves of the century…while you slept in."

I couldn't help laughing. "Get over yourself, Alex."

He laughed, eyeing me like he was waiting for some big news.

"What?"

"How was the wedding?"

"It wasn't a wedding. It was a reception, and it was pretty sucky." Carol had kept Nicole shackled to a giant plate of microwaved canapés for the best part of the afternoon. She dutifully offered them around the room for hours before escaping to drive me home.

Adam left much earlier than I did. I declined his offer to drive me home. The last thing I needed was a lecture from Alex about accepting lifts from strangers.

"Where were you anyway? When I got home, you were nowhere to be seen."

"Out and about," he said vaguely. "When I got home, you were asleep. It must have been some party, Charli."

"Everyone was there. The whole town was there," I said, drawing out my words as if I was explaining some big tragedy.

Alex leaned back, snickering at my drama. "Same old, same old then, huh?"

"Not quite. I did meet someone new. Adam Décarie, Gabrielle's cousin." I saw a flicker in his eyes at the mention of her name. "Mademoiselle Décarie," I purred in my useless French accent.

Alex began thumbing through the newspaper, too quickly to be reading it. Finally he gathered the paper together and thumped it on the table.

"What are you doing today?"

"Why are you asking?"

"Because I always ask. It gives me false hope that I'm actually managing to keep tabs on you."

"I'm taking Adam on a tour of Pipers Cove," I replied casually. It was no big deal and I hoped he agreed.

My relationship with Alex was complicated. We'd been on our own for so long that I couldn't remember a time when things were different. He was only twenty when he took me on, at a time when he should have been setting out to conquer the world, just as I ached to do. A certain amount of guilt came with that knowledge.

Part of me always wondered how things would have been for him if we'd had a normal family life. Raising a child is a responsibility that no twenty year old should have to bear, but Alex was extraordinary. I should have told him so more often.

"Are you going to be gone all day?" he asked, perfectly calm. Maybe he wasn't about to pull the my-house-my-rules card.

"It's a little town, Alex. A few trees, a few cliffs, maybe a wallaby or two and we're done."

"Will you call me if your plans change?"

"I would if I thought you'd answer your phone."

I'd arranged to meet Adam at the car park opposite the café because it seemed easier than giving him directions to the house. Alex wasn't doing me a favour by offering to drive me there. He wanted to check Adam out.

I saw the Audi as soon as we rounded the bend on the road, parked in almost the same place as the day before.

"Nice car."

"It is. And he drives it like a maniac." I wanted my comment to get under his skin. The way he chewed his bottom lip proved it had.

"Park at the café and I'll walk over," I said. As expected, Alex ignored me and pulled up along side Adam's car. "You don't need to turn the car off. You're not staying," I warned.

Still ignoring me, he took the keys out of the ignition. I should have known Alex would make a production out of it and I wasn't the least bit surprised when he got out of the car. He stayed behind me as I walked over to Adam. The three of us standing in the car park reminded me of a western movie, right before guns were drawn and carnage ensued. I introduced them before Alex had a chance to say something cringe-worthy.

"Adam, hi. This is my brother, Alex." I pointed at him in case Adam mistook him for a seagull or something.

Adam extended his hand and Alex met it with a firm shake. "Nice to meet you."

"You too," replied Alex.

I was a little shocked. My brother usually had a smart remark for everyone and everything. I gave him a look that would have killed him if I'd concentrated harder. "You can go now."

"Oh, geez, Charlotte. Thanks." Obviously the daze had lifted. "Call me if your plans change." He strode back to his car.

Adam looked to the ground in a failed attempt at hiding his smile. "He seems nice."

"So do most serial killers the first time you meet them."

Chuckling darkly, Adam opened the door for me. I got in and breathed out an unsteady breath of relief. I didn't need Alex there to screw things up for me. I was perfectly capable of doing that myself. Adam got in the car and a few seconds later the engine purred to life.

I instructed Adam to pull over just after we left the car park.

"Is there something to see here?" he asked. His confused expression made me giggle. "Why do I get the feeling that you're having a joke at my expense, Charlotte?"

He always seemed to speak formally, as if he chose the longest, most articulate way to say something. And there was something really sexy about it.

"No joke, Adam." I said, deadpan. "This is a major attraction in Pipers Cove." He looked sceptical but followed my finger as I pointed through the windscreen. I read the sign out loud. "Welcome to Pipers Cove. Population four hundred and sixty-eight." I spoke theatrically, as if I was reading from a neon billboard.

He looked at me from the corner of his eye. "And this is significant because?"

"You don't like it?" I asked, feigning disappointment. I added a pout.

He studied the peeling paint and outdated landscape. "It's a very nice sign. Is it special in some way?"

"Of course it is. See the picture of the lighthouse on the rocks?"

"I see it."

"Well, that's the kicker. There's no lighthouse in Pipers Cove. It's a big fat lie. This little Cove is so boring that they had to invent a lighthouse. Tourists spend days looking for it."

Adam slowly turned to face me, showing no sign of annoyance. "You're a stellar tour guide, Charli," he drawled sarcastically.

"I had to show it to you. I didn't want you to be one of the tourists who perish from exhaustion after searching in vain for days on end. I may have just saved your life."

"Thank you for the heads up, but Gabrielle's already warned me about the lighthouse, or lack thereof."

I cringed. "Did you tell Mademoiselle Décarie that you were spending the day with me?"

"I did."

"And what did she say?" I wasn't sure if I really wanted to know.

"She wished me luck." His warm grin took the edge off.

"She doesn't like me very much," I admitted. "I'm sure she told you that."

"I'm free to make up my own mind, Charli. So far, so good – you've already saved my life once."

I laughed. "Okay. We should probably move on. Is there anything in particular you want to see?"

Adam hesitated before reaching into his coat and pulling out a postcard. He smoothed it out as best he could before handing it to me. It looked like it had been folded and unfolded a million times. The heavy crease in the centre ruined a very familiar scene.

"Do you know this place? Gabrielle sent me this months ago. I'm hoping it was taken somewhere close by."

I knew exactly where the picture was taken. "It's not far from here," I replied casually, passing the postcard back. "I'll take you there."

Adam slipped the postcard back in his pocket. "You barely glanced at it. Are you sure you know where it is?"

I rolled my eyes. "I've lived here my whole life, Adam. Trust me. I know exactly where it is."

The sleek black Audi negotiated the turns to the top of the cliffs effortlessly. It was a far cry from my little old car that struggled to make it halfway up on its best day. Thick bush crowded both sides of the track. Adam winced each time a branch scraped the car, probably pained by the thought of the deep scratches being inflicted on his car. I pretended not to notice. He parked at the very end of the track, but there was nothing to see. It just looked like a dead-end road to nowhere.

Winter meant the bush was especially green, and obscured the view of the ocean. An unsuspecting hiker could fall off the edge by simply walking too far into the greenery, which is why the local council had abandoned the lookout years earlier and stopped maintaining the road. I watched through the windscreen as Adam wandered to the edge of the track, searching for his postcard landscape.

I'd spent more time up at the lookout than I'd ever admit. It was one of my favourite places to waste away an afternoon, sitting on the rickety old bench that had withstood a million storms. Only Alex knew of the time I spent up there. It was one of my best kept secrets.

The frigid air stung my face as I got out of the car. It was always windy on the cliffs, a few degrees colder too.

"Are you sure this is it?" he asked sceptically.

"Absolutely."

I strolled past him, towards a sandy opening between trees. I could feel Adam close behind me but didn't turn to check that he was keeping up. The roaring of the ocean got louder. I could feel salt on my face. When I broke through to the clearing, I stopped to let Adam pass. He took a deep breath as if the fierce wind had punched him. His expression was a mix of amazement and awe.

"Unbelievable! It's exactly the same as the picture!" He walked past the bench, dangerously close to the edge of the drop. He leaned forward to get a better look, making me extremely nervous. I ordered him back from the edge. Adam looked back at me, grinning impishly as he took a large step back.

"Thank you," I breathed.

"Are you afraid of heights?"

"No. I'm afraid of telling Gabrielle that I let you fall off a cliff," I replied sarcastically.

Laughing darkly, he sat on the bench and motioned to the space beside him. "Can we sit for a minute?"

I stood with my back to the ocean, fighting to keep my footing as the strong wind pushed me closer to him. My hair whipped forward, lashing my face. I brushed it back, holding it in place with my hand.

"Please, Charli. Before you blow away."

The change in wind force as I sat beside him was instant. I linked my hands around my knees, bringing them to my chest.

"Do you come up here often?" he asked.

"All the time. It's very quiet up here."

His smile was the most genuine I'd seen from him. "Well, I'm honoured that you shared it with me."

"Adam, why are you here?"

"You brought me here, Charlotte," he replied.

"You know that's not what I mean."

He smiled. "I know what you mean." I couldn't believe that Pipers Cove was his dream destination. I wanted to hear that he was on the run from the law or being chased by mobsters. "I'm on summer break. Visiting Gabrielle seemed like a nice change of pace."

Right. We were sitting at the top of a cliff, half freezing to death. Adam sank down on the bench, pulling his collar up. We sat in silence staring into the distance. The massive ocean looked grey and angry, dotted with white caps where the wind had broken the waves, and the dark clouds above complemented its mood perfectly.

"Are you glad you came?" I asked.

He kept his eyes on the ocean ahead.

"All my friends went to Europe, some resort in Spain. They're probably sipping cocktails on the beach as we speak."

"You must be wishing you'd gone with them." Heck, I was wishing I'd gone with them. "Cocktails versus hypothermia. Tough choice."

Adam looked at me. No quick glance, I could feel his lingering stare long before I met his gaze.

"Coming here was the right choice, Charli." He spoke slowly and deliberately.

I felt a blush prick my cheeks and fought to keep my eyes from drifting away. "But why here? What made you come here?" Nobody would voluntarily waste their summer in Pipers Cove.

Adam sighed. "You're going to think my reasons are lame."

I shook my head, promising I wouldn't.

He folded his arms across his chest to combat the cold. "Gabrielle's been here for a few years now. We've always kept in touch. I email her, but she likes to send postcards. She's old school." He winked at me and I smiled. "The picture of this place just got to me. I needed to see it. I'm not usually impulsive – in fact, I'm painfully predictable most of the time. Ditching my friends at Heathrow and jumping a plane to Australia is about the craziest thing I've ever done. But I *needed* to see it." He frowned at the ground.

"It's just a postcard, Adam," I teased, having no clue what else to say.

The frown melted. "Maybe it isn't about the postcard. Maybe there's a bigger picture. Do you believe in fate, Charli?"

"No." I almost spat out the word.

"What about love at first sight?"

I grimaced, refusing to entertain why he'd asked me. "Definitely not."

"So you would leave nothing to chance then?"

We truly were strangers. Anyone who knew me would know that I had a nasty habit of leaving absolutely every aspect of my life to chance, and not always to my advantage.

I kicked the dirt beneath my feet, digging a groove in the sand. "Probably not."

"Well, I plan every aspect of my life. I don't think I've been leaving enough to chance. I came half way around the world on a whim, searching for a place that might not have even existed."

"Well, thank goodness she didn't send you a postcard of the lighthouse."

He agreed, laughing.

"This view is really something," he said at last, focusing on the vast ocean.

"It is." The beauty of Pipers Cove couldn't be denied.

"You don't sound too impressed."

"I was… the first few hundred times I saw it."

"Maybe you should consider a vacation of your own, Charli. You sound like you need one."

"I'm in my last year of high school. I'll turn eighteen in December and then I'm out of here.," I announced with a touch of theatre in my voice. "That's always been the plan."

"Where will you go?" I wasn't sure if he was interested or being polite. His expression gave nothing away.

"I'm not sure," I admitted.

He threw his head back in a huge bray of laughter. "So you've been plotting your escape your whole life but you haven't actually planned where you're going to go?"

I grinned; I couldn't help myself. "The world's a big place. I'm spoiled for choice."

"It is. Does Alex want you to stay?"

I shook my head. "He wants me to finish school, though. I'm okay with that. It's the least I can do for him."

"How long have you two been on your own?"

It was a polite way of asking an ugly question. I felt no need to launch into the sad story of our lives. I was sure Mademoiselle Décarie would have filled him in on the details. It would have been her explanation as to why I was so damaged.

"Since I was three."

"You're close?"

"He's all I have." It sounded trite, but the truth often does. Adam looked forward again, processing the information.

I didn't want him to feel sorry for me. It was Alex who deserved the pity. I hardly remembered my mother. All I had was a hazy batch of recollections that dulled a little more each year. I barely knew her in life, so it was hard to stay close to her in death. I remembered even less of my father. According to Alex, he left just after I was born. We hardly ever spoke of them and I think Alex preferred it that way.

"Tell me about you," I blurted, to change the subject.

"What would you like to know?"

"Everything. Start at the beginning," I demanded, making him laugh.

"Okay. Well, originally I'm from Marseille. I moved with my brother and parents to New York when I was seven and…."

"How old are you now?" It was a question I'd been dying to ask since I'd met him.

"Twenty-one in October." I studied his features closely. The wind had dishevelled his dark hair, giving it a little more kink than when it was neat. His unusual cobalt eyes gave him a dark edge that didn't quite match his personality. He looked exactly twenty years old.

"What date?" I asked. The look he gave suggested it was a strange question.

"The thirty-first. Halloween."

I nodded and the conversation faltered. I tried to come up with a question intelligent enough to negate the last. Asking him to finish his story was the best I could come up with.

Adam was decidedly more American than French. He spoke of New York with the fondness of someone who truly felt he belonged there. He lived somewhere called the Upper East Side, between Central Park and the East River. He mentioned it casually, as if I would know where it was. I pretended I did, promising myself I'd research it later.

His father headed a law firm. Adam – the younger of the Décarie brothers –planned to follow in his footsteps. He wasn't exaggerating when he'd told me that he had his whole life mapped out. After his impromptu trip to Pipers Cove, he was heading back to New York to commence his first year of law school. This boy was so far out of my league it was embarrassing. I found myself staring at him, trying to find some minute flaw that might justify dragging him back to my level. Finding nothing, I decided that having a dimple on only one cheek was practically a deformity.

"So what about you, Charli?" he asked.

———

"What about me?" He needed to be more specific. I couldn't think of a single interesting thing about myself to put forward.

"Do you have any idea what you want to do, apart from travel?"

"That's all I want to do. I don't aspire to rule the world. I just want to rule *my* world." The words came out in a rush, sounding horribly conceited. I had no plans of a brilliant career. The biggest thing I aspired to do was get out of town. "I guess it must sound pretty unambitious to you," I added.

"I never said that," he said. "Don't put words in my mouth."

I suddenly felt wide open, fearing I'd just shown him enough craziness to make him want to cut me loose at any second. Determined to get in first, I stood and began walking away.

"Have I said something to upset you, Charli?"

I didn't turn around. "No. I just can't find any common ground between us."

"What does that matter?" I could hear the amusement in his voice, adding to my embarrassment. "I thought we were getting to know each other. I also thought it was going pretty well. I like you, Charli."

"You don't know me, Adam."

He wouldn't like me if he knew me. In fact, he'd probably despise me. Keeping him around was just delaying the inevitable.

"I know enough. Shall I tell you what I know?" His question stopped me in my tracks. "I think you're insecure, which is a shame. You're far too beautiful to be insecure about your looks, so maybe you're nursing a broken heart. Or perhaps I scared you with my postcard story. Could that be it?"

"No."

"I think you don't like people getting close."

I stared at him, for far too long to appear unaffected by his words.

"Whatever." My reply would have been perfectly adequate coming from a ten year old girl with a limited vocabulary. Coming from me, it sounded pathetic. I wasted no more time walking away.

"Charli, please," I heard. I didn't slow down until I reached the car.

Then I realised that my dramatic exit was for nothing. I had to face the humiliating fact that I'd arrived at the lookout in Adam's car. I had no choice but to wait for him.

The tortured French-American boy eventually strolled out of the bush, twirling his car keys around his fingers as if nothing out of the ordinary had happened.

My awkwardness had consumed me by the time we got in the car. I slumped in the cold leather seat, not looking at him. He turned the key and the engine purred to life. "I'd really like a cup of coffee right about now," he said. "Do you think we could go for coffee?"

He must have really needed the caffeine hit. I could think of no other reason for dragging out the agony.

"I've had enough for one day," I mumbled.

"Okay, I'll take you home," he replied quietly. The scraping of the bushes against the paintwork, amplified by the silence inside the car, didn't seem to bother him the way it had on the way up. Not a word was uttered until we were nearing the town.

"You can drop me off at the café," I told him. "You're going there anyway if you want coffee. You could try the Daintree's souvenir shop coffee but as far as I know, it's still instant and tastes like dirt."

He didn't answer me and I wasn't sure where we were headed until he pulled up at the café. We weren't the only ones parked there.

"What is it?" asked Adam, noticing my grimace.

I pointed at the little blue Ford Festiva parked crookedly across two bays. "That car belongs to Jasmine and Lily." He looked blank. "The Beautifuls."

He shuddered. "The Daintree's souvenir coffee is sounding good right about now."

"You'll be fine," I falsely assured. "Just don't make eye contact."

Just as we got to the glass door, the bell at the top jingled. It opened quickly, and before we knew it we were face to face with Lily Tate.

"Charli and Adam. Adam and Charli," she said, almost singing her words as she bobbed her head from side to side.

"Hi Lily," I mumbled. At least I spoke. Adam managed a half-hearted smile and a weak wave.

"I thought we had plans today." She stared accusingly at Adam. "Charli, can you translate please?"

"Ah, there was a little misunderstanding, Lily, but he'll make it up to you," I promised.

"I hope so. We went all the way out to Miss Décarie's house this morning. She wasn't expecting us at all! She said Adam had left early."

"Don't read too far into it," I told her, doubting she could read at all. "He went for a walk along the beach and lost track of time." The lie rolled off my tongue too easily.

Adam remained silent but his frown spoke volumes. It was amazing how much he understood considering he didn't speak English.

"Where do you fit in this story?" Lily asked, looking me up and down. Her snippy tone got my back up. Instead of trying to placate her, I found myself stooping to a level lower than pond scum.

"I ran into him down there. But I'm done with him now. You can have him back."

"You stole him?" she asked, widening her eyes in horror. "Jasmine's going to flip out when she hears that."

Adam looked at me, not so discreetly this time. I kept my focus on Lily, to escape his fierce glare.

"Like I said, you can have him back now." I offered him to her as if he was a toy we were sharing.

Lily stared at Adam but spoke as if he was invisible. "Maybe I could tell her he misunderstood, got the time wrong or something."

"Yeah. That'll work," I said.

"It doesn't matter anyway," said Lily. The loud slow voice she was using was obviously for the deaf, gorgeous, American, French boy's benefit. "He's here now." She hooked her arm through his.

Her territorial display didn't bother me one bit. What bothered me was the baleful look Adam gave me. I wanted to tell him that I wasn't really that wretched – that I was truly sorry for throwing him to the Beautiful wolves. But I didn't. I continued tormenting him.

"His English has improved too," I said, driving the final nail in the Adam-and-Charli coffin. "He spent the whole morning telling me how lovely he thinks you are."

Lily stood in stunned silence, for the first time ever.

Realising her mind freeze could go on for a while Adam took control. "Lily, I apologise for the mix-up." His smooth accent and low voice did nothing to unfreeze her brain. "I'm here for another week so I'm sure we'll have plenty of time to catch up."

It was an offer Lily was never going to refuse. And why would she? As far as she was concerned, Prince Charming was there for the taking.

"Walk me to my car and I'll give you my number," she instructed.

Adam was too polite for his own good. He followed her down the steps and I made my getaway, charging through the door of the café. Nicole was sitting behind the counter. Her grin was wide, as if she was expecting big news.

"Adam's going to come in here in a minute for coffee," I blurted, slamming both hands on the counter and making her jump. "Make him one and get him out of here."

"Why?" She leapt off the wicker stool. "What did you do, Charli?" She didn't sound anywhere near as surprised as she should have.

"Just get him out of here," I choked, trying to whisper and yell at the same time. "I'll be out the back."

Grabbing my sleeve, Nicole dragged me back to her side. "No way! You're not hiding out the back, you little coward!" she hissed.

"I royally screwed up," I whimpered.

I didn't need to explain to my best friend why the day had gone so far awry, which was a good thing because the telltale bell jingled. She was back behind the counter before Adam even walked in. I stood cemented to the spot as he bypassed me completely. He ordered coffee and kept her engaged in conversation while she made it. The few minutes dragged like hours. It was getting harder to breathe.

Finally, coffee in hand, Adam thanked Nicole. He almost made it to the door when I choked out his name.

Adam looked around, vaguely as if a stranger had called out to him.

"You told Lily you were leaving in a week."

"Yes."

"I thought you were staying for a couple of months."

"I said I *could* stay a couple of months," he corrected, coldly. "I'm going to spend some time with Gabrielle and then head home."

"I guess that makes sense," I agreed.

Nicole let out a groan. The slap I heard was her hand connecting with her forehead. Subtly had never been her forte. Adam's focus remained on me. Thinking about what he might be seeing made me want to bolt from the room.

"I had it in my head that this place held something for me. For a minute I thought it was you…." He shook his head like he couldn't believe he'd gotten it so wrong. "Thanks for showing me around. It was nice meeting you, Charli," he said, cold and polite. He walked out the door, leaving me standing there like the idiot I was.

"Are you just going to let him go?" Rushing over, Nicole grabbed a fistful of my coat. "You like him," she said, shaking me with each syllable. "Why are you making such a mess of this?"

Breaking free, I smoothed down my coat, buying time. She didn't wait. "Get out there and talk to him," she ordered, pointing towards the door.

"And tell him what?"

"Tell him that he wasn't wrong," she yelled, as if that was necessary to make me understand. She shoved me towards the door. "What are you waiting for?"

"He'll be gone now. It's too late."

"He won't be gone. He's standing by his car."

"How can you possibly know that?" Whoever built the store a zillion years ago had the good sense not to obstruct the view of the ocean. The small car park couldn't be seen from inside the café.

Nicole dangled a set of keys in front of me. "He's not going anywhere."

Snatching the keys from her, I marched to the door. I didn't even take time to string a reasonable apology together in my head. Adam was already walking up the steps, coffee still in hand. It took all my might not to throw the keys at him, run inside, bolt the door and hide until he was gone.

He could probably tell by the look on my face that he was going to have to speak first.

"I left my keys."

I shook my head. "Nicole took them to stop you leaving."

I dropped them into his palm.

43

"Why would she do that?" he asked.

"Because she knows I will have sabotaged this day. And she knows I need time to make it right," I explained.

"Charli – "

"You said that you thought it was me that drew you here." Interrupting him was all I could do. If I let him finish telling me how vile he thought I was, I would've lost my nerve completely.

His face contorted as if he wished he'd never said it. "You blew me off and handed me to the Beautifuls," he reminded me, outraged.

"I know," I replied contritely. "I'm sorry."

Adam backed down the steps. "You're so confusing," he muttered.

Before I knew it, I was following him to his car, taking two quick steps to keep up with each of his long strides. "Adam, you asked me if I believed in fate."

He balanced the cup of coffee on the roof of the car. His hand was on the door handle but he didn't open it. "And you said you didn't."

"I lied." He shook his head, incensed by me all over again. The car door opened and I wedged myself in the way to stop him leaving. "Please, I know I don't deserve it but let me explain."

He took a step back from me, folding his arms defensively. "No games," he warned.

"None," I promised, sealing the deal by crossing my heart, just to prove I had one. "If I'd told you the truth, you'd think I was crazy."

"As opposed to mercurial and jaded?" he asked.

"I'm only a little bit jaded and I don't know what mercurial means."

A hint of a smile ghosted across his face. "So what is the truth?"

I stepped out from behind the car door and pushed it closed. "I chance everything to fate. I always have. I'm constantly looking for shifts in the universe. My brother tells me that I'd find a deeper meaning in a hole in the ground." I paused and looked down, trying to slow my rant. "When you told me that the first chance you'd ever taken in life was to come here, searching for a place on a postcard, I just knew...."

I sucked in a breath. I'd reached my limit.

"Knew what, Charlotte?" he prompted. It was the first flicker of curiosity he'd shown since I'd begun speaking.

"Fate brought you here."

He replied quickly. "If what you're saying is true, fate isn't kind. Today was a disaster, so I'm struggling to understand why you're intent on salvaging this."

"It was only a disaster because I got ugly," I pointed out. "My head is very protective of my heart and it's a defect I'm well aware of. Keeping the Beautifuls out of my business has practically become my life's work. I'm so sorry you got caught up in it."

He shook his head, looking utterly confused. "I don't understand what you're trying to tell me."

"Things would be making a whole lot more sense right about now if I'd given you the chance to know me better." I bit my bottom lip, holding my breath, waiting for him to speak.

"Tell me who you are then, Charli," he suggested.

Bravely reaching into his coat pocket, I took out the ragged postcard. He stood completely still as I pressed it against his chest, smoothing out the crease.

"Well, for a start, I'm Charlotte Elisabeth Blake," I told him. "And if you look at the bottom right hand corner of your picture, you'll see my initials." I handed the postcard to him and he studied it closely.

Photography had been my passion for a long time. It wasn't a secret and I could think of no plausible reason why I hadn't told him about it the minute he'd shown me the picture.

It had been Alex's idea to publish them as postcards. It was never going to make me rich but the proceeds bumped my bank account up enough to make my dreams of travelling at the end of the year a possibility rather than a pipedream. Not surprisingly, I'd managed to corner the market. Every postcard in town was one of mine.

"I knew exactly where that photo was taken because I took it. A picture I took made it all the way around the world to you. And you came looking for it. It's fate. You had no choice but to come here. You said so yourself."

"How is that even possible?"

"Don't question the universe. Just go with it. We're practically guaranteed a happy ending."

He grinned at me. "Is that so?"

"Definitely so."

"So what happens now?"

I shook my head. "I'm not entirely sure but I'm hoping you'll stick around long enough to find out. Everything will be okay in the end."

Breathing suddenly became easier. I wasn't convinced he understood me but he hadn't jumped in the car and locked all the doors either. I was content to walk away.

For now, everything was exactly as it was supposed to be. I was never going to be able to turn the clock back but I felt confident that I had at least explained myself.

It wasn't a moment I wanted ruined by Nicole's relentless need for details so I bypassed the café and started walking home.

"What happens if it doesn't work out, Charli?" he called.

"Then it's not the end, Adam," I replied, barely slowing my walk.

---

4. Shifting Universes

The distance from the café to our house was ridiculously long. As soon as I was sure I was out of Adam's sight I took my phone and punched in Alex's number. "Can you come get me, please?"

"Hello to you too," he replied.

"I'm sorry. Hello. Can you please come and pick me up? I've just left the café," I amended, sounding sweeter.

"I've got a few errands to run. Do you want to come with me?"

Even after running errands, I'd still be home in less time than it would take me to walk. "Yes, please," I grumbled, tilting my head to look at the sky. The clouds were threatening rain now. I had managed to stay dry all day but was concerned that my luck was running out.

I heard Alex before I saw him. The V8 engine stuttered as he downshifted to take the bend. His beloved Holden Ute was one of his few guilty pleasures. He was the most sensible, level-headed man on earth except when it came to his car. It got washed every weekend – at least once. I swear he talked to it when he thought no one was listening. Every year he traded up for the newest, loudest model available and like a fickle schoolboy, his affections would quickly shift to the new car.

The engine dulled to a throaty rumble as he pulled up beside me. Alex leaned over and pushed the passenger door open. "What happened to Prince Charming? He couldn't give you a ride home?"

"I *chose* to walk," I said with dignity.

"But you didn't," he grinned. "You called me."

"Only to see if you'd answer your phone," I replied. "Do you want to hear about my day?"

"Well, you didn't call asking for bail money so I can only assume it didn't end too badly." The dark look I levelled at him had little effect but he amended his answer. "Of course I want to hear about your day."

"He dropped me off at the café and Lily was there. I basically fed him to her on a platter."

"Poor bloke." He laughed, knowing full well what the Beautifuls were capable of. "I'm sorry it didn't end well, Charli."

"I never said it didn't end well."

Alex glanced at me. "Okay, then."

If I had ended the conversation right there, he would have been perfectly content. Alex did not cope well with drama.

I waited a few minutes before speaking again. "Do you believe in fate, Alex?"

His face contorted into a frown as discomfort set in. "What's this all about, Charli?"

"What if fate brought Adam to me?"

His eyes remained on the road, but I had his undivided attention.

"The kid is here visiting his cousin, Charli," he stressed. "Fate has nothing to do with it."

I told Alex the postcard story in its entirety. "It can't be coincidental," I declared.

He groaned. "Look, you take beautiful pictures of the Cove. It's not much of a stretch to think someone who saw them would come here and check it out for themself."

I remembered the desperation in Adam's voice when he'd told me how he needed to see it with his own eyes. He'd spoken as if he'd had no choice.

"The universe hasn't shifted, Charli." He grinned. "I would have noticed something like that."

"So you don't believe in love at first sight?" I quizzed.

Alex shifted uncomfortably. "No."

"What about the fabulous Mademoiselle Gabrielle Décarie?" My pathetic accent sounded more like a fortune telling witch than a French socialite.

"Hardly," he mumbled. His protest was weak and I wasn't buying it. "What is she going to think when she finds out you're shifting universes with her precious cousin?" he asked, changing his tone.

The question had already crossed my mind. I was Gabrielle's least favourite person. We avoided each other like the plague, and that worked well for both of us. The most I saw of her was three hours a week during French class, if I bothered to make it.

Our road trip was quick. Alex ran a few errands and hardly anything was said on the way home, and that was okay. Alex was my safe place.

***

Monday mornings were always a problem for me. The feeling of dread was particularly bad that morning, knowing I had a double period of French after lunch. I considered ditching. I may not have been Gabrielle's favourite person, but fortunately the principal didn't share her opinion of me. The most severe punishments Mr Monroe dished out were half hour detentions, which I spent playing games on my phone or reading a magazine.

Lying in bed pondering my choices, I came to the realisation that I had none. Skipping French today was not an option. Adam would have filled Gabrielle in on the details of our day together. The relative safety of the classroom, where she couldn't scratch my eyes out in public, seemed like the best place to face her.

My alarm blared. Hitting the snooze button for the third time was tempting but nonsensical. Not much effort went in to choosing my outfit. I grabbed the first shirt I found in my drawers, a long sleeved green stretch cotton tee. My choice of pants was even easier; I owned more pairs of jeans than any girl should admit to. The hot blast from the hairdryer felt good as I waved it over my wet hair. One of the few benefits of having razor straight hair meant that it always dried that way, no matter how much it was tortured. There was just enough time for breakfast before Alex rushed me out the door.

My brother drove me to school most mornings, which was a godsend in winter. My little car took forever to start on cold mornings, and when it did, the heater would still be blowing cold air by the time I reached my destination.

"Do you need a ride home?" he asked, pulling alongside the ancient front gates of Pipers Cove High School.

The school wasn't as small as it should have been. Most of the neighbouring towns had no secondary schools of their own so students were bussed in, but even with the extra kids bumping numbers, it wasn't a big enough place to be anonymous, a fact made painfully obvious by the group of girls waiting for me at the gate. News travelled fast, and Adam Décarie was bound to be front page.

"No, I'll get a lift with Nicole. Thanks anyway." I got out and slung my backpack over one shoulder, feeling like I was about to walk into an interrogation. I got a moment of reprieve when Alex became the focus of their attention.

"Hi Alex," purred Lisa Reynolds, her entourage of friends cackling like geese in the background. Alex responded with a weak wave and drove off, far less cautiously than usual. Poor Alex. He seemed to be the unwilling object of desire of most of the female population in this town. I wasn't totally oblivious to how good looking he was, or what a good catch he would be. He was athletic, strong and in a constant state of dishevelment thanks to his extra curricular activities like tinkering in his shed and surfing. Too bad for them that his mind was strictly one track, and it was focused entirely on the Parisienne witch waiting for me in fifth period French.

Lisa jumped off the fence, smoothing the back of her skirt as she approached. She towered over most of the girls our age. It was easy to see why she was the spokesperson. Her shoulder length brown hair didn't shift an inch as the wind squalled around us. The only thing more excessive than the amount of hairspray she used was large number of silver bangles she wore. The way they jingled when she moved grated on me, and I don't know how it didn't send her crazy.

"You've been holding out on us," she accused, pointing her finger at me. Her friends followed closely, as if attached by invisible strings. I ignored her and quickened my pace.

"He's French, isn't he? How long is here for?" she asked, not taking a breath between questions.

"American. Why don't you ask him how long he's here for?"

"I saw you talking to him at the reception," she accused. "And Jasmine told me you spent the day with him yesterday. I just want the run-down. It's not every day we get fresh blood."

The notion that any boy who stumbled into Pipers Cove was fresh blood, up for grabs, was ludicrous but widespread. It strengthened my theory that the only way to transition into a well-adjusted adult was to get the hell out of town.

I managed to avoid Lisa for the rest of the morning. Nicole and I met at lunchtime, as always. We dumped our bags on the bench seats and sat on the picnic table, desperate to get closer to the warmth of the sun.

"She's still looking at me, isn't she?" I asked, dropping my head so my hair fell as a shield across my face. I couldn't rule out lip reading as a tool in their gossiping arsenal.

"Lisa?" I nodded, rolling my eyes. "She's talking to Lily."

"Oh, just perfect."

"You started this mess," she reminded me, totally unforgiving. "You're the one who stirred them up."

"I know I did."

Probably picking up on the regret in my tone, Nicole softened. "Do you think you'll see Adam again?"

"I doubt it."

I wasn't hopeful that I'd ever hear from him again. For all I knew, he was on the morning flight to Melbourne.

The bell rang. Fifth period French.

I sucked in a deep breath and opened the door. My eyes focused on my chair down the back and I walked straight to it before I noticed Lisa in the usually vacant chair beside mine. Escape was impossible. I sat, looking to the front of the class for the first time. Mademoiselle Décarie was nowhere to be seen. She was annoyingly punctual, irritatingly perfect...and ten minutes late for the first time in the history of year twelve French.

"Why did you tell Lily and Jasmine he couldn't understand English? I spoke to him and he seemed fine," Lisa hissed, as if speaking a foreign language was a sickness. I was working on a calm reply when Gabrielle Décarie breezed into the room. "My apologies for being late." Her accent made her words musical. I scribbled mindlessly on my notebook, keeping my head low.

"Where did you two go yesterday?" whispered Lisa, refusing to give up.

"Nowhere," I mumbled.

"Chapter four...chapitre quatre," instructed Gabrielle, pacing the length of the aisle between the rows of desks.

I flipped the book to the page and feigned interest as she began reading. I glanced up as she passed my desk and she met my glance with a homicidal glare. Her recital didn't skip a beat. Her words flowed effortlessly, giving no hint of the loathing she was throwing my way.

As soon as she'd passed, Lisa hissed, "Are you seeing him again?"

I shuffled to the left but she moved with me. "Shut up," I hissed through gritted teeth.

Never one to give in easily, Lisa scrawled her next question on a piece of paper and shoved it across the desk at me. Before I had a chance to pick it up, Mademoiselle Décarie's hand thumped on top of it.

"Do you have something to share with the class, Mademoiselle Blake?" Chairs scraped loudly as every person in front of me turned around to stare.

Suppressing the urge to throw up, I refused to meet her eye. "No. I have nothing to share," I replied, sounding far more confident than I was.

Her perfectly manicured fingers pushed the note towards me. "Read it to the class...in French."

A pin drop could have been heard. All eyes were on me.

I picked up the note and read it quickly, silently. Reading it aloud would have been a very bad idea. I did what I knew best how to do, infuriate Gabrielle even more.

I cleared my throat. "I hate French class," I pretended to read, uttering every word in English but putting a ridiculous French spin on it. The class burst into giggles and Gabrielle snatched the note, stuffing it into her pocket. I wasn't out of the woods yet.

Lisa's sigh of relief was audible. "Thank you," she breathed.

"I didn't do it for you," I spat.

Mademoiselle Décarie's heels clicked on the wooden floor as she marched up to the front.

"Read through to chapter six, silently," she said acerbically, dragging her chair loudly as she pulled it out.

The hour passed in total silence. I didn't read a word but kept my head down, pretending that I was. Even Lisa wasn't brave enough to talk. I looked up only once, in time to see Mademoiselle Décarie take the note from her pocket and read it. Her lips formed a thin line and I knew why her expression was sour. Lisa's words, scrawled messily, were hurtful and cruel: *I hope he's nicer than his cousin. Stuck up princess.*

Gabrielle's eyes met mine and I quickly looked away. I counted down the seconds until the end of class. The bell finally sounded and people filed out. Mademoiselle Décarie sat motionless – even Lisa made it past her desk unscathed.

I took my time, rearranging the books in my bag before throwing it over my shoulder. The walk to the door was slow.

"Charli," Gabrielle spoke so quietly that I wasn't sure she'd called my name. I stopped walking.

"Yes?" I asked, managing to sound artificially calm.

"Why didn't you read the note?"

I shrugged involuntarily. "I saw no need to embarrass us both."

Mademoiselle Décarie nodded but said nothing. I walked out of the room feeling free to breathe again.

5. Flee-itis

The student car park after school was the closest Pipers Cove came to rush hour. P-plate drivers waited impatiently to get out, pedestrians wove between cars and everyone was in a hurry to make a quick escape. It was all over in ten minutes, by which time I'd usually found Nicole.

Today she was nowhere to be seen. Parked in the spot her little yellow Hyundai usually occupied was the sleek black Audi. My heart skipped a few vital beats. It was in danger of faltering permanently when Adam got out and opened the door for me.

"It looks like you need a ride home."

"I thought I had a ride home," I replied.

"I relieved Nicole of her duties. I hope you don't object. If I've come all this way to find you, I should at least find out why."

"You should," I agreed, doing my best to keep my voice even.

I slid into the passenger seat, trying to appear hesitant but moving too quickly to be convincing. My eyes darted around the luxurious interior.

"Did you think I'd object?" I asked as he got in.

He shook his head. "No. At least, I hoped you wouldn't."

We were both quiet for a while. The car was so smooth, so much quieter than Alex's V8. Adam drove slowly, possibly because he didn't know where we were headed.

"Where are we going?" I asked finally.

"Where do you normally go?"

"Nic and I usually go to the café, and then I go home with Alex when he's done."

"So we're going to the café?" he asked casually. I found myself doing the airhead twirl with my hair. "Charli?"

I hadn't answered him. "We can go to my house. Alex gets home about six. We'll have the place to ourselves until then."

Obviously surprised by the suggestion, his eyes darted between the road and me, probably unsure what to make of it. It dawned on me that my statement could have had ten different meanings, at least eight of them explicit. I felt sick with embarrassment, quickly looking out the window to hide the fact that my cheeks were burning. Adam laughed, slightly putting me at ease.

"I didn't mean for that to sound the way it did," I mumbled. "It's not what you're thinking."

"You don't know what I think," he replied, smiling.

"I think I should rephrase, just so we're clear." He tried to stop the grin widening across his handsome face. "I'd rather go somewhere quiet. Hanging out at the café is just asking for trouble. You've been front page news all day and I don't want to be part of tomorrow's headline."

"I didn't think I was that newsworthy," he replied, laughing.

"It's a really small town, Adam. Filled with really small minds. That's a very dangerous combination."

"I'll just stick with you then, to be safe," he replied, reminding me of my less than stellar skills in protecting him in the past.

"You know, I'm probably going to screw this up again. It seems fair to warn you."

"Really?" I could hear the amusement in his voice. "How can you be so sure?"

"Call it intuition."

"You look panicked, Charlotte," he said, glancing across. "Like you're about to run away."

"I can't see myself jumping out of a moving vehicle."

"Shall I speed up, just to be sure?"

I grinned. "No, I won't run. But I do have a condition."

"A medical condition?"

"Yes. Its called flee-itis."

"I see. What are the symptoms?"

"Well, usually I have an uncontrollable urge to run...when I really should stay."

"Is it contagious?" he quizzed, still smiling but looking at the road ahead.

"Apparently not. You're still here."

"Well, let's hope there's a cure."

"I'm working on it. Learning to stay would definitely be beneficial. You can ask me anything, Adam. I promise not to bail." I sounded tons surer than I felt.

"Really? Anything?"

"Sure." My voice sounded casual but my heart felt like it was in danger of exploding.

He cleared his throat. I dreaded the question already.

"Okay, question number one." The long pause made me almost reconsider my stance on jumping out of moving vehicles. "How do I get to your house?"

We were already past the café and heading out of town. I wanted to tell him to keep going – the further the better – but common sense kicked in. The ten-minute journey had turned into half an hour by the time we turned and headed in the right direction.

Adam stood behind me as I fumbled the key into the lock. I couldn't explain my nervousness. There wasn't much about the last few days that I could logically explain. Finally the door unlocked and I threw it open, walking in ahead of him.

"Is Alex going to mind me being here?" he asked, looking around as if expecting Alex to jump out from behind the couch.

"I don't know," I replied, too honestly.

"Okay." He grinned. An uncomfortable silence crept between us and I found myself doing the airhead twirl with my hair again. "So are you going to give me a tour of the house? You're getting quite good at playing tour guide now," he teased.

I pulled a face. "Well, it might take a while. This house is huge." I threw my hands in the air, emphasizing the sarcasm.

"I can see that." He leaned forward slightly. "So this would be the lounge room in the south wing?"

"Correct. The lounge room in the north wing is much more impressive."

"I like this one," he replied, wandering around.

He was just being polite. The only impressive thing in the room was the huge, ostentatious TV, another of Alex's guilty pleasures. It sat atop an antique oak cabinet he'd picked up at a garage sale. The irony was not lost on me. Two brown leather couches took up the rest of the room. They were bulky and ugly, but the most comfortable chairs I'd ever sat on. The only visible sign that a girl lived there was the two pink throw rugs draped over the back of the couch.

Adam turned his attention to the bookshelves that ran the length of the side wall, peering at titles and pictures, studying each one closely. I felt nerves kick in again. He picked one picture up to get a closer look.

"Is this you?" he asked. I took the little silver frame from him and put it back on the shelf. It fell facedown and he righted it. "You were a very cute child."

"Thank you. We should move on." Adam followed as I walked through to the kitchen.

"Is flee-itis flaring up again, Charlotte?"

I was determined to see it through. "No. Ask me anything."

He grinned. "Anything?"

"Sure."

"How long have you been into photography?"

"Forever." I sighed. "When I was six or seven, I found an old Brownie box camera at the markets in Sorell. It was only a couple of dollars and came with a whole box of film spools. I think Alex just bought it to shut me up. I guess it worked. I was hooked from the very start. It gave me magical powers. Every kid wants superpowers, right?"

Adam chuckled, nodding his head. "I guess so. What was the superpower you acquired?"

"I could freeze time," I explained, a little too excitedly. "Every picture ever taken is a fraction of a second, frozen in time forever."

"I never thought of it like that. So that picture of you as a little girl is a moment in time?"

"It's simpler than that," I told him, pushing my chair back. I walked to the fridge, snatched two photographs from beneath a magnet and dropped them on the table. He studied both pictures. I watched the expression on his face change from a frown to a bewildered stare.

"What do you see?" I asked. He hesitated before replying.

"Ah, a couple of trees. They're the same picture."

"Try to look closer." I pointed from one picture to the other. "That picture was taken four seconds after that one. They're completely different."

"I'm sorry, Charlotte," he apologised. "I'm not following."

"Focus on one point. The leaves," I suggested. Adam leaned closer, studying each picture. He looked up grasping the point I was trying to make.

"They *are* different. The leaves are different," he said triumphantly.

"Now you're getting it," I praised. "A fraction of a second changes everything. Those pictures can never, ever, be recreated. I could take a million more pictures, standing in the exact same spot, and each one would be unique. The wind blows the leaves on the trees, waves crash to shore, tides change, sand shifts. Everything constantly changes."

"I guess we should all look at the bigger picture once in a while."

"Not bigger, deeper. We should all look at the deeper picture," I corrected. He nodded but didn't say anything. "What is it?"

His hand moved across the table, resting lightly on mine. "I think this is going to get serious, Charli," he said gravely.

"I know." All of my concentration was focused on remembering to breathe, voiding my ability to come up with anything more insightful.

I heard Alex's car pull up and wondered how time had passed so quickly. But it was just after five; he was early. I pulled my hand away from Adam's, straightening up as if I'd done something wrong.

"Is this the part where I should sneak out the back door?" teased Adam.

"No. Stay."

The familiar sound of keys hitting the hallstand broke the silence and Alex called my name. I wondered if it was to give me warning that he was about to walk into the room, but he strolled in as if nothing was out of the ordinary.

"Hi, Adam," he said casually.

"Good to see you again, Alex."

"Adam gave me a lift home," I blurted, answering an unasked question.

"Nice." His tone was insincere and it annoyed me.

"I really should go. Gabrielle will be wondering where I am," said Adam, totally unaware of the effect of the name. Gabrielle – Alex's kryptonite. A frown replaced any smart comment Alex had planned to make.

"You remember Gabrielle, don't you, Alex?" I baited.

"Sure," he mumbled, thumbing through the stack of mail on the bench.

Adam stood. "I'll walk you out," I offered, jumping out of my seat.

We were almost to the car before he spoke. "Did I miss something in there?" he asked.

"Alex has a hopeless crush on Gabrielle. The mention of her name sends him into a blind panic."

"Hmm. Interesting."

"Teasing him about it is kind of a hobby of mine. Alex isn't usually easy to rattle."

Adam pressed the button on his key, unlocking the car. He opened the driver's door and it suddenly felt like a steel barrier separating us, saving me from standing too close to him.

"I'll see you tomorrow," he said, drawing my hand to his lips and kissing my fingers.

At that moment, there was nothing I wanted more in the whole world. I stood staring blankly down the driveway long after the Audi was gone from view.

The interrogation I was expecting from Alex never came. We sat at the table, eating the dinner he'd spent all of ten minutes preparing, in complete silence. It was torturous, almost as torturous as enduring the leftover pasta dish we were eating.

Cooking duties were shared in our house. My attempts at culinary brilliance were mildly successful, edible for the most part. Alex's efforts left a lot to be desired. The menu at the café was seriously short because of it. The food he served was limited to cakes and muffins that he had delivered from the local bakery. If it were left to him, we would have lived on sandwiches. I would have preferred that. At least I could see what went into them.

I put my fork down.

"What?"

"Don't you want to ask why Adam was here?" Alex put a forkful of food in his mouth, shrugged and said nothing. "Why aren't you lecturing me? Why aren't you pacing around the kitchen threatening to lock me in my room?"

"Do you want me to?"

"No."

"As far as I know, you haven't done anything to make me want to lock you in your room, so we're okay." He had obviously put some thought into this. His words were too prepared, too rehearsed.

"Okay then," I mumbled.

"Okay then," he repeated, smiling at me. He began pushing food around his plate as if the conversation had never happened.

"He might be important, Alex," I warned, giving him one last chance to let me blow everything out of proportion.

He set his fork back on his plate, sighing loudly before speaking. "Just be happy, Charli...and go slowly."

Why was my brother being so uncharacteristically reasonable? I had no intention of taking things slowly with Adam; but he wouldn't have appreciated hearing that.

***

The next day was hellish. Minutes dragged like hours. I ended up taking my watch off and hiding it in my pocket so I couldn't keep checking the time.

—

Nicole and I sat together at lunchtime. I picked my sandwich apart while she picked me apart. No detail went unanalysed and no detail was too minor for her. Every time I passed something off as unimportant, she forced me to tell her more. It was a relief to hear the bell signalling the end of lunch. I threw my uneaten sandwich on the table, clapping my hands together loudly as I brushed off invisible crumbs.

"Say hi to Lily for me," teased Nicole, as I made my way to the last class of the day, English. Lily Tate waved at me as I walked in, silently calling me over to sit with her. If I didn't look at her, she'd give in eventually – at least, that was the plan. She picked up her bag, preparing to shift seats – foolishly I'd sat next to a spare desk. Mr Porter walked in, ordered her to sit back down, and saved me.

***

In the usual afterschool bolt for the door, even Lily didn't hang back. I dragged my feet, taking longer than usual to pack my books away. By the time I reached the car park, it was all but deserted, and that was a good thing. Adam had managed to slip under the radar again, avoiding Lily, Lisa and anyone else vying for his attention.

"Two days in a row. I'm impressed," I mocked.

Adam took my bag and slung it on the back seat. "Did you think I'd be a no-show?"

"I knew you'd be here," I said confidently.

"Do you have any idea what you want to do today?" He brushed my hair off my shoulder.

"We could go back to my house, check out the north wing," I joked.

"Or I could take you to *my* house," he suggested.

I slid into the car and used the time it took him to walk around to the other side to work out how to reply.

"Gabrielle's house?" My tone gave me away and he laughed.

"Sure, why not?"

"Well, I'm not sure what she's told you but I'm not exactly her favourite person." That was putting it mildly.

"She told me a few things," he admitted. I looked at him through narrowed eyes, apprehensive but too curious not to know more.

"Like what?"

"She told me about the last French assignment you submitted." His grin was wide.

I'd worked particularly hard on that assignment. The essay presented beautifully. It was grammatically correct – and written entirely in German. I knew even less German than French, but translating it on the Internet took no time at all. Needless to say, Mademoiselle Décarie failed me, and Alex barely spoke to me for three days.

"I'd had a bad week," I explained.

Adam's laugh was infectious. I smiled just long enough to let him know I wasn't upset.

"Do you always put so much effort into being bad?" he asked. "Imagine if you used your powers for good."

"I'd be passing French and your cousin would be looking for a new archenemy."

"Why do you hate her so much?"

"I don't hate her," I explained. Hate was too strong a word. "We've just never gotten along."

"Aren't you worried about failing?"

"French is the only subject I'm failing. France does not rate highly on the list of places I want to visit. Why would I possibly need to be fluent in the language?" I asked gruffly.

"There are plenty of reasons to learn the language."

"Name one."

"Well, you might meet a charming French beau and fall desperately in love with him. You'd never be able to truly tell him how you feel because he wouldn't understand you."

"I'd teach him English," I reasoned, making him laugh.

"Well, I hope for your sake you're a better teacher than you are student."

"Yeah, well, technically you're French and you already speak English."

It was too much to hope that he didn't hear my remark. I sank in the seat and watched him from the corner of my eye.

"Mademoiselle Blake." His voice was low and deliberately slow. "Are you desperately in love with me?"

"Not desperately," I muttered.

"I guess we'll have to work on that then," he replied, grinning like he'd won something.

When he turned south onto the main road, I knew he was serious about taking me to Gabrielle's house. Dread washed over me. "Ah, I really don't want to do this today. I think I'm going to have to ease into that one."

"I thought you were braver than that, Charli," he said, glancing briefly at me.

"I didn't expect to need bravery today. I was concentrating on cute and witty."

Adam laughed. "So where will we go? You're going to have to help me out. I'm new in town."

I leaned towards the window, looking up at the sky. It was dark and overcast but not raining. "Well, the weather seems to be holding. We'll go to the beach." I gave directions, leading him to the outskirts of the south side of town. Past the turnoff to Gabrielle's house a small road deviated off the highway, poorly marked – another secret place. The Audi hummed to a stop as we pulled up at the rusted gate blocking the track. Beyond stood a row of seven little shacks, dotted along the beach like children's cubby houses.

"Who lives here?" he asked.

"No one. They're fishing shacks," I explained. "People use them in the summer as holiday homes."

Most of the shacks were owned by locals. The rent they commanded over the summer months was phenomenal considering they were in such a poor state of repair. Tiny, two-room weatherboard houses with million-dollar views across the Cove.

We got out of the car and a large clump of brown clay fell at my feet.

"You should really wash your car," I teased, stamping to remove the muddy mess from my shoes. "Rental companies don't take kindly to people abusing their vehicles."

Adam slung his arm loosely around my shoulder as we walked to the gate. "It's not a rental car."

"You borrowed it?"

"I bought it, Charli. I'm here for a couple of months." His tone implied it was no big deal.

I overlooked the fact that he'd changed his mind about leaving early. My focus was entirely on the extravagance of buying an Audi to use on an eight-week holiday. "It's a *very* expensive car," I said, choking out my words.

He looked embarrassed. "It will still be a very expensive car when I sell it in a couple of months."

"Well, you might want to wash it first," I teased. Adam's arm slipped from my shoulders. I stopped and turned to face him. He avoided my gaze. "Are you a real life prince, Adam Décarie?"

When he smiled his whole face brightened. "Why would you ask such a thing?"

"If you were a rich prince, that would explain the car."

"No, Charli."

"The boss of a giant French drug cartel?" He rolled his eyes "No; no, you're right. Gabrielle would be the boss. You'd be her right-hand man. She'd make a much better tyrant."

"Her aide-de-camp," he said, scrambling my brain with his seductive accent.

"What does that mean?"

"If you paid more attention in French, you'd know," he pointed out.

I began walking again and Adam followed, as he did whenever I led him into the great unknown.

"I'm guessing you don't have a key for the gate?" he asked, as if he knew the answer.

"If they really wanted us to stay out, the gate would be twenty feet high with barbed wire at the top," I reasoned.

He shook his head. "I can't argue with logic like that."

Before I knew what was happening, he scooped me off my feet, effortlessly lowering me to the sandy ground on the other side of the gate.

"You look nervous Monsieur Décarie," I purred in my hopeless French accent. "Is this your first break and enter?"

"I get the impression it isn't yours." He arched an eyebrow suggestively.

"The harder the access, the sweeter the find," I quipped.

We made our way down the sandy track, past the shacks to the open beach. The sky was foreboding, threatening rain, and the wind squalled relentlessly. The stretch of beach near the shacks didn't have the protection of the cliffs further around the Cove, but it was quiet and deserted.

He drew in a deep breath. "The air is so clean here."

"I know. It's ironic really," I replied, brushing my wind-lashed hair off my face. "Sometimes I find it hard to breathe."

Reading between the lines was something Adam was becoming very good at. "And breaking rules makes breathing easier?"

"It keeps things interesting," I replied. "Small town girls lead small town lives, Adam. Jumping a few gates now and then is good for the soul."

"I doubt there's very much about you that's small town," he said dryly.

"I'm biding my time until my real life kicks in."

"How will you know when that happens?"

"It will be when I no longer have a list of things I've never done," I explained, still fighting the wind for control of my hair.

Our stroll slowed to a stop and I wondered if I'd said something wrong. Adam took a step back. "I'd like to see that list sometime," he said, seemingly preoccupied as he wandered away. He leaned down and picked up a long stringy reed, twirling it around his fingers. "Turn around," he instructed. He combed his fingers through my hair and managed to fashion a loose ponytail, securing it with the reed.

"Thank you," I mumbled, feeling behind my head to check his handiwork – which, remarkably, seemed to be holding better than Nicole's effort a few days earlier. I felt his hand on my shoulder and turned back to face him.

Adam swept his hand slowly across my forehead. "I wish I could trust what I'm feeling right now," he murmured.

His doubt punched through me. Of course he couldn't trust it. It was unfair to think he could overlook how awful I was to him in the beginning. I stepped away, giving him the space I was sure he needed.

"I want us to be friends, Adam." It felt like the blackest kind of lie but I was convinced it was what he wanted to hear.

"I don't want to be your friend, Charli." The words seemed to hitch in his throat.

I folded my arms across my chest like a shield, worried that the broken parts of my heart would fall at his feet enabling him to stomp on them some more. "All of this defies logic. I can't explain any of it."

I wondered if I had misinterpreted things. "I don't understand what you're telling me," I replied, admitting defeat.

"Explaining it may incite a terrible case of flee-itis," he warned, smiling just enough to make me think it wasn't all bad.

"Try," I pressed.

His arms dropped to his sides before he reached out to me, taking my face in his hands. "There aren't words for this," he murmured, frowning.

"You speak two languages. You can't string something together?"

"I'm sorry," he said, without one ounce of sincerity. "I'll try."

I watched his mouth open as if he was going to speak, but no sound came out. Instead, he lunged forward, reclaiming my face in his hands.

I tasted the salty ocean air on his lips as they crushed against mine, hard at first, then scaling back to a light touch that sent a hot rush through my body. The warmth of his hands on my face remained long after he moved them, trailing down my arms as he reached for my hands. He rested his forehead on mine. "I wished for you," he whispered, so quietly that I struggled to hear.

"What did that feel like? I've never made a wish in my life." My voice was as shaky as my words were stupid.

"Everybody wishes for something, Charli."

I put just enough space between us to be able to look at him. "Not me. I've saved them all up. Birthday candles, shooting stars, stray eyelashes...ladybugs. I've saved them all up. I figure I'm owed hundreds of wishes now."

Both of his hands moved to cradle my face, locking my eyes to his. "You're a complicated girl."

I turned away to break his hold on me. "I am. I'm like a great big jigsaw puzzle, with a few missing pieces."

"Which pieces are missing?"

"All the important ones unfortunately, courage being the main omission."

"You don't think you're courageous?" he asked, reaching for my hand and pulling me back to his side as we continued our stroll.

"Not when it counts. If I had been braver, I wouldn't have let you go on that first day. I would have been sickly sweet and enchanting, making it impossible for you to doubt that you'd come here for any other reason than me."

Adam stopped walking, jerking me to a stop. "So why do you think we were destined to meet, Charli?" His tone made it sound like it was the most important question on earth.

I shrugged. "I've never claimed to know the reasons. Maybe you've got my missing pieces."

He patted himself down, pretending to check his pockets. "Perhaps they're in my other coat," he teased, making me giggle.

The afternoon passed in a blur. Daylight in the Cove during winter faded quickly. Overcast days led to the blackest of nights, and trying to find our way back to the car on a moonless night would not have been anywhere near as romantic as it sounded.

"I should get you home," he breathed, perhaps realising this.

"You should," I agreed, very reluctantly.

***

I wasn't surprised to see Alex's Ute in the driveway. "I'll walk you in," offered Adam, undoing his seatbelt.

"No, it's fine. It's cold."

He eyed me suspiciously. "I thought you said Alex was okay with this."

"He is, I promise. But I was supposed to be covering a shift for him at the café this afternoon," I confessed.

"Are you in trouble?"

"Always," I said, matching his expression. "To varying degrees."

"I'll see you tomorrow?" He brushed my face with the back of his hand, making my heart fly. I nodded worried that my words would be gibberish if I tried to speak.

I wanted to throw my arms around his neck and never stop kissing him, but there was a fair chance that Alex was watching. He'd shown remarkable understanding when it came to my newfound love life – not even I was willing to push my luck. I was almost to the veranda when Adam called to me.

"You might need this," he said, walking towards me with my bag.

"Thank you."

He slung the bag over my shoulder. The lock he had on my eyes lingered a little too long. "What?" I asked, confused by the silence.

"Fais de beaux rêves, ma Coccinelle." His silky accent shattered my concentration. Any ability I had to comprehend what he was saying was now redundant.

"Okay." It was the absolute best reply I could muster. I didn't even wait for his car to leave. I raced into the house, heading straight for the bookshelf in the lounge.

"Charli?" Alex sounded mad already.

"Give me a minute." I ran my finger along the line of books, searching for my French dictionary.

"I want to talk to you," he demanded, ignoring my plea for time.

"Found it," I said gleefully, grabbing the book off the shelf and waving it at him.

Alex snatched the dictionary from my grasp and dropped it on the coffee table. "What happened to working this afternoon?"

"I lost track of time. I'm sorry," I replied, knowing I'd have to work much harder to appease him.

He started pacing the room, resting his hands behind his head as if his brain ached. It seemed to take an eternity for him to speak. I knew he was beyond angry now. I also knew it had very little to do with me not showing up for work. Finally he turned to face me. "This isn't a democracy, Charli. One of us gets to be the boss and guess what?"

"What?"

"It's still me." He didn't sound as menacing as he'd probably intended.

I kicked up anyway. "You're not the boss, Alex!"

"See, that's the thing," he taunted. "I *am* the boss. I have a big certificate to prove it." He drew invisible letters in the air, just to drive his point home. "Alex Blake is hereby the boss of Charlotte Elisabeth Blake. I should get it framed." The use of my full name was intentional. He knew it grated on me. "I do not want to go down this road with you." He struggled with the words but I knew what he meant. Meeting Adam hadn't just thrown me for a loop – Alex had no idea how to deal with it either. It was as if we were both sailing unchartered waters, without a map, in the dark. "I've almost managed to keep you on the rails until now. Don't let me down."

I didn't reply, and I think he appreciated the lack of backchat. He picked the book up, handing it to me like a peace offering. "What do you want the dictionary for? It's a bit late in the game for that, isn't it?"

"I wanted to translate something Adam said to me."

"What was it?" he asked.

I looked at him blankly, trying to repeat Adam's beautiful words in my head. I remembered the look he gave me but drew a complete blank when it came to the phrase he'd spoken.

"I forget," I muttered. At least it made him smile.

6. Charm

Six days was all it took for my pre-Adam life to fade. Spending time with him made everything else pale in comparison, which became painfully obvious when I considered the number of uncompleted school assignments I had due the next day.

This knowledge took none of the shine off seeing him waiting for me after school. Adam picked me up every day, always ten minutes late. It was the only sure-fire way I knew of avoiding the Beautifuls.

"Good afternoon, Coccinelle."

I repeated the word, botching the pronunciation so badly that he laughed.

"You haven't worked it out yet?" He pretended to be surprised.

"I don't speak French," I grumbled, shifting my stack of books from one arm to the other.

"Oh, that's right," he said, drawing out his words.

"You could just translate it," I said hopefully. He smirked, and I knew he had no intention of translating anything for me.

His strong arms wrapped around me the second I was within reach and I pressed against him. The stack of books separating us kept the embrace polite.

"I'll tell you one day," he breathed, landing a quick kiss on my lips. "Meanwhile, what are we doing today?"

I wanted to tell him we were going to the beach, or back to my house to watch a trashy movie that, from past experience, neither of us would pay attention to. But I couldn't. The road Alex didn't want me to travel was getting long and winding. Adam's knack for taking my mind off anything other than him was making me crazy, and my inability to get my homework completed was making me stupid.

"I have to go to the library," I said grimly.

Adam's face lit up like I'd just invited him on a trip to the moon. "Wow," he said, astonished. "I didn't see that coming."

I nudged my armful of books into his chest. Taking the books from my grasp, he pulled me in close again. My fingers laced through his as I stretched up to get closer to his ear.

"I hear they have books and stuff there," I whispered.

Adam laughed softly. "You're impossible."

"I know," I agreed, composing myself instantly by pulling him across the car park by his free arm.

"Is it going to be open?" he asked. "The whole place looks deserted."

"Mrs Young is always there. I think she lives there. She's a scary woman, Adam Décarie."

I knew he was intentionally lagging behind me. Changing tack, I let him walk ahead of me.

"I'll charm her," he teased.

"You won't be able to. She's un-charmable," I replied, prodding him in the back to hurry him along.

"Superb use of the English language, Charlotte," he mocked.

The library was deserted. Adam waited near the open door while I paced the end of the aisles looking for signs of life. I jumped when Mrs Young appeared out of nowhere and called my name.

"I don't think I've seen you in here in two years, Charli," she said gruffly. She was probably not exaggerating.

"I know, but I have a mountain of work due," I complained. "I just need a couple of hours."

Mrs Young shook her head so severely that I thought her wire-rimmed glasses would fly right off her face. She played the part of spinster librarian perfectly. Her ivory blouse was crease free and stiff, matching her upper lip. The heavy tweed trousers she wore probably played a part in keeping her posture so rigid. "I have a committee meeting in ten minutes," she said, tapping her watch. "Come back tomorrow."

Cue the gorgeous French American boy, who until that point had merely observed from the doorway.

"Ah, Mrs Young, I would be more than happy to ensure the library is locked up when we're done," he offered.

"And who might you be?" she asked, far less icily than she'd greeted me.

Adam extended his hand. She shook his hand, grinning like a smitten teenager. It made me smile. She wasn't a day under sixty.

"My name is Adam Décarie. It's a pleasure to meet you, Ma'am," he said, using the unfair advantage of a gorgeous accent and equally gorgeous face to stun her.

"Oh, ah, likewise," she stammered. "Are you any relation to Gabrielle?"

"Yes Ma'am. Gabrielle is my cousin."

"Lovely," she cooed.

"I will make sure Gabrielle gets the keys this evening. She can pass them on to you in the morning."

Adam wasn't asking permission and Mrs Young didn't care. She handed him the bunch of keys. Just as she got to the door, he called out, "Don't forget this." He handed her the dated grey cardigan from the back of her desk chair. She thanked him and walked out. Adam stood with his back against the door, twirling the keys and wiggling his eyebrows like a cartoon villain.

"You're shameless." It was impossible to keep the smile out of my voice.

"Un-charmable, huh?" he asked smugly.

"Is no one immune, Adam?"

He walked over to me, leaned down and rested both hands on the desk behind me, trapping me at an awkward angle. I couldn't have moved if I'd wanted to. And I didn't want to. And when his lips found their way to mine, I couldn't have cared if I never moved again. He murmured my name against my mouth and I managed a small groan of acknowledgement.

"You have work to do," he reminded me. He stepped aside, motioning towards the aisles of books with an upward nod.

"I do," I agreed, trying to calm my thumping heart.

By the time I'd completed enough work to scrape a passing grade, the heat between us was unbearable. Adam sat next to me, so engrossed in an Australian history book that I wondered if the feeling was one-sided.

"I'm done," I announced, slamming my book shut.

Adam barely glanced up. "Charli, did you know that Australia is the sixth largest country in the world?"

Groaning, I buried my head in my hands, making him laugh. He slapped his book shut, reached over and pulled me into his lap.

We stared at each other for a long moment. I tried to guess what he was seeing – something I'd done from the minute I met him. I swallowed hard, desperate for him to make a move but not confident enough to do it myself.

Finally he leaned forward, slowly skimming his lips along my jaw. Unable to slow my racing heart or thoughts any longer, I knotted my hands through his hair, drawing his lips to mine. I had no idea how far I was prepared to go. All of the lines I'd carefully set myself blurred into the distance. Being close to him was all I could think about and at that point in time, I couldn't get close enough. His hands slid up the back of my shirt and I felt small in his arms, totally absorbed in his touch, his smell, and the way he breathed unevenly.

"Charli, stop," he whispered. His hands moved to my shoulders, gently pushing me away. He inhaled deeply, pulling in one long breath.

"What's wrong?"

"Absolutely nothing," he said, smiling as he brushed the side of my face with his hand. I jumped off his lap, straightening my clothes. Adam stood too. "We should go, before we both ignite." He picked my coat up off the chair.

"Yes. Books are very flammable." My voice was small and hid none of the awkwardness I felt. I was barely able to look at him.

"Charli, I – "

"Don't say it."

"Don't say what?" he asked.

"Don't say anything," I muttered, trying to drag my coat on as we made our way to the door.

Getting out of the library was a good idea.

The drive back in to town was mostly silent. Adam concentrated on the road but my occasional glances in his direction were always met by a glance from him.

I played it out in my head over and over, trying to make sense of it all. Less than a week ago I was okay – bored, mediocre and uninspired but okay nonetheless. At this moment, sitting in this beautiful car, next to the most beautiful boy I had ever known, I realised I had no clue what I was doing.

He turned right at the turnoff, heading back into town. "Where are we going, Charli?" he asked quietly.

"Can you take me back to the café? I'll get a lift home with Alex."

"I can take you home if you'd like."

"No, no. It's fine."

It wasn't fine. Nothing about the whole situation was fine.

I glanced at him again but his eyes remained firmly on the road ahead. I hated the shift between us.

"Wherever you want to go," he said.

There were no cars at the café when we arrived and I breathed a silent sigh of relief. I fumbled with the clasp on my seatbelt as if I was desperate to escape the car.

"Flee-itis, Charli?" he teased.

"You're making me crazy, Adam. It's too much."

He reached for my hand, and kissed my fingers. "I'll make you a deal," he offered.

I sighed. "What's the deal?"

"You won't run away from this, whatever *this* is..."

"And in return?"

"I won't let you get too crazy," he said, smiling.

"Oh great." I rolled my eyes. "And they say chivalry is dead."

His hand swept my hair across my face. "It's all about timing, Charlotte," he breathed. I didn't hate my name so much when he said it.

"Deal," I whispered.

***

Nicole looked up from the magazine she was reading as soon as she heard the bell.

"Hi," she said, grinning expectantly.

"Hello."

"Where's Adam?"

"On his way home I guess. He just dropped me off," I replied casually.

It was too much to hope for to think Nicole would leave it at that. "Are you going to tell me *anything*?" she asked, grinning and frowning at the same time. "Are you okay? You seem a little weird."

"I'm fine. And I've always been weird."

Any intention I had of trying to explain the day's events disappeared the minute Alex walked in.

"What are you doing here?" he asked, surprised. Surprise was good. Surprise meant he hadn't seen my face glued to Adam's in the car a few minutes earlier.

He picked up the magazine that Nicole had absently tossed aside. She was usually better at concealing the fact that she read the new magazines as they came in.

"I had to come. I missed you," I explained, following him as he returned the magazine to the display stand.

He laughed. "Liar."

The bell jingled and Gabrielle breezed in. Her eyes flitted between Alex and the floor. Mercifully, she barely glanced at me.

It occurred to me that Adam might have mentioned Alex's crush to her. I couldn't think of another explanation for her nervousness. I'd never seen her anxious before and it was a good feeling. It felt as if I'd inadvertently managed to unhinge both of them without even trying.

Gabrielle approached the counter leaving Alex high and dry, glued to the spot like an idiot.

"Hello, Nicole," she greeted, smiling for the first time since she'd walked in. "I'd like ten stamps, please."

Nicole reached under the counter, counting out loud as she unwound the roll of stamps. "Anything else?"

Gabrielle walked to my display of postcards and slowly examined the pictures scattered across the shelf.

"Did you have something in mind?" asked Alex, seizing the opportunity to speak. By the time he finished his sentence he was standing beside her like a loyal little puppy. If he'd been cursed with a tail, it would have been wagging.

I looked across to Nicole, still behind the counter with a strip of postage stamps wound around her fingers. The look on her face wasn't what I expected. She looked irate. She tossed her head, rolling her eyes when she saw I was looking. The smile I gave her was weak and unreassuring.

"I have been collecting these," she explained, pointing at the row of postcards. "I thought I had them all but Adam is under the impression that there are four different pictures from the cliffs overlooking the Cove. I wondered if I might have missed one."

"Charli?" queried Alex, probably eager not to appear as oblivious as he actually was when it came to my photography. He levelled a look at me that Gabrielle didn't see, warning me to behave.

"There are four," I reluctantly confirmed. "We're waiting on more being printed. They should be here next week."

Gabrielle nodded. It bothered me that she was collecting them. Perhaps my postcards were being used in some strange Parisienne witch ceremony to cast evil spells on me. I knew she wasn't from Paris – Adam took pleasure in reminding me that she was from Marseille every time he heard me refer to her as the Parisienne Witch. Marseillaise Monster didn't quite have the same ring to it.

"What do you do with them?" I asked.

If she thought it was a dumb question, she didn't let on. "I've sent some to my family and friends. I am also making an album, commemorating my time here," she replied.

"Are you leaving town?" asked Nicole, a little too excitedly.

She looked embarrassed then, and I almost felt sorry for her. "Ah, no. I have travelled rather a lot in the past. I like to keep track of places I've been to. These pictures are just beautiful. I've tried taking my own but none have been quite as special as these." She spoke slowly, as if trying to string words together in the right order although her English was more articulate than mine.

"I'll make sure Nicole puts some aside for you when they arrive," said Alex.

"Sure." Nicole's tone was acidic, but Alex was too dazzled to notice.

I spoke again. "I can print the original pictures for you if you'd like. They'd look much better in an album than postcards."

Alex stared at me, his umber eyes boring through me as if looking for the ulterior motive – probably because there always was one. It felt as if tiny shards of glass were stabbing at my stomach as I waited for her to shoot me down with a French expletive.

"Thank you, but I actually like the charm of the postcards."

"Okay." I shrugged indifferently.

"I know you've been spending a lot of time with Adam lately. If you come to the house I could show you my albums."

I searched for the catch, but found nothing. "I would like that," I replied, horrified. It was easy to convince Adam that hanging out at Gabrielle's house was a bad idea. It wasn't going to be so easy when she'd openly invited me.

"Would you like to come for dinner tomorrow night?" Her voice almost seemed shaky. I'd never seen a single chink in her armour, until now.

"She'd love to," Nicole shamelessly chimed in.

I ignored her. "No thank you...I'm busy."

"Doing what?" Alex frowned at me.

I glared at him, scolding him with my eyes. It was a gesture that didn't go unnoticed by Gabrielle. She looked to the floor, clearing her throat before speaking. "Maybe another time. Talk it over with Adam."

"Um, okay." I murmured, leaving Alex's question unanswered.

An awkward silence swept over the café. Nicole finally broke it. "So, just the ten stamps then?" she asked cheerily.

Gabrielle walked to the counter. "Yes. Thank you," she said, smiling politely. She bestowed a small smile upon Alex as she walked past him. It was the most simple of gestures but enough to make my six-foot-two brother buckle.

"See you, Charli," she said.

That was inevitable. Even if I could think of a way of getting out of going to dinner, I still had to face her at school. I was beginning to feel overwhelmed, too far out of my comfort zone to find my way back.

7. Heavy Head

Weaselling out of shifts at the café was becoming increasingly difficult. Alex was on to me. Hanging out at the library for a day didn't make me studious – it alerted him to the fact that I was falling behind.

Agreeing to cover a shift for Nicole while Carol dragged her to the dentist in Sorell for a check-up was a strategic manoeuvre on my part. According to Alex I was becoming unreliable and preoccupied, and I needed to prove him wrong. I wasn't expecting to see Adam that day, so seeing the Audi parked at the café was a surprise. Skipping my usual afterschool rendezvous with him had done nothing but make our liaison in the library the day before seem even more awkward. I'd spent half the night analysing it and by morning my confidence was shot. He'd told me it was a timing issue, but I let darker thoughts creep in. Maybe it was a Charli issue. I was hopeful of stealing the minute I needed with him to set everything straight but the instant I got out of the car, I knew it wasn't going to happen.

Adam sat at one of the two tables on the veranda, deep in conversation with Jasmine Tate. He looked up and saw me.

"Charli," he breathed, sounding relieved.

"Charli, we were just talking about you." Jasmine's voice oozed innuendo.

"I'll bet you were." I dragged myself up the four small steps.

"I had no idea you and Adam were such good friends," she purred. Adam shifted uncomfortably in his chair.

"I think you've been misinformed. We barely know each other." My tone was ice. "Maybe you should vet your sources a little better."

Jasmine threw her head back and gave her trademark shrill cackle. "Oh, poor Charli. You just can't catch a break can you?"

I knew exactly what she was referring to – and it made me want to crush her like a bug.

Adam seemed to be having trouble understanding my about-face. "Charli, please sit down," he said politely, motioning to a chair next to him.

"Yes, go ahead. I was leaving anyway," said Jasmine, as if I needed her permission.

"No, I'm not staying," I said.

Adam groaned. We'd been down this road before. I didn't know how not to hurt him when flee-itis set in. I just wished it wasn't playing out in front of a Beautiful.

"Of course you're not staying," he said. "You're going to run away."

Content that her evil work was done, Jasmine smiled. "I'm just going to leave you two to it," she said, and tottered down the steps in her dangerously high heels.

Neither of us acknowledged her. Neither of us even looked at her. The look Adam gave me wasn't kind, and I deserved it.

"Sit down, Charlotte."

I sat.

"I can't believe that its only just occurred to me that all the time we spend together is alone – which suits me fine. The problem is, I've been so wrapped up in you that I never realised we were hiding. I've just endured twenty minutes of interrogation from Jasmine."

"What did you tell her?"

"Nothing scandalous," he said, matching my sore tone. "You never told me this was supposed to be a secret."

"It's not a secret."

Adam pulled in a deep breath through his nose. "You're reckless and impulsive, yet guarded and secretive at the same time. You can't have it both ways."

"You don't know what she's capable of," I warned.

"Do you seriously think she'd ever get the best of me? I don't think so, Charli."

"You wouldn't even see it coming."

He shook his head, muttering something under his breath.

"Jasmine Tate is a twin," I told him, right out of left field.

"Lily and Jasmine are twins?"

I shook my head. "She has a twin brother. His name is Mitchell and he is the reason I'm so jaded and mean a lot of the time."

"I'm sorry Charli, but for what it's worth, she never mentioned a word about it."

"No, of course she didn't. She's saving it for another day."

Adam reached across the table for my hand but I pulled away. "Beat her to it." His tone was rough, like he was daring me to be brave.

"Excuse me?"

"If you're worried about her telling me something, tell me yourself," he urged.

I wished I could say there was nothing to tell. I hated that I had to suffer the indignity of explaining it to him, but if I didn't, he might finally break and wash his hands of me.

The Tate family lived in a majestic-looking house on a huge vineyard on the south side of town. Their father had made his fortune producing wines that rivalled the best in the country. The Beautifuls seemed to think they were society debutantes because of it.

Mitchell was nothing like his sisters; his ideas were different. He moved into a shack on the property as soon as his parents allowed. The epitome of free-spiritedness, he wanted to conquer the world by surfing every beach on it. He never played by the rules, never cared much about consequences and I gravitated towards him because of it.

Our relationship was tricky to define. It was like a strange dance, always stepping sideways and never quite meeting in the middle.

When he and his best friend Ethan decided to embark on a journey around the world with nothing more than a couple of hundred dollars in their pockets, I had no right to object. We were friends and nothing more. But in the days before he left, when the excitement in him was brewing, the total hopelessness of it all started to crush me. I didn't want him to leave. I toyed with the idea that it might have been because I loved him. Looking back, I think it was just that I needed to have him around.

The single biggest regret of my life occurred on the day before he left. I lied to Alex, telling him I was staying at Nicole's, and headed to Mitchell's place after school, convinced that I could make him stay.

"I was dumb enough to think I was enough to hold him here," I told Adam.

"So you told him how you felt?"

I looked across the table at him, wondering how I was going to tell him I'd done something much worse.

"I spent the night in his bed – as if that was the very best I had to offer." I paused, expecting him to stand up and leave. But he didn't. I sucked in a sharp breath and continued. "I gave him every single part of me and he left anyway." I looked into his eyes, expecting to see the revulsion I felt for myself. All I saw was concern. He was honestly good to the core. "His sisters found out. The whole town knew before I even got home."

"I'm sorry," he said quietly. "That must have been horrible."

"My name was mud. My name is *still* mud. It was a stupid thing to do and the only one who regretted it more than I did was Mitchell."

"How do you know that?"

"Mitchell told Ethan, and goodness knows who else. Ethan told Nicole that he'd called me one of the biggest mistakes of his life." I was surprised by how much it still hurt to say it out loud. "So now you know. Pieces of me aren't missing. They've been smashed up."

Adam reached across the table, palm up. I couldn't respond. "I know what you're thinking."

"How heavy is your head, Charli?" he asked.

"Excuse me?"

"You're always claiming to know what I'm thinking. Your head must be so heavy, weighed down by both our thoughts."

"I'd much rather guess your thoughts than hear them right now," I muttered.

"Tough. I'm going to tell you exactly what I'm thinking."

I closed my eyes, and braced myself for the worst. He was too smart not to figure this out. I was damaged.

"Firstly, I'm annoyed with myself for being so polite to Jasmine. I was under the impression that she was just classless and dim-witted. I had no idea she could be so vile and cruel. Secondly, I'll never believe you again when you tell me that you lack courage."

I opened my eyes, confused, and focused on his dimple, unable to meet his eyes.

"I'm going to foul this up, Adam. I just know it." My voice took on a strange edge of panic.

He leaned across the small table. "I'm not going to let us mess it up. If you want to keep this quiet, we will. And if you should change your mind and decide that you're ready for the world to know how crazy I am about you, I'll be there, shouting it from the highest point in town."

When I wasn't concentrating, I had a stupid habit of saying exactly what I was thinking. "You won't have far to go. Gabrielle's house is the highest point."

"Great," he quipped. "Let me know when you're ready."

I slid my chair back. "I have to go. I'm supposed to be working."

Adam caught my hand as I passed him. "You're so much more beautiful when you're not tearing yourself to shreds, Charli," he said quietly.

"I'll try to remember that," I promised.

8. Penguin King

The perfect weather managed to hold into the late afternoon. The fading sun left a bright pink streak across the cloudless sky. It would have been the perfect summer evening except that it was freezing and the end of June.

We turned off the main highway and negotiated the four small side streets to get to Gabrielle's home. The car crawled to a stop at the end of the short driveway, right in front of the pretty seaside cottage.

Nearly two weeks had passed since she'd made her invitation. Adam mentioned it only once. I made a vague promise to think about it, but in truth I thought about little else. The easiest way to simplify my time with Adam was to call a truce with Gabrielle. Shipping Jasmine Tate to the Sahara Desert would also have been simplifying – and possibly easier to do.

Gabrielle's home was a small white brick house with a weathered red tin roof, neatly trimmed lawn and fussy cottage garden, full of plants that would have been bursting with flowers if the season was right. It looked like a fairy-tale cottage. I wondered how Snow White would feel knowing that a wicked witch had moved into her house, then felt guilty for the thought.

"What are you thinking about?" asked Adam, snapping me back to attention.

"Fairy tales actually. Do you know Snow White?"

"Not personally, no."

"Hmm, you're definitely not royalty then," I replied, making him snicker.

"Are you ready?" he asked.

"Can we set some ground rules first?"

"Its just dinner, Charli. Do we really need rules?"

"Please?" My voice was pathetic and whiny but it seemed to work.

"What are the rules?" he asked, giving in immediately.

"Don't leave me alone with her."

"Fine."

"And no speaking French. I'll automatically assume you're talking about me."

"Anything else?"

I thought hard, making sure all my demands were covered. "No, that's it."

"Great. Can we go inside now?"

"I'm not sure I want to do this."

"What happened to your courage?"

"You promised I wouldn't need any courage. It's just dinner right?"

"Exactly. So let's go inside." I studied his impatient face. He knew I was being ridiculous. I knew it too.

"Fine." I surrendered.

***

Adam took my coat as I shrugged it off. My eyes darted around the front room, trying to take in as much as I could before the Parisienne appeared.

The cottage seemed much bigger than it looked from the outside. It was light and airy, with white walls and oak floorboards. Huge windows on the east wall boasted a view of the ocean. The sun cast a pink glow over the room and combined with the warmth of the open fire; I couldn't help feeling a little more at ease.

Gabrielle breezed into the room, drying her hands on a tea towel. "Hello." She smiled. "I'm so glad you could make it, Charli."

I wondered if she thought I wouldn't come. I knocked all prejudices aside, determined to play nice. "Thanks," I replied, forcing a smile.

Gabrielle's demeanour gave nothing away. The only hint of nervousness she showed was the fact that she was still wringing her hands on the tea towel. "I hope you don't mind eating early. I teach an art class on Thursday nights so I have to leave at eight."

"No, it's fine." I meant it. I welcomed anything that would make this ordeal shorter. Maybe she did too and that was why she had suggested I come over that particular night. "What sort of art classes do you teach?"

My intrigue was genuine. I wasn't surprised that she was artistic – every fibre of her being screamed artfulness.

"Gabi's a painter," Adam announced proudly. It was the first time I'd ever heard him shorten her name. He pointed to a wall of framed paintings. "Those are all hers."

Most of the paintings were landscapes. Some were places I recognised; others were places I had only dreamed about. They were undeniably beautiful and I stood staring at them for too long to pretend to be unimpressed.

"These are amazing," I exclaimed.

"Thank you. It's just a hobby."

"You're very talented."

"Thank you," she repeated, sounding embarrassed. "Please, excuse me for a minute while I check on dinner."

I turned my attention back to the paintings. Adam stood behind me. "So what about you?" I murmured, "Are you artistic?" I knew he was perfect, strong and brilliant, but I'd never figured out what made him that way. My photography and my love of the ocean were my bliss. It bothered me that I didn't know his.

"Not at all," he replied at once.

"So what do you do, Adam? What's your bliss?"

"He studies too much, and he reads," said Gabrielle as she laid dinner plates on the table. "And when he's not doing that he's running up the beach or doing some other excruciating form of exercise."

"Gabrielle, tais-toi, d'accord?" hissed Adam. I nailed him with my glare, reminding him of our ground rules.

"You promised," I whispered.

Gabrielle giggled. "What did you promise her, Adam?" she asked, concentrating on the table setting.

"He promised me that you would only speak English tonight." I kept my eyes fixed firmly on Adam's, too intimidated by Gabrielle to look at her. "I don't understand French and I don't speak French. I am my French teacher's worst nightmare."

Gabrielle took me completely by surprise by laughing. "You have no idea." She changed the subject tactfully. "I cooked salmon, Charli. I hope you like fish."

"It's my favourite actually," I replied, completely truthfully.

"Adam, why don't you show Charli around?" suggested Gabrielle. We walked down the hallway and he paused at a door, ushering me ahead of him.

"This is your room?"

He nodded.

It looked too lived in to be a guest room. To the left was a wooden desk, roughly painted white in keeping with the rest of Gabrielle's shabby-chic furniture. It was scattered with heavy textbooks and well-worn novels.

"So this is what you do with all your spare time?" I asked, thumbing through a thick book.

"Somewhat," he replied.

"You're on holiday. You study on holiday?"

"Some of the time."

I set the book back down and moved towards the window.

"What else do you do?" I quizzed, pulling the curtain to peek outside.

"Not much. It's a very small town."

I smiled at him and he smiled back before quickly looking away. "You must do something, Adam."

———

92

"Do you really want to know what I do?"

I nodded.

"I count down the minutes until I can see you. I have even resorted to watching daytime soap operas just to distract myself." He looked sheepish.

"Soap operas?" I grinned.

"And cooking shows," he added, making me laugh.

"You need a hobby," I teased.

"I have one in mind. I'll show you if you'd like," he said.

The fact that we were in Gabrielle's house changed nothing about the way my body reacted when he came near me. My knees went to mush and I was sure that she could hear my heart from the kitchen.

"It's outside," he murmured, planting a kiss on my lips, so soft that I couldn't be sure he'd actually touched me.

We bypassed Gabrielle by sneaking out the back door. Adam led me across the lawn to a shed in the back corner. The shed – not much smaller than the house – was in a terrible state of repair. The corrugated iron structure was rusty, and I was doubtful that he could open the door without it falling off. He proved me wrong, and flipped the old-fashioned light switch.

"A boat?" I choked in disbelief. "You bought a boat?" I ran my hand along the hull.

He laughed. "Apparently she came with the house. I'm thinking of restoring her."

The old wooden sloop, perched on dodgy wooden trestles, looked to be about five metres long and was covered in layers of weathered blue paint. A messy pile of rigging and an ancient mast lay on the ground.

He was certainly ambitious.

"What do you know about boat restoration?"

He walked around the structure, running his hand along the gunwales. "Absolutely nothing. But I'm a fast learner."

I didn't doubt him for a second. "Do you know anything about boats in general?"

"My dad used to take my brother and me sailing when we were kids. Nothing as grand as this old maiden, though." He patted the boat, gazing at it with the same expression he liked to stun me with.

"You can sail in New York?"

The surprise in my voice made him laugh. "You can sail in New York," he confirmed. "I'll take you sailing on the Hudson someday," he promised, stepping sideways and taking me with him. He danced me around the dilapidated old shed, waltzing to silent music, laughing. "Down to Battery Park, past Ellis Island and across to the Statue of Liberty."

"We can do that?"

Our dance slowed to a stop. "I'm pretty sure we can do *anything*, Charlotte," he whispered, before leaning in to kiss me.

Even the softest kisses he bestowed on me burned down to the tips of my toes. Finally we broke apart, because we had to – wooden boats were flammable too.

"Did you know this boat is special?" I asked, pointing in the general direction of the boat behind me as I tried to regulate my breathing.

He chipped a few flecks of paint off with his fingers. "It will be, as soon as I can get all of this paint off."

"It's already special."

Adam's attention turned back to me. I never got tired of seeing him smile.

"I get the distinct impression that you know something I don't, Charli." His formal vocabulary didn't surprise me anymore.

"Call it a hunch," I said, grinning. I'm sure my lack of refinement when it came to choosing my words didn't surprise him either.

Spotting a crate full of old tools, I picked up a screwdriver. Scraping it along the side of the boat, I peeled away layers of paint.

"Charlotte." Adam groaned. "Please don't hurt the boat."

"Underneath the paint it's almost perfect. No rot or decay…strange for an old boat like this, don't you think?" I ran my fingers along the wounded wood.

"What does that mean?"

Dropping the screwdriver back into the crate, I dusted off my hands. "There's a wood here called Huon pine. It's endemic to Tasmania. Huon trees live to be three thousand years old. They used to make boats out of it because the wood has a special oil in it that stops it rotting. The trees are protected now so they don't log them anymore. Huon pine only grows a millimetre a year. It's hard to imagine how long it would take a big tree to grow."

Adam looked stunned, trading glances between the boat and me. "Charli, that means this boat is about a billion years old!"

"I told you it was special." Triumph saturated my voice.

He pulled me in close. "*You're* special. How could you possibly know the things you do?" he asked quietly.

"I don't know for sure that it's Huon, but it might be. You may have found yourself a hidden treasure."

"I already knew that," he whispered.

***

The oval dining table seemed too small and intimate. I found it difficult to make eye contact with either of them and was grateful for the beautiful view of the ocean from the large window. I silently wished the last few minutes of daylight would hold just long enough to get through dinner. Staring into the darkness might have seemed a little odd.

"The view is perfect isn't it?" asked Gabrielle, passing a bowl of salad so perfectly arranged that it could have been mistaken for a piece of her art.

I forced a smile. "You have the best beach. We come here a lot."

Gabrielle's house was just south of the Cove. The stretch of beach below her cottage was the straightest stretch for kilometres, popular with surfers in the winter and overrun with tourists in the summer.

"With Alex?" Her accent made her words musical. It also made it impossible to decipher her tone.

"Yeah, mostly," I replied casually.

"You swim down there?" asked Adam incredulously. He stared through the window at the dark sea, blackened by the low light.

"Of course," I said, confused. "You like to swim too, don't you?"

"Sure, in a pool. A nice clean pool where you can see exactly what's underneath you."

"This is one of the best surf beaches on the south coast, Adam," I said, a little too defensively.

"Ugh. Surfers," groaned Gabrielle.

I fought the urge to scream my words at her. "Do you have something against surfers?"

"She thinks they have no sense of self-preservation. And they mess up her view. She calls them penguins," he said, seizing the opportunity to rib her.

"Well that's what they remind me of," she grumbled. "Sitting out there on their boards for hours on end, huddled in a group." Her tone was irritated, as if the hours the surfers spent on the water cut in to her own personal time.

"You should give it a try. You might understand it better," I said.

Gabrielle absently ran her finger around the rim of her wine glass.

"I couldn't imagine Gabi venturing out there," said Adam, his smile wide.

I looked to the window, seeing nothing but my reflection. The light had completely disappeared and sombre blackness was in its place.

"They wouldn't have her out there," I retorted. Braving the nasty glare that Gabrielle threw at me, I maintained eye contact. "Surfers are very territorial."

Gabrielle's usually porcelain cheeks turned crimson. Now seemed like the perfect time to throw Alex's name into the mix.

"Alex is the penguin king. He's out there every morning."

"I know," she replied. Maybe she really did study them.

"You should ask him to give you lessons," I suggested.

Gabrielle brought her napkin to her mouth, making a small coughing sound. I wondered if I'd made her choke. Adam looked torn, like he wanted to slap on her on the back but wasn't sure if he needed to. "Are you okay?" he asked finally, sliding his glass of water across the table to her.

"Fine," she replied, recomposing herself. She glanced at her watch. "I actually have to go. I'm sorry to leave so early." Her voice was surprisingly sincere. "I'm very pleased you came, Charli. I hope you know you're welcome here always. And now I really have to go."

Adam sat motionless at the table long after Gabrielle had left.

"Maybe I should put them both out of their misery and set them up on a date," I said at last.

"And what happens if they fall in love, get married and have five children?"

"I would slash my wrists."

"What am I going to do with you?"

"Can you take me home?" I asked.

"Already?"

———

"Yeah. I've done enough damage for one night," I replied sheepishly.

"You haven't damaged me."

"I have, you know. One of these days you'll wake up and realise how horrible I truly am."

He read the distress in my face and pulled me to my feet, holding me tight. I didn't feel the usual rush of blood to my head. I was safe in the arms of someone who didn't care how wicked I could be or how positively unreasonable I was at times.

"Never going to happen," he whispered.

9. Secrets and Lies

The illuminated clock in the car held my attention for much of the drive home, reminding me that eight o'clock was a ridiculously early time to be returning from dinner.

Nearly a whole week without rain had worked magic on our driveway. The deep puddles had dried into muddy potholes that cushioned the blow of driving over them. Despite the pitch-blackness of the night, Adam negotiated them perfectly.

The house was in darkness when we arrived, meaning Alex wasn't home. He probably wasn't anticipating me screwing dinner up so badly that I'd be home that early.

"Adam, will you wait with me until Alex gets home?" I asked.

"Of course I will."

He held my hand and I clung to the back of his coat with the other as I followed him up to the veranda. Reaching into my coat pocket, he grabbed my keys, unlocking and opening the door so quickly, I barely had to slow my walk. I flicked the light on, flooding the lounge room with light.

"Okay?" asked Adam.

"Fine," I replied as I made a grab for his lapels, pulling him close to me.

He kissed me just long enough to get my heart racing before mercilessly freeing his lips from mine. I groaned in protest and he chuckled. "I need to let Gabi know I might be late home," he said, reaching for his phone.

He punched buttons on his phone with one hand, inches from my ear. I continued kissing his neck, wondering how he'd slow his breathing when she answered. It was a thought that lasted only a few seconds, soon replaced by confusion and shock.

We stood as still as statues, listening to the muffled sound of a phone ringing from the kitchen. My head snapped up to look at Adam. He looked as surprised as I felt. He pressed a button to end the call and the phantom phone stopped ringing.

Gabrielle's phone was in my house.

I heard Alex before I saw him. His bedroom door burst open and closed quickly. Judging by the way he practically fell through the doorway, he must have run down the hallway.

"Charli," he breathed. He was dressed only in a pair of jeans, still dragging one arm through his white T-shirt.

My reply was choked. "Hi."

The look on his face was familiar to me. We shared the same genes. I shouldn't have been surprised that his trying-to-come-up-with-a-plausible-lie face was exactly the same as mine.

"Ah, Gabrielle's phone is here," said Adam, pointing vaguely towards the kitchen. "Is she here?"

My brother glanced at me but couldn't hold my gaze. He looked back to Adam.

"Yes." His voice sounded strained, like he was confessing to a murder or something equally as heinous. Perhaps he was.

That was Gabrielle's cue to enter the room. I was perfectly positioned to see her breeze down the hallway, every bit the runway model. Unlike Alex, she had the decency to make sure she was fully dressed. She nervously raked her hand through her bedroom hair, looking everywhere but at us.

"Art Class, Gabrielle?" asked Adam. Her burning cheeks answered for her. "Why didn't you just tell me?"

Alex seemed more concerned by my reaction. He tried to speak but I cut him off.

"How long has this been going on?"

I wanted him to tell me it was a one-off, a sordid little one-night stand. That would be the easiest scenario to deal with, but the minute I noticed that his pinkie finger was linked around hers, it was game over. This was no one-night deal. He loved her.

He spoke hesitantly. "Over a year."

I sucked in a breath as if I'd just been hit.

"It will be okay, Charli," promised Alex.

He was foolish to think I'd be so easily placated. "You lied to me. How is that ever okay?"

The reality was that this wasn't as simple as him telling me one little untruth. Alex would have had to string a million lies together to keep his affair with Gabrielle a secret for so long.

"It's not okay," he said, backpedalling.

I tried to work out whether to stay or go. If I wanted answers, I had to stay. "Just tell me why!"

"I'll tell you everything," he replied, without actually telling me anything.

"Well, speak!" I demanded. "Please, just tell me something, anything!"

I scowled across the room at him but he was looking at Gabrielle. He wasn't answering me because he was protecting *her* feelings.

I was suddenly thankful I'd left my coat on. "I have to get out of here," I blurted.

"Charli, stay," urged Adam. I shrugged him away.

"No. I can't be here."

I half-expected him to joke about my flee-itis flaring up but he didn't. No one was in the mood for jokes. I pulled open the drawer of the hallstand searching for my car keys. My dramatic exit was hampered by the fact that I couldn't remember where I'd left them.

"Take my car," offered Alex, pointing at his keys. "It's in the garage." That explained why we hadn't seen it when we arrived. I imagined her sporty little Mazda was hidden next to it. Thinking about how far they'd gone to conceal this was making me nauseous. The guilt must have been killing him. Never before had he offered me the use of his car.

"Don't let her go while she's angry," mumbled Gabrielle, tugging his arm.

"If you want to leave, I'll come with you," offered Adam.

I shook my head but didn't reply. My moment of rebellion was lost. I couldn't even remember the point I was trying to make. The bunch of keys sounded like a much larger object as I slammed them down on the hallstand.

"Why did you cook salmon for dinner?" I asked, aiming my extraneous question squarely at Gabrielle. If I had nowhere to run, she certainly didn't either. I was going to make sure of it.

"I told her it was your favourite," Alex admitted.

"So it was all part of the plan, pushing me to go to dinner? The interest in my photography was a nice touch, Gabrielle."

"I am interested in your photography, Charli," she insisted.

"How uncomfortable did it get when Adam came into the picture? Oh wait...it probably made things easier, didn't it? I have a distraction now. You get to spend more time with Gabrielle. In fact, things are probably much easier..." My voice trailed off as I came to a horrible conclusion.

Alex got there before me and was shaking his head before I'd finished. "No, no. Adam knew nothing about this."

"Not a thing, Charli," assured Adam, flatly. His voice was void of emotion. Maybe he was in shock too – or maybe I'd been right all along. He was too good to be true. I searched his eyes for the truth. He looked as confused as I was.

I saw no more point in talking, wanting nothing more than to disappear. Without another word I pushed past Alex and Gabrielle and marched to my room, slamming the door so hard that I expected it to fall off the hinges.

I leaned my back against the closed door and without much grace, slid to the floor. I sat quietly for a long time, dazed. I could hear muted conversation coming from the lounge room but I couldn't bear to listen. Alex wouldn't give me answers when I stood before him, begging like *I* was the one who had done something wrong. Too scared of what I might hear by eavesdropping, I covered my ears with my clenched fists to make sure I heard nothing.

***

It didn't surprise me that Alex was already up when I woke the next morning. I trudged into the kitchen as if my shoes were made of concrete blocks. I wanted to pretend nothing had changed, that the whole night before was a bad dream. The minute he turned to face me, I knew it was impossible.

"I've cooked breakfast." Alex never cooked breakfast. Looking at the plate of food that vaguely resembled eggs I remembered why.

"No thanks," I mumbled, wondering how eggs could be burnt black and yet be runny at the same time.

"Please, Charli," he pleaded. "Consider it a peace offering."

He pushed the plate towards me and I slid it straight back. "A peace offering would be a big, fat chocolate cake Alex, not...scrambled eggs," I said, hoping I'd guessed right.

"It's an omelette," he corrected, allowing a smile to creep across his face.

I pretended to retch. "Well, assuming you're not trying to kill me, I'll give it a miss."

The smile disappeared from his face and he was suddenly serious. "I'd never intentionally hurt you, you know that."

"Keeping your girlfriend – or whatever she is – a secret from me hurts a lot more than a few bad eggs ever would."

His expression was irate but resigned. "I just couldn't tell you. The longer it went on, the more difficult it became. You, better than anyone, knows what this town is like, Charli."

"Don't make this about me."

"I didn't want to complicate things. Gabrielle is your teacher." His tone implied he was doing me a favour.

"She's not my girlfriend, she's yours. It makes no difference to me. You're the one who would have to put up with the stupid gossip, not me. Don't pretend you were protecting me. You were protecting her," I said contemptuously.

Alex spoke too quietly. "I protect you, Charli, always you."

"Look, she makes you happy. Don't you think I want you to be happy?" I asked, annoyed that he'd made it about me again. Alex held his palms out. "Am I that horrible?"

"No, of course not." He replied without hesitating, which reassured me just enough to keep me in the room.

"Why her? You could have any girl in this town."

"I only want her."

I believed him.

"Jasmine Tate is in love with you."

He smiled. "Jasmine Tate frightens me. Both the Beautifuls do."

"Yeah, well, Gabrielle Décarie frightens me," I muttered.

Alex sat down. Looking at the plate of eggs in front of him, he grimaced. "Look, how about we do something today? Just you and me."

"I have school," I reminded him.

"I know. Sometimes you just need the day. I think we need the day."

"Are you worried that I'll go to school and create a scene? Blow your little charade to pieces and embarrass your witch?" I snarled.

"No. I know you would never do that." He sounded certain, and I suddenly felt guilty for suggesting it.

"I have to go," I said.

"I'll drive you if you can wait a few minutes. I just need to –"

"It's okay. I'm going to take my car. It needs a run."

"You *are* going to school, aren't you?" asked Alex, looking at me through narrowed eyes. He knew me better than I knew myself at times.

"Do you want me to lie?" I asked.

He shook his head, grimacing.

"I won't lie, then."

In the rear vision mirror I saw Alex watching me as I drove away. I could only imagine what he was thinking at that point. I hoped he trusted me enough to know that I would never be the one to tell the Beautifuls that Alex Blake was off their list of most eligible bachelors. I also knew I'd said nothing to convince him of that.

10. French Attack

School was the last place I felt like going, and Alex's offer of spending the day with me was practically an invitation to ditch. I considered going to see Adam but talked myself out of it. I'd almost accused him of being Alex and Gabrielle's accomplice – their aide-de-camp. Even Adam had to have a limit. I was sure I'd pushed him beyond it.

I watched monstrous dark clouds rolling in across the bay. The approaching storm matched my mood perfectly and I decided to make the most of it. I grabbed my camera bag from the passenger seat. I'd found my calling for the day. I slung the bag over my shoulder and ventured up the steep hill.

The top of the paddock was relatively flat, at least level enough to sit comfortably while I steadied my camera on the small tripod. I was still setting up my equipment, trading glances between the viewfinder and the angry sky above when something I wasn't expecting caught my eye.

"No freaking way," I mumbled, looking through the viewfinder to be sure it was actually her.

Climbing through the wire fence by the road was Gabrielle – not an easy manoeuvre in a pencil skirt and the most beautiful black heels I'd ever seen.

I considered lying down in the long grass – watching her staggering around in heels while she searched for me did have its appeal – but decided that seeing her stumble her way towards me like a drunk beauty queen was pleasure enough.

She was halfway up before she gave up on preserving her pretty shoes. I giggled as I watched her pull them off one at a time, futilely dusting them off as she stumbled closer to me.

Finally she was close enough to hear me speak. "If you were planning to drag me to school, you might have considered wearing more sensible shoes," I told her, fighting the urge to snap a picture of her.

"I'm not planning to drag you anywhere," she replied, still breathless from her trek.

"How did you know I was here?"

"I was passing and saw your car."

"Your house is that way," I said, pointing south. "Were you on your way back from my house? Did he let you stay over and sneak you out after I left?"

She overlooked my sarcasm, dropped her shoes on the ground and replied without skipping a beat. "No, he snuck me out the window before dawn."

I had to hand it to her; she was playing the game to perfection.

"What do you want, Gabrielle?"

She pointed to the grass. "Can I sit?"

"Sure. Pull up a blade."

Her usually flawless demeanour faltered as she flopped on the grass beside me, tugging at her tight black skirt. Turning my attention back to the viewfinder on my camera, I studied the black clouds rolling in.

"It's kind of fitting, don't you think?" she asked.

"What is?"

"The weather. The calm before the storm."

"Are you expecting a storm, Mademoiselle Décarie?" I asked, feigning disinterest.

"I am expecting nothing less," she revealed smugly.

"Is that because I am malevolent and full of animosity?" I asked, reciting one of her previous descriptions of me.

"No, it's because you're hurt. And when you're wounded, you do what you need to in order to protect your heart."

"You don't know me," I scoffed, annoyed that she was right.

"I know you adore Alex."

"So do you, apparently."

"I'm glad that you know that, Charli. I truly do love him." There was no mistaking the sincerity in her voice. "I wanted to tell you months ago but Alex was nervous. He knows what you went through last year. He was worried about the gossip flaring up again."

"Why would it? It's nothing to do with me. Imagine every girl in town finding out that he was off the market because *you'd* stolen him."

The bright smile she gave reminded me of Adam. "Alex loves this town but he doesn't trust it. He tells me that the small-minded gossip has been viral for years. I was always under the impression that that loathsome Jasmine Tate was at the root of it."

"You don't know the half of it."

"I knew everything, Charli. I teach at that school. I *tried* to protect you."

"What do you mean you tried to protect me?"

"Don't you remember spending every afternoon for two weeks in detention?"

Of course I remembered. That was the fortnight I'd decided that she was a witch. I couldn't understand why she'd been so hard on me.

"I just wanted to give you a break from them, Charli. But I ran out of excuses to keep you there after a while so – "

"So you started keeping Jasmine back after school."

Gabrielle pulled a disgusted face. "For three weeks. I was so glad when that wretch finally graduated."

Looking back, spending afternoons hiding out in detention had been my salvation. At the time, dealing with the wrath of Mademoiselle Décarie was so much easier than dealing with the rest of the world.

"She very nearly broke me." It was an admission I never intended to make to her.

"I know," she said gently. "Alex knew that too. We started seeing each other around that time. He was terrified of making things worse for you. By the time it all blew over, too much time had passed. It had turned from a secret to a lie."

"It's not an excuse."

"No, it's an explanation."

"Don't you think I have I right to be mad at him?" I asked. "He lied to me, for a really long time."

"You lie to him all the time," she accused.

I shouldn't have been surprised that Adam confided in Gabrielle. He saw no reason to keep anything from her.

"Do you report back to Alex?" I quizzed suspiciously.

"Absolutely not." She answered with complete certainty.

"Why?"

"We're not that different, you and I. I think that's why you despise me so much."

I frowned. "I don't despise you. And we're very different."

"You're not as bad as you think you are. You should never believe your own press," she said, grinning wryly.

"Do you believe my press?"

"How tragic it would be if I did." Gabrielle spoke more formally than Adam at times.

"Very nasty things were said about me. They thought I was trash."

"You're not the first girl to make an error in judgement, Charli. Don't let it be for nothing. And I find it bizarre that certain girls in this town could consider you to be trash. I assumed that wearing sequins in the afternoon would make one trashy."

She made a valid point. Jasmine, Lisa and Lily's fondness for short, sparkly clothing was questionable to say the least.

"It sounds like you find this place just as suffocating as I do."

"Yes. That is true."

"So why don't you leave?"

Gabrielle absently picked at blades of grass. Her face seemed strained.

"I can't just yet. I have been fortunate enough to find the man who loves me."

I frowned uneasily. It was strange to hear her speak of Alex that way. The longest relationship I could remember him having was over and done with after just a few weeks. Thinking hard, I couldn't even remember her name, and then wondered if he could.

"Despite what you might think, I want him to be happy. You make him happy."

Gabrielle gave a tiny smile. "Thank you."

I started packing away my equipment. "The rain is coming," I said.

We looked to the sky. The black clouds had taken on an angry purple tinge. Faint rumbles of thunder could be heard in the distance and I could see she was starting to feel anxious.

"Your pretty shoes are going to get wet."

"I don't care. I fear that if we don't have this conversation now, it might never happen."

Gabrielle was definitely a girly girl. Imagining her voluntarily sitting in a field in the middle of a storm was a stretch. I, on the other hand, lived for days like this.

"When you leave Pipers Cove, where will you go?" I asked.

"I want to go home to Marseille. I left when I was eighteen and it's been a long journey, nearly nine years." Her voice was thoughtful, as if she was digging deep for the right words. "I'm ready to go home…conditionally."

Instantly, I knew what the condition was. "You want Alex you go with you?"

It wasn't a question that needed answering. "Isn't love a dreadful thing?" she asked, as if she was enjoying a private joke. "It makes you do all sorts of unreasonable things."

"Alex will go with you. He won't have reason to stay much longer. He knows I have plans to travel," I told her.

It had always irked me that I'd kept him tied down for so long. Knowing I was partly to blame for Gabrielle staying much longer than she had planned made me feel even worse.

"Are you planning to follow Adam back to New York?" she asked, shocking me to the core.

The look I flashed her was so fierce that she should have burst into flames. "What? No! We've never even talked about that! Why would you ask?"

My distress seemed to amuse her. "As I said, love makes you do all sorts of unreasonable things."

I allowed myself to dream for a second. I had honestly never considered going to New York. Perhaps I should have congratulated myself for being sensible for the first time ever.

Gabrielle had asked me the question so casually that it sounded like a realistic prospect, except we both knew it wasn't. Alex would lose the plot completely, probably locking me in the house for years, which in turn would put a huge dampener on Gabrielle's romantic trysts with him. I lay back in the grass, staring at the sky, laughing at the absurdity of the idea.

Gabrielle laughed too but in a much more demure way. "Don't you think Alex would approve?" she asked between giggles. "New York is the perfect place to start an adventure. That's where I started mine."

"Alex would hit the roof."

"He would, but I'm trying to get him to keep an open mind...just in case." She looked at me from the corner of her eye. "I have an advantage because I can vouch for Adam. He's the most decent person I know, and I've been telling Alex that every chance I get."

That explained a lot. Alex had been very lenient when it came to Adam – too lenient. Of course he wasn't mellowing. It was all down to the Parisienne witch, who was shaping up to be more of an unlikely ally than my archenemy. It was becoming impossible to hate her.

Finally, the sky gave out and we were pelted with rain. Surprisingly, she seemed unaffected by it. I shielded my camera bag as best I could but Gabrielle didn't move an inch. Her ivory shirt clung to her skin as if it was painted on. The clip holding her hair failed under the weight of the rain and hung loosely at the base of her neck. Wiping streaks of black mascara off her previously perfect face was the only hint of vanity she showed. I couldn't help smiling at her.

"You're enjoying this aren't you?" she asked. She stood up, brushing as much mud off her clothes as she could manage. "I've got to go. I have to go home and change before I go to school. Are you going to school today?"

Her tone suggested I had a choice. I decided to push my luck right to the limit. "I should, but I'm probably not going to make it. I have third period French. My teacher is a witch."

She chuckled. "I have heard that. Maybe she's just misunderstood." She scooped her ruined shoes up. "Will you promise me something, Charli?"

"Maybe."

"Resist the urge to follow Adam too soon. At least see out the last few months of school. Alex needs you around a little longer."

I nodded but didn't reply. Skipping town and chasing Adam back to New York was a stretch by any imagination, even one as wild as mine.

I watched as she made her way down the hill, stumbling on the uneven ground. I knew an unlikely truce had been forged between us. A desire to make one last iniquitous stand took over.

I scraped together a handful of mud and flung it as hard as I could. To my delight, it hit her square in the back. The rain washed it all the way down her back. She slowly turned around to face me, holding her arms away from her body in a way that made me think she was about to sprint back to me and pounce. I considered running but wasn't sure I could outrun her now that she'd ditched the heels.

"What was that for?" she shouted.

"For making Alex fall in love with you," I shouted back.

Gabrielle scooped a lump of earth into her hands, probably too angry to consider the damage it was doing to her perfect manicure. I flinched as she pegged the mud at me with the precision of an Olympic athlete. I felt the black muck ooze down the sleeve of my coat but didn't look down to survey the damage.

"What was that for?" I asked, failing miserably in my attempt to appear angry.

"For ruining my shoes."

When the storm began to wane and the rain slowed to drizzle, I found it had taken my dark mood with it. I made my tentative way to my car, slipping on the muddy incline. I was relieved that Gabrielle wasn't still there to see.

I didn't consciously make the decision to go to Adam but that was where I ended up.

I expected things to be different between us. I sat in my car on the driveway, forcing the ridiculous memory of the night before to the back of my mind. Thinking about it only added to my vexation.

Eventually, I summoned the courage to knock on the door.

"Charli?" His voice was unexpected, making me jump. The only thing separating us was the screen door, but it might as well have been iron bars.

I couldn't place the emotion in his voice. For all I knew, I was about to be unceremoniously cut loose. I took comfort in the fact that he'd be painfully polite about it. Polite to the extreme. I stood silent, staring at him through the mesh.

"Are you okay?" he asked finally.

"I just wasn't sure if you'd want to see me."

"I always want to see you but I'm not sure I should let you in." He held the door open with his foot. I shied away. "Only because you look remarkably like a creature from the black lagoon," he clarified, smiling the one-dimpled smile I loved so much.

I looked down and realised what he meant.

"Is that the only reason?" I asked cautiously.

"What other reason would I have?"

"I just thought...after last night –"

"Last night was nothing to do with us," he chided.

"I thought you'd be running for the hills by now," I said, making him smile.

"Why would I leave? I just got here." I shrugged but didn't reply. "Maybe we should hose you down," he teased.

"Is that what you did to Gabrielle?"

He smirked. "No, she had a plan. She called ahead and asked me to put her robe near the door. I think she stripped off in the garage."

"Did she tell you what happened?"

"Not exactly but she warned me not to let you in the house if you looked like her."

"She said that? Wow. And all I really wanted to do was roll around on her white couches for a minute."

He laughed loudly. "I'm definitely not letting you in then."

"I'll be good," I promised.

"I can't be sure about that. I actually like it when you're not good so that would make me an unwilling accomplice. I definitely think I should hose you down."

"No need," I replied, kicking off my sodden shoes. I dragged off my heavy coat and dropped it to the ground. "Better?"

"Marginally," he replied, waving his hand to usher me inside.

"You don't sound too convinced," I said.

"I make it a habit never to trust a girl caked in mud."

"Oh, fine," I huffed in mock annoyance. I started unbuttoning my shirt. Adam grabbed my hands.

"I'd trust you even less if you were naked." He grinned wickedly at me. "I'll get you a robe."

He disappeared inside, returning with an oversized whiter-than-white robe. He winked as he handed it to me before turning his back. I stripped off my shirt and jeans, swapping them for the plush robe.

"Okay. You can turn around now," I said, waving the sleeves that hung well below the end of my hands.

His lips pressed into a hard line as he fought against smiling. "I did."

I took an unnecessary step closer to him as he started rolling up my sleeves. "Does it take a lot of work to be so good all of the time?"

"I wasn't being good, Charlotte." His voice was velvet. "Far from it, actually. I got a perfect view of you through the mirror over there."

He pointed to a huge bevel edged mirror hanging on the far wall. I should have been mortified. But I wasn't.

Grabbing the cord on the robe, he pulled me through the door and into the confines of a strong hug. I buried my head into his shoulder, breathing in his scent.

"Do I have you for the whole day?" he asked, stroking my wet hair.

"When one is truanting, it is usually customary for one to take the whole day," I said, trying to mimic his formal diction.

"So what are we going to do with this day?" he asked, smirking at me in a way that made me think he had a few ideas.

"Wash my clothes?"

***

A long time passed before I even thought about moving from the couch. I was too comfortable – until the subject of the night before came up. I'd done a complete about-face where Gabrielle was concerned, which confused Adam.

"You were so angry last night. I thought they'd have to work a little harder to get you on side."

"Everything seems to make so much sense now. The whole time I thought he had a mad crush on her, he was torturing himself by lying about it."

"He chose to lie about it, Charli. They both did."

"I'm not sure they meant to, not for so long anyway. Sometimes Alex gets weird, like he wants to tell me something but then chickens out. Now I know why."

He frowned. "Gabi could have told me."

"No, she couldn't. She didn't want to put you in the position of having to lie to me."

His hold on me tightened as he pulled me in closer. "I wouldn't have lied to you. I would have told you everything I know."

I laughed. "That's why lying is sometimes the best option."

"So your mud fight with Gabrielle was a bonding experience?" he asked, lacing my fingers through his.

The oversized robe slipped off my shoulder and he ran his finger along the strap of my bra.

"Yeah, in part," I mumbled, pulling the robe back.

"Anything you want to share?" he asked, murmuring the words against my neck. He wasn't playing fair. His touch acted as a truth machine and I'm sure he knew it.

Gabrielle's words still rang in my ear. I wanted to tell him that thoughts of following him to New York were trickling into my head. I just couldn't explain it to him in a way that didn't make me sound crazy.

"Another time," I whispered, pressing my lips to his.

I heard the clothes dryer beeping, signalling the end of our imprisonment. I prised myself free of his arms.

"Where are you going?"

"To get dressed. Then we can get out of here." My jeans were scorching hot on my skin as I dragged them on. The metal button burnt my stomach, making me wince.

Adam appeared in the doorway. Looking far from sympathetic, he watched me jump around, trying to keep the button clear of my skin. "What's the hurry? You're not even prepared to wait for your pants to cool?"

"The day's nearly gone. The rain's stopped. We need to find something to do," I replied, rushing through my sentences.

"You're so pretty when you're trying to avoid third degree burns," he said.

"Thank you. Now let's go," I replied, reaching for his hand and dragging him out of the room.

The mad rush seemed pointless ten minutes later when we were still sitting in Adam's car, trying to decide where to go.

"Are we hiding today or are we going public?"

It was a fair question. I was more than happy to keep him all to myself. The fact that I wasn't at school would set tongues wagging anyway. Hiding was just delaying the inevitable, but I wasn't ready to throw us under the bus just yet.

"We're definitely hiding."

"Okay then. How about you take me to the hardware store? It's supposed to be on the main street. I've driven up and down a hundred times but haven't managed to find it."

The Pipers Cove shopping precinct consisted of a handful of shops along main road. Window-shopping was hardly an all-day event. Even the most serious shopper could browse all the shops in less than an hour, which made missing the hardware store frustrating for him.

"You should have asked Gabrielle for directions," I suggested, trying to keep a straight face.

"I did. She told me it was on the main street and then laughed," he griped.

Unable to keep a straight face any longer, I giggled. Adam glanced across at me, mumbling something in French.

"I'll take you there," I promised.

11. Sparkly Things

Following my directions, Adam pulled into an angled parking bay in front of the shops on the main road.

"Are you sure this is a hardware store?" he asked.

It took great effort to keep my tone serious. "Would I lie to you?"

"I apologise," he said insincerely. "The sign on the roof confused me." He ducked his head to look up through the windscreen at the huge sign mounted on the roof. "Floss Davis. Master Jeweller."

Everyone in town knew where Norm Davis's hardware shop was located, which was fortunate because the only hint of what he sold was the wheelbarrow out the front, filled with a mass of pansies. His wife Floss's jewellery business was extremely well represented by a massive sign that nearly buckled the roof.

I dragged Adam inside.

"Did I hear voices?" boomed Floss from down the back of the shop. She appeared a few seconds later and Adam flinched. Floss's wild curly hair was a very unnatural shade of red, and she wore a brightly coloured striped smock – free flowing and loose but doing very little to hide her size. She pulled me in close, shaking me like a rag doll as she hugged me.

"It's been so long," she crooned. "I'll make us some tea. I want to hear all your news." She was speaking to me but looking at Adam – who obviously was the news.

"Floss, I'd like you to meet a friend of mine. This is Adam Décarie."

Floss shook Adam's hand so enthusiastically I feared his arm might fall off. "Well, now. It's always nice to meet a friend of Charli's."

She looked Adam up and down and I silently dared her to find fault. I knew she wouldn't. Floss Davis was a good soul.

"Adam is restoring an old boat. We came to get supplies," I explained.

"Fabulous. I'll get Norm," she said, just before turning around and screaming out his name.

The beaded curtain separating the store from the back office rattled violently and Norm came running down the aisle. Unlike Floss, Norman Davis was fairly nondescript. Much slighter than his wife, he wore a flannelette shirt and moleskin pants. It was token attire for any country shopkeeper – except Alex, who wouldn't be caught dead in flannelette.

He announced his arrival by clapping his hands together. "What can I get you kids today? Two for the price of one on shovels, in case you're interested."

"Ah, no," I said, thrusting Adam forward. "I'll let Adam explain."

Norm placed a firm hand on his shoulder and marched him down the aisle, repeating the two-for-one offer on shovels.

Norm was either extremely knowledgeable or a great salesman. I sat drinking tea with Floss at the tiny jewellery counter at the front of the store, watching Adam through the window as he walked to the car laden with enough supplies to build a boat from scratch.

"He's easy on the eyes, isn't he?" whispered Floss, leaning across the counter.

My head dropped, embarrassed that I'd been caught staring at him.

"What's the story Charli?"

Maybe I was acting stranger than usual. Perhaps the Décarie effect was more powerful that I'd thought. I told Floss everything, and when I finished that tale, I spilled the beans on Alex and his Parisienne. There was no reason not to confide in her. Floss Davis was the trustworthiest person I knew.

"I knew there was something going on," she said. "That tiny slip of a French girl! Amazing."

"Do you know Gabrielle?"

"She comes in occasionally for canvas and turpentine. She's an artist, I think."

"A very talented one," I confirmed.

"Well, she has fantastic taste in men."

A bad case of the giggles overtook me. If the Beautifuls were members of Alex's fan club, Floss was the president, but much less scary and with a heart of pure gold.

When Adam walked in, looking far more settled than when he left, Floss effortlessly pulled him into the conversation. "Did you get everything you need?" she asked, pouring him a cup of tea from the gaudy teapot.

"Yes, Ma'am. Thank you."

She squinted. "I detect an accent."

"American."

"No, something else," she accused.

"French?" He sounded like he wasn't completely sure.

I cringed. I'd just got through telling her everything about Adam – including the fact he was the tiny-slip-of-a-French-girl's cousin.

"Yes! Of course!" she replied, excitedly.

Adam glanced at me from the corner of his eye as Floss launched into a long monologue. I was the worst French pupil that ever lived, but even I knew that not a word out of her mouth was French. She looked at Adam, anticipating a reply.

"Ah, I'm so sorry," he said. "I didn't understand a thing you said."

Floss slapped both hands down on the counter, so hard that I thought that the rings she was wearing were going to crack the glass. "What part of France did you say you were from?"

"Marseille," he replied, sounding a little frightened again.

Floss threw her head back in a bray of loud laughter. "Well, that explains it. We clearly speak different French."

Adam stared wide-eyed at her for a long moment, probably trying to gage whether she was serious. "Yes. We speak different French." He spoke slowly and the imbecilic choice of words was very unlike him.

She reached out and patted his hand, soothing him as if he'd done something wrong. "It's okay, darling."

I couldn't help laughing, and something about my laugh set Floss off. She stretched across the counter, crushing me against her huge bosom in a hug. She finally released me, but only to pinch my cheeks.

"Have you ever seen a prettier girl, Adam?" she crowed.

Adam looked straight at me. "No, Ma'am. I never have."

My cheeks burned, possibly due to embarrassment but more likely because of the way she'd pinched me.

Not another person entered the shop in the next half hour – including Norm. The phone ringing was the only reason Floss finally excused herself from our impromptu tea party.

"Don't go anywhere," she ordered, pointing at us as she shuffled backward down the aisle.

As soon as she was gone, Adam tipped his tea into a pot plant near the counter. "I think I've just met your number one fan, besides me of course."

"Yeah, she's pretty great. Alex used to bring me here when I was little. Floss would sit me up here on the counter to show me the jewellery." I tapped my finger on the glass top. "He used to freak out, worried that I'd fall through it."

He peered down. "Is this the whole collection?" The glass cabinet wouldn't have been more than a metre wide. I nodded. "And this warrants the huge sign out the front?" he asked, whispering as if someone was listening.

"Sparkly things trump shovels, Adam. These are special," I replied, making him laugh.

"You think everything is special." His tone was sympathetic. Perhaps he felt sorry for me.

"It's true," I insisted. "Take that one for instance." I pointed through the glass to a silver filigree ring with a dark blue stone. "Sapphires have been treasured for thousands of years. The ancient Persians believed that the earth rested on a giant sapphire and its reflection is what coloured the sky."

"No kidding?" he asked. His blue eyes were suddenly wide and bright.

"I kid you not. And diamonds, well let me tell you about diamonds," I said theatrically, sweeping across my forehead with the back of my hand, pretending to swoon. "When diamonds are set in gold and worn on the left side..." I pointed to my ring finger. "They're supposed to have the power to ward off devils and drive away nightmares. And when a house or garden is touched at each corner with a diamond it's supposed to be protected from storms and lightning."

Adam seemed awed by my trivia. "You, Charlotte Blake, are extraordinary."

"The purple stones are amethyst," I continued, tapping my finger on the glass. "Leonardo Da Vinci wrote that amethyst was able to make evil thoughts disappear."

A kiss brushed my neck. "I'm having a few evil thoughts of my own right now."

"Most gemstones are supposed to protect from evil, or bad weather or disasters. I don't know of any that ward off the evil thoughts of cute French American boys, though," I teased.

"That is a shame," he breathed into my neck.

From the corner of my eye I noticed Norm. I broke Adam's hold and put some distance between us. He wandered past, muttering something about fencing wire and an overdue account. As soon as we heard the beaded curtain rattle, Adam stepped closer, pulling me in again.

"Can I continue with my evil thoughts?" he whispered, making me laugh.

"Yes. Please, feel free."

"Where were we?"

"I was telling you about gemstones."

"Oh, that's right," he said, turning his attention back to the display cabinet. "How do you know all of this?"

I smiled. "My youth hasn't entirely been misspent, Adam."

"I thought you didn't believe in reading educational books."

"I don't. I believe in magic."

***

Daylight had faded by the time I arrived home. It wasn't until I stepped up on the porch that I began to regret staying out so late. I had no idea what sort of mood Alex would be in. I could smell something cooking and it made me shudder.

He's punishing me, I thought.

In the kitchen, Alex stood at the stove with his back to me, stirring the concoction he would soon be passing off as dinner. I wasn't sure whether to speak or sneak down to my room.

"Where's your car, Charli?" he asked, doing nothing to disprove my theory that he had eyes in the back of his head.

"Adam brought me home. I left my car at Gabrielle's."

He lifted the pot and carried it to the table. I slide a placemat underneath it to stop him burning a hole through the laminate. Ignoring my save, he pulled out a chair and sat.

"Are you hungry?" He almost sounded hopeful.

"Is this another peace offering, Alex?" I asked. "I keep telling you, chocolate cake would be much more appropriate."

"I didn't think I needed another peace offering. You ditched school. That makes us even." He motioned for me to pass my plate.

"I only want a little bit," I murmured, trying not to sound offensive.

"I didn't cook this, so you'll live to see another day," he said sarcastically.

"Gabrielle cooks for us now?"

Alex smirked – before he loaded up my plate to the point of overflowing. "No, Floss does. She stopped by the café this afternoon to give me a casserole and a lecture about not keeping her in the loop where my love life was concerned."

"She won't tell anyone, Alex," I assured him. "Besides, I think people should know." It was the truth. I saw no reason for them to be sneaking around. And I was looking forward to seeing the crushing blow served upon Jasmine Tate when she found she'd lost out to the Parisienne beauty queen. She'd either retreat with her sequined tail between her legs or fight harder to win Alex over. Both options had their appeal, and thinking about them made me smile. "Gabrielle puts up with a lot for you. You know that, right?"

"I keep telling her I'll make it up to her."

"She wants to go home, to Marseille."

Alex rubbed his brow, as if my words had caused him pain. Maybe it was the food. Floss was a hard-core vegan. The only way her green bean casserole could have tasted worse was if Alex had cooked it.

"I know she does." He spoke slowly, edging his food around his plate with his fork. Suddenly the conversation had taken a serious turn.

"You should go with her," I urged, keeping my tone casual.

"Impossible, Charli."

"You know I'm leaving at the end of the year. There's no reason for you to stay. You'll be a free man."

Alex was unamused. He stared at me as if I'd just sworn at him. "I've always been free. I'm not tied here." His voice was low. "I've given up nothing for you."

"We both know that's not true," I murmured.

He changed the subject. "This is really awful, isn't it?" he asked, looking at his plate of food.

I nodded.

Alex's chair scraped he pushed it back. He scraped his food into the bin, clearly keeping his temper in check. Any reminder I gave of the sacrifices he'd made for me instantly got his back up. Following his lead, I dumped my dinner and rinsed my plate.

"I'm going to my room," I said, pushing past him.

"We're okay, Charli. Nothing has changed."

I turned to look at him and he met my gaze. "Plenty has changed, Alex. And none of it's bad. I just wish you could see that."

I went to bed that night feeling smug. I had been right all along. The universe was shifting and Alex's misguided attempt to reassure me that nothing had changed proved that he was feeling it too.

12. Translation

Some days, surfing was more important than breakfast. Unless I got at least an hour in at the beach before school, those days seemed doomed from the start.

Alex sat at the table, reading the newspaper while he ate. "Quarter past six, Charli," he announced, reminding me that I was late.

I rushed past him, swiping a piece of his toast along the way. "I'm not waiting for you," I told him, annoyed that he wasn't ready. I swung the front door open with the zest of someone making a prison break... to be met by a startled – but still impossibly beautiful – French woman, hand raised to knock.

"Alex is inside," I told her, waving my toast.

I wasn't surprised to see her. I'd seen so much of her in the past week that I wondered how on earth he'd managed to keep her a secret for as long as he had. Stepping aside, I ushered her through the door.

The excitement of stealing a few minutes with the one she loved was obvious. She practically skipped into the kitchen, into the arms of my brother, who pulled her in close the minute she was within reach. I left them to it.

My mood wasn't great. The minute I got out of the car I could tell the waves would be nonexistent by the direction the wind blew my hair. The early morning rush to get there had been for nothing.

Onshore winds are the worst for surfing. The wind blows in from the ocean making the waves crumbly and shapeless. I cursed Alex. He didn't bail on me because Gabrielle was coming over. He knew the swell was useless but letting me trek down here anyway was a great way to get me out of the house early.

The frigid water lapped at my feet but that was as far as I was prepared to go – until I caught sight of the Beautifuls. Jasmine and Lily walked their revolting dog most mornings so seeing them wasn't a surprise, but I was usually better at avoiding them.

"Charli," purred Jasmine as soon as I was within earshot.

"What?" I snapped, focusing my attention on the ridiculous dog. Mitchell had presented his sisters with a cute designer puppy – bizarrely named Nancy – a few years earlier. The Beautifuls thought she was the ultimate fashion statement, carrying her around in a handbag and dressing her up. Unfortunately, Nancy developed a bad case of eczema, which made big patches of her fur fall out. The designer puppy soon became the most hideous dog in the southern hemisphere. Two years on she was still half bald, but at least she no longer had to wear a plastic cone around her neck to stop her biting herself. I laughed every time I saw her.

"No surf today. Whatever will you do?" Jasmine asked condescendingly.

She was definitely the brain of the operation. Nothing Lily ever did or said seemed to be as caustic as her sister. I was certain that somewhere underneath the grey velour tracksuit was a fairly decent person. But I wasn't going to see it today.

"You look like a little baby seal," said Lily, scrunching up her nose as if I smelled like one too. Jasmine threw back her head and cackled, giving Lily the approval she needed to continue. "I hope no one comes along and clubs you."

The wetsuit I wore wasn't designed to be pretty. The thick neoprene was necessary to protect against the twelve degree water. If someone came up with a suit that protected against the Tate sisters, I would have worn that.

"What do you want?" I asked, still focusing on their aesthetically challenged mutt.

"We don't want anything. We're just out walking Nancy." Jasmine tugged on the small dog's lead. The pooch gave a meaty little growl and stumbled into line.

It was too much to think they'd leave it at that. They had the gall to follow me as I walked up the trail to retrieve my gear.

"The car park is that way," I said, pointing to the sandy path.

Jasmine continued smirking at me but Lily turned around and looked. "Oh, look who it is!" she said excitedly.

I couldn't help turning. Adam jolted to a stop so suddenly, it was a miracle he didn't sprain both ankles.

Running recreationally, without the threat of something terrible chasing you, seemed pointless to me. But Adam loved it. He jogged the length of the beach along the Cove most mornings, so seeing him there was no great surprise.

He ripped the headphones from his ears and swept his brow with the back of his hand. The thick scrub concealing the beach until the very end of the track had blinded him. The music blaring through his headphones had rendered him deaf. And the fact that he didn't turn around and run straight back the way he'd come as soon as he saw us made him dumb.

"Ladies," he said cautiously, his eyes darting between Jasmine and me and bypassing Lily altogether.

Jasmine gave him a limp wrist and a pouty look. "I'm glad we ran into you," she said. "We haven't seen you around much lately."

He stared at her, focused and granitic. "Don't lose too much sleep over it."

I knew he couldn't stand the Beautifuls, especially since I'd told him why they were so despicable but it was still shocking to hear him speak so rudely to them. Judging by their looks of horror, they weren't expecting it either. Jasmine recovered quickly, clearing her throat and glancing down at Nancy while she pulled herself together. Adam took the opportunity to wink at me.

"You should come to our house sometime," suggested Lily, leading me to wonder what planet she'd been on during the last few seconds of conversation.

"Yes, you should," agreed Jasmine. "You too, Charli. You haven't come to the vineyard in ages."

A disgusted groan escaped me. "Never," I muttered, slinging my bag over my shoulder and preparing to make my getaway.

Jasmine blocked my path. "You used to visit all the time. Remember?" Her mascara caked eyes narrowed. I hesitated too long, prompting her to continue. "The last time you came over was to see my brother...to give him his going-away present, if I remember correctly."

"How embarrassing," whispered Lily before bursting into a fit of giggles.

Adam's promise of keeping quiet was not going to hold. His arms were folded tightly, and as hard as I tried to catch his eyes, his glare remained solely focused on Jasmine.

I pushed past Jasmine so forcefully that she stumbled in the sand, almost stepping on Nancy in the process. I'd only made it a few steps when Adam called my name. I turned around, praying I wouldn't regret it.

"Are you going to leave me here with them?" The amusement in his voice put me at ease. "I couldn't stand it."

Both girls stood still, their expressions confused and disbelieving. The only movement came from Nancy, who was also trying to make a getaway by chewing through her pink diamante-encrusted lead.

"What's the worst that could happen, Adam?" I teased.

"Please, Coccinelle," he said, moving towards me. "I'd save you if you needed me to."

"I know what that word means, Adam," I said sourly. "I looked it up."

When Adam spoke French, it was intoxicating. I never cared that I didn't understand it. Alex called Gabrielle sweetheart. It was cringe-worthy and unoriginal, but it was *her* word, and to Gabrielle, no one said it better than Alex. Coccinelle was my word. It was the sweetest expression on earth – until I spent ten seconds translating it online.

"You did your research. I'm impressed." He grinned victoriously.

"I'm not," I snarled. "It's not nice to call someone a piglet."

Adam burst into hysterics, laughing so hard he clutched his stomach. The Beautifuls – obviously reading the humiliation on my face – began cackling like demons. I didn't wait for him to compose himself. I turned to walk away, but he caught my hand, stopping me.

"Your translation skills need some work," he said, still laughing.

I snatched my hand away, giving him a look that should have reduced him to ash. The Beautifuls suddenly went quiet, probably anticipating an argument.

"Coccinelle. Piglet," I hissed.

"No. Cochonnet, piglet," he corrected. "It doesn't even sound similar."

"Oh." I looked at the ground.

"Are you mad?"

"Very," I muttered, digging my feet into the cold sand.

"Too mad to rescue me from the clutches of the Beautifuls?"

I finally looked up. "Oh, fine," I grumbled, sounding inconvenienced. "But let's not make a habit of it, okay?"

We left the Tate sisters standing. The view of the beach disappeared the minute we entered the trail. Strangely enough, all thoughts of the Beautifuls did too.

13. Gift

There had been method in Adam's madness. He'd given the Beautifuls enough information to keep them guessing, but not enough to keep them talking. Not only had they not bothered me for days, they'd changed tack completely and begun ignoring me.

"How long do you think they can keep it up?" asked Nicole on the way to Biology class.

I smirked, partly because of her comment but mostly because her hair was a garish shade of red. "Nic, did you voluntarily do that to yourself?" I asked, pointing to her hair.

"You don't like it?" she asked, fluffing it with her fingertips.

"It looks like something bled all over your head."

"I know," she said wistfully. "I'm going to change it this afternoon."

I would have been sobbing in a corner somewhere if my hair looked that awful. Nicole saw it as an inconvenience rather than a tragedy. It was amazing she had any hair at all considering the hours she spent in her mother's salon torturing it. Other than turning a progressively darker shade of blonde as I got older, my hair hadn't changed much since I was a kid. Even the style had remained the same.

"You have a lot of time on your hands lately, huh?"

"I don't mind." She smiled reassuringly but I still felt a twinge of guilt. "Besides, four more weeks of staying out of trouble sounds like a good thing."

"What do you mean?" I asked, slow on the uptake.

"I've realised that I don't get in to nearly as much trouble when you're not around," she explained, grinning impishly. "When Adam goes home, things will go back to normal."

Nicole's words rang in my ears for hours. I had always known he was here temporarily, but having her put a time frame to it was like being sucker punched. I'd gone from feeling like I'd just found Adam to the much darker place of having to prepare to let him go.

I wasted no time in getting out of class at the end of the day. It wasn't until I got near the car park that I began to worry that he might not be there. Standing around waiting for him meant dealing with at least one of the Beautifuls. He'd picked me up every afternoon for weeks. The covert operation was executed flawlessly each day; but now I was tired of it. He never complained but I'm sure it grated on him too.

I saw the little blue Festiva immediately. I'd picked the wrong day to get out early. Jasmine Tate stood leaning on the car while she waited for Lily.

Jasmine had worked in Carol Lawson's hairdressing salon since leaving school the year before. It was unusual for her to be here. I wondered if she'd been fired and made a mental note to ask Nicole later.

Thankfully she didn't speak, but the icy lock her eyes had on me as I walked across the car park was unnerving enough. The Audi peeled into the car park not a minute too soon, and I quickened my pace.

Until that moment, I'd been confident of making a clean getaway. All hope disappeared the minute I saw Lily and Lisa walking across the car park, eyes firmly on Adam's car.

Lisa tapped her arm and pointed at me. "I knew it!" yelled Lily. Even if she had been capable of showing some decorum, she was too far away to berate me discreetly. "You *are* messing around with him." Her tone was angry, as if I'd stolen something from her and was refusing to give it back.

They stopped walking as I passed them, probably expecting me to stop and explain myself. It could also have been because it was a better vantage point than Jasmine's car.

Adam had the sense to stay in his car until the last minute. He met me with a smile bright enough to remind me that I had no reason to hide anything. Without a second of hesitation I dropped my bag and threw my arms around him. My feet left the ground as his arms tightened around my waist. We were eye to eye and my lips easily found his.

"Hello," he said, choking out the word as soon as I released his lips from mine. Loosening his grip on my waist, he lowered me to the ground.

"I'm not hiding any more. No more wasting time."

A grin swept his face. "I'm glad you feel that way," he murmured. He glanced in the direction of Lily and Lisa. I didn't bother turning, their poses wouldn't have changed much in the ten seconds since I'd passed them. I think the smile he gave was designed to be reassuring. "We should go. I'm getting nervous. They seem to have expanded their pack."

I turned around. Jasmine, who was still leaning on the open car door, was scowling at me, and Lily and Lisa, still in the same spot, had arms folded with matching pouts on their faces. Soon, everyone in town was going to know about us, and unbelievably, I didn't care.

But old habits die hard, which probably explained why we spent the rest of the afternoon in Gabrielle's shed – or boathouse as Adam now jokingly referred to it. He was keen to show me the progress he'd made, and I had to admit it was impressive. In little over a week he'd already scraped a good few layers of paint off.

"So what do you think?" he asked, reminding me of a keyed-up child.

I paid more attention to him than the boat. His paint spattered jeans looked old and battered but I remembered him wearing them before he started playing with paint. The faded blue jeans looked old and distressed in all the right places then too, and I didn't doubt that he'd paid a fortune for the privilege. Clearly his family were wealthy. He was extremely well travelled, impeccably dressed (even with the paint stains) and considered buying an Audi A6 to drive around in for eight weeks no big deal.

"Charlotte," he said, reminding me that I hadn't answered him.

"I think you'll be finished in no time," I said, embarrassed that he'd caught me staring.

Adam ran his hand along the boat in a long sweeping motion, openly proud of his progress. "I hope so. It would be a shame to have to leave her half finished."

"What are you planning to do with her when you leave?"

Adam reached for my hands, pulling me in to him. "I thought you could sell it, bump up your travel kitty a little."

I leaned back. "If that boat is Huon, it's worth thousands of dollars," I pointed out.

"I'm not going to just leave it to rot for another fifty years, Charli," he reasoned. "It's not like I'll be coming back for it."

His words unintentionally cut me to the quick. My reply didn't come easily. "No, I guess not."

"I hope it is worth thousands," he mused. "You and Nicole could go anywhere you wanted."

New York is where I want to go! I silently screamed. Why didn't he know that?

Either the internal screaming didn't show on my face or Adam ignored it.

"Alex mentioned that Norm Davis knows a lot about boats," he said. "I've asked him to come and appraise it for me."

I escaped the circle of his arms with a sharp shove. I paced the shed, trying my best to appear unaffected by the dark thoughts in my head.

"Have I said something wrong?"

"No, no of course not," I mumbled. "It's a very generous gesture."

"It's just a boat, Charli."

"How can you give her up so easily? You've put so much in to it." My voice was shaky, doing little to disguise the fact that I wasn't talking about the boat any more.

"It's just a boat," he repeated.

I feared I had become a poster child for idiocy, repeating mistakes of old. Falling head over heels for a boy who was never going to stay with me wasn't a good idea the first time round. Allowing myself to fall even further a second time, knowing from the beginning that it wasn't going to work out was nothing less than soul destroying.

"You're absolutely right," I agreed, smoothing the front of my coat with my hands as if that was all I needed to do to pull myself together.

"We're talking about the boat. If you'd like to discuss things about Pipers Cove that I *am* going to have trouble leaving behind, please feel free."

"I know what – "

He cut me off. "Here comes the heavy head. You don't know what I'm thinking, Charlotte. You can't possibly know how many nights I've lain awake trying to figure out a way around this."

Perhaps regretting the outburst, he looked to the floor, unable to maintain eye contact.

"What did you come up with?" I asked.

Leaning down, he kissed my forehead. It wasn't the usual heart stopping, lingering touch. I felt pitied – until I leaned back and noticed that his eyes looked just as stricken as I felt.

"I'm not selfish enough to ask you to come with me. Who am I to do that?" he whispered. "You dream bigger than anyone I've ever met. I could never ask you to give it all up for me. New York is not for you. Not yet anyway."

"I think I belong with you."

Adam released me and began pacing around the shed as if he was looking for an escape route. "You don't know where you belong. That's the whole point."

"So that's it then?" I asked throwing up my hands in defeat. "I crash and you don't even stumble?"

He turned back to face me and gave a half-smile, as if amused by my theatrics. "I stumbled and fell hard, Charli, the minute I met you." He thumped his heart with his palm. "We found each other once; what makes you think we won't find each other again?"

"I might get lost. The world is a huge place."

He laughed humourlessly. "When you're done conquering the world, I'm going to be there, ready to pick up right where we left off…if you'll still have me."

"Nothing will change. I'm always going to want you," I replied, finally speaking with enough strength to sound like I actually meant it.

"I'm counting on it, Charli."

I closed my eyes, trying to convince myself that it wasn't as hopeless as it seemed. We were both in exactly the right place, for now. I was prepared to endure the pain of an unhappy ending, as long as he was with me at that moment.

***

The dreaded fallout happened sooner than I anticipated. Like any good bully, Jasmine waited until I was alone. Adam hadn't seen her when we arrived at the café. If he had, there's no way I would have been left on my own.

Jasmine ambushed me before I even made it to the steps. The silent treatment had given way to her usual form of insult.

"Some things never change, do they?" she hissed.

"Nope. Some things never do," I smugly agreed.

She tottered over to me. Already taller than me, she was downright menacing in heels. Her perfume was practically chemical warfare. "You should be really careful, Charli. You wouldn't want to make a name for yourself...again," she warned.

"I don't think I'm that important, Jasmine. I feel sorry for you if I'm the best you've got to talk about." I took a step back from her to regain some personal space.

A sly smile crept across her face and I wondered if she was going to lurch forward and rip my throat out. As I turned, she grabbed my arm. I snatched it away and took a step back, out of reach.

"You have no idea what's coming," she said menacingly.

I rolled my eyes and sighed. "Do your worst." My tone was intentionally blasé. I refused to think about what her worst entailed. I was certain I'd seen it before.

It took great effort to appear apathetic as I walked into the café, leaving the chief Beautiful high and dry outside. My heart thumped so hard I could feel it in my toes. Alex stood at the counter, glancing up to smile at me before turning his attention back to the day's takings.

"Are you okay?" he asked, making me wonder if I looked like I was about to throw up.

I stood with my back against the door as if I was barricading us in, not completely sure that Jasmine wasn't about to storm the building. "Never better."

"Jasmine's still out there, huh?" He already knew the answer.

"How did you guess?"

He chuckled, only half paying attention as he reconciled the till. "She's been out there for ages, waiting for you presumably. What have you done to upset her this time?"

"What makes you think she's upset?" I tried to sound innocent but he saw through me, as always.

"Charli, her mood is dark enough to steal sunlight."

"She found out about the whole Adam thing," I explained, trying to appear nonchalant.

His head snapped up and I suddenly had his undivided attention.

"What Adam thing?" he pressed, walking around the counter.

I whispered as if we weren't alone in the room. "The Adam-and-Charli thing."

He nudged me out of the way of the door so he could bolt it. I couldn't understand what he mumbled under his breath and I was pretty sure I wasn't supposed to.

14. Jailbreak

Every one of the thirty-two days since Adam had nearly mown me down in the car park had slipped by much too quickly.

School was an annoying commitment that bit hard into my social schedule.

"Miss Blake," said Gabrielle, too loudly. Both of her hands slammed down on my desk, snapping me back to reality.

"Yes?"

"Am I keeping you from something?"

Being the sister of the love of her life wasn't exactly working to my advantage. There had been an unlikely truce forged between us in the weeks since I'd discovered her relationship with Alex. Out of school we were friendly. She was supportive of my relationship with Adam, managing to talk my pigheaded brother around on several occasions when it came to me pleading for more freedom. During school hours she rode me just as hard as she always had.

"Excuse me?" I asked. My voice buckled at my blatant attempt to buy more time to think of an acceptable answer.

"Am I keeping you from something?" she repeated, slowly this time as if I was mentally slow.

"Someone, more like," mumbled Lisa Reynolds from three rows behind.

I'd given up reacting to the snide comments. Everyone assumed Gabrielle's treatment of me was down to the fact that I'd shamelessly stolen her cousin. The truth was much simpler. She was hard on me because I deserved it. Meeting Adam had done nothing to improve my French, or my motivation to learn French. I was a terrible pupil for her before, and just as terrible now – possibly worse.

The Beautifuls had taken my newfound love life particularly hard, baiting me at every opportunity. I didn't even know what was spurring them on any more. At first I'd put it down to jealousy, but even though they had long since given up the chase for Adam's affections, I remained fair game. None of them missed an opportunity to blow things wildly out of proportion. Being the subject of gossip and baseless rumour wouldn't have bothered me so much if not for the fact that it always made its way back to Alex. It annoyed me that he felt the need to question me about it. I guess I'd spent so long doing the wrong thing that nothing seemed impossible to him.

Gabrielle strode down the aisle. "Time is up. Pass in your papers please." Even her authoritative tone was musical. Blind panic set in as her heels clicked closer to me. In the forty-five minutes I'd had to complete the impromptu French comprehension test, I'd finished only a handful of questions. More pathetically, it was multiple choice.

Before I could circle any more, Gabrielle was standing with her palm outstretched. She gave up waiting for me to hand it to her and snatched it out of my grasp. Her eyes scanned the page for a second before thumping it back on the desk.

"Perhaps you need more time," she suggested, in a tone nowhere near as gentle as her words. "I look forward to the pleasure of your company this afternoon, Charli. In detention."

I heard Lisa's cackle behind me. Gabrielle was two desks ahead of me now and didn't give me another look. By the time she reached the blackboard at the front of the room, two more classmates had made the detention list.

"At least you won't be lonely, Charli," goaded Lisa, too loudly for her own good.

Mademoiselle Décarie dropped the chalk on to the ledge of the board and spun around. "No, she won't. You will be here too."

"No. I can't," she protested. "I have plans."

"And now your plans have changed."

"Well, thank you, Charli," sang Lisa, saying my name like it was poison.

"You're welcome," I replied, cheerily.

The next sound I heard from Lisa was practically a growl. I swear I saw the corner of Gabrielle's mouth curl as she tried to suppress a smile.

The first opportunity I had to call Adam came at lunchtime. "Don't worry about picking me up this afternoon," I said, easing into the tale.

"Oh, you have a ride?" he asked, sounding disappointed.

I tried to mimic his formal tone. "No. I am being detained. Gabrielle sentenced me to afternoon detention."

"Nice one, Coccinelle. Was it your fault?"

"Entirely," I admitted.

Sharing lunch with Nicole was about the only thing that hadn't changed in my life. Every day we met at the same picnic bench we'd been frequenting since the beginning of our high school careers. I dumped my bag on the table; fossicking for the less than impressive lunch I'd packed that morning.

"Hello," she greeted, not looking up from the book she was engrossed in.

"Hi. What are you reading?"

"Nothing you'd be interested in." She had a point. She marked her page and slipped it into her bag and looked at me for the first time. "What's the matter?"

I rushed through the details of my upcoming detention, glossing over the fact that it was well deserved. Nicole looked so bored that I expected her to take her book out of her bag and begin reading again.

"So that's my afternoon ruined," I complained.

She shrugged. Her indifference was beginning to annoy me. Even more annoying were the text messages she kept receiving every few seconds.

"You're popular today." I forced a smile but she didn't notice. Her fingers furiously tapped at the buttons on her phone as she typed her reply. "Okay. I give up." I threw my hands in the air in frustration, slapping them down loudly on my knees. "Who are you texting?"

"Lisa."

That was one answer I wasn't expecting.

"Ugh! What is she up to?" My eyes quickly scanned the crowded quadrangle, looking for any sign of an impending ambush by the Beautifuls.

"We're going to Sorell after school today, shopping." She spoke absently, implying it was no big deal.

"Lisa scored detention too," I said gravely.

Suddenly, I had her undivided attention. "Because of you?" Her eyes widened. She gathered her belongings off the table and threw them into her bag. "Well done, Charli. It's the first time in ages I've made plans without you and you still manage to mess them up," she scolded.

"Yeah, well a shopping trip with Lisa Reynolds would end up messy anyway, with or without me."

To me, the idea of a long car ride to Sorell with Lisa followed by hours of window-shopping was equal to Chinese water torture. I'd assumed Nicole felt the same way.

"That isn't the point. You're upset because your plans with Adam have been ruined. At least you had plans. You always have plans. I'm just trying to do the same." Her voice trailed off.

I felt selfish. Lunchtime was practically the only time we had spent together lately, and it was completely my fault.

"I'm sorry, Nic."

"Ugh. Don't be. I don't want really want to go shopping with Lisa," she replied, dropping the choler from her voice.

"So why did you agree to go then?"

"She caught me at a weak moment." A smile swept her face and I knew I was forgiven.

"Well, if you think about it, I've actually done you a favour. I think we should do something tomorrow. Just the two of us."

"What about lover boy?" Her face was serious but her tone wasn't.

"I'm sure he'll be able to fend for himself for a while," I replied casually.

It wasn't Adam I was worried about. I was the one who seemed to have the most trouble operating when we were apart.

I took my time getting back to Mademoiselle Décarie's classroom after school. My bag felt as if it was full of bricks. The rest of the inmates were already there. She handed me a new test paper as I walked past.

"Can I leave when it's done?" I asked, not hopeful.

She replied without looking at me. "Yes."

"When do I get to leave?" asked Lisa caustically.

"When Charli's finished," replied Gabrielle. She was enjoying herself a bit too much.

Lisa huffed, folded her arms and leaned back. "I hope you're happy," she said, glaring at me. It was hard to imagine she could see when she squinted like that.

"Thrilled," I replied, turning my attention to my test paper.

We'd been holed up for less than half an hour when Lisa's theatrics began. Huffing and puffing followed by snide little whispers. Gabrielle ordered us to behave before excusing herself from the classroom with her empty coffee mug in hand.

As soon as she was out sight, Lisa moved to the row behind me. A vicious tug on my ponytail a few seconds later followed.

"Don't touch me," I hissed.

"That's the first time you've said that in a while," she said crassly.

Todd Wilson and David Hamilton, the other inmates, leered at me.

Gabrielle returned, and sat without a word. Twenty minutes passed in silence. Lisa's glare boring into my back did nothing for my concentration. Flicking through the pages in front of me, I groaned, wondering how I'd fare statistically if I guessed the answers.

Gabrielle's ringing phone sounded ten times louder than usual in the silence. She walked out of the room to answer it in private.

I waited for Lisa to start on me but it didn't happen. She was distracted by rapping on the window. The afternoon suddenly got brighter. Unable to hide my smile, I walked to the window and slid it open.

"What are you doing?" I asked, grinning down at him.

"Is Gabi in there?" Adam whispered, pointing past me. I shook my head and smiled. "I came to break you out," he said, grinning.

"She won't let me go," I said, half whispering my words.

Lisa's chair made a screech. I rolled my eyes at Adam, warning him that she was coming.

"Hi Adam," she purred.

"Hello," he said politely.

"Are you here to save us?" she asked.

"Inadvertently."

"Cool," she replied, probably thinking he'd answered her in French.

"Charli, pass me your paper."

I dropped the papers down to him. Caught by the wind, they fluttered to the ground in a messy heap.

"Sorry."

Adam filled in the answers quicker than I could have read the questions.

"You're cheating," hissed Lisa.

"Technically," I muttered, speaking more to myself than to her.

Adam passed the papers back. I didn't even bother looking at them, focusing on him as he winked at me.

"You're going to get caught," warned Lisa, folding her arms and tapping her foot on the floor.

"She'll only get caught if you tell," said Adam, using his velvet voice to daze her.

"I would never tell. I'm not a snitch. I'm just pointing out that one way or another, Charli always gets caught."

"I won't let that happen," he said. I couldn't be sure that she'd recognised the menace in his tone. "Go," he ordered, grinning at me.

I slid the window shut.

"How are you going to keep them quiet?" asked Lisa, pointing to Todd and David like they were the enemy.

I sat back, looking at my fellow inmates. David grinned at me but Todd remained stony-faced.

"Alright, from the beginning. A C C B C D...." I read, rattling off the answers on my page.

I heard the familiar sound of Gabrielle's heels clicking on the hard floor. My voice got quicker and more frantic as she got closer and so did their writing. By the time she walked in, I'd given away all but the last four answers.

Jumping out of my seat, I was at her desk before she was, waving my papers at her. "Can I go now?"

"Eighty percent is a pass. Do you think you passed?" she asked, intent on torturing me some more.

"I'd bet money on it," I replied, too smugly for someone begging for parole.

The room was so quiet I could hear her pen scratching across the page as she marked. Finally she spoke. "Eighty-six percent. Not too bad," she praised.

Eighty-six percent? Impossible! Adam's French literacy skills were slipping.

"Can I go?"

"Yes. I have better things to be doing too, you know." Her tone was sharp but I was fairly sure she'd forgiven me already.

"Finally," said Lisa, groaning out the word.

She picked up her bag and stormed out of the classroom before I'd finished packing my books. Todd and David handed their papers in and I walked out before Gabrielle finished marking them, hoping they'd had the sense to change a few of their answers. It was after four. Cursing myself for wasting so much of the afternoon, I rushed to the car park. Every atom of stress disappeared the minute I saw him. He leaned against his car, arms casually folded, looking more like an angel than a devious criminal who had managed to prematurely free me from detention.

Stretching up to link my hands around his neck, I smiled at him.

"What?" His voice sounded worried and I wondered if he knew the urge to kiss him to death was spreading across my chest.

"Nothing."

He leaned so close that his lips brushed my mouth as he spoke. "How did we score?"

I couldn't remember the mark on my test. I was having trouble remembering the subject matter at that point. "Ah, eighty something," I murmured. "A very disappointing result."

He laughed. "I could hardly give you a perfect score. I doubt today would have been the best time to showcase your newfound appreciation of the French language." The mischievous sparkle in his eyes threatened to destroy my train of thought again.

"No, I guess not," I breathed, leaning my face in closer to his again.

His lips brushed mine, just once, softly and sweetly. "You know what today is right?"

"Friday?" I was so flustered that I actually sounded unsure.

"Exactly."

Alex and Gabrielle usually escaped town on Friday nights. They were prepared to take the long drive to Hobart for dinner, just so they could walk around town anonymously. Gabrielle was tired of the secrecy, but she loved him. The small gesture of being able to walk down the street while he held her hand made her remember why.

Adam's hand rested on the small of my back, crushing my body against his. "So where are we going?" he asked.

"The beach," I replied.

The sunshine was a welcome intruder on the winter's day. It wasn't enough to make me take my coat off, but it was bright enough to make-believe it was warmer than it was. The beach seemed like the best place to enjoy it.

We headed to the surf beach below Gabrielle's cottage. Alex usually picked me up from her house when he dropped Gabrielle off after dinner. Maybe he thought I was more likely to behave there than at our house.

It wasn't exactly deserted. A handful of surfers hung on the break and a few people making the most of the unseasonal sun meandered along the beach.

"Well this is cosy," said Adam.

I sat on the sand and pulled him down beside me. "Do you want to leave?"

"No."

I smiled and looked away, turning my attention to the ocean. The bright sun glinted off the spiky waves like diamonds.

"I saw you and Alex out there this morning," he said.

"Did you?" I asked. "Were you down here?"

"No," he said, "but you should probably know that I spy on you a lot when you're out there." His voice was unrepentant, his smile too cheeky to be sorry.

"Wow. Really?" My tone was dry, not at all surprised.

"I'm sure you've seen the binoculars Gabi has in the lounge room. She would never admit it but she uses them to keep tabs on Alex when he's playing penguin king. I find it much more interesting to spy on the penguin princess." He suddenly looked pensive. "You're different out there, you know."

"How?"

"You're strong out there. Fearless and unafraid, which confuses me. I hate the thought of swimming out there because it's dark and you can't see what's underneath." His low voice was thoughtful. I frowned, unsure of where he was heading. "It's like the blackest kind of night, Charlotte, endless and dark, and it's the place that you're most comfortable."

I felt embarrassed that he'd put so much thought in to it. "It's not endless, Adam."

"No?" he asked, turning back to me.

"No. The ocean has a horizon, sky above it, a beach on at least one side, and if I was unlucky enough to sink below the water I'd eventually hit the bottom."

He raked his hand through the sand. "I love the way you see the world," he marvelled.

"La La Land," I said.

"Excuse me?"

"Alex tells me I live in La La Land," I explained. "I think he worries that when I go away, I'll find some hippy commune on a deserted island, start wearing hemp clothing and stop shaving my legs."

He grinned. "Nicole will be pleased."

My face twisted at mention of her name. It was a reminder of the ground I had to make up. I hadn't treated Nicole well over the past few weeks. We'd spent years wasting away hours planning our big adventure, but since Adam had hit town, it had barely rated a mention. Nothing about our travel plans had altered since we were eight years old. But I was beginning to realise that was a lie. When all was said and done, if the perfect boy laying beside me in the sand were to change his mind about taking me with him, I would go.

Had I become that fickle? Would I seriously consider breaking my best friends heart to preserve my own? Yes I would. And I hated myself for it.

"What's the matter?" he asked.

I shook my head.

He gently pulled me back onto the sand. I gazed upward, lost in the view of the clear sky, but his eyes never left my face. For some reason, he only ever saw the good in me.

15. Surprise

Time alone with Adam was the thing I craved most. More than sunshine, clear skies and food, as it turned out.

"You're not hungry?" he asked, watching me from the opposite side of the dining table.

"Not really," I admitted, placing my fork on my plate.

Gabrielle was like Jekyll and Hyde. One minute she was holding me against my will in her dreadful French class, and the next she was making sure there was dinner in the fridge for us.

"So if we're not going to waste time eating, maybe we could use this time together a little more productively," he suggested, flashing me an errant grin.

"Did you have something in mind?"

The calculating look on his face told me he did. He made enough room for me to sit on his lap. I twisted one of the buttons on his shirt – which is where I kept my focus, avoiding his eyes.

"We could work on the boat," he suggested.

The way he held me tighter when I tried to stand up made me think he seriously considered scraping paint off a boat a good way to spend a night alone.

"No," I said crossly.

I struggled harder against his grip and he released me immediately. I put some distance between us. Adam remained seated, a bulletproof look on his face, obviously plotting his next move.

"Just for an hour or two," he pleaded, unsuccessfully trying to conceal his smile.

"You're crazy. It's dark and cold, and that's a stupid way to spend our night together." I waved vaguely at the black windows.

"I have a surprise for you," he admitted.

"What? A new power sander?"

"No," he murmured. "The one Alex lent me works just fine."

"So, what is it?"

"You'll see," he replied, giving nothing away.

He stood and pulled me to him, and as his lips melted on to mine I closed my eyes, concentrating on nothing other than remembering how to breathe. I felt too weakened by his touch to speak. I didn't even notice when he stepped away to grab our coats. By the time I opened my eyes he had his on and was holding mine out. The metal press-studs snapped loudly as he buttoned my coat all the way up to my neck, as if I was five years old.

"I don't want you to be cold," he explained, grinning craftily. "Okay. Ready?"

"No."

"I'll make a deal with you." His tone was sweet but the look on his face convinced me he was still scheming.

"No deals."

"I'll go surfing with you in the morning if you come out to the shed with me tonight."

I saw no lack of honesty in his eyes. He'd made no secret of his acute dislike of the ocean – the thought of swimming in it at least.

"Really?"

"You have my word, Charlotte." He placed his hand on his heart.

"Fine," I surrendered. "Let's get this over with." He picked the throw rug off the couch on our way out.

His surprise had nothing to do with the boat. He slid the huge shed door open and the fluorescent light flickered a few times before settling, casting enough light for me to see that the boat looked exactly as it had the last time I'd seen it.

Something in my expression made him smile. I watched in silence as he walked to the far end of the shed, picked up an old milk crate and brought it back. Bundling up the throw rug as a makeshift cushion, he dropped it on the crate.

"Sit, please. I just have to find something."

I got the impression we were going to be there a while. Adam rifled through boxes of tools and the pockets of a coat he'd left there earlier, searching for the surprise.

"If you tell me what it is, I could help you look for it," I suggested.

"I can't believe I've lost it," he said, glancing across at me as he upended a box of junk on to the shed floor. "I only picked it up this afternoon."

"Is it big or small?"

"Small."

"Well, the light in here is not very good," I reasoned. "Why don't you wait until morning?"

Ignoring the mess he'd just made, Adam stepped over the pile of tools and headed back towards me. I met him half way, happy to take his hand when he reached out. He stood in front of me and I studied his face closely. His eyes were never cold and piercing as blue eyes often are. They were cerulean, intense and deep, like the rest of him. Finally, his lips, cold from the night air connected with mine, sending a shudder through me.

"Charlotte," he whispered, leaning back to look at me again.

"Yes?"

"You have to breathe," he reminded me.

I felt my body tense as I sucked in a much needed breath. My fingers began to tingle and I wasn't sure if it was due to a lack of oxygen or the cold night air. His hand moved to my neck and he popped open the first two buttons of my coat. My chest was heaving with each gulp of air that I forced into my lungs but I didn't flinch as his cold hand slipped inside my coat.

"Your heart is hammering," he said, sounding bewildered by my over-the-top response to his touch.

"I know," I said, struggling to regain some control of myself.

His hand slid free of the warm confines of my coat. His body shifted away and I wished I hadn't said anything.

"You are so beautiful," he said, walking back to the tools he'd dumped on the floor.

"Why do you do that?" I asked, failing to conceal my frustration.

He continued throwing tools back in the box, pausing to glance at me.

"Do what?"

"You know what."

For a moment, I had been hopeful that the not-so-good side of him, the side that peeked at me through the mirror while I was half naked and helped me cheat my way out of detention, was winning. The heat radiating from our bodies might have been enough to numb the chill of the air but it wasn't enough to numb the good, responsible side of Adam.

"Do you really want to do this here, Charlotte?" he asked quietly, making me wince as he threw a spanner into the box at his feet. "In a cold shed?"

"*I* wanted to stay inside," I reminded him, making it known why I'd protested leaving the house in the first place.

His eyes drifted up to meet mine. He spoke seriously. "When the time is right, we're going to have the whole night together, not a few rushed hours while Gabi and Alex are at dinner."

The mere mention of Gabrielle and Alex killed the mood instantly. He might as well have doused me with iced water. An entire night alone was impossible. There was no way my brother would loosen the reins that much. Adam should know better than to even hope for that kind of scenario, and I told him so.

"So he'd rather you sneaked around behind his back?"

"Of course he would," I snapped. "That's exactly what he expects from me."

A tool crashed into the box, making me wince. He was annoyed.

It was a pointless argument that neither of us was going to win. Thankfully Adam wasn't as stubborn as me. He knew when to quit, expertly changing the subject to something trivial. He was also good at compromise, spending only a few more minutes looking for the mystery package before giving up for the night.

We returned to the warmth of the house and I spent the rest of the night curled in his arms on the couch, half watching a movie that was so tacky it had gone straight to DVD. Adam gave up even pretending to watch it after a few minutes, opting for one of Gabrielle's French novels. A foil gum wrapper fluttered out of the book as he flipped it open. Leaning across, I picked it up from its landing spot. I'd never known Gabrielle to chew gum. The sticker on the spine of the book indicated that the tattered novel was a library book. Realistically, the forgotten litter could have come from anywhere.

Something about my expression made him question what I was thinking.

"I remember my mum used to chew a lot of gum," I said, smoothing the wrapper on my knee. "The smell of peppermint, and gum wrappers as it turns out, always reminds me of her."

He smiled, snapped the book shut and gently placed it on my lap. "What else do you remember?"

"Not much. I remember her singing to me, always singing to me."

"They're nice memories to have, Charli," he whispered, tangling his fingers through my hair.

I picked the book up and handed it to him. "Will you read it to me?" I asked, craning my neck to look at him.

"Shall I translate?" he asked, amused.

"No, read it in French."

"You won't understand it."

"I don't need to understand it. I just need to hear it."

I had been drunk only once in my life. Nicole and I had stolen a bottle from her parents' liquor cabinet when we were fifteen. The way Adam sometimes looked at me reminded me of my headspace after first few mouthfuls of whiskey – warm and giddy, tinged with euphoria. Thankfully the puking, headache and morning-after lecture from Alex never followed.

"You're so incredibly special, Coccinelle," he said, manoeuvring my body so my head rested in his lap.

"Just shut up and read, piglet," I replied, making him laugh.

I closed my eyes, concentrating on his voice but not attempting to decipher his words. He could have been reading from the TV guide for all I cared. His accent captivated every bit of my attention, which is why I didn't hear Alex and Gabrielle arrive home.

"Ready to go?" asked Alex, jolting me back to reality.

I sat up, peering over the back of the couch to look at him.

"Now?"

"It's after eleven, Charli." Something about him was off.

Our night was over and a twinge of sadness hit me. Our nights together were limited – and that knowledge was beginning to sting.

The drive home was quiet and tense. Alex had a habit of stewing over things. If he was upset about something, I was sure to hear about it eventually. I leaned my head against the cold car window, gazing upward at the night sky as it whizzed past.

"Do you want me to wind the window down?" teased Alex.

I smiled. "No. How was dinner?"

My gaze returned to the darkness outside as he replied. I was only half paying attention to his reply until he mentioned something about Nicole working the next day. It jogged my memory and I realised I'd double booked myself.

"Oh, Nicole can't work tomorrow. We've made plans," I told him.

The look Alex gave me was dark. I smiled at him, still marvelling over the fact that my social life had picked up enough for me to be double booked in the first place.

"If she doesn't work it, I'll have to," he said.

"I know. Please, Alex. Please, please," I begged, batting my eyes at him.

He laughed hard, just once. "Does that look work on anyone?" he asked.

I grinned. "Yes. You. Every time. You just don't realise it."

16. Confession

It wasn't until I arrived at Gabrielle's house the next morning that I realised it was a ridiculously early time to be visiting. Adam Décarie was clouding my every thought and any common sense I once had was long gone. I crept on to the veranda in stealth mode, unsure if I was going to be waking anyone.

I hated sleeping in on weekends. The thought of wasting a single minute of a free day sleeping was ridiculous. Obviously the Décarie's thought differently. It was so quiet that if I didn't know better, I'd have said the house was deserted. I didn't want to knock. Visions of Gabrielle coming to the door, furious with me for waking her from her beauty sleep, popped into my head. I *really* did not want to knock on the door.

I tiptoed along the veranda, heading towards the back of the house. The sun shone brightly for the second day in a row, glistening off the ocean like a multifaceted jewel. I stood for a minute taking it all in, wondering how Gabrielle managed to score the most prime real estate in the Cove.

Something else caught my eye. Lying on the wet grass was the white mohair blanket from the night before – except it wasn't white any more. It was dirty and stretched out in an odd shape. I was definitely glad I didn't knock on the door. If she didn't kill me for waking her up early on a Saturday morning, she would surely kill us for ruining her blanket. I scooped it off the ground, rolling it up.

The blanket wasn't the only discarded item on the lawn. Next to it was a small brown velvet box. It took a long minute before I bent down and picked it up, gingerly as if it might explode in my hands. Shoving the box into my pocket and ignoring the small voice in my head screaming at me to open it, I continued around the house to Adam's window.

The white curtains were sheer but peering through them, I saw nothing. Tapping lightly on the glass didn't rouse him so I changed tack and tried my hand at breaking and entering.

The window slid open remarkably easily considering the frames were wood and constantly battered by salty ocean air. I smugly considered a career as a cat burglar until my entrance through the window brought me back to my senses. There was nothing catlike about it. My foot got stuck on the ledge as I levered myself up, sending me toppling to the floor with a thud. Unbelievably he didn't wake. He didn't even stir.

I watched him sleep for a minute, his face even more perfect than usual. His body was covered by a thick quilt, leaving only his bare arms exposed. I had to touch him. My fingertips were only millimetres from his skin when I jerked back with fright at the unexpected sound of his voice.

"I'm awake, Charli." He smiled but kept his eyes closed.

"For how long?" I asked, too mortified to be angry. "I've been staring at you like an imbecile and you've been awake the whole time?"

Reaching for my hand, he pulled me the short distance across the bed. His warm arms wrapped around me as I lay with my back to him. He rested his chin on my shoulder, smoothing my hair with his hand to keep it out of his face.

"I woke when you fell through my window," he murmured. "Is there a reason you're gracing me with your presence so early?"

"Are you complaining?"

"Never," he whispered.

He tightened his grip around my chest and planted a quick kiss on my neck. Suddenly the brown box was burning a hole in my pocket.

"I brought Gabrielle's blanket in. We left it outside," I told him. "It's ruined, Adam."

"I'll buy her a new one," he replied, unconcerned by the damage we'd done.

"I found something else."

"Really?" he asked, failing miserably at sounding surprised. "What did you find?"

I knew even without looking at him that he was smiling. He knew exactly what I'd found and he was going to make me tell him.

"This," I said, reaching into my pocket and pulling out the dew-soaked box.

"Did you open it?"

Twisting myself in his arms, I turned to face him. "No. I didn't open it. It doesn't belong to me."

Adam took the box from my hand and balanced it on my hip. "It does belong to you. Open it," he urged, grinning.

"What is it?"

"Open it," he repeated, tapping the lid with his finger. I caught the box as it began to slide off me. "It's just a trinket, I promise."

I could handle a trinket. It wasn't going to be the magnitude of the million-year-old boat. I wasn't going to have to find a way to politely refuse.

"Do you know what it is?" he asked, watching my face as I flipped open the lid.

I held the necklace above me. The teardrop-shaped black gem encased in the silver pendant shone as it caught the morning sun. Beautiful ribbons of red and green flickered through it.

"I've never seen anything like it," I breathed, awed by the unusual stone.

"What do you know about opals?" he quizzed.

"They're symbols of hope, courage, happiness and truth," I whispered.

"Très bien. I thought it was the perfect gift for someone about to set out on a voyage of the world. I had Floss make it for you," he said, murmuring the words against my throat.

I touched his face with the hand that held the necklace. The fine silver chain tangled around my fingers as I pressed them to his cheek. He leaned forward to kiss me again but I gently held him back, needing to see his eyes.

"You are the best person I know," I whispered.

A sweet, perfect smile swept across his face and I wondered how I'd got so lucky. I didn't want to move. I could have stayed there forever and never moved again but the hold he had on me lasted only a minute.

"Are we surfing today?" he asked. "I assume you're here to make sure I honour my side of the bargain."

"No. I'm here to let you off the hook, actually. I have to cancel. I forgot that I made plans with Nicole yesterday," I said regretfully.

"I'm *so* disappointed, Charlotte." The wily grin betrayed him. It was the look of a boy who'd just been given a reprieve. He'd probably regretted making the deal since the offer tumbled out of his mouth.

"Liar." I laughed, breaking his loose hold so I could slide off the bed.

"Are you leaving already? You just got here."

I had to leave. He was in danger of making me stay, just by the way he was looking at me, and that wouldn't have been fair. Poor Nicole had been pushed to the backburner so many times over the last few weeks that changing today's plans would have been nothing less than criminal.

The thought of Gabrielle catching me in his room that early in the morning was another incentive to get out of there. I heard the shower running and knew it would be a good time to escape.

"Are you going out the window or through the door?" he teased.

"Which would you prefer?"

"I'd prefer that you stay here with me."

His dark blue eyes locked mine. I turned away because I needed to. Untangling the chain from my fingers, I draped the necklace around my neck, fumbling with the clasp for a few seconds before he appeared behind me. He swept my hair across one shoulder and quickly fastened the clasp. I wasn't paying attention any more. I was too focused on staring at him through the mirror.

Standing in front of him shielded little of my view. It was as if it was the first time I'd ever really looked at him. Strong, muscular arms wrapped around my chest, holding me to him. Much taller than me, his body hunched forward to rest his chin on my shoulder, emphasising every muscle on the side of his chest that wasn't obscured by my body. Obviously, there *was* merit in running recreationally. He had gifted me the beautiful gem as a token of protection and strength. At that moment, I didn't need it. He shone brighter.

Dragging myself away, even for a few hours, was harder than I imagined it could be. I should have been preparing to let him go. The smart thing to do would be to start distancing myself from him now. But I wasn't smart. I wanted to leave with him – to never have to face time without him – but even in my hazy reasoning I knew it was impossible.

My preoccupation was obvious to Nicole the minute she met me at the front door.

"Nice bling," she complimented, pointing at my necklace. "It's like those ones we saw in Floss's shop, remember?"

I did remember. It was the sole reason I'd accepted it so willingly. A trinket that Floss had made was much easier on my fragile psyche than the Huon sloop.

Nicole led me to her bedroom. The Lawson house was bigger than ours but it always felt crowded. That probably explained why she spent so much time at mine. I'm sure the fact that Alex lived there had something to do with it too. She'd shared a bedroom with Joanna right up until the wedding, and even after all of her sister's belongings had gone, the bright pink room still seemed tiny.

I sat on the low stool at the cluttered dressing table. There were more creams and potions than I'd ever seen in my life – the legacy of having a hairdresser and beautician for a mother. I often wondered how I would have been different had my mother been around while I was growing up. I absentmindedly unscrewed the lid on a pot of cream and sniffed it. The pungent fruity smell that stung my nose snapped me back to reality. Alex had done just fine.

"Where's Carol?" I asked, looking past her.

"I don't know. Why?"

"I have to tell you something." I wanted her mother well out of earshot.

"Can you talk and fold?" she asked, pointing to a basket of clothes on the bed. She didn't seem worried. Maybe she knew what I was about to say.

"I've been thinking about going with Adam when he leaves. I really want to but he's sensible. He talked me out of it." The words came in a rush as if I had to say it before I lost my nerve. Nicole glanced at me before turning her attention to the shirt she was folding. "Say something, please." I snatched a denim skirt from the basket.

"Were you planning to bail on me, Charli? Ditch me at the last minute?"

I looked away, pretending to concentrate on the skirt. "It sounds awful when you put it like that. I don't know what I was thinking," I mumbled.

"What *were* you thinking?"

"I don't know. Do you know?"

I wanted her to make sense of it for me. I wanted her to make me understand why I had been prepared to abandon my dreams and destroy those of my best friend in the process. I wanted to know why hearing Adam tell me he couldn't be without me made me hopeful that he would be with me always.

The skirt was impossible to fold. I rolled it up, much as I'd done with the wet blanket, and threw it back in the basket.

"I don't know much about him, Charli, other than the fact that he's drop dead gorgeous." She grinned at me and I couldn't help smiling back. "You tell me why he's so freaking special that you'd give up all your dreams to be with him."

I sat back on the stool, needing the support, while I recounted every event of the last few weeks. My voice sounded embarrassingly wistful as I filled her in on the details.

Nicole was really the only person who could understand how I felt about him. She'd watched seventeen years' worth of my insecurities unravel in a few short weeks – only to have new ones surface. I told her that I needed to be with him. My voice took on a tone of desperation as I punched out the words. Such a trite affirmation would never have crossed my lips a few weeks ago, but now it was a statement that held meaning. I'd never been surer of anything in my life, but nothing I said made it sound strong enough, true enough...or gut-wrenchingly painful enough. I could feel my face twisting with emotions I wasn't sure how to explain.

The shirt Nicole was folding was forgotten. She stared at me strangely, like she was trying to make sense of my words or at the very least come to terms with the fact that I had just said them. I was the girl who thought boyfriends were for bored girls with no ambition. I was never the girl who believed a boy like Adam existed, let alone dared to hope I'd find him.

"Wow." Her voice was understandably incredulous.

I slumped forward, burying my head in my hands. Something was very wrong with me. "I know, you think I'm an idiot."

Nicole sat down on the edge of her bed, sighing heavily. "You're not an idiot. You love him. I totally get that."

My head snapped up to look at her. "Is that what this is?" I asked, speaking as if I'd just been diagnosed with some foreign tropical disease.

She burst into giggles and I didn't know why. "You do make things hard for yourself don't you? You're such a control freak, Charli. You can't control this. You just have to go with it."

"How am I making things hard for myself?" I asked, continuing my run of stupidity.

"Well, you could have picked a guy who lives a little closer than a million miles away. And the fact that his cousin is a witch doesn't help either," she explained. I cringed when she referred to Gabrielle as a witch. I'd called her far worse in the past, but it seemed wrong now. "So what did Alex say when you told him?" she asked, choosing another random item of clothing to fold.

"I didn't," I confessed. "I'm not going to New York so it makes no difference."

"But you will end up with Adam eventually. That means you're not planning to come back here. He should know that," she said disapprovingly.

"I know," I agreed wearily.

She tossed the shirt back in the basket. I endured an uncomfortable minute of silence before she finally spoke.

"Poor Alex. He'll be heartbroken. He's cared for you for so long and – "

"He's easily distracted these days." I cut her off mid-sentence and my tone was unfairly severe.

No one was more aware of the sacrifices Alex had made than me. I found it infuriating to be reminded of it and I know he despised being thought of as the martyr just as much as I hated being thought of as the damaged little orphan.

"What do you mean?" she asked.

The frown that swept her face made me wonder if I should explain or not. I knew she'd want to know. The whole town would want to know about Alex and Gabrielle.

"He's kind of seeing someone," I confessed, downplaying it by epic proportions.

"Who?" Her voice sounded urgent – like knowing was a matter of life and death – and I understood at that moment that it was. To her, it was more than a crush. It was her reason for getting out of bed in the morning. I just wish I'd made the connection a few sentences earlier. It was too late to get out of telling her now.

I looked at the floor and spoke barely louder than a whisper. "Gabrielle Décarie."

She sucked in a quick, sharp breath. "Oh."

"I know. Weird, huh? I'm still trying to get my head around it. Things are pretty serious. It's been going on a long time, over a year." It wasn't really an explanation. It seemed more like damage control.

"Gabrielle," she mumbled, stunned.

"I'm so sorry," I told her.

Nicole stood, fluffing up her newly brunette hair with her hands – a mannerism I'd seen a lot of lately. "Why are you apologising?"

"I guess...I guess I've always known that you like him."

My eyes flitted between her and the floor. I felt like I'd just called her out on her deepest, darkest secret.

A weak smile crossed her face. "It was never going to go anywhere, Charli. I'm not stupid. He's thirty-four."

"I know. He's old." I grinned, trying to raise a more genuine smile from her.

"Alex is one of the good guys. It's easy to like him. He deserves someone nice, not someone like Gabrielle." She said her name as if it was a swear word.

I wasn't sure if I could be the one to enlighten her about the woman formally known as the Parisienne witch. She was not a witch and Alex did deserve her.

Her face suddenly changed. The pained look disappeared and she smiled half-heartedly. "How could they have kept it secret for so long? Why would anyone want to do that?"

"I don't know."

"Do you think they'll ever tell anyone?"

"Gabrielle is leaving it up to Alex. I think it's his decision to keep quiet."

"Charli, that's why she's stayed here so long." She spoke with certainty. It was as if all of the mystery that had shrouded Gabrielle had disappeared once Alex was added to the equation.

"I know. She's ready to go back to France and that's why I'm hoping that when I leave town, he will too. I'm the reason he's dragging his feet."

She smiled but it wasn't convincing. I smiled back, but I doubt I looked confident either.

The morning disappeared quickly, just like old times. It seemed months since Nicole and I had spent any time together and I realised just how much I had missed her.

Knowing I was coming over that morning, her mother had assigned her a mountain of chores to get through, believing that idle hands did the devil's work – and that I was the devil. I helped her load washing, tidy her room and sweep the back patio while we chatted. I'd always maintained that nothing ever happened in Pipers Cove, but hiding out with Adam had pushed me so far out of the loop that hearing even the most mundane gossip was interesting.

"So Jasmine has decided that Adam is not her type," explained Nicole.

"Poor Adam. He'll be so disappointed," I replied.

"Imagine her reaction when she finds out that Alex is off the market too."

"At least it takes the heat off me."

"Has she left you alone lately?"

"Sort of." I grimaced. "She's plotting something. She told me I had no idea what's coming. Do you know what that means?"

She frowned. "No clue."

We stood to attention when Carol appeared at the back door a few minutes later, eying us suspiciously.

"I forgot to bring the towels home from the salon last night," she said, her eyes darting between us. "Perhaps you girls might like to fetch them for me."

Her snippy tone didn't bother me. It beat doing chores and hanging around the house. We were out the door and in my car before she could add any conditions to her request.

17. White Knight

The main street of Pipers Cove resembled a ghost town on weekends. Rolling tumbleweed wouldn't have looked out of place. None of the shops were open except Norm's hardware store, which traded until three.

The row of angled parking bays lining the street was empty with the exception of the infamous blue Festiva, crookedly parked right outside the salon.

"What is *she* doing here?" asked Nicole bitterly.

I had no clue why the Beautifuls' car was parked there but had no doubt we were about to find out. Nicole was never one to hold back. She stormed the building with the gusto of a police raid, pushing open the glass door with her entire body. The candy pink vertical blinds wobbled in every direction as the gush of outside air caught them.

The Beautifuls seemed to wobble a bit too. Lisa – who had been lounging along the pink velvet couch in the waiting area – sat bolt upright, knocking the cotton wool balls that were stuffed between her newly pedicured toes flying in every direction. Jasmine was at the basin, rinsing Lily's hair when we walked in. They were now both covered in water. The only one who didn't jump out of her skin was Lily. Poor, oblivious Lily. A bomb could have gone off and she would have continued reading her magazine.

"What do you think you're doing?" snapped Jasmine, reaching for a towel to dry herself off.

"I could ask you the same question," spat Nicole, angrily.

Jasmine gave up trying to dry the front of her tight fitting red shirt and turned her attention back to her sister. She rubbed Lily's hair so brutally that her voice shook as she spoke. "What does it look like we're doing?"

"It looks like you're treating your posse to free products."

The chief Beautiful chuckled darkly, infuriating Nicole. I watched from the doorway as she marched over to Jasmine and ripped the towel from her grip. Lily squealed loudly and grabbed the back of her head. I wondered if Nicole had managed to tear out her over-bleached hair in the process.

Nicole spelled it out for them in no uncertain terms by speaking slowly and loudly. "You're stealing."

Jasmine's shameless snicker proved something we already knew. They were morally bankrupt. "It's not stealing. It's market research," she said, raking through Lily's hair with a wide-toothed comb.

Lisa stood up, waddling toward Nicole with the grace of a drunken duck, trying to not disturb the remaining cotton wool between her toes.

"We come in every few Saturdays when the new stock comes in, to try it out," she explained. She had the intellect of the world's dumbest criminal and I bit my bottom lip to stop myself laughing out loud at her stupid admission.

Jasmine shushed Lisa, directing a poisonous glare square at her but it was too late. Nicole pieced it all together instantly. One of Jasmine's duties as Carol's apprentice was ordering new stock. Judging by the way Lily was studying the product catalogue; they were ordering whatever they fancied and intercepting it without Carol ever knowing.

"You wait until my mother finds out," warned Nicole, unfortunately sounding juvenile.

Jasmine didn't look alarmed. If anything she looked even more demonic than usual as she stepped toward Nicole, waving the plastic comb at her. "Are you planning to dob on us, Nicole? Because that would be a huge mistake."

"You're a thief!"

Jasmine sauntered back to Lily's chair. "What would happen if I got in first?" she mused. "I could call her and tell her everything."

I didn't buy it for a second. Her tone was too cunning for someone entering a plea bargain.

"You'd tell her what you've done?" asked Nicole, understandably sceptical.

"Oh, Carol," she mocked, holding the comb to her ear as a makeshift phone. "I came to the salon to tidy up a little and Charli and Nicole are here. I hate to be the one to tell you, but Charli's been filling her pockets with as much stock as she can carry."

"She'd never believe you," I scoffed, speaking for the first time since we'd walked in.

Jasmine sucked in a long breath, exhaling loudly as if talking had become arduous. "But what if she did? Your name has been bounced around this salon a million times…and never in a nice way. It's not going to be much of a stretch to convince her that you're not only slutty, but a thief too. Everyone already thinks you're damaged goods, Charli." She shook her head, tutting. "Everybody talks about it. You're just an attention seeker…such a disappointment to Alex. Of course Carol will believe you're a thief."

Her speech burned like acid but I refused to appear affected. "I'll take my chances."

"Will you, Charli? Really? She'll press charges. You know she will," she goaded. "A criminal conviction will spell the end for you. Your travel plans might be cut short. Most countries don't take kindly to criminals seeking entry visas."

"You are such an evil bitch," said Nicole glumly.

"It's true," said Lily, breaking in. "Our cousin, Sarah, couldn't get into Canada because she had a drink driving conviction."

Nicole groaned and slapped her own forehead. "Sarah couldn't get into Canada because she spelled Canada wrong on her visa application."

Lisa's giggle was extinguished by another lethal glare from Jasmine.

"It, doesn't matter anyway, Nic," I said, sighing heavily for effect. "Jasmine's right."

"What are you talking about?" she hissed.

"I can't risk it. I know what Carol thinks of me." It took great effort to sound so defeated.

Lisa guffawed, obviously impressed by the outcome of Jasmine's attack on me. I glanced at Nicole, silently trying to reassure her that I hadn't lost my mind.

The Beautifuls claimed the win, going about their business as if we were no longer in the room. I walked toward the back room on the pretence of collecting the soiled towels. Nicole followed. "Here, take this one too," demanded Jasmine, throwing a sodden pink towel at me as I passed. I let it fall, refusing to demean myself by picking it up.

As soon as we were through the narrow doorway, Nicole grabbed my arm "What's gotten into you?"

I nudged her aside and began rummaging through the lotions, potions and powders lining the shelves of the back wall. I had a plan – and the inspiration had come from a most unlikely source.

Floss Davis was fanatical about living organically and chemical free. I knew Carol had done her hair for years, and thanks to Gabrielle Décarie, I had a fair idea how she managed to make her hair such a bright shade of red without chemically dyeing it. Gabrielle was an experimental artist. She loved trying out new mediums and painted on everything from canvas to ceramic. Her latest project was staining leather with henna. I'd watched her working on it one day, carefully and slowly ensuring none of the dye touched her bare hands. When I asked her how long it would take for henna to wear off skin, she answered by painting a tiny heart on the inside of my wrist, which was still bright orange nearly a week later.

"I found it," I said, thrilled that my hunch had paid off. I spun around to show her the container of henna powder. "Find me some hand lotion or something."

Nicole looked confused but she did as I asked, handing me a tub of moisturiser. I decanted the gritty brown powder into the white cream, mixing it with a spoon I found next to the sink. With a bit of luck, Jasmine would be stirring her coffee with the same spoon on Monday morning.

"What is that stuff?" asked Nicole.

I grinned, already tasting victory. "Tate bait," I whispered. I put my finger to my lips before casually strolling back into the shop. Nicole followed behind, struggling to carry the bundle of pink towels she'd collected.

Everything in the salon was pink. It was pink overload. If there had been a cluster of seizure patients in town, they would surely trace the source back to the bright pink fittings in Carol Lawson's salon.

"Are you sure your mum won't find out?" I asked, hoping Nicole would be clued up enough to follow my lead.

"Err, yeah," she muttered, unconvincingly.

"I've always wanted to try this," I said, holding the pot of lotion out in front of me, giving Jasmine ample opportunity to snatch it from me as I walked past – which she did. She didn't notice me glance at Nicole and give her a wink. She was studying the label.

"It's nothing special," she scoffed.

"It is if you use it properly. Gabrielle Décarie swears by it."

"How would you know that?" asked Lisa.

"Because I spend a lot of time at her house, whoring around with Adam," I said dryly. A thrill rushed through me. I could see them mulling it over. "She smothers her hands with it, leaves it on for ages and then washes it off."

Even if a sense of decency had kicked in – which it hadn't – it was too late to let them off the hook. Jasmine had already unscrewed the lid and begun slathering her hands in the grainy gunk.

"Like this?" she asked, seeking approval.

"Perfect."

Nicole and I left the trio of Beautifuls sitting in a line on the pink velvet couch, identically posed, resting their elbows on their knees to ensure their hands received the optimum treatment. I instructed them to leave it on at least half an hour, but they were greedy. They'd put on twice the suggested amount and leave it on much longer.

I managed to contain myself long enough to suppress my dance until we were out of sight. Nicole threw her head back in a bray of laughter. "We're going to hell in a hand basket," she told me, laughing. "You know they're going to be gunning for you now, right?"

I did know; which is why I had mapped out the rest of my afternoon in my head. I figured I had a few hours reprieve – an hour for them to finish their *treatment* and another few hours while they tried scrubbing the orange dye off their hands. All bets were off after that. They'd come looking for me, and past experience told me that the safest place to be when that happened was wherever Alex was.

I drove Nicole home before heading to the café. Alex's Saturday shift should have been more bearable considering Gabrielle had surrendered the first day of her weekend to hang out there with him, but for some reason the atmosphere was tense. I frowned. He couldn't have found out what I'd done so soon. There was no way the Beautifuls could have been hunting me down that quickly.

Gabrielle sat at the end of the counter, perched on the wicker stool with her legs crossed in a ladylike, but uncomfortable-looking pose. Alex stood a few feet away, arms folded and body rigid.

"Am I interrupting something?" I asked, knowing the answer.

"No," replied Alex tensely.

"Yes," retorted Gabrielle, staring at him.

Alex glowered at her. I'd seen that look a million times. He was silently ordering her to hush – only it didn't work. She hesitated for only a second before continuing.

"There is an art exhibition next weekend that I would like to go to. Alex is refusing to accompany me."

"Why?" I asked, making my way over to the counter. It wasn't like Alex to refuse her anything.

"Because it's in Stanley and we'd be gone for the whole weekend." Gabrielle was speaking to me but glaring at Alex. His demeanour didn't waver.

Stanley, a pretty seaside town in the northwest, was about as far away from Pipers Cove as they could go without leaving the state. It was a full day's drive. Excitement bubbled inside me and I concentrated hard on not letting it show. But it was pointless. To Alex, I was completely transparent.

"Not going to happen, Charlotte," he warned.

"I didn't say anything!"

"You didn't have to."

"They are not children, Alex," snapped Gabrielle.

Everyone recognised the conundrum without anyone mentioning it. There was no way Alex would consent to leaving Adam and me to our own devices for an entire weekend. The only person with half a chance of convincing him otherwise was the French beauty queen staring him down from the other end of the counter.

"How was your morning with Nicole?" Alex finally asked, trying to change the subject.

"Interesting." He looked at me for a long moment before speaking, probably debating whether to ask me to elaborate. Thankfully, he decided against it. "So, why are you here? I thought you would have gone to see Adam."

I grinned craftily, making him smirk. "I'm pacing myself. I don't want to appear too eager."

"Let me guess. You've already called him and he's on his way to pick you up."

"Exactly," I confirmed, levering myself on to a stool beside Gabrielle.

It was a relief when Adam showed up. When Gabrielle was upset with my brother, she had no qualms about letting him know. She was unyielding, refusing to let go of her lovely but impossible plan for a weekend up north. Alex refused to budge. Her reasoning soon deteriorated to bursts of French, complete with hand gestures. I couldn't blame her. His bags would have already been packed if not for the fact that he had an irresponsible minor in his charge.

Gabrielle dropped the attitude as soon as Adam walked in, but Alex's ire remained. After all, Adam was fifty percent of the reason why they were at loggerheads. I leapt off the stool, throwing myself at him with the enthusiasm of someone with separation anxiety. Gabrielle said hello before spouting something in French. Adam nodded but said nothing, taking my hand.

"English, Gabi," scolded Alex, visibly unimpressed.

She didn't get a chance to interpret. The bell on the glass door jingled violently and Jasmine Tate burst into the café, looking as deranged and furious as I could have hoped. I quickly moved behind the counter, standing beside Alex as if that made me bulletproof.

No matter how trashy Jasmine looked, she was usually seamlessly pieced together. Now she was almost unrecognisable in the holey grey windcheater and mismatched brown track pants she wore. Her brassy blonde hair was dishevelled and pulled in a messy ponytail.

"What have you done to me?" she screeched, holding gloved hands in the air.

I cowardly said nothing.

"Charli, what's going on?" Alex didn't take his eyes off Jasmine.

The chief Beautiful dragged the gloves off her hands to show him. I heard Gabrielle gasp. Her bright orange hands glowed. It was a better result than I could have hoped for; I wished Nicole was there to see it.

"We've tried everything to get it off. Give me the antidote." Her tone, still angry, had taken on a desperate edge.

"We didn't poison you, stupid. There is no antidote. You'll have to wait for it to wear off."

"How long?" she demanded.

I shrugged. "A couple of months at most."

Her face grew almost as flushed as her hands. The seriousness of her predicament was starting to sink in.

"Bitch!" she screamed, lunging across the counter. She managed to catch the sleeve of my shirt and began pulling me forward. Alex grabbed me around the waist, lifting me off the floor as he reclaimed me. Adam did the same thing to Jasmine, but had to struggle a lot harder against her flailing ginger hands. Gabrielle sat perfectly still, wide-eyed.

"Enough!" roared Alex, motioning with his hand for her to stay back.

"Look what she's done to me!" shrieked Jasmine. Her lurch forward was thwarted by Adam's grip around her middle. She managed to shrug free. "You think she's so precious. She's not you know," she screamed.

"All Charli has to do to aggravate you is exist," returned Alex. "Everyone has a limit, Jasmine."

Alex didn't even know what I'd done to her. It was astonishing that he always defended me without question – especially when I least deserved it.

"She dyed my hands orange," she bellowed, waving her hands under his nose.

"I see that."

"Yeah, well…." Her voice trailed off. "There's plenty you don't see. Her reputation around town is as damaged as she is." She spun around, pointing at Adam. "You could do so much better than her, you know that, right?"

Adam didn't seem too worried. He actually looked like he felt sorry for her. I felt no pity whatsoever. I felt furious.

"Why are you doing this? You need to shut your mouth!" I yelled. "If you so much as say another bad word about me, Carol Lawson is going to know that you've been stealing from her," I threatened.

"You won't tell her," she said, calling my bluff.

"Are you prepared to take that chance?" I asked, hoping I sounded just as vile as her.

Her eyes narrowed. "You're despicable."

Gabrielle let out a sharp laugh. "That is the pot calling the pan black."

There was a long silence before Alex finally corrected her. "Kettle, Gabs."

"Pardon?"

"Kettle. The pot calls the kettle black."

"Why would the kettle be black?" wondered Gabrielle.

"I'll explain it later, sweetheart," he said gently.

Never before had I seen her grasp on the English language slip. But her blunder was nothing compared to Alex's. He was either so distracted or so caught off guard that he had called Gabrielle *sweetheart* – right in front of the mouth of the south.

Jasmine let out a strange gurgling sound and stared at Gabrielle. Gabrielle was still frowning, fidgeting with the gold charm bracelet she was wearing, apparently trying to understand the black kettle situation. Jasmine returned her attention to Alex, and the look she gave him wasn't kind. "You and *her*?" she asked in disbelief.

Alex smiled sweetly. "I'm not telling you anything. That's how rumours start." The biggest secret in the Cove was out, and judging by the Machiavellian look on his face, he didn't care one bit.

"Ugh!" she growled, throwing her carroty hands in the air in defeat. "You all deserve each other!"

Her eyes flitted between the three of us. None of us spoke. She tugged on her gloves and stamped out.

179

Alex's smile disappeared along with her, and an eerie silence set in. It was as if we'd all witnessed a terrible train crash and were too shocked to speak. I could feel his glare but kept my eyes on the front door.

"You have ten seconds to explain," he informed me.

I punched out the explanation so quickly, I had five seconds to spare. I could almost see his mind ticking over as he processed my confession.

"Of all the stupid things to do." His reproach was warranted, and defending myself would only have added fuel to an already raging fire. "You're like a mini terrorist. Are you trying to get us run out of town?"

Gabrielle tried to stop a giggle escaping. I turned my attention to Adam.

"I think it was ingenious," he murmured, revealing the dimple on his cheek.

"You are too easily charmed," complained Alex, waving his hands as if he was showcasing the major prize in a game show. "Charli Blake is the kind of girl your mother warned you about, Adam. Nothing but trouble."

So much for defending me to the death! If he hadn't been so worked up it would have been funny. The only people in the room game enough to see the humour were those of French lineage.

"I would be more than happy to claim her," Adam told him.

"Me too," added Gabrielle, much to my surprise.

Alex shook his head. He marched to the front door and flipped the sign, declaring the shop shut for the rest of the day.

"Are you closing?" asked Gabrielle, checking her watch. "It's early."

"I'm done. If I don't get out of here, I might explode," he muttered, pushing past me to collect his coat.

I knew Alex was close to breaking point. Escaping the café before he had a chance to lock the door seemed like a good idea. I reached for Adam's hand. "I'll see you later." I moved quickly, giving Alex no chance of calling me back. Adam turned to face him as we reached the door.

"I'll have her home early."

"I honestly don't care," Alex said wearily.

He sounded broken. For a horrible second I wondered if I'd finally pushed him too far. Perhaps in the process of slaying the Beautiful dragons I'd accidentally assassinated my white knight too. I peeked at my brother. "Do you mean that?" My voice was small because I feared his answer.

Alex looked back at me for a long time. He didn't look angry any more, just beaten. "No," he said simply. And I believed him.

Adam and I sat in his car while I explained the whole sorry saga to him. Even armed with all the details he didn't seem to think I was as wicked as I clearly was. Alex and Gabrielle came out of the café soon after us, and left in separate cars. Not a good sign. Poor Alex had been pulled in too many directions that day, and knowing him, he was heading home to stew.

Alex was a big fan of brooding. I arrived home a few hours later to find him in the yard chopping firewood. Giving me the silent treatment while he took his frustration out on the woodheap was common practice. He'd hacked through enough wood in the last year to see us through at least three winters.

"Are you going to chop it all?" I asked, leaning against a veranda post, not willing to venture any closer while he was wielding an axe.

The axe smashed down on a block of wood. "I might."

"Alex, I'm sorry."

"No, you're not." I couldn't dispute it. I wasn't feeling a skerrick of regret for dyeing the Beautifuls, but disappointing him was never part of the plan. "Do you ever think, Charli? Before you do stupid things does any part of your brain stop to consider the consequences?"

"Not often," I admitted.

He leaned on the axe handle as he wiped sweat with his forearm. "What am I supposed to do with you?"

"I think you should take Gabrielle to the art exhibition in Stanley," I said, ignoring his question.

He punched out a hard laugh. "I'm sure you do. Leaving a criminal mastermind and her awestruck boyfriend alone for a weekend sounds like a great idea."

"You can't baby me forever," I grumbled.

He smashed the axe down on another defenceless block of wood, so hard that splinters hit the garage. Staying on the veranda was a wise decision. "If you're so big and brave, how come you came running to me when you knew Jasmine was on the warpath?"

"I'm not brave, Alex. I'm scared of everything, but lately I've become hopeful of changing that."

"It's fleeting, Charli. Adam is leaving in a few weeks. Then what?"

It bothered me that he'd mentioned Adam. He had nothing to do with anything that had happened that day. And now the speech I'd prepared during the drive home didn't seem applicable any more. He'd gone off on a completely different tangent.

"It won't be the end. I'm sure of it."

Alex let out an appalled groan, swinging the axe over his head as if it was weightless. The ear-splitting crack of the wood made me flinch. "You're absurd. You are so.... seventeen," he said, puffing with exertion. "If you're thinking of running off to New York, you're making a huge mistake. You'd be giving up everything. You'll get stuck somewhere you don't want to be and you'll hate every minute of it."

"Like you did?"

Those three words grabbed him. Even from a distance, his hazel eyes looked as hard as glass. "Don't you start," he warned.

"You know it's true," I insisted. "I don't even know what your dreams were but I know you gave them up to look after me. You give *everything* to me. You can stop doing that now."

He dropped the axe on the grass and leaned down to pick up the chopped wood. "You do stupid things, make dumb decisions. I wonder if I gave you enough. Maybe there's some major life lesson I forgot to clue you in about."

Abandoning the safety of the veranda, I stepped on to the lawn.

"Alex, the things I do are no reflection of the job you've done. Sometimes I'm just a jerk. Don't take it so personally."

He pointed to the pile of wood with his free hand. It was a mute ultimatum that I understood perfectly. I picked up the smallest pieces I could find. Unimpressed with my effort, he offloaded a much larger log into my arms.

He smirked. "Sometimes I'm a jerk too."

"This is too heavy," I complained.

"Suck it up, princess." He was already walking towards the garage carrying more wood than I could have shifted in a week.

I'd pushed the envelope too far that day to consider claiming pity points. Pretending to drop the bundle on my foot and faking a mortal injury wouldn't wash. I followed him the to the neatly stacked woodpile.

"Don't throw it all away for a boy, Charli," he said as soon as I was close enough to hear.

It was a confusing exchange. He flitted from chastising me about the dumb decisions I made to my relationship with Adam. Why did he think the two were linked?

I dropped the wood on the ground. Alex began stacking it against the wall. It felt like I had only half of his attention and I found myself raising my voice to compensate.

"I would never regret it, no matter how short-lived it might be. I'd rather have five minutes of something amazing than a lifetime of nothing special. Staying here, playing it safe and never dealing with anything more challenging than Jasmine Tate would kill me."

Alex walked past, ignoring the fact that I was yelling at him. I groaned in protest, dragging my feet across the damp grass as if I was physically damaged. He waited until my arms were laden before speaking.

"I'm not blind, Charli. I knew before you even did that there wasn't enough in this town for you. A few months away will be – "

The two logs thudding to the ground as I dropped them cut his sentence short. "I'm not coming back here, Alex, ever," I blurted. "When Nic and I are done travelling, I'm going to New York." I'd had no intention of revealing that little gem quite so soon, but as usual, my mouth got the better of me.

I might as well have drilled him in the side of the head with the blocks of wood he'd just chopped. He looked so devastated that I wished I could suck the words back in. Calming down and explaining my reasons was the only chance I had to make him understand – except I didn't know how. "I *need* to be with him."

Trite, I thought. He's never going to buy it.

"You're not supposed to *need* him, Charli. You're supposed to just *want* him. Needing him is what I'm afraid of. You're going to follow him to New York and get stuck there because you need him…and trust me…when need kicks in, you're not going to want him any more."

"I love him," I added, hoping it was a more acceptable reason.

"Well, it sounds like you've got it all worked out. You've come to this conclusion in just one month? Nice work."

"I feel sorry for you!" I yelled. "You've become jaded." Frustration was making my blood boil.

Alex must have noticed that I was on the brink of a major meltdown. His demeanour changed. "What do you want me to say, Charli?" he asked gently. "What do you want to hear?"

I stared at him, doubtful that I was capable of giving an answer any less banal than the last few. "I just want you to have faith in me. I'm never going to have it any more together than right now."

"I promise you, in time you will."

"I'm always going to see things differently. I'm going to continue to chance things to fate. I'm always going to believe in magic and I'm always going to trust that things will work out in the end." I pointed a log at him. "Those are the lessons *you* taught me. That's who I am."

His hands flew up, but at least he reacted. It was the only proof I had that he was actually listening to me. "You forgot to mention that you also have a defective sense of judgement and zero common sense," he said, leaning to pick up more wood.

"I'm working on it," I said sourly. "Please, just consider the bigger picture for a minute. What if I'm so unbelievably lucky that I've found the one I want to be with forever?"

"And what are the odds of that, Charli?" he asked as he walked back to the garage.

"I'll take my chances. I'm not wrong about this," I insisted, following empty-handed.

"And if you are?"

"I won't regret a single minute of it. I can promise you that much. That has to be enough for you."

"Look, Adam has been a good distraction for you. I see that. But you have to see it for what it is. This isn't his real life, Charli, and I doubt you're going to fit into his world. What do you know about his family?"

"It couldn't be any weirder than ours," I replied morosely.

A smile ghosted across his face and he turned away, dumping the wood with more might than necessary. "I don't think you know anything," he muttered.

"I know all I need to." My tone lacked certainty for good reason. It was a big fat lie. I'd pieced enough together to know that Adam's life was nothing like mine but I'd never asked him about it. Perhaps I was afraid to.

Stubborn, idiotic and stupid were all words I mumbled under my breath as I stormed across the yard to the house. Behind me I heard the whack of the axe slamming down on wood again.

It took almost an hour for Alex to give up torturing himself and the woodheap. I said nothing as he moseyed to the fridge and sculled juice from the carton. I sat at the table, sifting through a stack of pictures that I'd been meaning to sort until my new brilliant life got in the way.

Alex pulled out a chair and sat opposite me. I hoped he would speak. Dishing out the silent treatment had never been my forte and I wasn't sure I could keep it up.

"Charli, I want to ask you something," he said seriously.

"I'm not sleeping with him."

It was a knee-jerk response that made Alex duck his head as if I'd just thrown something at him.

"I wasn't going to ask that."

"Oh. Good." I wondered if my cheeks looked as flushed as his. I tried my best to look casual while ignoring the growing pit in my stomach.

"I just want to know how you can be so certain about all of this. Tell me why Adam is so important."

The mere fact that he was willing to continue this conversation was a huge step forward. He was throwing me a lifeline, giving me a chance to explain my shady reasoning. I swallowed hard, praying I could articulate a half-decent response.

"He sees the good in me, Alex. And for a long time I didn't think there was any. You give me one good reason why I shouldn't be making plans with a boy like that."

He nodded. I couldn't place the emotion in his eyes but I was hopeful that he'd go easy on me for being so cliché and seventeen.

"You'll be a long way from home if it ends badly," he said, finally.

"But not so far from Marseille. That's where you'll be, right?"

He avoided my question. "Do you remember the arguments we used to have when you were little?"

Of course I remembered. I started most of them. They were usually trivial, like me wanting to wear pyjamas to school or eat cereal for dinner.

"You used to climb that big tree in the front yard and I'd have to spend an hour coaxing you down," he said, smiling at the memory. "The conversation was always the same. I'd tell you to jump and you'd ask me if I'd catch you. Do you remember what I used to tell you?"

"Word for word."

"Tell me."

"Every single time you jump, Charli, I will catch you," I recited. His eyes drifted down again, pretending to look at the pile of photos, but he was smiling.

"I meant it. I'm always going to be there to catch you."

"I know that."

"Even if I'm in France."

The effort it took to appear calm was colossal. "So you're going?"

"I love her. I have to go, right?"

"You absolutely do," I said. It was impossible to hide my delight. "You know why you've never spent much time jumping out of trees, Alex?"

"Tell me, oh-wise-one," he urged, leaning back in his chair.

"It's because no one's ever been at the bottom to catch you."

"Yeah, well, sometimes it's better to just stay in the tree."

"Why?"

"Because the view is much clearer. Some of us need a clear view."

If my life had been a book, Alex had read from the very beginning – including the preface. True to form, I had only flicked through the pages, paying very little attention to the plot.

If his life had been a book, I was the unnecessary postscript at the end – the annoying add-on that should never have been included. I never understood why my mother chose to have me so many years after Alex. Maybe I wasn't planned – that would explain my father's quick departure after I was born. He obviously suffered with flee-itis too. If things had worked out the way they were supposed to, my brother and I would probably be strangers. He would have grown and left town, my mother would have raised me, and our paths might have crossed once a year at Christmas. That should have been the plot of the Alex Blake novel. There wasn't supposed to be an irritating postscript. I said nothing as he walked away. For once, he deserved to get the last word.

18. The Parisienne

Pipers Cove quickly descended to crazy town. News of Gabrielle and Alex's not-so-secret love affair spread like wildfire, and our little café did more trade in the next three days than it had done in a month.

Alex never coped well with crazy. I steered clear of the café – and so did he, closing early each day to go surfing.

Mademoiselle Décarie's life seemed even more difficult, but she took it in her elegant stride. The Beautifuls and their associates filled in the many blanks with details of their own. Lily and Lisa didn't miss a day of school, overcoming the problem of iridescent hands by wearing gloves – teamed with matching newsboy hats as if Winter Barbie was the look they'd been aiming for. Jasmine hadn't surfaced since the incident in the shop, calling in sick with a terrible case of the flu. Nicole saw no need to enlighten Carol. Collateral, she called it.

The only good part about Gabi and Alex becoming the victims of the ruthless local gossips was that Adam and I were left in peace. It was like a get-out-of-jail-free card. It no longer felt like all eyes were on us. Mercifully, we'd become yesterday's news.

It didn't stop us hiding, though. The boat was nearing completion and most of our afternoons were spent in the shed. I didn't mind watching him work but had long since given up offering to help. Adam humoured me for a while, giving me menial jobs like sanding already raw wood, but it never lasted long. There was something lacking in my technique. He'd watch me for a few minutes with a look so pained, anyone would have thought I was sanding the flesh off his bones. It always ended the same. I'd stop what I was doing just to put him out of his misery. Instead, I busied myself doing what I did best, taking pictures. I photographed Adam a million times, never once finding a flaw.

"You're going to wear that thing out," he teased.

I snapped a quick picture, trapping the brilliant smile he flashed me. "A small price to pay," I replied, looking at him through the viewfinder.

"For what, Coccinelle?" he asked.

I grinned up at him, high above me on the deck of the boat.

"A moment in time that I'm never going to get back."

He ruffled his fingers through his hair, creating a cloud of sawdust.

"That sounds so sad," he said finally.

"It's not sad," I insisted. "It doesn't matter that I'm never going to get it back. I was there at the time."

The distance between us dulled none of the shine in his sapphire eyes. "I love hanging out in La La Land," he declared.

Behaving at home was the least I could do. I made sure I was home on time every night and did my best not to rattle Alex's cage too often, which was difficult considering he was teetering on the edge of a meltdown.

I was in the kitchen, trying to scrape something half decent for dinner together when I heard his keys hitting the hallstand just before he rounded the doorway.

"What are you up to?" he asked accusingly.

"Nothing. I'm just trying to sort something out for dinner," I said, staring vacantly into the fridge.

"Charli, no more," he said wearily. No more what? I'd been an angel all week. "I can't work out if you're up to something or if you're just being good. Up to something I can deal with. Being good…well that's just creepy."

"Whatever do you mean?" I shut the fridge door much harder than necessary.

Alex sat, looking a lot like someone with the weight of the world on his shoulders. "Madame Décarie reported that you passed your French assignment. That troubles me."

"Would it help my case if I told you Adam did it for me?" Hopefully, I wouldn't regret telling the truth.

"Yes," he said wearily. "Yes, it would."

"See." I tapped my forehead. "Always thinking."

"Gabrielle thinks your French has improved because you're spending so much time with him."

I smiled. We both knew that wasn't true.

Dinner conversation was trivial, and that was okay. We made a start on doing the dishes when he floored me with a most unexpected offer.

"I'm going to give you a chance to misbehave," he said, reaching for a tea towel.

I grinned craftily. "I'm always up for a challenge."

"I think we're going to head up to Stanley for the weekend, if Gabi still wants to go."

I turned the tap off, shaking suds off my hands while I gathered my thoughts and worked out how to play it cool.

"Really?" My voice seemed to be an octave higher.

"Really," he confirmed, wiping plates with vigour. "But I haven't asked Gabrielle yet. She might have changed her mind."

That was never going to happen. After the week they were having, escaping the Cove for a few days would be a godsend.

I grabbed the phone and thrust it at him. "Call. Now."

Alex took the phone and retreated into the lounge. I didn't bother trying to eavesdrop. There was no more room in my brain for any more information. He returned a while later, expertly timing the end of his phone call to coincide with the last of the dishes being put away.

"Well?"

"Done deal. We're going to leave Friday afternoon. If Nicole's happy to work Saturday and Sunday, I'm free until Monday."

I breathed a huge sigh of relief. Everything was falling into place. "Great," I enthused, concentrating hard on not sounding too happy.

"It is great. So, there's only one thing left to do," he said, handing me the phone. I took it from him as if it was scorching hot. "You need to call Carol and make sure it's okay if you stay with Nicole this weekend."

"What?" I gasped.

Slowly, he repeated his sentence.

I nodded in defeat, edging towards the door with the phone in my hand.

"Call her, Charli." Alex's instructions were clear and precise, just the way he planned.

"I will," I promised, walking away.

Alex left the house early the next morning, determined to get an hour in the water before opening the café. As soon as he was gone, I left too.

Sleep hadn't come easy the night before, but not because I was plotting a way of taking Alex up on his offer of misbehaving. I laid awake trying to figure out a way of doing the right thing. I came up with only one solution, and it all hinged on the Parisienne.

Walking up to Gabrielle's door felt exactly the same as walking into detention – I didn't want to be there but I didn't have a choice. She came to the door before I had a chance to knock, startling me enough to make me jump back a step.

"Charli." Her eyes widened, possibly in shock. "Adam is not home. I think he went for a run along the beach." She pushed the screen door open and gestured me inside. "I was just making some tea."

"Thanks," I mumbled, feeling out of place without Adam there.

We sat at the small oval table and Gabrielle poured tea from a mint green teapot into two matching cups. Of course they matched – everything in the entire house matched.

"I'm glad we have a bit of time alone actually. I wanted to show you something," she said, sliding a cup towards me. Her eyes darted in every direction but mine, making me think that something horrible was on its way. She rummaged through her tote bag, pulling out a collection of notebooks. She hesitated slightly before sliding the book across the table towards me.

I opened the black canvas-covered book. The handmade pages were a dirty white with red flecks of cotton melded through. Thumbing through, I saw page after page of my postcards. The tailored presentation was impressive, but the details that took my breath away were the handwritten notes and sketches that decorated every spare space on the pages. The cursive handwriting was so perfect it looked like a computer font.

"Is this a diary?" I asked quietly.

She smiled. "Of sorts."

I closed the cover and slid it back towards her. "I shouldn't be reading this, it looks private."

She pushed it back to me. "Relax, Charli. It's in French. Unless you've suddenly become bilingual, I'm not concerned that you'll learn any secrets."

I opened the book and carefully thumbed through the pages.

"These are truly beautiful."

"So are your photographs. My interest is genuine, Charli. I've been working with them for months."

"I see that."

I couldn't deny it. Much work had gone into that journal. I had accused her in the past of feigning interest in my photography. It seemed impossible to me that someone with so much talent of her own could find my work beautiful.

Embarrassed by her praise, I laid the journal back on the table, swapping it for another book that caught my eye. It was brighter, a mix of heavily layered marbled pastel paints. I ran my hand over the roughly textured cover.

"This is Marseille, my home," she announced proudly, patting the cover with her hand.

I turned each page, studying each picture for as long as I could without appearing weird. The third page held a photograph of the most incredible house I'd ever seen – if it could be called a house. It was more like a castle straight out of a fairy-tale.

"Who lives there?"

"It's our family home. I grew up there."

My jaw fell open in shock. Gabrielle was a secret Snow White after all. Her cousin was keeping a few secrets of his own, and if I was being truthful, I'd say I suspected that too.

"What has Adam told you about our family Charli?" she asked, twisting her head to look at the page I was staring at.

"Not very much," I admitted. In fact he'd told me nothing, and it was getting harder to ignore.

"I'm not surprised. He is very modest," she said, smiling the same smile that Adam used to stun me.

"Will you tell me?"

Gabrielle hesitated. "The Décarie family is centuries old, Charli, practically aristocratic," she explained.

"Like royalty?"

"Not quite, just very wealthy. I think it's referred to as old money."

I sat silently for a long time, trying to process what she was telling me. "Does Adam live in a castle?"

If it was a stupid question, she didn't let on. "No. His family lives in New York."

I tapped the picture of the castle with my fingertip. "Are you excited about going home?" I asked.

"I have Alex now." She smiled like he truly was the best thing in the world. "But I miss my family terribly."

"Alex will go with you." I said it with too much certainty. It wasn't a statement I was qualified to make.

Gabrielle looked down at the cup of tea she was cradling. "Time will tell."

"He told me so. When I leave town, he's going to go to Marseille with you."

She frowned as if she'd lost the ability to comprehend English. "He hasn't told me," she uttered quietly.

I leaned back in my chair, dragging in a breath like I was drowning. I did feel like I was drowning – artificially calm on the surface and frantically treading water underneath.

"I think he's saving it for the weekend. He wants to tell you when the time is right." I spoke slowly, which was a mistake. I ended up sounding like I was lying.

"You're not coming back here, are you?" she asked. "You're going to New York."

"I need to be with him. I know you understand that," I said, sounding much stronger.

She looked at me for a long moment but didn't speak. Her reaction, or lack thereof, confused me. We were both getting what we wanted. I thought she'd be jumping for joy, breaking out the French champagne or doing whatever it was that arty French beauty queens did when they celebrated.

"I see," she mumbled finally.

"Alex's decision has nothing to do with me. He loves you, that's why he's going to Marseille," I said.

"And how do you feel about it?"

It wasn't a question I expected her to ask and I had to think about my answer. "I want Alex to be happy. You make him happy."

Finally she smiled, just enough to be slightly reassuring. "Isn't love a dreadful thing?"

I nodded, feeling the anguish twisting on my face.

"What is it, Charli? I can tell there's more to this."

I shifted nervously in my seat before edging into the real reason I was there. "Alex has cut me a huge amount of slack by leaving me at home this weekend and I don't want to ruin it by lying to him."

"Okay." She drew out the word.

"I want to stay here. And I want you to help me tell him."

"Oh, Charli." That was the only part of her sentence I understood. A long French monologue followed, complete with hand gestures and over-the-top facial expressions.

"Yes or no?" I asked as soon as she paused. I saw a flicker of pity in her green eyes. Maybe she knew how Alex would react. Perhaps they'd already discussed it. "I'm not asking you to tell him, Gabrielle. I'm just asking you to be there when I tell him," I clarified.

It seemed an eternity before she spoke.

"Okay. Dinner tonight. Here. We'll tell him over dinner. I'll cook." She spoke absently, as if she was trying to string a plan together in her head.

"Thank you," I breathed. I made my way around the table towards the door.

"One more thing, Charli," she said, reaching for my hand as I passed her. "You need to talk to Adam." She tapped her Marseille diary. "He's only perfect for you if you know everything about him."

I knew exactly what she meant. "Do you think Alex is perfect?"

"Except when he calls me Gabs." She pulled a face. "What a ridiculous appellation to bestow on someone you claim to love."

I burst into a fit of giggles. Sometimes I felt as if I needed a French *and* English dictionary on hand to understand what she was saying.

"I'll see you tonight," I told her, still laughing as I made my way to the door.

19. Confusion

My school day dragged, and its slowness was compounded by the fact that I was stuck in detention until five.

For once, Mademoiselle Décarie had nothing to do with it. Mrs Young had sentenced me for the crime of failing to return two library books by the due date. Until then, I wasn't even aware that she had that kind of power. I got no sympathy from Alex when I called to tell him. Adam was slightly more understanding, although disappointed that I'd managed to cut into another of our afternoons together.

By the time I arrived at Gabrielle's, Alex was already there. His red Ute stole three quarters of the narrow driveway. My heart thumped mercilessly as I made my way up to the porch.

"They're in the shed, working on the boat," Gabrielle told me, obviously not concerned.

The thought of them spending time alone together was disturbing. Adam didn't always understand the complications between Alex and me. He thought for us to spend the weekend together while Alex and Gabrielle were away was logical, unable to grasp that Alex saw it as leaving a child in a brushwood house with a can of petrol and a box of matches. If Adam mentioned it before I did, anything was possible – and every scenario I played out in my head as I walked the short distance to the shed ended badly.

Spying on them felt criminal but I was powerless to stop myself. I stood motionless, peeping through the crack in the door. Alex stood near the stern with his arms folded. I couldn't see Adam, but heard the very sound of sandpaper scraping along wood. Mercifully, the conversation was light. They were talking about the boat, debating the million dollar question – was it Huon or run of the mill pine? Adam had no clue. Alex was undecided.

"Norm will be able to tell you," said Alex. "Are you sure you want to sell it?"

"I have no use for it," replied Adam casually. "Besides, Charli could use the extra travel money."

"That's very generous of you." Alex's tone was strange. "But I guess thousands of dollars is just a drop in the ocean for you, right?"

The sandpaper sound stopped.

"It bothers you, doesn't it?"

"It wouldn't bother me if Charli knew about it," Alex replied.

"You know as well as I do, it wouldn't make any difference to her."

"How do expect her to adjust to your life in New York, Adam? She's pinning everything on this working out. That *does* bother me."

Adam laughed but it was somehow wrong. It was sarcastic and hard.

My thoughts drifted to the French castle that Gabrielle called home. Alex had some adjusting to do too. I wondered if *that* bothered him.

"Do you even see her when you look at her?" asked Alex. His arms were still folded across his chest.

"I see *everything*." Adam spoke without hesitation. His answer couldn't have sounded any truer if he'd had time to rehearse it. "She's stronger than you think she is."

Alex finally uncrossed his arms, moving both hands to the back of his head like he was warding off a migraine. "Everything is fine then. I'm worrying unnecessarily," he said.

"You don't like me very much do you?" asked Adam.

His question floored me. Considering it took Alex a long time to speak made me think it staggered him too. I'd never heard either of them say a bad word about the other. How had I not seen the tension before now? Part of me didn't want to hear the answer. A bigger part of me was too cowardly to move. So I stood, waiting for his reply.

"I don't like the effect you have on her."

The sound of tools crashing into the metal toolbox made me flinch. When angry, Alex liked to chop wood. Adam liked to make noise.

"Why do you have such a strong hold on her?" Adam asked. "I don't understand it. You need to let her go. She's more than capable of making her own decisions." He spoke calmly but the frustration in his voice was undeniable.

"In case you haven't noticed, she's capable of getting in to a lot of trouble too," replied Alex.

Through the tiny gap in the shed door, Adam walked into view carrying the box of tools, dumping it on a shelf. "So you've made it your life's work to keep her on the straight and narrow? How's that working out for you, Alex?" he asked, glancing back at my brother.

"Pretty well, until you showed up."

"I don't buy that for a second. Charli has never toed the line. That's why you're having such a hard time letting go of her. She was impossible to hold in the first place." His words were abnormally harsh. Adam was usually much more low-key when it came to telling people off.

Alex's response confused me. I expected an angry comeback. I held my breath, waiting for the ranting to begin but it didn't happen. Instead, he relaxed. "Charlotte has a high tolerance for risk, she's a slave to the sea and she takes pictures of time," he said, ticking off my list of weird character traits on his fingers, making them sound more bizarre by the tone of voice he used.

I was glad that I couldn't see Adam's face. I imagine he looked horror-struck. There was no way Adam could ignore the list when it was being spelled out for him. I could see Alex's face clearly, though. His smugly calm expression hinted that he thought Adam was about to come to his senses and make a run for it.

At last Adam spoke. "Those are the things I see when I look at her," he stated. "They're not faults or flaws. That's who she is and I love that about her."

"That's what you see?" Alex sounded incredulous.

"That's exactly what I've seen from the minute I met her."

There was an extremely long pause.

My heart wasn't sinking any more. In fact, there was a fair chance it was going to float right out of my chest. Adam walked out of view again and I leaned closer to the gap.

"You weren't expecting to find her, were you?" asked Alex quietly.

"No. I've never met anyone like her. She's changed the way I see everything. Have you ever felt that for someone?"

"Once," he vaguely admitted.

"Gabrielle is hoping that you'll go back to France with her," said Adam, connecting the dots.

Alex tried to sound offhanded and unexcited. "That's my plan."

"Maybe you should fill Gabi in, put her out of her misery. Do you love her?" quizzed Adam.

"Completely." He finally spoke with the fervour that a statement like that deserved and I was relieved.

"So why did you keep her a secret for so long?"

"You've been here long enough. You've seen how the rumour mill works."

"So it comes down to you not wanting to be talked about?"

"No, it's even more selfish than that. I never believed someone like Gabi could ever want me for very long. There was no point going public if was going to be short-lived."

"So what changed your mind?"

Alex's hands moved behind his head again. "Gabrielle knows everything about me. Every. Last. Thing."

"And yet she still loves you?"

"Yeah. Imagine that. Perhaps you should give Charli the same chance."

Adam walked into view again, dragging his arms through his coat sleeves. "I'm going to tell her everything this weekend...while she's staying here...with me."

The thought of Adam finally coming clean about his prince charming status now seemed trivial. I stopped breathing. Waiting for Alex's reaction (and the lack of oxygen) was killing me. I shouldn't have been surprised that Adam had told him about our plans. He'd seen no point in making a big deal of it in the first place.

"That's what this dinner is about, isn't it?" asked Alex. "She's planning to break it to me using you and Gabrielle for moral support."

"That's about the gist of it," replied Adam calmly.

"Fine. Consider me told."

"That's it?" asked Adam, sounding understandably cautious.

Alex held both palms out before slapping them against his sides. "What do you want me to say? I'm loosening my grip."

"No catch?"

"None."

"Why?"

"You said it yourself, Adam. *You see her.* And I believe you when you tell me that. But I have to warn you, if you hurt her...if you so much as disappoint her, I'm going to break both your legs."

"Understood," replied Adam in a tone that suggested he didn't really believe him.

Both of them started walking towards the door and unless I moved quickly, I was about to be sprung. I made the dash back to the house.

"What's the matter?" asked Gabrielle as I burst through the front door.

"Nothing," I replied, shrugging off my coat and hanging it by the door. "Adam told Alex I'm staying here for the weekend."

Her voice was melodic and calm but her eyes flickered. She straightened already-straight placemats and tidied perfectly aligned silverware. I wondered if she had some form of obsessive-compulsive disorder that required everything to be perfect – except boyfriends.

"And he took it well?" she asked.

He'd taken it brilliantly. He hadn't killed anyone.

"He's okay."

"Très bien. We can enjoy dinner then."

Neither of us had a chance to say anything else before Adam walked in.

"Where is Alex?" she asked.

"Coming. He's just cleaning up."

"And you?"

He raised both hands, paint-free. "I know the rules," he told her, like a good child.

Alex appeared seconds later, unceremoniously dumping his keys and phone on the table, knocking Gabrielle's place settings askew. She didn't move, blowing my theory about her obsessive-compulsive disorder. Her obsession was something entirely different, and he was standing beside her, both hands on the top of the dining chair – staring at me like he was waiting for a confession.

I glanced at Adam and he winked. Gabrielle was focused only on Alex.

"Sit down," she instructed.

Alex did as she asked without breaking the lock on my eyes.

"Anything you want to tell me?" He spoke to me like I was five years old. He knew full well why we'd summoned him to dinner, but he was going to make me explain it anyway.

Adam frowned. "Why are you doing this?" he asked. "I've just told you everything."

Gabrielle offered the bowl of salad to Adam, but he ignored it. "I'd like to hear it from Charli."

"Why are you acting like I'm invisible?" I snarled.

"I'm not," Alex said.

Gabrielle cleared her throat. "We need wine," she announced, already walking away. I wanted to leave too but couldn't come up with a plausible excuse to do so.

It was confusing. I thought they'd just cleared the air in the shed. Why was Alex intent on keeping the drama going?

"You're bullying her." Adam was clearly baiting him and as expected, Alex bit.

"And you're speaking out of turn."

Gabrielle came back and carelessly set a bottle on the table. As she pulled her hand away, the bottle fell, saturating Alex's shirt. He jumped up, wiping the red stain with a napkin. I couldn't be a hundred percent sure it wasn't intentional. Gabrielle was hardly the clumsy type.

"Oh, I'm sorry. Quickly, take it off." Gabrielle unbuttoned his shirt as she spoke. "I'll soak it."

She rushed off to the laundry with the stained shirt, leaving me alone with the two idiots. Alex folded his arms, more out of menace than modesty. Adam mimicked his pose. The only difference between them was the looks on their faces and Alex's bare chest. Alex still looked annoyed but Adam looked aghast. I squeezed his knee under the table but it did nothing to snap him out of whatever dark thought he was lost in.

The silent standoff continued until Gabrielle returned.

"Here." She draped a shirt over Alex's shoulder as she walked past him. Of course he had clothes there. He probably had a toothbrush there too. As soon as she sat down Adam asked her something in French, punching out the words urgently.

Gabrielle frowned. "Non," she said simply.

Alex didn't seem anywhere near as confused as I was. Maybe she'd taught him French. Perhaps I was the only person at the table who had no idea what was going on.

Adam repeated the question, and before he'd even finished Gabrielle launched into a tirade of her own that ended only when Adam stood and slammed his fist on the table, making crockery, cutlery and glass rattle. He pulled me to my feet.

"We're leaving," he snarled to no one in particular.

Alex said nothing. Gabrielle began to speak but Alex shushed her.

I snatched my hand free. "I'm not going anywhere until someone tells me what's going on," I demanded.

"Go with Adam, Charli. Its fine," Alex suggested weakly.

I didn't protest as Adam reached for my hand again and led me out.

We drove so far into the night that we were halfway to Hobart before he finally pulled over. He'd hardly said a word since we left, and even in the darkness I could tell he was furious. I wasn't sure what I was feeling. I still had no idea what was going on.

"You do realise Tasmania is an island, right? There's only so far you can drive."

His hands gripped the steering wheel and his head dropped.

"Promise me something?" he said, ignoring my last statement.

"Anything."

"Don't change your plans, not for anyone."

I knew he meant Alex. "His opinion counts, Adam."

It was hard to build a defence when I had no idea where the hostility was coming from.

Adam glared at me like I'd just cursed him. "Why, Charlotte? Why do you feel so indebted to him? I hate that you carry this guilt," he ranted.

It wasn't like Adam to be so insensitive. He knew our history. It was annoying that I had to justify my feelings again, so I said nothing. He shook his head, muttering to himself.

"English!"

He spoke painfully slowly, as if my English comprehension was poorer than my French. "You owe him nothing."

"Whatever just happened between you and Gabrielle is nothing to do with me. There's no need to bring Alex into it either."

Adam reached across, stroking the side of my face. Even in the low light, his cerulean eyes looked wounded. Continuing the conversation was senseless. We were going around in circles. My brain seemed to be short-circuiting, overloaded by a whole lot of nothing.

"I think we should go back," I suggested.

Adam's hand moved to the keys. "I will take you anywhere you want to go."

"Do you mean that?" It was important to look at him as I asked the question.

His expression didn't waver. "I've never meant anything more in my life."

I didn't object when he turned the car around. There was nowhere else to go, for now.

Alex was on the porch we arrived back at the cottage. I wondered if he'd been waiting there all along or if he'd come out when he heard the car pull up. Adam quickly kissed me goodnight, heading straight into the house and unnecessarily pushing past my brother on the way.

"Goodnight, Charli," said Gabrielle, appearing out of nowhere.

"Thanks for dinner," I replied. It was a strange thing to say considering we didn't get as far as eating.

The journey home with Alex was weirder than the drive to nowhere with Adam. Every one of my thoughts at that moment was so discordant that I couldn't string a sentence together in my head let alone out loud. It was Alex who finally spoke.

"You and I really need to talk."

"So, talk."

He grimaced. "Not right now."

Everything was becoming too serious.

"What happened in there, Alex?" I asked.

"We'll talk when I get back from Stanley," he promised.

"Is it bad?"

"Oh, Charli." He spoke so sympathetically that I was beginning to regret not taking Adam up on his offer. Perhaps we should have kept driving. "I promise it's nothing bad."

I deliberated for a long moment, still trying to make sense of nothing. I glanced across at Alex who was staring straight ahead at the road. His whole body was rigid and his expression was grim. Pressing him for information wasn't the solution. I wasn't sure what was. How do you fix something when you have no idea what the problem is?

"Fine. We'll deal with it later then," I agreed, reluctantly.

***

I managed to catch Nicole the next day at lunchtime.

"Hey," I said glumly, dumping my bag on the table.

She was preoccupied, furiously texting. She glanced briefly at me, to let me know she'd heard me. "I called you last night. You didn't answer," I told her.

"I know. I had an early night," she replied absently. Finally she slipped her phone into her pocket and shifted to face me. "How was dinner?"

"It sucked."

"Why?"

I told her everything that had happened in great detail – just as I would have if she'd taken my phone call the night before.

"Oh ,well." Her tone grated on me almost as much as the way she shrugged her shoulders.

"That's it? Something huge is going on. I have no clue what or how to deal with it, and you say 'Oh, well'?"

Nicole started packing up her stack of books and her untouched sandwich, as if she was in a major hurry.

"Look, families fight," she reasoned, pausing for a second. "The witch obviously did something to upset Adam and he arced up. I doubt it's anything to do with you."

"But nothing happened. He was having a spat with Alex, Gabrielle spilled some wine and Adam lost the plot, ranting at her in French."

She jumped off the table and I knew I had her attention for about three more seconds.

"Maybe he caught her casting an evil spell on you."

The witch references were getting old. "Not funny, Nicole."

"You're overreacting. No one was upset with you. Wait until Alex gets back on Monday and hear what he's got to say," she reasoned. "I have to go."

I checked my watch. We had another twenty minutes. "Go where?"

Nicole slung her bag over her shoulder and flashed me a crafty grin. "Not class. I've had a better offer."

"You're ditching me?" I asked incredulously.

She huffed. "Like you haven't ditched me at least ten times in the last month?"

She had a point. She wasted no time in walking away and I had to raise my voice. "Where are you going?"

She turned, but continued walking backwards. "Tell you later. Have a good weekend."

"You too," I called, but she was out of earshot.

Mentally, I had reached my limit. On an ordinary day I would have chased her down, demanding to know what offer could be powerful enough to make her skip fifth period. It wasn't as if Nicole never ditched school – I managed to talk her in to it occasionally – but it was not something she enjoyed. I usually had to spend the afternoon reassuring her that we weren't about to be arrested for delinquency, while giving her my word that Alex would bail us out if we were. Something was going on. Pipers Cove was crazy town.

The day had been rough from the start. I was sleep deprived and my brain didn't seem to work properly because of it. Alex had laid down the law over breakfast, reminding me that my unsupervised weekend was conditional. One of the conditions was that I went straight home after school so he could give me the keys to the café. Nicole had agreed to work both weekend shifts, but it was up to me to lock up and secure the takings. That was condition number two. I had no idea what conditions three through sixty-five were; I lost interest long before he stopped talking.

Keeping Adam and my brother separated for a few days seemed like a good idea, although I wasn't entirely sure why. I drove my own car that morning, negating the need for Adam to pick me up after school.

At least the weather was holding. I loved days without rain. It was still bitterly cold, but nowhere near as gloomy. My little car, temperamental at the best of times, started spluttering before I'd made it halfway home.

"Don't you dare die on me," I growled, whacking the dashboard to warn it. Angry threats gave way to pleading. I was still pleading when the car finally conked out at the base of our driveway, dead in the middle of the gravel road, in the path of anyone driving past.

It took Alex all of two minutes to get there when I called him.

Gabrielle sat in the passenger seat. School had only been out half an hour. She must have ditched fifth period too. It appeared that I was the only sap stuck indoors on a Friday afternoon for educational purposes.

"Pop the hood," instructed Alex.

I flicked the lever under the ancient dashboard. He lifted the hood, shielding my view of him for a few seconds until he closed it, crashing it down with loud metallic clap.

"I can't see anything wrong," he said, wiping his hands on an old rag he'd brought with him.

"I don't know." I shrugged. "It just coughed a few times and stopped."

Alex smirked.

"What?"

"When was the last time you put fuel in it?"

"Huh?"

"Petrol, Charli."

I glowered at him. "Um, I don't know. Sometime in June?"

He rolled his eyes. I got out of the car as he retrieved the can of petrol he kept for stupid moments like this.

"Are you leaving town now?" I asked, thinking of no other reason why Gabrielle would be with him.

"Yeah. I want to get to Hobart before dark. We'll set off to Stanley in the morning." He reached into his coat pocket, pulling out the keys to the café.

"Nic has a set too. She'll open up but you need to close, okay?"

I nodded, taking the keys. Nothing more was said while he funnelled the fuel into my parched little hatchback. He screwed the cap back and turned to face me. "Are you alright?" he asked.

"Of course," I replied, twirling the keys. I don't know what made him ask me. Perhaps I looked battle-weary.

"Say the word, Charli, and I'll stay," he offered.

I replied without hesitation. "Go."

The look Alex gave me was the strangest I'd ever seen. It was as if he wanted to speak but couldn't find his voice.

"I'm listening, Alex," I whispered.

"I didn't say anything."

"I'm listening to what you're *not* saying."

He half-smiled. "What do you hear?"

"That you love me and we'll talk on Monday."

He kissed my forehead. "That's exactly what I'm saying," he whispered.

Whatever had happened at dinner was of epic proportion. I'd never seen him so conflicted. But whatever it was would have to wait. I waved as they drove away, hopeful that all the drama of the night before had left with them.

I didn't stay a second longer than I needed. I showered, grabbed my already packed overnight bag and left. I stopped for more fuel in town, only half filling it because I couldn't be bothered, and headed to Snow White's cottage.

20. Weekend

My mood had brightened considerably by the time I parked behind the suave black Audi. I sat in the car for a while, contemplating the next few days. I realised that I might have inadvertently cashed in my first ever wish – then decided that wasting a single minute of it by sitting in the car made it a very poor investment.

I wandered to the front door, trying not to appear too eager. The effort was in vain. He wasn't there. Prince Charming had stood me up.

I marched across the lawn to the shed. The door was open, which was a pity considering part of my plan included furiously sliding it open. I stood in the doorway, watching him for a long time.

Adam sat painting, high up on the deck, in a world of his own. The white earphones in his ears explained his trancelike state. His jeans and shirt were spattered with blue paint, indicating he'd been at it for a while. Even with a smudge of paint on his face he was obscenely good-looking. And he was supposed to be all mine for the weekend. I wasn't meant to be sharing him with an ugly, rundown old sloop.

Knowing he couldn't hear me, I embarked on a frustrated monologue purely for my own entertainment.

"Adam Décarie. If you think for one second I'm going to play second fiddle to this stupid boat tonight, you're mistaken. I will burn it to the ground if that's what it takes to get you out of this shed." I paused to catch my breath, elated by how good it felt to unload without upsetting anyone. Adam continued painting; unaware he was on the receiving end of one of my best tantrums ever. "I will take every bit of my clothing off, piece by piece, risking frostbite, hypothermia and certain death until you notice me."

"Charlotte Elisabeth Blake," he said smoothly. I stumbled back, grabbing the rusted edge of the doorway to keep myself upright. Adam continued stroking the paintbrush along the deck. "You play second fiddle to no one. But if you're serious about taking your clothes off, I'm not going to stop you."

"You weren't supposed to be listening," I gasped.

He grinned. "Then why are you talking to me?"

"You've got your headphones on. You're supposed to be listening to music."

"The playlist ended ages ago."

"What kind of idiot wears headphones when he's not listening to music?"

He grinned down at me. "The kind of idiot who doesn't want to touch his iPod when he's got paint on his hands."

The concrete floor didn't open up and swallow me whole. Perhaps I should have cashed in another wish to make it happen.

"Can we go inside now, please?" I asked in a small voice.

"I'll go anywhere with you," he announced.

"Inside will be fine, for now."

He climbed down, wiping his hands on his shirt as he walked towards me. It was an awkward embrace as he tried to keep me paint free, resting his elbows on my shoulders as he leaned in to kiss me.

"Hello," he whispered.

"Hi."

"You look tired today."

Damn. Irresistible and gorgeous was the look I was aiming for. I was wearing lip-gloss, for crying out loud.

"And you look like a caveman," I retorted. "Maybe I should belt you with a plank of wood and throw you over my shoulder."

He beat me to it, pretending to lean in to whisper something before throwing me over his shoulder in a move a fireman would have envied.

"You're covered in paint! I can walk! Put me down, right now!"

"I think we both know that's not going to happen, Charlotte," he said, like he was suddenly the king of everything.

He carried me all the way to the house slung over his shoulder like a sack of flour. Once inside, he lowered me on to the exquisite white couch and stepped away.

"I need a shower," he said, showing me his painty hands. "Five minutes."

I didn't want to wait five minutes. I'd waited my whole life for him; surely that was long enough.

Adam didn't seem surprised when I walked into the bathroom. He turned off the water, reached for a towel and wrapped it around his waist.

My plan of playing it cool fell by the wayside very quickly. Cool was unachievable. The bathroom was full of steam, the most beautiful boy I had ever known was naked and the blood flowing through my body was practically at boiling point.

"Adam Décarie, you have to kiss me," I ordered.

"I *have* to kiss you?"

"I cashed in a wish for you," I explained. "I've never done that before."

Unfazed by my madness, he stepped closer to me. "You spent a wish on me?" he whispered so close to my ear that I could feel his words on my skin. He was warm and smelled divine, like soap.

"I'm wish rich, Adam. I've been saving for years," I reminded him, craning my neck as he kissed a long, slow line from my ear to my throat.

His free hand drifted to my shoulder, sweeping slowly down the length of my arm.

214

"I can't believe I found you," he said, murmuring the words against my mouth.

I was certain my bones were about to ignite at any second. I couldn't even fake confidence. My whole body was shaking.

"I've been here all along," I pointed out.

I felt his smile on my skin.

Abandoning his grip on the towel, his arms wrapped tightly around me and his lips finally pressed against mine. Blood raced through my body as I tried to slow my breathing. When we finally did break our embrace, I was fighting for air.

"Flee-itis, Charli?" His voice was slow and controlled but his hard, shallow breathing betrayed him.

"No." I inhaled deeply. "Décarie-itis; it's different."

He laughed, kissed me as if his life depended on it – then scooped me into his arms and carried me to his room.

***

The sheer curtains in the tiny bedroom blocked out none of the morning light and I woke early. I lay listening to the rain peppering the tin roof, caught in a perfect moment, tangled around him, listening to him breathe as he slept beside me.

My head rested uncomfortably in the crook of his arm but I didn't care. Every other part of my body felt blissful – heavy and weightless at the same time. I would have floated to the ceiling if his arms weren't around me. His hold on me didn't waver as I twisted to see his face. Tracing a light line around his lips with my fingers made him flinch, enough to loosen his grip but not enough to wake him. He murmured my name – not the shortened, preferred version but the extended, ridiculous version that was more suited to a character from a Jane Austen novel.

"Are you awake?" I whispered.

The silence made my heart fly. He'd whispered my name in his sleep. Running my hand down the length of his arm made him move just enough to free me.

Moving slowly and quietly, I gathered my clothes and made my way to the bathroom.

My overnight bag hadn't made it out of the car, and everything I needed to make myself look human was in it. Fossicking through Gabrielle's cabinets looking for a hairbrush seemed more intrusive than going through her handbag, and I couldn't bring myself to do it.

A bag of toiletries on the counter brought me a little hope. Obviously it wasn't Gabrielle's. The black leather bag contained everything from razor blades to cologne that reminded me of him – even without smelling it. The small comb I found had no hope of making it through my hair so I gave up, repacked the bag and repositioned it on the counter, hoping it looked as it had before.

Determined to elevate my status to smug but pretty, I headed to the car to retrieve my bag. But the mission was all but forgotten when the sound of the ocean pounding on the base of the cliff distracted me. Some days it couldn't be heard from the house and other days the waves were deafening. This day was different, a happy medium. Even without seeing them I knew the waves were rhythmic and slow.

I walked across the back lawn. The minute I saw the surf I was sold. I wondered if leaving would be misconstrued as regret if he woke and I wasn't there.

Glancing around quickly to make sure I was alone, I dropped the towel and dragged on my wetsuit, which had a permanent home in my car. The overgrown trees lining the side boundary shielded me from anyone lurking in the neighbouring garden – an unlikely scenario considering the early hour. I dragged my brush through my hair before pulling it into a messy bun.

Carrying my board under one arm and everything else with the other, I stumbled barefooted down the crude track to the beach. Gabrielle was spoiled rotten by the easy access, yet I couldn't remember ever seeing her down there.

Standing ankle deep in the icy water, I couldn't help turning to look up at the house perched on the cliff to make sure it was still there. Shaking all thoughts of him from my head, I refocused on the ocean. The dark water, greyed by the overcast sky, crashed in slowly. The rain had dulled to a light sprinkle that I couldn't even feel.

"Charli Blake," called a smooth voice from somewhere behind me.

I didn't turn around. I didn't need to. I knew exactly who it was. If there was a chance the little cottage on the hill might disappear in a puff of smoke this would have been the time.

"Mitchell Tate." I tried to keep my voice even.

"Did you miss me?" He sounded closer, right behind me.

I shrugged my shoulders as I worked on my lie. "Were you gone?"

"Aren't you going to look at me?" I could hear the smile in his voice.

I saw him in my head. Scrappy shoulder length sandy blonde hair bleached by the sun, broad shoulders and a year-round tan that his sisters would have killed for.

Turning around, I paced the few feet necessary to get back to the water's edge. Nothing was said for a few seconds and I made no secret of the fact I was staring at him. The unkempt blonde hair was gone, replaced by a short buzz cut. Other than that, nothing had changed. He was just as I remembered him. Tall, tanned and handsome. Mitchell loathed the Beautifuls moniker, yet he was the only one who deserved the title.

"Where have you been, Mitch?" I asked, working to sound casual.

He clasped his hands, blowing a warm breath into his clenched fists before launching into his reply. "Everywhere. South Africa, Bali, Tahiti, California – "

"So why did you come back?" I cut him off. I got the impression his list of conquered surf beaches was long.

"Ethan's back too. It was time," he said simply. His grin was infectious and I smiled at him for the first time. "You look good, Charli."

There was a time when I wanted to hear him say it – but he never did. It was too late now.

"When did you get back?"

"A few days ago." His smile didn't waver.

"And you're down here already? You must be keen."

"I knew you'd be here. I wanted to see you but I wasn't expecting such a chilly reception." He raised one eyebrow, shooting me a look that once upon a time would have dropped me to the floor. Now it just annoyed me.

"What *were* you expecting, Mitchell?"

A nervous laugh hitched in his throat. "I'm not sure."

"I don't think there's much to say. I laid it all on the line before you left, remember?"

Every bit of rejection I'd felt that day flooded back. Making the decision to change a friendship comes with the risk of losing everything. Alex claimed that I had a high tolerance for risk. Seeing Mitchell standing in front of me reminded me that it rarely worked in my favour.

"You were barely sixteen, Charli. Alex would have killed me."

"I can still arrange for him to do that," I said seriously.

"Are you still mad?" A grin crossed his face again as he rocked back on his heels.

"I don't even think about you." I punched out my words but he overlooked the harshness.

"I've thought about you every day."

"You never even wrote, Mitchell, never called, nothing. Your sisters didn't even know where you were most of the time," I hissed through my teeth.

"So you *did* ask about me," he said triumphantly.

Frustration overtook me. I scowled, pushing past him to pick up my bag and board. "We're done," I said, walking away.

I could feel his eyes pulling me back, willing me to turn around, but I held strong, refusing to look back at him. I was almost at the beginning of the trail when he called out again.

"Would it have made a difference, if I'd written to you?"

"No!"

I don't know how long he stood there. Not once did I turn back to check. Mitchell Tate was not a complication I planned on spending time thinking about.

A strange kind of nervousness fizzed inside me as I approached the cottage, dissolving the euphoria I'd felt when I woke. It hardly seemed fair. Mitchell had blown back in to town after being absent for over a year as if nothing had changed. *Everything* had changed.

Sneaky, underhanded and more than capable of stretching the truth were all fair statements when it came to describing myself. They were not attributes to be proud of but it was an angle I'd worked for a long time. I didn't want to take that road with Adam. He deserved more from me. Telling him that Mitchell Tate was back in town before he heard it from anyone else was the only option I had.

Dumping my gear on the porch, I brushed as sand off my feet as best I could before pushing the door open. The squeaky floorboards made creeping through the house impossible but there was no need. He leaned on the archway that separated the kitchen from the dining room, nursing a cup of coffee, smiling as if it had been months since we'd seen each other.

"You weren't gone long," he noted. "I thought I would have lost you for hours."

Ordinarily he would have. The waves that morning were faultless. I could have wasted an entire morning in the water and not felt a wisp of guilt. Instead, I had run back to the house after less than half an hour feeling as guilty as sin.

"I have to tell you something," I said bleakly.

So much for easing into it.

Adam's hand, warm from the mug, moved under my chin and tilted my head, giving me no option but to look at him. I stared at him for too long, desperately trying to string a sentence together in my head.

"It must be important if you abandoned the beach," he said.

I looked to the ceiling – preparing to be struck down at any second as I launched into my confession the only way I knew how, bluntly. "Mitchell Tate was on the beach. He's back in town."

Adam leaned back to look at me, only loosening his grip on my waist slightly, staring for a long time.

"Does that news change something, Charlotte?" he asked finally. He didn't look bothered in the slightest.

I fervently shook my head. "Nothing," I promised.

"Good. So neither of us need to waste another minute talking about it," he murmured, leaning in for the kill.

That was too easy, I thought – easier than I deserved, anyway. I don't know what reaction I was expecting. Mitchell meant nothing to Adam, which was exactly how it should have been. In a less complicated, less smashed up world, he would have meant nothing to me either.

Adam's hand trailed a line up my back, reaching for the zipper at my neck. It crackled as he slid it down, stopping when he reached the end of the line at the small of my back. I backed away. I had no qualms about him seeing me naked – playing coy after last night would have been absurd – but getting out of a wetsuit is about as elegant as trying to squeeze into jeans two sizes too small. "Hold that thought," I instructed him, and slipped away to the bathroom.

I stood under the shower too long, letting the water run over my head. I didn't expect Adam to walk in but wasn't unhappy when he did. I cleared the foggy shower screen with my hand, smiling at him through the temporarily clear patch of glass.

"I just got a phone call," he announced, waving his phone at nothing in particular. "I've been waiting all week for a parcel and Mrs Daintree just called to let me know she's holding it at the post office."

Holding it to ransom more likely. The Daintrees ran the post office and adjoining souvenir shop, and Valerie Daintree was as nosey as Carol Lawson. She'd probably demand to know the contents of the package before she handed it over.

"Do you want me to come with you?" I asked. "Val is a scary woman."

His laugh echoed. "There are a lot of scary women in this town, Charlotte. I think I can handle her. Besides, Nicole called too. She wants you to go to the café. She said it was urgent."

Of course it was urgent. Nicole would have been champing at the bit to break it to me that Mitchell was back in town. Truthfully, I wanted to see her too. Even if I hadn't, going to the café was still preferable to fronting up at the post office with Adam.

It turned out that Adam had a few errands to run that morning, all boat related and boring, so we took our own cars with the vague plan of meeting somewhere in the middle later.

For the first time ever I was actually glad that my car lost the capability of hitting the speed limit somewhere back in the eighties. I was in no hurry to reach the café, already knowing what I was in for when I got there.

Nicole didn't disappoint, meeting me at the door before the bell had even stopped jingling. "I'm so glad you're here," she said, reaching for the sleeve of my coat and pulling me through the door.

"Why? What's the emergency?" I asked, pretending to look around for signs of fire or some other catastrophic event.

"No emergency. Look, I know I promised Alex I'd be here today but something's come up."

The wicked smile that crept across her face was not one I saw often. Her plans for the day didn't involve working. And I'd been wrong about the reason for wanting to see me. Mitchell had nothing to do with it.

"Ethan?" I asked.

She nodded. "And Ethan had something to do with the offer you got yesterday afternoon, right before you ditched me?" She continued nodding through my entire sentence, looking nowhere near as contrite as she should have. "Why didn't you just tell me they were back in town?"

"I didn't think you'd appreciate the distraction," she said wryly. "What was I supposed to say? 'Oh, and by the way, remember when Jasmine told you that you had no idea what was coming? Well, I just found out what she meant by that.'"

As much as I hated to admit it, she was right.

It was inevitable that Nicole would gravitate back to Ethan the minute he hit town, even knowing he was wrong for her. He knew he was never going to be the one she was looking for. To her credit, she had made that very clear. Ethan knew exactly where he stood, which probably explained why there were no tears when he left town. Nicole used her time with Ethan like a practice for the real thing. Unlike me, she had always expected true love to be blinding and fierce. I'd laughed when she first told me that she'd know the instant she found the one for her. I wouldn't laugh now.

"I'll stay. You go," I said unwillingly. But it wasn't as if I had anything better to do. Adam wouldn't be back for ages. Valerie Daintree could hold him against his will for hours.

"You're sure?" Her words implied I had a choice but she was already reaching for her bag and coat.

"Yeah. Go."

The second I'd finished speaking, Ethan walked through the door, and judging by the dumb grin on his face, he'd been waiting in the wings the whole time. "All set?" she asked, too enthusiastic to appear casual.

He nodded.

"Ethan. Hi," I said, a little too loudly, to compensate for the fact that I was invisible.

"How are you, Charli? You look good." He hadn't even looked at me.

Ethan hadn't changed much in the past year. His hair was longer than he used to wear it, which made me wonder why Mitchell's was so severely short. It bugged me that I'd even made the comparison. I did not want to spend a single second of my time thinking about Mitchell Tate. Ethan was quite short, not much taller than me and about the same height as Nicole. He shared the same physique as most surfers, stock standard for any boy who spent hours a day cutting through water with his arms.

Nicole asked me one more time if I was sure I wanted to stay, already halfway out the door when she asked the question.

Manning the café on the first morning of my weekend alone with Adam seemed nothing less than sabotage. I wasn't sure if Nicole was the culprit or if I was the one to blame. I'd browsed through most of her contraband magazine collection by the time the bell at the top of the door finally jingled.

Floss Davis's large frame shuffled through the door and I grinned, truly thrilled to see her. "Hello, love," she beamed, walking towards the counter in her usual slow manner.

"Where have you been, Floss?"

It had been days since I'd seen her, and that was almost unheard of. I'd been lying low, but it was still unusual to go so long without seeing her somewhere around town.

"Well, we went on a whirlwind tour of the big smoke a week or so ago, up to Adelaide for a few days," she explained.

"Oh, nice," I purred. "That Norm sure knows how to treat a girl right."

Floss looked confused. "It wasn't Norm's idea. It was that lovely boy of yours."

"Adam?" I asked incredulously.

Floss's eyes darted around as if she was looking for an escape route. "I assumed he would have told you, considering he's already given it to you," she said, pointing to my necklace.

"Told me what?" I demanded, clutching the black pendant at my throat.

"Oh, Charli, I'm not sure if – "

"Just tell me, please."

"He commissioned me to make that necklace for you. He had very specific ideas about what he wanted. It had to be a black opal. There was no way I'd buy a black opal sight unseen." She huffed out a breath at the end as if it was the most ludicrous idea on earth. "I told him the only place to buy such a stone would be from a reputable dealer on the mainland. He told me to do whatever I needed. Norm and I had a fabulous three-day, all expenses paid trip to Adelaide, and tracked down the most spectacular black opal I've ever seen. Don't you think it's a stunner?"

I nodded, astonished by her tale.

Once Floss started talking, there was no shutting her up. I continued nodding as she went on to explain the characteristics of the perfect black opal but truthfully I was only half listening – until she mentioned Norm's fabulous negotiating skills.

"It took some wheeling, he wanted over six thousand for it initially. I got him down to five and a half thanks to Norm. He always was good at bargaining," she said proudly.

Adam had assured me it was a cheap trinket. A five and a half thousand dollar opal was no cheap trinket.

"What's the setting, Floss? What's the chain made of?"

224

"Platinum," she said, grinning at me. "I've never worked with platinum before."

Of course she hadn't. Floss crafted semiprecious jewellery out of metals like nickel and silver. And I'd actually taken my pendant off before showering, worried that the cheap metal would make my skin turn green.

I needed to sit down. I was mortified by my own naivety, but mostly I was angry. Since when has jewellery worth thousands of dollars been an appropriate gift for me? I didn't deserve it. I hardly felt that I deserved *him* most of the time.

I was beginning to realise that Alex was right. I knew nothing important about Adam Décarie and it was time I started asking questions. The minute Floss was out of sight, I took the necklace off, burying it deep in the pocket of my jeans.

Even if my ridiculously extravagant black opal had spontaneously combusted, it wouldn't have come close to the discomfort I felt half an hour later when Lily Tate and Lisa Reynolds sauntered through the door, followed by Jasmine.

It was the first time the trinity of Beautifuls had been seen in public for a week. Any plans I had of serving them quickly and sending them on their way were dashed when they sat down. They hardly ever ordered in unless they were in the mood for tormenting my brother with an hour of flirty innuendos while they pretended to drink coffee.

"What do you want?" I asked from the relative safety of behind the counter.

"Customer service really isn't your forte, Charli. You should work on that," said Jasmine in a syrupy tone that must have taken hours of practice to master. Lily and Lisa giggled, a piercing shrill that reminded me of fingers scraping down a blackboard – a feat none of them were capable of considering they were all still wearing gloves. I tapped my pen on the counter.

"Two cappuccinos and a skim milk latte," said Jasmine in her superior tone.

I stared at her blankly like I didn't understand her order.

"Do you need to write it down?" she asked, making the other two girls giggle again.

"No. I've got it," I replied dryly.

Ignoring them was impossible. The whispered comments seemed louder than the fake casual conversation they threw in for effect, even over the sound of the coffee machine. It wasn't until I took their coffees to the table that they spoke directly to me.

"What's this?" asked Jasmine sourly.

"It's what you ordered," I said, pointing to the cups in front of her. "Three flat whites."

"You are so stupid," said Lily. She didn't say it meanly, it sounded more apologetic. I smiled at her, safe in the knowledge that I wasn't the stupid one.

"Did you hear the news, Charli?" asked Lisa. Her friendly tone offered false comfort. I held the empty tray to my chest like a shield. I had a feeling I was about to need it.

"Does it matter? You're going to tell me anyway." My childishness was beginning to echo theirs, which added weight to my theory. If you hung around them for any length of time, there was a chance you'd turn into one of them.

"Mitchy is back in town."

As usual, Jasmine was the spokesperson for the group. I wondered if rank was based on age or hair colour.

"I know," I replied, wondering how he'd react to being called Mitchy.

"How could *you* know? He only just got back," spat Lisa.

"I saw him on the beach this morning."

Lisa's face crumpled and I realised there was a new game in play. It had only taken Lisa a few days to set her sights on Mitchell Tate, no doubt with the full support and encouragement of his sisters.

"I told him to stay away from you," snarled Lily.

"Good. I hope he listens," I said, making my way back to the counter.

More muted whispers followed before Jasmine spoke again. "It's our birthday soon. We're having a huge party. We've organised everything. It's black tie."

It was hard enough to get Mitchell to wear shoes, let alone a suit and tie. The Beautifuls used any excuse to get dressed up, and a birthday party was obviously a prime opportunity, even if one of the guests of honour was sure to hate it.

"Why are you telling me?"

"We *have* to tell you about it. It's not like you'll be there to see it for yourself," replied Lily.

"Thank goodness for small mercies," I muttered.

The Beautifuls stopped talking to me when they realised I wasn't taking the bait. Their irritating banter slowly faded to background noise. The only time I looked up was to serve the odd customer that came through the door. I had four in an hour, and the day was dragging.

The Beautifuls still showed no signs of leaving when the telltale bell at the top of the door jingled.

"Mitchell!" shrieked Lisa, launching herself at him. Snaking her arms around his waist, she squeezed him tightly.

"Hey, Lisa," he mumbled, prising her off. He stared at me the whole time, paying no attention to Lisa who was unashamedly trying to maintain her grip on him.

"Sit with us," instructed Jasmine, pulling out a chair.

"In a minute." He was walking towards the counter.

"What do you want?" My tone was cutting but, as usual, he ignored it.

"To see you."

227

I felt my heart unfairly skip. "I'm busy," I lied.

"What time do you finish?"

"I'm busy then too, Mitchell."

"I'll wait. We need to talk." He leaned too far across the counter as he spoke and I instinctively took a step back.

From the corner of my eye I had enough vision to see the Beautifuls hanging on every word. It was an impossible conversation and I hated being pushed into having it in front of an audience.

"We talked this morning," I hissed.

"No. I tried talking to you this morning and you walked away from me." His voice was low and muted but our audience missed nothing.

"There's nothing to discuss. Leave." My voice sounded strange, like I was trying to whisper and yell at the same time.

"Fine," he said, shrugging. "We'll talk later."

Part of me hoped he'd join his sisters at the table. That might have made it seem a little less like he'd come there just to see me. But he didn't sit down. He walked out of the shop without another word and the minute the door swung shut, all eyes were on me.

"You need to leave him alone," ordered Lily.

"Does it look like I'm trying to do anything but that?" I demanded.

"You have Adam," said Lisa, as if I needed reminding.

"Yes, I do," I spat.

"So what are you doing? Do you want both of them now? That's not very ladylike, Charli." Jasmine chided. The smile she gave me didn't match the choler in her voice. She was grinning like she'd just won the lottery.

"Why does he want her? Why do they *always* want her?" asked Lisa in a tone so theatrical I could only half believe she was serious. She looked like she was about to cry and I did *not* want to see her cry.

"He doesn't. He's just confused," Lily soothed, making me laugh out loud. She whipped her head round and shot a look of sheer poison at me. Lisa burst into tears, a weird guttural sob.

"He's all yours, Lisa. Take him. *Please*, take him," I begged.

Jasmine's smile remained, which added to my vexation. I had somehow become the villain and it happened so quickly, I didn't see from which direction it came – until I connected the exultant smile on Jasmine's face to the emotional mayhem in the room.

Lisa had designs on Mitchell. Lily was doing her best to ensure they came to fruition, but Jasmine was more intent on torturing me.

"*You* called him," I accused, pointing at her from across the room.

Lisa and Lily stared at Jasmine.

"I thought he'd like to know." She folded her arms and leaned back in her chair.

"Like to know what?" asked Lily, patting Lisa's back.

Jasmine's icy glare was replaced by a sympathetic look. "That Lisa was here of course. You know what Mitch is like, he needs a little encouragement."

I was actually beginning to feel sorry for the junior Beautifuls. Unrequited love was one thing, but Jasmine was playing on a whole level above those two.

"We need to keep him away from Charli," said Lily, turning to glare at me again.

I said nothing. There wasn't any point.

Adam walked through the door just in time. I got the feeling they were about to lynch me or burn me at the stake. I'd never been so grateful to see anyone.

A quick sideward glance at the table of Beautifuls was the only attention he paid them. "Is everything okay, Charli? You look a little bit flushed."

"She's embarrassed, or at least she should be," said Jasmine acerbically.

Adam didn't speak but raised his eyebrows, questioning me silently with his eyes.

"Tell you later," I promised.

The corner of his mouth lifted. "Are you here by yourself?" he asked, leaning across the counter to speak quietly. It made no difference. The Beautifuls had supersonic hearing.

"Yes she is," confirmed Lily dutifully.

Adam turned to face her for the first time since he'd walked in. "Well, I guess she's lucky you've been here to keep her company."

"Charity work is good for the soul," said Jasmine, reaching under the table for her handbag. It wasn't the first time I'd noticed the huge advantage Jasmine had over her sister and Lisa. She recognised sarcasm and was capable of responding appropriately. Her dumb blonde act was just that.

Lisa and Lily followed her lead as if she'd silently given them orders. Lisa's crocodile tears stopped, proving that she was the second best actress in the shop. Jasmine waited until her entourage had walked out before speaking again.

"Adam, my family is hosting a black tie dinner soon, to celebrate our birthday. You won't be there of course, it's after you leave. But I think you should know that Charli with be there. She'll be my brother Mitchell's date."

Adam turned back to me with the confused expression that overtook him whenever he was cornered by a Beautiful.

I shook my head in disbelief and he turned back to Jasmine.

"Excuse me?"

Jasmine smiled, flicking her hair off her shoulder. "She'll be my brother Mitchell's date," she repeated. "I don't like it any more than you do but it was bound to happen. He's been back in town for two days and they're already gravitating towards each other."

"Jasmine!" I choked out her name. I wanted to choke her. "*You* called him. He came here because *you* told him I was here."

"Texted him," she corrected as she waved her phone at me.

"You know Lisa likes him. She thinks you're helping her chase him." My tone had an edge of revulsion now.

"I know. Poor thing," she lamented. "As if Lisa Reynolds would ever make the grade."

Adam said nothing. His eyes darted between Jasmine and the floor, but never at me.

"Why would you do that?" I asked, sounding more defeated than angry now.

"Because it would be a tragedy to see Adam invest so much time in you when it's hopeless. He could be spending these last few weeks here broadening his horizons." Her grin was reserved only for him.

Adam found his voice at just the right moment. "My horizons would never be that broad, Jasmine." His tone was respectful but his words were not.

She overlooked the monumental insult he'd just paid her but I didn't doubt that she understood. She breezed towards the door, turning to face me one last time.

"Honesty is always the best policy, Charli." The superior tone was back with a vengeance. I watched as she walked out the door, fighting the unbelievable urge to drag her back in by her hair. How dare she get the last word in! How dare she assume that Mitchell being back in town would change anything! I picked up the first thing I could reach, a magazine I'd been reading, and pegged it as hard as I could at the door. Adam flinched. The bell jingled furiously and then there was the inevitable silence. Silence because neither of us knew what to say. I was so angry I could feel myself shaking.

It was Adam who spoke first. "I am in competition with a Beautiful?" he asked, only half jokingly.

"Believe me, there is no competition." I said it too weakly to sound convincing.

I could feel the tears beginning to well in my eyes and I looked up to the ceiling, hoping to stop them brimming over.

"She really got to you didn't she?" he asked, reading the situation entirely wrong.

Finally the tears escaped and there was no point trying to hide the fact I was crying. Gripping my sleeve in my clenched fingers, I wiped my eyes. I'd woken that morning feeling completely blissful. I struggled to understand how it had turned so ugly.

Adam swept the tears from my cheek. "I know what we have, Charli. I'm not concerned by anything Jasmine has to say."

I knew he was trying to reassure me but his words were irritating. After my encounter with Floss, I didn't even know what we had. I snatched my hand free.

He waited.

"Ask me if I love him," I demanded, still focusing on the floor.

"Perhaps asking if you love me would be more appropriate."

I stopped pacing and looked up him, seeing confusion and sadness in his eyes.

Ignoring his question, I answered my own. "I do *not* love him but I know everything about him."

"Alright," he said simply.

Stepping on only the white squares of linoleum and avoiding the black, it took four paces to reach him.

"I know nothing about you." I stared at him, refusing to unlock him from my gaze. His mouth moved a little bit, as if he was going to speak but thought better of it. "You know everything about me, my heart, my head and my body. But I know nothing important about you."

The look he gave me was one of sheer agony. "Do you want to get out of here?" he asked.

I shook my head. "I can't. Nicole's off doing goodness knows what with her substitute Prince Charming and Alex would kill me if I closed early. It's been a quiet day and the takings are way down."

I walked back around the counter and opened the cash register. The amount of money in the drawer seemed pitiful.

Adam reached for his wallet. He took out a wad of notes and slapped them on the counter. "The takings are way up today," he replied. "Can we please get out of here now?"

Tentatively, I picked up the money, smoothing out the notes. I estimated hundreds of dollars but was too scared to count it.

"You need to talk to me." My voice faltered, no authoritative tone whatsoever.

"Just put the money away and we can leave. Then we'll talk," He sounded much stronger than I was.

All my energy had been used fending off Mitchell and the Beautifuls. I didn't have it in me to argue with him. I stuffed the money in the till and reached for my coat. Adam stood silent as I followed Alex's closing up routine, locking the door and flipping the closed sign. He caught my hand as I walked past but I refused to stop, pulling him towards the back door.

The silence continued into the car park. His car flashed orange as the doors unlocked and he opened the passenger door. I stood looking at him for too long, unsure what I wanted to do.

"Please, Charli," he said. "We can come back for your car later."

It took me a while to realise it had started raining again. Adam made no attempt to escape it, reminding me of the very first day we'd met, in the car park over the road. Water streamed down his face but he ignored it. Realising I wasn't in a hurry to get in, he closed the door.

"I know about the necklace," I burst out. "Floss told me everything. I can't accept it now." I reached into my pocket and held it out to him but he didn't move. "You have to take it," I insisted. I grabbed his hand and slapped the pendant into his palm.

"I have never met anyone like you, Charlotte." His eyes drifted away from me for the first time as he looked at the black gem in his hand.

"That's because I'm strange. It's a well-known fact. Ask anyone."

The corner of his mouth lifted. He took a few probationary steps towards me.

"Stay back," I warned, throwing my hands in front of me. "You still haven't told me anything."

He stopped. "What would you like to know?"

He bounced the necklace in his hand as if it was scalding, and I felt the need to let him off the hook. Confessing to what Gabrielle had told me seemed like a good idea.

"I know that your family is filthy rich, Adam. Gabrielle told me."

The pained look on his face didn't slip. It seemed an eternity before he spoke again.

"What about the life that comes with the money, Charli?" His voice faltered, like he'd considered changing his question half way through. "You couldn't possibly know about that. I'm concerned that you're going to hate my world. I'm not sure there's enough magic in it for you."

"You'll be there. The rest I can deal with."

"My family does have a lot of money," he conceded. "They've always had a lot of money." He spoke as if he was confessing to a crime.

"It makes no difference to me," I insisted.

"I wasn't trying to hide anything from you. I just enjoyed the fact that it meant nothing to you. Until I got here, I'd never made my bed or done a load of laundry. I'd never even made my own cup of coffee. I am the ultimate spoiled brat," he confessed. He slipped the necklace into his pocket. "Anything I give you, Charli, can never compare to what you've given me."

I fervently shook my head. "I don't want anything from you."

The small space between us felt charged. "Truthfully, I could buy you whatever you wanted. I'm manipulative like that."

"You think I'm not manipulative? I manipulate everyone I know. You've seen what I'm capable of."

He laughed shortly. "It's not the same thing."

"It's exactly the same thing."

"I fear you might be a little biased."

The dimpled smile he gave me won out over my anger. I felt like we were finding common ground where I'd feared there might not have been any. A few tiny chinks in his armour brought a kind of hope to me. I had always known I was flawed and insecure. Finding out that he was too put us on a more even keel.

"I'm not biased. It changes nothing," I said triumphantly.

"I might not be worth it, Charlotte," he warned, looking confused.

The smartest boy I had ever known just wasn't getting it. "You said my name while you were sleeping. Someone who thinks of me even as he sleeps is definitely worth it."

The look he gave me was becoming familiar. It was the same puzzled expression that made me wonder if he thought I was a little unbalanced. Perhaps I was the one who wasn't getting it. I stood for a long moment, searching for whatever it was that he thought I was missing.

He saw my preoccupation and misinterpreted it. "If you're having second thoughts about coming to New York – "

I put my finger to his lips. "I never have second thoughts. I always go with the first."

"That's what I'm afraid of," he murmured against my finger.

***

Being at Gabrielle's house no longer felt like we were breaking rules. Adam got out of the car and I followed, not giving him a chance to open my door for me. We were almost at the house when I spotted two little red tulips jutting out from the rockery, bright against the mass of greenery that would be overflowing with flowers in spring. He saw them too and leaned down to pick them.

"No," I protested.

He straightened up. "Why not?"

"I'll tell you another time," I promised, turning back towards the house.

"Not so fast, Coccinelle," he said.

"I still have no clue what that means." After my first attempt at translation, I'd been reluctant to research it again.

"I am prepared to make a deal with the devil. I will translate for you if you tell me why you just reacted as if picking flowers is a federal offence."

As if on cue, my phone beeped. "Are you not going to reply?" he asked, studying me closely as I glanced at the message and retired my phone to my pocket.

I felt the colour fade from my cheeks and I wondered if I looked pale. "Its Nicole again."

"The flowers," he persisted.

"The translation," I demanded.

Without warning, he dipped me backwards, so low my head was just inches from the ground.

"What are you doing?" I gasped.

His voice was serious but the smile was warm. "Ladybug. Coccinelle is French for ladybug."

Adam loved small details. I'd all but forgotten the conversation we'd had on the beach where I'd confessed to saving ladybug wishes. I shouldn't have been surprised that he'd remembered.

If a beep could sound urgent, that would have described the sound coming from my pocket. "Nicole must really need to talk to you," he said, righting me. "Maybe you should call."

I reluctantly took the phone and read the message. I struggled to look at him and he moved his head, trying to follow my eyes as they flitted everywhere but at him. No wonder he found it so difficult to read me. It was like watching him trying to navigate a road that I'd already smashed up.

I was about to do the unthinkable.

"It's not Nicole," I said. "It's Mitchell. He's at my house. He wants to see me."

His lips formed a straight line. "So you're going to drop everything and go running?"

"I have to put an end to this, Adam. Please understand."

He nodded stiffly. He didn't understand and unfortunately for me, I was too inept to explain it to him.

The journey home should have taken half the time that it would have in my old car but I drove ridiculously slowly. Caution and safety had nothing to do with it – I was buying time.

21. Memory Lane

I sat in the car longer than I should have, trying to prepare myself for the conversation ahead.

Mitchell leaned against the railing of our veranda with an unreadable expression on his face. It occurred to me that he probably wasn't entirely sure it was me sitting in the Audi.

I enjoyed seeing him squirm for a short minute before getting out of the car and storming the veranda like I was about to charge at him. "You have five minutes and I shouldn't even be giving you that."

"I just want to talk, Charli. I've been trying to talk to you since this morning," he said smoothly.

I could feel him standing behind me as I twisted the key in the lock of the front door. "You need to leave me alone." I wanted to sound stronger and considered repeating the sentence with more anger – and maybe a growl. The gesture of throwing my keys down on the hallstand seemed to have the same effect.

"Calm down, feisty one. We'll talk and then I'll leave you alone," he promised, reaching for my hand. I snatched it away.

"Four minutes," I warned.

He smirked and walked through to the kitchen, unaffected by my hostility. "Do you still drink tea?" he asked, flicking on the kettle with the familiarity of someone who lived there.

"Can you please get to the point? I have better things to be doing right now."

Mitchell sat down at the place usually reserved for Alex. "By better things, you mean the American?" I couldn't pick the emotion in his voice. The expected tone of jealousy was absent, leaving me wondering if I'd become conceited as well as mean.

"Adam. His name is Adam," I replied, trying to lose the attitude.

"So you're going to shack up with him when your trip is over?" I raised my eyebrows. "Nicole told me."

"I can't wait," I told him. "Have you been to New York?"

His lips formed a thin line. "Can't say I have. I've heard that the surf isn't that great there."

"I'll cope," I muttered.

He leaned back in his chair. "Does he know you, Charli?"

It was a vague question but I understood perfectly.

"Completely."

"Completely? Wow. Impressive."

It was a bold declaration and he had every right to be sceptical. Mitchell knew everything about me by default. – knowing someone her whole life makes familiarity inevitable. To think I'd shared everything with Adam in just a few months would have seemed impossible.

"It's the truth."

"He knows that you have the ocean in your blood?" I nodded. "And he thinks New York is the place for you?"

I continued nodding. Mitchell was quiet. The cogs turning in his head were almost audible as he searched for something else to put forward – something he thought I would never share with anyone. I waited in silence, safe in the knowledge that he'd come up blank.

"What about *us*, Charli? Does he know about us?"

"He knows, and there is no *us*," I said casually. "There never really was. You made sure of that."

He straightened up. "Tell me something? If I had stayed, would you still have chosen him?"

I leaned back. "He knows everything about me and even after all that, he doesn't think I'm crazy. I love him, Mitchell."

He smiled but looked like it took effort. "I never thought you were crazy."

"That's because you're off kilter too." I kept my tone light, shying away from the direction the conversation was heading.

Finally he looked at me. "I wish things were different, Charli. I should never have left you the way I did."

"You should never have let me spend the night with you in the first place. Nothing changed until then. Everything fell apart because you weren't brave enough to stay with me." I said it too loudly, putting too much meaning in it.

I could see the frustration building. It took a lot to rile Mitchell. Having the Beautifuls as sisters gave him superpowers when it came to keeping his cool, but his calm demeanour was fading fast. "You were just sixteen." He spoke through gritted teeth. "Your brother would have slaughtered me."

"So you left."

"What was I supposed to do?" he asked in exasperation. "It wasn't fair to ask you to wait for me. I couldn't ask you to come with me. What could I have done differently?"

"Not telling everyone that I was the biggest mistake of your life might have been a start. Your sisters buried me after that," I spat, raising my voice to match his.

"I never said that, never," he insisted, drumming his finger on the table.

"Of course you did. That's what elevated my social status to skanky whore," I replied bitterly.

"No. I said that *leaving* you here was the biggest mistake of my life."

I allowed my mind to wander as I tried to process his words. My life had all but fallen apart because I chose to give everything to a boy who'd changed his mind. I'd spent a year hating him because of it. Now that I had finally heard his side of the story the anger was slipping.

"It doesn't matter now." I sighed. "None of this matters now."

Mitchell nodded. "I'm not going to bother you again. I just wanted to make sure you knew the truth."

The truth wasn't supposed to hurt so much. It was a strange moment and the only comfort I drew was from knowing that even if I had never met Adam – if my life had remained on pause since the day Mitchell left – I would never have taken him back. Regardless of what Alex might think, my tolerance for risk just wasn't that high.

22. Conte de Fée

Adam never mentioned Mitchell when I returned. I was relieved and hopeful that maybe we'd manage to get through the rest of the day unscathed. It worked for several blissful hours until there was a knock at the front door.

Adam leapt up like he was expecting it.

"Who would that be?" I asked, peeping over the back of the couch towards the front door.

"Dinner, I hope."

Maybe I'd misheard him. No one in Pipers Cove delivered. Our café closed at five-thirty and that was considered late night trading. He stepped out and closed the door, making it impossible for me to eavesdrop.

Back inside, he dropped a box on the coffee table, sat beside me and draped his arm casually around my shoulder.

"Dinner is served," he announced, grinning.

"Pizza?" I asked, leaning forward to lift the lid – just to make sure there was actually a pizza in there. "How did you do this?"

"I love pizza," he said, drawing out his words and avoiding my question.

I wasn't about to press him for an explanation. He must have paid a phenomenal amount of money to have it delivered from Sorell. We were about to indulge in the world's most expensive pizza, but I didn't care. The list of things I knew about Adam had just grown. He loved pizza.

"I didn't know that."

His cerulean eyes looked warm, totally unguarded. "That's because I've never told you. I was under the misconception that trivial details were unimportant, but I've changed my stance."

"Since when?"

"Since I realised how much I like the trivial details," he replied, flipping open the box.

I picked up a slice, terrified by the thought of dropping it on the pristine couch. Noticing my discomfort, he disappeared to the kitchen, returning with plates and far too many serviettes.

"This is the nicest thing ever. Thank you," I whispered, nudging him in the side with my shoulder.

He looked at me from the corner of his eye. "*Ever?*"

"Maybe not ever," I amended. Unable to look at him, my focus locked on one of Gabrielle's pictures on the far wall.

Adam dropped his half-eaten slice of pizza back in the box and brushed his hands together. "I have something to show you outside." He stood, extending a hand to me.

The minute he started leading me towards the door I had some idea what I was in for. It involved a cold shed and a big ugly boat.

"Adam, no," I protested, tugging on the sleeve of his shirt with my free hand.

He stopped. "I've spent the entire afternoon trying to work up the courage to show you this," he said.

His statement intrigued me. Unless he'd filled the hull of the boat with venomous snakes I doubted he had any need for courage.

"Let me get my coat."

"You won't need it," he assured me.

I felt the temperature drop before we'd even reached the door. The windows at the back of the house emanated frigid air.

He took a small step towards me, dissolving the space between us, and I stretched my arms up, linking them around his neck. "It's much warmer in here," I murmured, with a pouty look that was meant to be seductive but probably just looked strange.

"I'll keep you warm. I promise." He kissed the corner of my mouth, sending a shudder through my body. Suddenly hypothermia didn't seem like such a bad way to go. I held his hand as he led me towards the back door.

As expected, it was bitterly cold, but there wasn't a wisp of wind. Adam kept a protective arm around me as we stumbled across the lawn. My eyes were shut at his request, making walking tricky.

Releasing his hold, he brushed his fingertips across my eyes. "Open your eyes," he whispered, shifting me slightly as he positioned me for the big reveal.

Opening them for a fraction of a second was long enough to catch a glimpse of something totally unexpected – a flicker of light in front of me. Something about my expression made him laugh.

"I know you saw it," he accused.

Ignoring him, I drew in a breath and opened my eyes fully.

We were in the back yard, far away from the shed. At the edge of the dew-soaked lawn, backed against the garden rockery, stood a tiny tent adorned with a string of coloured lights. Adam had navigated us through an obstacle course of long extension cords that snaked back to the house.

"When did you do this?" I asked in disbelief.

"After you left, this afternoon." Even in the muted light, his smile was grand.

The lights sparkled like little coloured stars. The backdrop of the fussy cottage garden made a magical setting. I snaked my arms around his waist. His hand slipped under my shirt, rubbing my back. My body went rigid at his cold touch.

"It's perfect." I kissed him as high I could reach without stretching, pressing my lips to the base of his neck.

"Not perfect, exactly. The Santa lights weren't quite what I was looking for but I had to work with what I had. Who knew Gabi had such a penchant for tacky Christmas decorations?"

He led me to the tent, releasing me only to unzip the opening. "After you, Mademoiselle." His accent alone made me wish I were strong enough to drag him in after me.

The light didn't quite cast far enough. It was blacker than black inside and I hesitated. "Hold on," he said, leaning inside to retrieve a torch. The tent was instantly transformed into a tiny dome-shaped palace.

A mattress took up all the floor space. I cringed as I pictured him dragging his cousin's furniture across the saturated lawn, folding it awkwardly as he forced it through the small opening of the tent.

Kicking off my shoes, I crawled inside and buried myself in the mass of bedding to keep warm. Adam followed me in, shining the torch on the roof, maximising the amount of light.

He lay on his back, stroking my hair as I rested my head on his chest. His eyes were fixed on the illuminated canvas ceiling. All of my focus was on the cardboard box in the corner, by his feet.

"Adam," I said, concentrating on the sound of his heart beating.

"Charlotte," he replied, formal as ever.

"What's in the box?"

"I'm going to show you who I am."

"And that requires courage?" I asked, mimicking his formal tone.

"More than I'm used to," he admitted.

His eyes never left the roof of the tent. I lifted my head, propping my chin on his chest but he wouldn't meet my gaze. Changing tack, I threw my leg across his body, pulling myself on top of him, forcing him to look at me by holding his face in my hands.

"Tell me what's in the box," I demanded.

His hands locked around my wrists. "You might have to move first."

I didn't want to, but curiosity was winning out. Reluctantly I freed him to retrieve the box – which he did with the slow speed of someone trying to diffuse a bomb.

"I've been waiting for this parcel for days. I intended telling you everything...even before you yelled at me," he explained. He tore the strips of packing tape off ridiculously slowly, as if it was causing the box pain. It was causing me pain, the same kind of torture that Alex inflicts on me when unwrapping his birthday presents one strip of tape at a time.

"So what is it?" I asked impatiently.

"A few of my favourite things," he said, wiggling his eyebrows suggestively as he plunged his hand into the mass of Styrofoam beads.

"Raindrops on roses and whiskers on kittens?"

Pushing the box aside, he leaned forward, kissing me hard enough to push me back on to the mattress. He covered my body with his, kissing a line from my lips down to my neck.

"No kittens or roses," he murmured.

"Adam, the box," I reminded. I craned my neck and wrapped my arms tightly around his neck, pulling him tighter against me – hardly an appropriate reaction considering I was trying to get his mind back on the task at hand.

He groaned, burying his head in my shoulder. A breathless giggle escaped me and I let my arms fall limply to my side, leaving him with the option of moving or crushing me to death. Thankfully he rolled off me, turning his attention back to the mystery box. "Close your eyes," he instructed.

"It's dark, Adam. How much darker do you need it to be?"

He smirked and I wished I could see his eyes better in the low light. He placed something small in my hand, closing my fingers around it. I grabbed the torch and uncurled my fingers.

"A memory card?" I asked, more than a little confused.

Adam didn't wait for my reaction, nor did he explain why he'd given it to me. The next item left me even more bewildered.

Wordlessly, he took the tiny card from my hand and pushed it into a slot on the side of the machine he was holding. I vaguely shone the torch in his direction, waiting for an explanation.

"This is a digital projector," he said finally, glancing at me.

"Like an overhead projector?" I asked, thinking of the antiquated machines used for presentations at school.

"Exactly."

"Don't you need a screen?"

He tapped the side of his head with his forefinger. "You're so much more than a pretty face, Charlotte."

Hopefully he saw me roll my eyes but the speed in which he made his way for the door of the tent made it unlikely. I leaned forward, watching him from the doorway as he dashed to the clothesline. He unpegged a large white sheet that unfurled like a sail on a yacht. He weighted it down with some rocks from the garden – no doubt gathered in the planning stages that afternoon.

I laughed as he extended his arm and took a bow, as if it was the finale of some grand production rather than the beginning. He balanced the projector on a block of wood he'd stolen from the woodpile and hurried back to the tent.

"Very resourceful," I exclaimed, still laughing.

He grinned back at me. "I'm learning to use my imagination. I have a great teacher."

He connected the cords, crossed his fingers and flicked the switch. The projector flooded the sheet with a bright white light. A round of applause seemed appropriate – until my overzealous clapping reminded me that it was the sort of gesture the Beautifuls would make.

"Are we watching a movie?"

"Not exactly." Rolling to the side, he reached for the box again.

"There's more?" I asked.

"Of course there is more. It wouldn't be much of a show without snacks, would it?"

Perhaps the element of surprise was the game. If so, he was definitely victorious. Styrofoam beads fell like snow as he upended the contents of the box on our makeshift bed. Amongst the snowy mess lay an assortment of junk food, most of which I'd never heard of.

I picked up a drink. "Dr Pepper."

Adam unscrewed the lid and handed it back to me. "Try it."

I hesitantly took a sip, fairly convinced by the smell that I wasn't going to enjoy it. Something in my horrified expression amused him as I forced myself to swallow the ghastly liquid.

"That is vile! It tastes like the cough medicine Alex used to force on me as a kid."

"Okay, so you're not a fan." He managed to compose himself long enough to speak before dissolving into laughter again.

I reached for something else.

"Doritos." My tone was triumphant – and rightly so. I'd eaten them a million times before, usually while watching some sappy movie of Nicole's choice on a Friday night.

"Not so fast, Coccinelle." He ripped the bag from my grasp just as I opened it, sending chips flying around the tent. "These are my favourite. You'll have to fight me for them."

"You can buy them here, you know."

"They're not the same," he replied.

I pulled a face. "These are the foods you like?"

"Sometimes I am, tragically, more American than French," he admitted, putting his hand to his heart and speaking with false sorrow. "I like all these things except the chocolate. I can't stand chocolate."

He picked up a bag of chocolate, waving it in front of me.

"You don't like chocolate?" I asked outraged.

"Not one little bit."

I dramatically swept my forehead with the back of my hand as if I in danger of passing out. "I don't know if we can go on. I'm not sure I can be with a man who doesn't like chocolate."

He leaned forward, kissing me as I fell onto my back. Corn chips and Styrofoam beads crunched beneath me. "I could convince you otherwise," he suggested.

"How?" I asked, surprised that one word could take all the breath I had in my body.

"I'll show you..." I was convinced my heart was about to punch through my chest "...later," he added, breaking my hold and leaving me gasping for air. He pulled me back into a sitting position and drew the thick blankets around us.

"Are you ready?" His voice was a little shaky. The nerves were taking over. He rifled through the packets of chips and chocolate bars, finally locating the remote control. He clicked a button, pulling me out of the darkness and into his world.

The next half hour was a whirlwind tour of New York City. He showed me pictures of everything, from clichéd tourist spots to places only people who lived there knew about, pausing between pictures to answer every question I asked.

Still awed by the bright lights of the Manhattan skyline, I wasn't expecting the next photo that flashed up. I stared at the candid picture of Adam with his arm draped around a pretty brunette woman, but I felt him looking at me. They shared the same unusual blue eyes, but even with that hint, I couldn't make the connection. I frowned, leaving him no option but to spell it out for me.

"That's my mother, Fiona," he said quietly.

"She's beautiful," I said truthfully.

He clicked, forwarding to another picture.

"And this is my dad," he announced.

So much for the distinguished, slightly greying man in his fifties that I had pictured. He'd already told me that his father's name was Jean-Luc. That information alone conjured up a scary image of a powerful, intimidating man. But the handsome man in the picture looked more like someone my brother would hang out with. His perfect smile was a carbon copy of his son's, making the resemblance undeniable.

"There was no chance you were ever going to be ugly." It wasn't something I meant to say out loud. Adam seemed embarrassed, clicking through the next pictures too quickly for me to see any of them.

"My brother Ryan is the ugly one," he said, smirking.

"Really?" I asked, thrilled at the prospect of discovering the Décarie black sheep.

"No, not really," he replied, embarrassed again.

"Adam, how come you two don't have long-winded French names?" I asked, curiously.

He took no offence to my strange question. "Like you do, you mean?"

"Very funny," I scowled, pretending to be cross. He was right. Charlotte was one of those tragic French names that should have been made obsolete centuries ago.

"Our mother is a stubborn Londoner," he explained. "That might have played a part."

"Your mum's English?"

He nodded.

"You're just a wealth of information tonight, aren't you?" I teased, surprised by his candidness.

"That was my plan, Charlotte."

The way we were both huddled in the tiny doorway of the tent, surrounded by a ton of blankets, made it impossible to think we could get any closer. He proved me wrong, edging close to murmur in my ear, "Do you want to see where I live?" And with a click of the remote we were inside his house.

Gabrielle had assured me there were no castles in New York. I wasn't so sure. Our whole house would have fitted into the lounge of the Décarie home. Opulent was not a word I used often, but I could think of no other. Insecurity twisted in my stomach like splinters of glass.

No wonder he was calling on courage to share this with me. I'd never been more tempted to run away. He reached for my hand, holding it tightly. He probably thought I was about to bolt too.

He'd laid it all out for me, just as I'd begged him to do. How I handled this moment would determine whether I was strong enough to make the leap with him.

Harder than surrendering my heart and more intimate than sharing my body was facing up to my own truth. False bravado was my forte. If there was to be a moment of admission – a point where I told him I wasn't able to go through with this – this was it.

He looked at me as if he expected me to do just that.

"Adam," I began, my tone too grave for him to draw any positivity from it. "I just don't know if I can be with someone who doesn't like chocolate. I might need some more convincing."

The remote bounced off the wall of the tent. Pinning my hands behind my head he straddled my body, leaning down close.

"I love you, Charli Blake."

My soul gave me no choice but to believe him. I didn't know if I could fit in to his world but I did know that Adam didn't belong in a tent in the backyard – and yet here he was, for no other reason than he loved me.

Looking into his jewel-like eyes I could see every possibility, and none of them scared me.

Conversation became sparse over the next few hours as talking gave way to a quieter form of communication. Warm beneath the covers, secure in his hold, my skin tingled as he ran his fingers down the length of my arm. Lacing his fingers through mine, he brought my hand to his mouth and kissed it. My body felt too unhinged to move – not that I wanted to – so I concentrated on stringing a coherent sentence together.

"Do you have a garden?" I asked.

He seemed used to my questions now, just answering them instead of frowning and looking at me like I was odd. "A huge garden. It's called Central Park." I could tell he was smiling. "I'll take you there every day if you want me to...under one condition."

"What?"

He shifted beneath me, moving my head from his chest back onto the pillow.

"You haven't told me about the flowers."

I'd forgotten. I should have known he'd remember.

"*Peter Pan* – it's my favourite book of all time. I must have read it a hundred times as a kid. Not the Disney story, the original version," I explained. "J M Barrie wrote about fairies."

"Go on," he cajoled, grinning.

"He wrote that when the first baby laughed for the first time, its laugh broke into a thousand pieces and they all went skipping about and turned into fairies." I recited the quote as best I could remember – a good effort considering his gaze was scrambling my brain.

"You buy into that theory?" He already knew the answer but I replied anyway.

"I had to. Fairies can't live unless a child believes in them. And every time a child claims not to believe, another fairy falls down dead. I didn't want that on my conscience."

Despite my deliberately ominous tone, he laughed. "Of course not. So what does that have to do with flowers?"

"Well, being pro fairy comes with certain responsibilities," I explained. "So I researched everything I could, determined to protect the endangered fairy population. I became very proactive. Poor Alex was forced to plant hundreds of tulip bulbs in our garden every winter because fairies use the flowers as beds for their babies."

"So picking the flowers probably is a federal offence," he said finally.

"Equivalent to child endangerment, I'd say."

"And have you ever actually seen a fairy?" he asked.

"Fairies generally come out at night, so unfortunately not. We've always had scheduling conflicts. I'm more of a morning person. Alex used to tell me he saw them all the time, but there's a chance he was lying."

"Maybe we could work on that. Do you think many fairies hang out at Central Park?"

"I'm not too familiar with American fairies but I know the French are big believers."

"Really?" he asked, amused.

"Sure. Take La Dormette de Poitou for instance." I stumbled over the pronunciation. "She's a sleep fairy. It's her job to make sure children have sweet dreams."

"I'm not surprised a French fairy would be your favourite," he teased, tightening his grip around me.

"I never said she was my favourite. My favourite happens to be Italian. Basadone. He rides in the wind and steals kisses from unsuspecting women."

"He sounds creepy if you ask me. The French fairy is obviously much classier."

"Not all of them. I haven't told you about Bugul Noz from Brittany. That poor creature is so ugly that humans *and* fairies reject him. Even the animals stay away from him because he's so hideous. People have keeled over from the sheer shock of seeing him. I can't even describe him to you because he's so awful looking."

"Poor guy," he said, battling to keep a straight face.

"Don't you fret." I patted his chest condescendingly. "I'm fairly certain he's not related to the Décaries of Marseille."

Without warning, he rolled to the side, covering my body with his. The look he gave me was strange, like he was looking beyond my eyes, searching for something. Self-consciously, I looked away.

"Why won't you look at me?" he whispered, pinching my chin between his finger and thumb, forcing me to meet his gaze.

I hoped it was too dark for him to see me blush. "Because it's all a bit silly, isn't it?" I mumbled.

"I wish you could see yourself through my eyes. You'd never have another moment of self-doubt as long as you live."

"Everybody should believe in conte de fée," I whispered.

Adam stared at me as if I'd just insulted him. Finally, he raised his eyebrows and smiled. "Charlotte, how can you maintain that you don't speak French when you throw words like conte de fée into casual conversation?"

"Fairy tales," I said, shrugging my shoulders.

"I know what it means. I'm just surprised that you do."

"I know all the important French words."

"And what are they?" he quizzed.

I ticked them off on my fingers. "Bonjour, conte de fée and croissant."

His laugh echoed through the tent and I couldn't help laughing with him.

As if on cue, the batteries in the torch began to fail. The light flickered. Adam fumbled for the switch and with one click we were in the dark.

***

Adam lay beside me, breathing in a way that only comes with deep sleep. I listened for a long time, trying to take my mind off the racing thoughts of everything he'd shared with me that night. As usual, he'd learned more about me than I had about him, but not because he'd kept anything from me. Every question I put to him was answered. When he began to shift restlessly I wondered if his mind was swimming too.

The light filtering through the thin walls woke me the next morning. I felt achy and tired, far too wrecked to have woken of my own accord. Adam was finally still. Maybe he knew he was a restless sleeper and anticipated stealing the covers from me. There were enough blankets in the tent for us to survive an Antarctic storm – even after most of them ended up on his side.

I was hopeful of getting out of the tent without waking him until I saw my jeans wedged between him and the mattress. I tugged at them and Adam woke with a start, launching himself at me as if I'd tried to steal his wallet.

"Whoa!" I cried as he landed on me, his face inches from mine.

He looked confused for a second, as if he wasn't sure where he was. His eyes closed and he groaned, holding me tightly as he rolled us over.

"Sorry," he murmured.

"Too early for you?"

He rolled us back over, more carefully this time so I felt none of the weight of his body.

"Hardly," he murmured, kissing my neck.

If I were a magician I would have made the rest of the world disappear at that moment. Life was more perfect than I ever expected it could be.

"Adam," I whispered, moving his face with my hands so he was looking at me.

"Charli."

"You sleep, and I'll go to the beach for a while."

He smiled lazily. "Charlotte Blake, you have a deal."

He leaned in and kissed me in a way that made me consider renegotiating our deal – until I heard the waves crashing below.

23. Sunday Surfers

Sunday was the one day of the week that my brother never surfed.

His problem with Sunday surfers is that they are just that – surfers on a Sunday – which meant it would take a lifetime for them to actually acquire any skill. Alex didn't suffer fools easily, so forfeiting his beach for that one day a week while overconfident amateurs took over grated on him more than I did.

The only other person with such a low opinion of anyone who dedicated less than twenty hours a week to the sea was Mitchell Tate, so I was surprised to see him there.

"Hey." He jumped at the sound of my voice. "I didn't mean to scare you."

"I wasn't expecting any crazy girls sneaking up on me from behind."

I stood beside him, looking out to sea. Clearing the air the day before had worked wonders. The anxiety I'd felt had completely disappeared.

"Sundays never used to be your day, Mitch. I'm surprised you're here."

He stood, arms folded, glowering at the handful of Sunday surfers hanging on the break, like they'd stolen something from him.

"I had to get out of the house. Did you know my sisters are planning a birthday party?"

"I did know that. I never made the guest list though," I said, trying to sound disappointed.

Mitchell glanced at me from the corner of his eye. "Half your luck."

"Can't you get your parents to rein them in?"

"You'd think so, considering they're footing the bill."

I laughed, harder this time and he turned to scold me with a sharp look. I stared back, a stare that lingered too long, leaving room for an awkward few seconds of silence to creep in. I didn't want awkwardness. Fighting to keep things casual, I looked back to the ocean.

"Where's Ethan today?"

He leaned across and whispered as if it was a secret. "With picky Nicky, at the café."

Nicole had earned the unenviable title of picky Nicky for being exactly that – too picky. Ethan clearly adored her but Nicole stood firm. He was not the one for her – she just acted like he was, which confused everyone. Obviously time apart had changed nothing. Ethan was still in no-man's-land, waiting for her to either surrender or find the real Prince Charming.

"Where's Captain America this morning?" he asked in turn.

He seemed unfazed by the look of poison I shot at him. Maybe that was a good thing. Self-absorbed, mean-spirited Mitchell was bound to be easier to deal with than the sweet, kind-hearted Mitchell I should be keeping my distance from.

"That's very unattractive behaviour, Mitchell." I tried to sound harsh but it came out sounding like a trite lecture from a schoolteacher.

"I thought you'd appreciate my less attractive side."

"Idiot."

He unfolded his arms for the first time since I'd arrived, moving his hand to my hair. I quickly slapped it away.

"Wait," he protested. "You have something in your hair."

I wished the sand would open up and swallow me whole when he picked a piece of Styrofoam out of my hair. The wind caught it and it quickly blew away, taking none of the mortification I was feeling with it.

"So Alex is wrapping you in foam before you come out to play now?" he teased.

"Something like that."

He didn't ponder my answer too long, moving to the subject of the surf. "So, are we going out there?" He pointed out to sea as if I needed direction.

"Why? Do you need a buddy?"

"Maybe." He was looking past me now and I turned to see what had caught his attention. "Maybe he could be my buddy," he said. Adam was walking along the beach towards us.

Gripping his arm, I hissed, "You be nice."

Mitchell's smile gave me no comfort at all. Rather than waiting for Adam to reach us, I dropped my board and ran to him.

Adam stopped walking just as I started running, probably anticipating the ambush as I launched myself at him.

"What happened to sleeping?" I asked, throwing my arms around his neck.

"The tent wasn't quite as comfortable without you in it," he replied.

"I would have stayed."

He lowered me to the ground and grinned. "No, you wouldn't have."

I took his hand, leading him towards Mitchell. "There's someone I want you to meet," I said, walking a little faster than usual.

Even without introduction, they knew exactly who the other was. I wasn't worried about anything Adam might say. He was excruciatingly polite, all of the time. Mitchell, not so much.

I called out Mitchell's name and he turned to face us. I could feel my face contorting as I silently begged him to be good.

"What's wrong, Charli? Do you have something in your eye?" baited Mitchell.

I should have known better. Letting these two meet defied common sense.

"This is Adam," I replied sourly.

"Nice to meet you," said Adam extending his hand. "I've heard a lot about you."

Mitchell shook his hand but his eyes stayed firmly fixed on me. "I doubt that. Charli tends to gloss over details."

Adam barely hesitated. "Only the unimportant ones."

I was beginning to feel ill. He probably thought Mitchell was a dick. I knew Mitchell was being a dick. My glare must have had some effect because Mitchell's eyes drifted back to the ocean. Then he turned back to Adam. "Are you going out there?" he asked. "I have another board and wetsuit in my car if you're interested in having a crack. I'm sure Charli could teach you the basics...probably enough to keep you alive at least."

"Thanks, but no," he said, squeezing my fingers again.

"Yeah," said Mitchell, screwing up his face as if he'd tasted something horrid. "I'm going to give it a miss too."

"Why aren't you staying?" I asked, too curious to keep quiet.

"Sunday surfers, Charli."

The kindest thing I could do for Adam was get him off the beach. The second kindest thing was not to inflict Mitchell on him ever again. Leaving seemed like a good idea.

"You could have stayed," suggested Adam as we ambled towards the cottage.

"I don't like Sunday surfers either," I told him.

***

A lazy day together was the plan. Alex and Gabrielle weren't due back until late afternoon and I knew once that happened, something huge was on its way. Adam knew it too, which probably explained why he'd avoided the subject all weekend. I'd asked what his argument with Gabrielle had been about, hoping it might give me a heads-up. Whatever Alex wanted to discuss was so important that he needed a few days away to rehearse it. I'd drawn my own conclusions from the very little information I was working with.

"I think Gabrielle is pregnant. Either that or they're getting married," I told Adam over breakfast.

He nearly choked on his toast. "Where did that come from?"

"Call it a hunch."

"Your hunch is wrong, Coccinelle." He shook his head.

I had to believe him. Adam knew exactly what was going on. I was the only fool being kept in the dark.

"What were you arguing with your cousin about?" I asked, for the umpteenth time.

A look of dread washed over him, an expression that happened every time I asked.

"I've already told you, we weren't arguing. I simply asked her a question and she replied," he said, shrugging his shoulders to suggest indifference.

I was getting nowhere. "You should tell me what you know. It's the right thing to do."

Adam's confounded expression didn't waver. "I can't tell you this. If I told you what I know, you'd be left with a million more questions that I don't know the answer to."

"Fine," I huffed, folding my arms and leaning back. "I'll wait for Alex to tell me."

"Awesome idea," he breathed, visibly relieved.

The subject was closed – but it didn't stop me thinking about it. I'd managed to push most thoughts of Alex out of my mind until that morning. Once I started counting down the time until he was due home, I became fidgety and preoccupied. He'd told me he'd be home by six. Before six, I was free and easy. After that, all bets were off.

24. Romance Languages

An hour earlier than I needed to leave, Adam drove me to the café to collect my car. It wasn't that I wanted to leave early; I just couldn't sit still. I also needed to secure the takings from the previous day before Alex found out that I hadn't.

My beaten up little car stood alone in the car park.

"Oh, it's still here," I said, feigning melancholy.

"Did you think it wouldn't be?"

I had no qualms about leaving my car there overnight. Car thieves are fussy. If I'd left the engine running and a free-to-good-home sign on the windscreen, it still would have been there a month later.

I reached for the door handle but he pulled me back. "Adam, I have to go," I said, grabbing his wrist to stop his hand creeping any further up my shirt.

"Not for ages," he breathed, totally unremorseful.

"If I didn't know better, I'd say you were trying to keep me here."

He straightened up, grinning craftily. "You do know me, and I *am* trying to keep you here."

"Should I be worried about going home?" I wondered.

"Of course not," he replied, hesitating too long. "My reasons for keeping you here are purely personal."

I wasn't convinced. Picking up on my angst, he held my hand tighter than usual. "Someone incredibly smart once told me that everything works out in the end."

I looked across at him. "And if it doesn't?"

"Then it's not the end."

His grin was contagious and I smiled back. "Wise words, Adam Décarie."

"Fighting words, Charlotte Blake," he declared, sounding more American than usual.

I was halfway out of the car when I turned. "Did you mean it when you said you'd take me anywhere I wanted to go?" I asked.

He nodded but the gesture didn't match his woeful expression. I remained still, waiting for him to add something.

"Where would you like to go?"

"Back to last night, in the tent, when nothing else mattered."

Adam stared at me for a long time. I wondered if I'd said something stranger than usual. Finally he reached into the console of the car, pulling out a notebook and pen. He scrawled a few words, tore out the page, folded it and handed it to me.

"What's this?"

"Everything I know," he replied, flatly.

He couldn't have written more than a couple of sentences. I had to consider the possibility that Adam really didn't know anything. I started to unfold the paper but he stopped me.

"If you don't get the answers you need, read it then. But give Alex a chance to tell you first," he urged.

Unable to find my voice, I nodded, clenching my fist around the note.

"I love you, Charlotte." He spoke strongly, like those four words were a big bandaid for my soul.

I scurried into the café before I could change my mind about leaving.

Seeing Ethan perched near the counter wasn't unexpected. It was actually a relief. It meant Nicole was occupied and her questions would be minimal. I grabbed a calico bag from under the counter and filled it with the money from the till – just as I should have done the day before.

"What's your rush?" she asked, bumping the till shut with her hip.

"I've got to get home. Can you lock up for me?"

"Sure I can," she replied, glancing at Ethan.

I glanced at Ethan too, and caught him rolling his eyes at her. Obviously my request had cut into their plans. I felt no pity. I'd covered for Nicole the day before and if he dared to kick up about it, I was prepared to remind him of that.

"Thank you," I said, glaring at Ethan.

Nicole must have noticed. She cleared her throat, pulling my attention back to her. "I'll see you tomorrow," she said, granting me a small smile that I knew was false.

I slipped out of the café without another word. Dealing with that little stage show could wait.

My little car started on the first try – perhaps appreciative of having fuel in its rusted tank. The engine didn't falter but I still drove slowly.

Beating Alex home wasn't part of the plan, but as soon as I pulled up to the house I knew I had. I didn't go inside. Instead, I sat waiting on the front steps, growing more anxious by the minute.

What could he possibly have to tell me? I wondered if he was going to try talking me out of my trip. Perhaps I'd done something to make him think that travelling was a bad idea. *Unlikely*, I reasoned. Alex always played fair. He'd made no secret of the fact that he was unhappy that I'd decided to end my trek in New York, but encouraging me for years and then talking me out of it at the last minute was not his style.

Adam's note felt like a lump of lead in my pocket. I spent a long time watching the daylight fade as I weighed up the pros and cons of reading it. In the end – true to form – curiosity won.

Digging deep, I retrieved the paper. It was so scrunched that it took a few seconds to unfurl, giving me time to reconsider reading it – but I didn't. Compromising with my conscience, I unfolded only half of the note.

The words didn't make any sense, and for good reason. They were written in Latin.

"Mea filia, mea vita," I recited, doubting my Latin pronunciation was any stronger than my French.

I'd seen the words before. My brother had two tattoos, an intricate Celtic band around his right arm and the Latin script across his heart, both acquired when he was a teenager. I'd never asked what it meant, assuming it was some phrase that was meaningless now he was grown-up and over the tough-guy-tattoo stage.

Adam had seen the tattoos when Alex took his wine-stained shirt off.

Adam's major in college had been Romance Languages. He would have understood the Latin script perfectly. Languages were his thing. Drama was my thing, and judging by the way my hand was shaking, I sensed my drama was about to get a whole lot worse.

I unfolded the second half of the note, knowing Adam would have translated it for me. I was right. Nausea set in as I studied the words on the page, swallowing hard as bile rose in my throat.

"My daughter, my life." I repeated it aloud over and over, so many times that it began to make no sense.

Alex had a daughter?

Impossible!

Before Gabrielle, there had never been anyone he was serious about…except me. I'd taken up his entire adult life…

And I suddenly realised why.

Pieces began falling into place at a crushing rate. I fell forward onto my knees, crawling to the edge of the veranda, reaching it in time to throw up in the garden bed below. I clutched my stomach, half sobbing and half retching, unable to stop until my body was too exhausted to continue. I laid my head on the cold stone paving, unsure if I'd ever have the strength to move again.

I don't know how long I lay there before Alex arrived home. It was still light, so it couldn't have been long. He ran to the veranda, shouting my name, probably thinking I was dead. I felt dead. My world had stopped – and from the little I knew, it was entirely his fault.

"Get away from me, Alex," I murmured, too numb to throw any anger behind it.

He levered me to a sitting position, pulling me in close to him. He took the paper from my fingers and I felt him freeze.

"Let me explain," he pleaded. "I need you to understand everything."

I tried shaking my head but the hold he had on me made it impossible. "Tell me that it's not true. Tell me Adam is wrong and I'll believe you." It took forever to get the words out.

It took longer for him to reply. "I can't do that, Charli."

"You have to, Alex," I demanded. "I remember things. I know it's not true."

I could feel his hand trembling on my cheek. "The woman you remember was my mother, not yours. You're *my* daughter." His voice cracked with under the weight of his confession.

I pulled away, suddenly unable to draw enough oxygen out of the air. Alex pushed me forward, rubbing my back as I rested my head between my knees. I was dying.

"No," I whimpered.

"It's true, Charli."

"No," I repeated, sounding no stronger than before.

"I was only seventeen when you were born. Your mum's name is Olivia. She was seventeen too. You were born in Sydney." He rattled the information quickly. It was like he wanted to state as many facts as he could before I got up and ran away. If my legs had been functioning, I would have.

I couldn't believe him. My whole life had been a lie. I couldn't bear to hear any more. I covered my ears with my hands, pleading with him to stop.

"It's the truth, Charli," he groaned.

I found the strength to break his hold. "I will never believe a thing you tell me for the rest of my life."

Alex was on his feet before I'd finished. He grabbed me by the wrist and roughly led me to the front door while he fumbled for the key. Once inside, he strode down the hallway, dragging me behind him. In the spare bedroom was the filing cabinet, and he dropped my arm to rifle through it. I rubbed my wrist as if he'd hurt me. If he thought he had, he ignored it. Finally he thrust a piece of paper at me.

"Read it," he demanded.

It was my birth certificate.

I couldn't deny it any longer. Even blocking my ears, closing my eyes and singing loudly couldn't drown out the fact that I was indeed the daughter of Alex Blake and Olivia Fielding.

I slammed it into his chest. "I won't hear it from you. I don't ever want to hear another thing from you!"

Alex looked devastated. "Then go to Floss," he said, defeated. "She knows everything."

I glared at him as I backed away, and left the house without another word.

***

Floss and Norm lived in the centre of town, one street back from the Lawsons'. Floss was waiting for me on the porch, so Alex must have warned her. I ran across the lawn, throwing myself into her arms.

"Hello, love," she said, hugging me tightly. "Let's go inside and make some tea."

I clung to her as we walked through the small front room into the tiny kitchen. "Alex is my father," I blurted.

"I know, love," she said, like it wasn't all bad.

I surprised myself by crying. I thought I was all cried out. Floss passed me a big box of tissues and I grabbed a wad.

"Donna Blake was Alex's mum. She was a good friend of mine. I'd known her for years but I hadn't seen her since Alex was a boy," she explained. "One day she turned up on my doorstep, all the way from Sydney with a tiny baby, just a few months old."

"Where was Alex?"

"Working up north on a fishing boat. I didn't think much of it at the time. He was a young man. It made sense for him to be out on his own," she said, shrugging. "She said that the baby was her daughter, but something wasn't right."

"Why?"

"Donna had her demons," she said gently. "She was a big drinker. I knew after just a few days that it had completely taken over her life. You were perfect in every way, certainly not the product of an alcoholic mother."

"Alex left me with her?" I asked, horrified at his carelessness.

"No," she replied emphatically. "Your mother relinquished custody to Alex when you were born. He was going it alone and struggling financially. He was offered a week of work and he had to take it, leaving you with Donna." I scowled at the table, pretending to dab my eyes with the tissues to hide my disgust. Floss laid her hand on mine. "He was desperate, Charli. He had no idea she packed you up and brought you here. When the poor boy got home, you were gone. For nearly a month he had no idea where you were."

"How did he find me?"

"I tracked him down." She paused. "He arrived in town the very next day."

"Why didn't he set the record straight? Why didn't he just tell people I was his?"

Floss sighed. "Donna was his mother. She'd created this huge fairy-tale about you, telling a million lies. Alex never knew his father, not even his name. He felt protective of his mum – even after what she'd done. So he went along with it, settling in as best he could on the pretence of being your brother. I took care of you during the day so Alex could work. Donna slipped deeper into drink. Alex was forever dragging her out of the pub, paying her debts, enduring her antics."

"That's so awful," I gulped

"She was his mother, Charli," Floss said tenderly. "He looked after her for years, hoping that she'd eventually conquer the drink."

"But she never did," I guessed.

Floss's eyes were shiny with tears. "She went on a huge bender one day and just went to sleep. She had a massive stroke. She was just forty-one," she said, sounding puzzled, like she still had trouble wrapping her head around it.

The hazy recollections of the woman who sang to me were of my grandmother. I'd remembered nursery rhymes and lullabies – not drunken tunes crooned at ten in the morning. How had I got it so wrong? Poor Alex never had a chance.

"Life got much better for the two of you after that. He scraped enough money together to buy the café. A year later he bought the house. He never intentionally lied to you, love. He's been fighting for you since the day you were born. I hope you can see that."

"What happened to my mother? *Who* is my mother?"

"I don't know. You're going to have to ask Alex."

I groaned. It was all too hard.

Floss leaned over. "I've seen what that man has endured over the years, Charli. Anything less than total understanding from you will not be tolerated. Do you understand?"

"Would taking a few days out to get my head around it all be tolerable?" My voice was tiny, implying I was scared of her. Perhaps I was.

"Yes, love," she said kindly, squeezing my hand.

***

The Décarie house was in darkness. Considering the late hour, I wasn't surprised. If I had been thinking straight I would have gone home to bed, waiting until morning to see Adam. But I wasn't thinking straight. Part of me doubted that I'd ever be capable of lucid thoughts again.

I wasn't too jumbled to know that knocking on the front door would be a mistake. Dealing with Gabrielle could wait. The knowledge that she'd transitioned from a Parisienne witch to my stepmother was cringe-worthy. I remembered overhearing Alex tell Adam that Gabrielle knew everything about him. I wondered if that included his early admission to parenthood at seventeen.

Adam's window slid open easier than expected. Climbing through it was easy, probably because I'd done it before.

The sheer curtains meant that even at night the room was never completely dark. I could see him lying completely motionless, so I knew he was awake. He never stopped tossing and turning in his sleep.

He threw back the covers and patted the space beside him.

I kicked off my shoes and crawled into his waiting arms, fighting back tears. "I have so much to tell you."

He kissed the top of my head. "It can wait," he soothed.

Being with him brought instant relief. I didn't have to listen and I didn't have to explain. Lying in the arms of the very best thing in my life was exactly where I needed to be. I had found my new safe place.

Four days passed before I even contemplated going home. Gabrielle, who was spending more time at our house than at her own, kept Alex in the loop.

"He misses you, Charli," she told me over and over. The pressure from her was subtle but constant.

I wasn't a complete monster. I knew Alex was hurting – I was just tragically inept to deal with it.

School had become an unlikely escape. No one there knew of the turmoil I was going through at home, and the thought of the Beautifuls catching wind of it made my stomach turn. Thankfully, torturing me wasn't high on their list of priorities that week. All talk was of the gala event they were planning. The guest list had ballooned to include just about everyone in town, except me.

Confiding in Nicole was a given. I'd never kept anything from her, but pinning her down long enough to break the news proved difficult. Her romance with Ethan was consuming her – and it wasn't attractive. She cut more classes than she attended, to spend time with him. Far from discouraging her, Ethan parked down the street from the school, waiting to pick her up. Nicole dropped everything the minute her phone rang. Ethan Williams was starting to irritate me.

"Nic," I called, trotting to catch up with her as she moseyed towards the art room.

She turned and stopped walking, but didn't stop tapping away at her phone. "Where've you been?" she asked, only half paying attention.

"Around. Where have you been?"

"I've been busy, really busy," she said, grinning at her phone.

"How is Ethan?" I asked dryly.

She shoved her phone in her pocket and finally looked at me. "Everything is going exactly to plan. He's lovely."

I wanted to be happy for her but an uneasy feeling niggled at me. I wondered if I was jealous. Nicole was doing nothing that I hadn't done since Adam arrived in town. But I loved him. Nicole had always considered Ethan more of a hobby.

The bell sounded and the corridor suddenly became deserted.

"I really need to talk to you," I told her, glancing to make sure the coast was clear.

"What?"

I drew in a long breath, wondering how I could get through the soap opera that had become my life. Short, fractured sentences were the best I could muster.

Nicole stared at me, wide-eyed, long after I stopped talking.

"Say something," I urged.

"Tell me again," she said, struggling to speak.

"Alex is my father," I replied, breaking it down for her.

Her expression was appalled. "Since when?"

"Since birth, presumably," I snarled.

"Wow, Charli. What a freak show."

"Thanks for your support." My tone did nothing to mask my hurt.

I turned to walk away but Nicole grabbed the hood of my jacket, pulling me back. "I didn't mean it like that – it's just… weird."

I shrugged her off. I had just told her the biggest news of my life and my best friend found it weird.

"It's not weird, it's my life," I hissed.

"I guess that explains why Alex has been acting so strangely all week," she mused, still ignoring the bigger picture. "I thought it was because I'd quit."

"You quit?"

"It was taking up too much time."

"Nic, we're supposed to be saving money. We're leaving in a few months," I scolded.

She shrugged. "Adam is giving us the money from the boat. That's more money than we'd ever earn selling postcards and working at the café. Ethan said it's probably worth twenty grand."

The girl in front of me was no one I knew. Her words revolted me. Adam had worked on the boat day and night for weeks. I'd never felt comfortable with him gifting me the proceeds when it was sold. While it was true that we were pooling all our money, Nicole claiming a stake in the proceeds of his boat was a stretch by any measure.

She didn't notice my growing fury. "We can go anywhere with that kind of money, Indonesia, Fiji, Africa..."

In all the years we'd been planning our trip, Africa had never rated a mention. Alex had a list of no-go zones. Africa was one of them, along with a zillion other places he deemed unsafe for two girls travelling alone. The ideas spewing out of Nicole's mouth were not her own. And I knew who had put them there.

I knew that Mitchell and Ethan would breeze out of town as quickly as they'd arrived. All I had to do was ride out Nicole's abominable behaviour until then. Even if she was foolish enough to invite Ethan to tag along on our trip, he wouldn't wait that long. We were stuck in the Cove for another four months.

The ride home from school that day wasn't the usual leisurely drive. Adam just pushed the passenger door open for me rather than getting out to open it.

"Where's the fire?" I teased, slipping into the seat.

"No fire," he replied. "I have to get back to meet Norm at four. He's coming to check out the boat."

"So it's done?" I asked, excited that he had finally finished it.

"Completely, even the name. Gabi painted it on for me."

Norm was waiting when we got there, his ancient station wagon parked right in front of the shed, so close that we had to squeeze past it to get in the door. "Well, isn't she a beaut?" he asked, sweeping his hand along the hull.

I had to admit, Adam had done brilliantly. The boat was far from ugly now. The wood was smooth and freshly painted royal blue. The exposed wood on the deck gleamed under new varnish, and her name was written in white letters across the stern.

La Coccinelle.

"How can you sell it? Are you sure you don't want to keep it?" I whispered, grabbing Adam's sleeve.

"I have the original Coccinelle," he whispered. My heart missed a few vital beats.

Norm paced around the boat, tilting his old towelling hat a hundred times, deep in thought. "I'll give you thirteen thousand for it," he offered.

Adam folded his arms, staring blankly at the boat, obviously much better at the poker face than Norm, who misconstrued his silence for rejection and upped his offer.

"Can you give us a minute, Norm?" he asked.

"Sure, sure," replied Norm, turning his back as if that would dull his hearing.

Adam pulled me down to the bow.

"I had no idea he was interested in buying it. I thought he was here to offer a valuation. What do you think?" he whispered.

"I think it's Norman Davis. He'll love this boat," I replied.

"He was very quick to make me an offer, Charli." Absentmindedly, he swept my hair off my shoulder. "That leads me to think it probably is Huon, and it's probably worth twice what he's offering."

I knew Adam well enough to know that seeing his boat go to a good home would win out in the end.

"He'll treasure it," I promised.

Adam turned back to Norm, who was pretending not to listen.

"Mr Davis," he said, clapping his hands together, "you have a deal…under one condition."

"Name it," said Norm, looking a little scared.

"You don't change her name. The name has to stay."

Norm looked at the white lettering on the stern, and tried to pronounce it. "What does it mean? It's not voodoo is it? Floss would never approve of anything voodoo."

Adam laughed and I nudged him in the side.

"It's not voodoo Norm," I assured. "It's French. It means ladybug."

Norm leaned forward, shaking Adam's hand so hard that his whole body jerked.

"Pleasure doing business with you, young fella," he said, revelling in his negotiating skills. "What about payment? Would you prefer cash or cheque?"

"Cheque. Make it out to cash and see that Charli gets it," he instructed.

Norm looked at me and winked. Perhaps he thought my negotiating skills were as stellar as his. Embarrassed, I looked to the floor.

We were making our way back to the house when Gabrielle burst out the front door, handed me an overnight bag that Alex had packed for me and put in her car. He'd been sending her home with clean clothes for me all week – one outfit at a time.

"Call Alex. He misses you, Charli," she said, backing down the driveway, dangerously close to the letterbox.

Adam motioned to her to stop. Too late. "That's going to hurt," Adam murmured.

Gabrielle got out and inspected the damage. "This is a sign," she yelled, pointing at me.

"No," I uttered, terrified. "It's a letterbox."

Adam choked.

"No, silly girl. I have played postman for Alex all week, passing on his messages. I have just run over my mailbox. I can receive no more messages!" she yelled, brushing her hands together as if she was dusting them off.

"Perhaps we should shoot the messenger," suggested Adam, riling her even more.

Gabrielle looked so angry that I stepped behind Adam for protection. "Charli, go home. Give Alex a chance to explain. He loves you and in case I haven't made myself clear, he misses you." She barely slowed her pace as she passed.

Adam waited until she was in the house. "I think she just went postal," he murmured, making me giggle.

I'd had four days to get used to my new life. There was no going back, but the only person stopping me from moving forward was myself. Alex had reached out to me a hundred times via the strung out Parisienne, but I'd been stubborn and selfish and kept my distance.

It was time to go home.

25. Compromise

Alex was in the lounge pretending to watch TV. The setting was staged – the splinters on his shirt gave it away. He'd been chopping wood, probably up until the second he saw me pull onto the driveway. The woodpile must have grown tenfold that week.

As soon as I walked in he switched off. "Ask me anything, Charli," he said, getting straight to it.

"Okay. How much wood did you chop today?"

Realising he'd been caught out, he pulled a face. "A bit," he conceded.

I flopped onto the couch opposite him. Alex picked splinters off his shirt while he waited for me to speak.

"Tell me about my mother," I said finally. It was one of the most important things I'd ever ask him, but I sounded uninterested.

"I loved her, Charli. You have to know that. She was bright, sweet and unbelievably beautiful. I don't think we spent a day apart for two years."

His eyes drifted away. He smiled slightly as he spoke and I knew he was visiting a good place.

Box number one had been checked. At least he loved her.

"Were you scared when you found out she was pregnant?" I asked.

Alex gave a sharp laugh. "Scared doesn't even begin to describe it."

"She could've had an abortion." My glib tone suggested that would have been an easy option.

Alex frowned.

"Or adopted me out," I added.

"That was the plan. Olivia knew from the very beginning that that was what she wanted to do. She wanted to get her life back." He smiled at me. "Her plans were always big."

"What were her plans?" I wanted him to tell me something that I could align myself to. Maybe she was the reason I was a little weird.

"She wanted to be a dancer. A ballerina," he clarified. "I can still remember the way she moved. Olivia didn't walk in a straight line if she could help it. She glided and twirled everywhere she went. She was gorgeous." His voice trailed off at the end. His smile started slipping.

"So I get my looks from her, then?" I suggested, trying to keep him talking.

His face brightened. "Definitely from her."

I reached for the throw rug and pulled it forward, needing the distraction while I worked up to my next question.

"Why didn't you go through with the original plan of adopting me out?"

"You gave me no choice, Charli. I fell in love with you the second I saw you."

"But Olivia didn't?"

Alex shook his head. "She was stronger than me. We were young, broke and clueless. She was adamant that giving you up would mean giving you the best life possible. I was the selfish one. You are the very best part of me, Charli. How could I have given you away?"

"What happened to her?" I asked in a small voice.

He grimaced as if my words caused him pain.

"She had her plan, and to her credit she stuck to it. She never held you or named you or even really looked at you. I guess that made it easier for her to cope. She moved interstate to live with relatives soon after you were born. I never heard from her again. I've always made sure our number was listed, just in case she changed her mind, but I've never heard from her."

"Do you hate her for that?" I asked, wondering if I did.

"How could I ever hate her? She gave me you."

It was quiet for a while. I watched him, studying his face carefully. In a lot of ways, I was looking at him for the very first time, drawing comparisons that I'd never made before.

We both had brown eyes. But now I had *his* eyes – my *father's* eyes. The concept was strange.

"Would you ever have told me if Adam hadn't found out?"

"Of course I would have," he insisted. "Boy Wonder's mad translating skills just sped up the process."

"When?"

"I had a deadline. You need a passport to travel. You need your birth certificate to apply for a passport."

Nicole had organised her passport months earlier. When it came to doing mine, Alex had kept delaying me. Now I knew why.

Floss had demanded total understanding from me where Alex was concerned. At first I wasn't sure I could give it. But over the past few days I'd lost the anger. I'd also lost a lot of the curiosity. Initially I'd wanted to know everything. Now my questions were more basic. Most of Alex's answers were basic too. He stuck to the facts, telling me only what I asked.

I went to bed tired enough to sleep for days, but woke at four in the morning with one more question burning at me. I stood in his doorway, calling his name loud enough to rouse him.

"What's wrong?" he asked sleepily.

"I have to ask you something."

He reached across, fumbling with the lamp as he switched it on.

"Now?" he asked, shielding his eyes from the light with his forearm.

I crawled onto the bed, laying my head on the pillow next to him. "It's really important."

"I'm listening," he mumbled groggily.

"You said that Olivia didn't name me," I reminded, hoping he was awake enough to keep up.

"No, she didn't. I named you."

I leaned over, pulling his arm away from his face so he'd look at me. It made no difference – he kept his eyes closed.

"Since when have you been a fan of nineteenth century England?"

Alex laughed. He knew I detested my name.

"I'm not. I'm a fan of *Charlotte's Web.*"

I groaned. "You named me after a spider?" I pulled the pillow from under my head and thumped him with it. "What's wrong with you?"

Alex threw the pillow back. "She wasn't just a spider, Charli," he said with reverence. "She was gifted. How else do you describe a spider that can weave words into her web?"

"That's the most outrageous thing I've ever heard," I complained.

"Charlotte is the perfect name for you," he insisted.

I huffed in mock outrage. I'd spent the night gathering information about my mother, believing that sooner or later he'd tell me something that I could use to tie myself to her. Learning the origin of my name brought everything into perspective. He could deny it all he wanted, but the truth was Alex Blake spent as much time in La La Land as I did.

I was stuck in a strange place. My white knight, the man who had protected, advised and guided me through my entire life, had had a status update. He was my father. Peculiarly, not much had changed. His tight hold on me never wavered. My curfew stood, my lack of aptitude when it came to my schoolwork was still a bone of contention, and boy-wonder-with-the-mad-translating-skills was still on the outer for encouraging my excursion to New York. Adam and Alex barely spoke any more. I don't think it was intentional – they just never seemed to be in the same place at the same time.

Gabrielle spent a lot of time at our house, and with her never at home, the cottage had become my favourite place to be. Every minute with Adam was treasured – even when we were in the shed.

La Coccinelle was gone and the empty shed looked massive. I sat on the old wooden workbench, watching as Adam packed up the last of the tools. I'd seen him do a lot of packing recently, and hated every minute of it. I didn't need reminding that I only had him for another eight days.

"What are you going to do with this stuff?" I asked, picking a screwdriver out of the pile of tools beside me.

He took it from me and dropped it into a crate already overflowing with tools.

"Most of it belongs to Alex," he said.

"So Alex gets his tools back, Norm got the boat…I'm going to have little reminders of you all over town," I said, forcing a smile.

Adam wedged himself between my knees.

"I have a confession to make," he said, leaning in close.

"Oh?"

"I sold my car today. You're going to be seeing that around too."

"Sold it to who?"

Adam returned to the tools. "I would have given it you but I knew you'd never accept it." He was stalling.

"Tell me," I demanded.

"The Beautifuls...well, technically I sold it their father, but I'm pretty sure he bought it for them."

"Oh well," I sighed. "There goes the neighbourhood. Maybe we could hide some rotting fish in the glove box or something."

He smiled at me. "Does your evil know no bounds?"

"I have boundaries," I asserted.

He manoeuvred his hand under my knees and lifted me off the bench.

"Where are we going?" I asked as he carried me towards the door.

A grin swept his face. "To the house...to cross some boundaries."

***

Nicole had quit her job without giving notice. Since she'd gone Alex had worked every shift, and the long hours were beginning to take a toll.

I kept to my routine of arriving just before closing so he'd give me a lift home. "Alex, I have something for you," I said, waving a bunch of papers at him as I approached the counter.

"Sounds ominous. What is it?"

"Nothing bad," I assured him.

"So I don't need to meet with your principal or hire a lawyer?"

I pulled a face at him. "It's my passport application. I've filled most of it out, so you just need to sign it so we can lodge the papers."

I put the stack of papers on the counter.

He barely glanced at them. "We'll go to Sorell next week, if I get time. We'll lodge them there."

"We can do it here, at the post office."

Alex stared at me like I was missing something obvious. He picked the papers up and waved them at me. "You want to give these papers to Valerie Daintree?"

I nodded.

"You're out of your mind. If you wait a few more months you won't need my signature anyway."

"I don't want to wait, Alex," I informed him. "I don't care if people find out …unless you do."

Throwing it all out there would only be empowering if both of us were prepared to let the secret go. His frown showed he wasn't ready yet.

"It's not that I don't want to," he said, handing papers back to me. "Just give me a while to figure out *how*."

I nodded but said nothing. There was nothing I could have said that would have reassured him. Alex was dealing with issues much older than me and I had to give him the time he needed. In fact, I was prepared to let it drop indefinitely. At worst I'd have to wait until I turned eighteen in December and no longer need his signature.

It was Alex who broached the subject again, over breakfast the next morning.

"I'll close up early today, pick you up after school and we'll lodge the papers," he told me.

I swallowed. "You're sure about this?"

He scraped butter across his toast while he deliberated. "Charli, keeping quiet was never anything to do with you. You know that, right?"

I nodded, hoping I looked convincing.

"When I was a kid, we moved around a lot. My mum would spend a few months running up debts, drinking away her money. Eventually the wolves would come knocking." He smiled, but there was nothing humorous in what he was saying. "So we'd move on. It was that way for years. When I had you, all I wanted was a stable life for us. Mum was so far gone by then that there was no way she could be on her own. Whatever plans I made had to include her. A guy I knew offered me a week of work on one of his boats. It was an opportunity to make some quick money and set us up somewhere new. All Donna had to do was stay sober for a week to look after you."

"But she couldn't do it?"

"Apparently not." He grimaced. "She packed up and brought you here on a drunken whim."

"Thank goodness for Floss, huh?"

"Floss took very good care of you until I got here," he agreed. "By the time I arrived, Donna had already begun spinning the same crap I'd heard a hundred times before, telling everyone that life was good and she had it all together. But now her story included the sweet little daughter that she dragged everywhere with her, including the pub."

I dropped my eyes to the table, unable to look at his tortured expression.

"The point I'm trying to make is that by the time I got here, I was tired of starting over all the time. I liked it here. I wanted you to grow up here. People in town were already talking about Mum, but it was harmless. Everyone just thought she was a lush – which she was." He winked at me and I smiled. "I stuck to the story she'd started. I couldn't bear explaining the truth back then."

"And now?"

He stared straight at me, deliberating. "Now, I'm not sure that I care. No one can say I've done a bad job, right?"

I rolled my eyes, grinning. "You're right, Alex. I'm almost normal."

"Exactly," he said exultantly. "My kid grew up to be ten times smarter, prettier and more brilliant than theirs."

Apparently he still liked to hang out in La La Land.

***

The last period was supposed to be free study. I used it to double-check my passport application. By the time Alex picked me up that afternoon, I was confident that it was flawless.

Alex parked in front of the post office and got out of the Ute. He was almost at the door before he realised I wasn't following him. "Are you coming?" he asked, dropping his head to talk to me through the open window.

"Adam opens the car door for me," I said, adding a pout.

"I'm not your date, Charlotte." He opened the door anyway.

Valerie Daintree kept us waiting at the counter a long time, sorting mail into pigeonholes, knowing full well we were waiting to be served. Alex's patience eventually ran out. He thumped his hand on the service bell so hard that it distorted the sound of the ring.

"Yes, Alex. May I help you?" she asked, finally turning to acknowledge us.

She was stringing him along for good reason. Alex had once dated her daughter, Sabine. Valerie had high hopes for them but as usual, Alex lost interest after just a few weeks, dumping her on Christmas Eve. Poor Sabine recovered quickly, moved to the mainland and married an accountant. Valerie, however, never seemed to get over it, which explained why she was trying to bump him off with a fierce stare.

Alex pushed the papers across the counter. Mrs Daintree took her time reading through them. It was excruciating, like waiting for Gabrielle to grade my French homework while I was still in the classroom.

"I'm sorry, Alex. It's erroneous," she said, thrusting the application back.

Who uses words like erroneous? I'd never even heard a Décarie say it.

He pushed them back to her, speaking slowly and smoothly. "Val, if you check the details, you'll see that every detail is exactly as it should be."

Mrs Daintree flicked forward a few pages to the copy of the birth certificate, studying it with wide-eyed interest. "Err, yes," she stammered. "It appears to be in order."

Alex leaned over the counter. "I assume that all information received at the post office is confidential and private?"

285

"Of course," she replied snakily.

"Then I have no reason to think that this information will go anywhere other than the passport office." He patted the papers with his palm.

Mrs Daintree's mouth fell open as if she was going to speak but Alex beat her to it.

"You have a lovely day," he said insincerely. He winked at me and grabbed my elbow, leading me towards the door.

I was glad we got out of there when we did. If we'd been a minute later, we wouldn't have seen the pretty black Audi driving down the street.

"Is that Adam's car?" asked Alex incredulously.

I couldn't blame him for being unsure. The sleek black car had undergone some changes. Most noticeable were the huge glittery butterfly decals adorning the side windows.

I gagged. "Not any more."

The sale of the Audi had been rushed through much quicker than Adam had anticipated. His original plan of handing it over just before he left town fell by the wayside once Jasmine started calling him incessantly, pleading with him to give it up early. He was mystified how she got his number. I suspected Nicole, but kept my thought to myself.

It pulled into a bay in front of Carol's salon. The doors were flung open. Alex began to laugh. The hot pink velour seat covers, purple dash mat and fluffy thing hanging off the rear vision mirror made it look like the inside of a seedy nightclub.

Jasmine, Lily and Lisa piled out. The juniors headed straight into the salon, but Jasmine spotted us staring at her.

"Hi Alex," she called, ignoring me. "What do you think?"

"I think I want to scratch my eyes out," he muttered, too quietly for her to hear. He gave her a thumbs-up and sought refuge in the Ute. I was still giggling when I got in.

"Adam will cry when he sees it," I told him.

"Adam should have known better," he replied.

Before he started the car, his phone rang. Alex answered it without checking the number. "Yes Val, that's correct," he said formally.

After answering a few more questions with one-word answers, he ended the call, groaning. "Val's going through your application as we speak. She had a few burning questions," he said wryly. "She's probably in there right now Googling Olivia's name."

"Have you ever Googled her name?" I asked in a small voice.

He turned the key. "Why would I do that?"

"Aren't you curious? Don't you ever wonder what became of her?"

"I'm sure she did just fine," he said, looking over his shoulder as he backed out. "But I'll understand if you're curious. If you want to find her, I'll help you."

I couldn't make sense of his attitude. He'd loved her. They'd had a child together. How could he not be curious?

I wasn't interested in finding her. Olivia Fielding meant nothing to me. All of my curiosity was based around her relationship with my father.

Neither of us said much on the journey home. Once we got out of the car, the conversation would be over. If I wanted to know more, I had to ask now.

"How could you just forget about her, Alex?"

He looked at the bunch of keys in his hand. "I'll never forget her. I see her every time I look at you." He looked across at me, looking embarrassed by his admission. "We went our separate ways and that's how it was supposed to go. We weren't destined to be together forever."

"How do you know that?"

"Because we were so different, Charli. I wanted a quiet life where I could surf all day. She had hopes of living in a big city and touring with a famous ballet company. The only thing we had in common was the fact that we were hopelessly in love with each other."

"Perhaps you should have thought about that before you made a baby," I snapped.

"There are reasons why society discourages teenage pregnancy, Charli," he said, tapping the side of his forehead.

"Why did you stay with her for so long if you knew it wasn't going to work out?"

"Because I loved her." He enunciated each word like it was a stupid question.

I let out a disgusted groan. "Trite."

"It's the truth," he insisted. "You're so sure I don't understand what you're going through, aren't you? I *lived* it, Charli."

"It's completely different."

"Of course it is," he said sarcastically. "Because you and Boy Wonder are peas in a pod, right? So similar it's scary."

I hated the condescending tone he adopted whenever he dragged Adam into a conversation. No good ever came of it.

"There's no comparison. I'm not about to make any accidental babies," I hissed.

"The baby had nothing to do with it. I know that because you're very young, you're hopeful that things will work out for the long haul. I also know that you're going to absolutely hate New York. Adam will win out for a while, but eventually you're going to have to make a tough decision."

"What decision?"

"You're going to have to decide when to call it quits."

Why would I ever have to do that? I loved Adam. There would never be a time when I wanted to end it. I was certain of it.

Alex shifted in his seat. "Charli, I know logic isn't your strong point, but work with me here. Adam is about to start law school. That's his dream. You have a dream. He has a dream. They don't match up."

Adam had his whole life meticulously mapped out. A career in law awaited him. That was his bliss. None of that was achievable unless he spent the next few years working towards it. My hopes for the future were much more simplistic but just as valid. I wanted to tell Alex that I'd found a way to tie it all together, that we could be happy together in New York for as long as Adam needed to be there. But I couldn't.

"Things might change." My voice sounded weak even to me.

"If you alter his course, you'll never be able to live with yourself," he warned. "There should be no compromise at your age, for either of you. You're both supposed to get what you want. The best you can hope for is that you meet somewhere in the middle later on."

"I wasn't planning to change Adam's path."

"You know you have the power to do that though, right?"

Ridiculous, I thought, shaking my head emphatically.

"I've seen the way he looks at you, Charli. He's at the point where he'd do just about anything to keep you in his life and for Adam, that's completely new territory. He's used to getting everything he wants. He's never had to work for that to happen."

Ordinarily, Alex could go days without saying anything insightful. Deep conversations were a rarity. Perhaps that's why I was so confused.

"Tell me what you think I should do," I muttered.

"I can't tell you what to do."

That was a lie. Alex was always telling me what to do. The fact that I'd never actually done it was failure on my part, not his.

"Once you stop being ruled by your heart and start actually listening to what your head is telling you, things will become clearer. There just shouldn't be compromise at seventeen."

Alex's words burned like acid. I thought hard, struggling to find a flaw in his theory. "I won't change my mind about him," I insisted.

"Love affairs at seventeen are about intensity, Charli, not longevity," he said gently.

I didn't want to hear it. Getting out of the car, I slammed the door as hard as I could. It was childish, and it was the best response I could come up with.

Alex got out and slammed his door as hard as I'd slammed mine. "Who taught you to run away when conversation gets tough?" he said angrily. "I never taught you that."

"You don't get to take credit for everything." I stormed over to my own car. Now that Adam had no car, we were reliant on mine.

"Curfew, Charlotte," he growled, walking past me to the house.

I glowered silently. The last word was his – again. That was happening a lot lately.

Unlike Alex, my beaten-up little car endorsed young love, behaving perfectly all the way to the cottage. I was glad to see Gabrielle drive past as I turned into her street. Desperate to see Adam, I ran to the door, prepared to kick it in if he took too long to answer. Fortunately, he was there before I made it to the porch. I launched myself at him, throwing my arms around his neck and hooking my legs around his waist.

"Are you happy to see me or is there some other reason for your enthusiasm?" he asked, murmuring the convoluted question against my mouth.

I tightened my grip, trying to hold him closer to me as he walked us across the room, lowering me to the white couch and blanketing my body with his. I moved my hands behind his head, knotting my fingers through his hair as I drew him to me, kissing him with my whole body.

Adam was always better at drawing the line than me. The point of no return was my favourite place to be these days. He pulled away, moving to the other end of the couch.

"Tell me what you did today," he said, breathing a little unsteadily. "I did absolutely nothing so you'll have to share your day with me."

It was going to be a long week for Adam. Not only had he parted ways with his treasured boat, he had been prematurely separated from his car. I stretched my legs across his lap, sinking deeper into the couch and trying to think of something interesting to tell him. Rehashing my spat with Alex wasn't remotely interesting – it was becoming old hat and overdone.

"I got my passport application lodged," I said, hoping that was newsworthy.

His face lit up. "You know what that means, don't you?"

"No, what?"

"You're now officially a flight risk." He wiggled his eyebrows, making me giggle.

"Where will we go?" I asked.

"You, Coccinelle, will go everywhere. And then you'll come back to me."

"I wish you were coming with me. We could find a nice deserted island somewhere," I told him. "Would you be happy living on a beach with me?"

He smiled, but it was strained. My suggestion was ridiculous, but Alex's words screamed at me. Adam wasn't a boy who belonged on a deserted island. And maybe – horrifically – that meant that he wasn't a boy who belonged with me.

Alex had the uncanny knack of making me rethink conversations long after the event. Maybe it was a gift, or maybe he'd spent my lifetime perfecting the craft. Either way, alarm bells in a distant vault of my mind were growing louder.

I prayed it wasn't common sense kicking in. I'd managed just fine without it so far.

Travelling the earth in search of the perfect place was the biggest dream I'd ever held. In my mind, *my* place was warm and sunny. The ocean was the bluest shade of blue and the sand was pure white. There were no skyscrapers, no traffic and no snow in winter. New York – Adam's perfect place – had all those things.

Effectively, I had made the decision to cut one dream short one for another. My entire heart belonged to the French American boy with the cerulean eyes. I would want him forever. But my soul belonged to a place I hadn't found yet and the truth was that when I did, Adam wouldn't be there.

I looked across at him. "If I ask you something, will you answer honestly?"

"Of course."

I chose my words carefully. "When I go on my trip, if I find my perfect place, will you come?"

Adam's face contorted as if I'd punched him. He looked to the floor for a long time before his eyes drifted back to mine. "Happiness isn't a place, Charli. Just be."

I stood, and brushed at my clothes as if they were covered in sand. "You didn't answer my question." The brushing had become slaps. I was literally beating myself up while I waited for him to speak.

"I love you, Charli." I stopped smacking myself. "I would go anywhere to be with you."

"But if that turns out to be the place I belong, would you stay there with me?"

Adam hesitated, making me hopeful of receiving an honest answer. "I would. I guess we'd have to work something out."

"What could we work out?"

"Charli, I don't know. I guess maybe I'd have to defer school for a while or something." His tone was rough. I'd dredged up his worst-case scenario and he wasn't handling it well.

"You'd do that?" I asked in a tiny voice.

"If I had to."

I believed him and it terrified me. Alex was right. The capacity I had to change Adam's path was huge. He loved me enough to put everything he'd worked for his whole life on hold – and I couldn't promise him the same in return.

"I have to go home," I said, staring vacantly at him.

"Why? You just got here. Stay," he urged. His dark eyes were pleading with me. I couldn't find my voice.

I needed time to think. I walked out into the cold air, praying that I'd find a way to deal with the fact that my heart had just waged war on my soul.

***

I tried to appear normal as I walked through the door. Alex was sprawled on the couch with his head on Gabrielle's lap.

"You're home early," he said, glancing at his watch. "Really early."

"I didn't feel like sandwiches again. I thought I'd come home and cook dinner." The lie came easily. The twinge of guilt I usually felt when I lied to him didn't come at all.

Years of school teaching had given Gabrielle extraordinary powers of perception. "I'm going to head home," she announced, patting Alex's chest for him to sit up and free her. I walked through to the kitchen, leaving them to debate the real reason why I was home early.

I was hacking through a head of lettuce with a blunt knife when Alex appeared in the doorway.

"So what's for dinner?"

"Sandwiches," I mumbled.

"So you changed your mind about cooking?"

"I've changed my mind about a lot of things."

"Like what, Charli?"

"Wholemeal bread," I ranted extraneously. "I *hate* wholemeal bread." I picked the loaf off the table and shook it at him like some weird prop.

He grinned. "I do too. I also hate low fat milk and brown rice, but Floss told me my kid needed those foods to live. They're good for your heart."

I needed all the help I could get where my heart was concerned.

I thumped the loaf of bread on the table, squashing it. Alex tried to salvage it by reshaping it with his hands.

"Tell me what to do, Alex," I demanded.

I didn't need to elaborate.

"I can't. You have to figure it out," he said quietly.

I looked to the floor, trying to hide the fact that I had begun to cry. It was frustration more than sadness. Alex dropped the bread and enveloped me in a hug. "If you already knew the answer, what would it be?" he whispered.

My mind worked surprisingly quickly.

Going to New York had never seemed like a long-term plan. It was something I needed to do to be with Adam, but I'd always considered it temporary. It was an adjustment I was too selfish to make permanently. It wasn't surprising that I'd never looked at the bigger picture before now. Leaving everything to chance was my usual modus operandi, but Adam – the boy who loved small details – had somehow managed to overlook them too.

Once broken down, it was simple. I was not a girl who had it all together. The list of things I'd never done was far too long. Adam knew his place in the world, but he was prepared to bend and twist his life to keep me in it. I couldn't let him do that. I had to let him go.

26. La La Land

If Adam thought it odd that I called him at six in the morning he didn't let on. Nor did he question me when I told him that I needed to see him. I don't know what made me suggest meeting at the lookout on the cliff. We hadn't been there since the day after we'd first met.

He borrowed Gabrielle's car. I took mine, never suggesting that we go there together. He never questioned that, either.

Nothing about the view from the top of the cliffs ever changed. Even the weather remained the same. Cold blustery winds that sting your face and freeze your hands the second you get out of the car are constant. The only thing that had changed since the last time was us. We no longer sat at opposite ends of the rickety wooden seat, cautiously trying to figure each other out. We sat together, bound by something neither of us had ever really managed to understand.

"What are you thinking, Charlotte?" Adam's eyes were locked ahead, fixed on the angry ocean below us.

I tightened my grip on his hand, sucked in a breath and prepared to let go of everything.

"Going to New York would be a mistake for me, Adam. It would be a mistake for both of us. I don't belong there." I wanted to sound strong but my tone smacked of indecision.

"Would you like to tell me why?" he asked seriously.

I pulled my hand free. "This isn't your real life. Your life before me was exactly as it should have been."

"I'll happily make room for you in my real life," he said, forcing a smile.

"I don't want you to. It won't work," I said coldly, watching his expression crumple. "You have everything worked out. You've always known who you are and what you want. I don't know anything."

His frown intensified into a scowl and he focused back on the ocean. "Perhaps it seems that way because until a week ago, you didn't know where you'd come from. Your father has to own that one. Seventeen years of angst and guilt and displacement could have been avoided if he'd just been truthful."

It was the first time Adam or anyone had ever referred to Alex as my dad. I wasn't sure how I felt about that. Perhaps that *was* the crux of my problem. I might have been far less complicated if I'd known the truth from the beginning.

"Please don't bring Alex into this."

"I know he's been in your ear, Charli," he replied.

Annoyed with the direction the conversation was headed, I stood up, unsure of my next move. Adam made it for me, grabbing my hand and pulling me back down.

"Alex has nothing to do with this," I insisted. "I'm trying to tell you that – "

"You're trying to run away," he interrupted. "I know we have some figuring out to do, but I'll do whatever it takes to make sure you're happy in New York. And if I can't, then we'll work something else out."

He made it sound simple, but I couldn't swallow away the lump in my throat. There was no way I could let him change anything about his life for me. I wasn't a safe bet at the best of times. Gambling his whole future on me was the riskiest long shot ever.

"It's not enough," I said grimly. I made no attempt to stem the tears down my cheeks. I deserved to feel woeful.

"Tell me why," he demanded.

"It'll never work, Adam. Eventually I will make you miserable and all the little quirks you find so endearing now will drive you crazy."

"Charlotte – "

I snatched my hand away, overcome by frustration. He was still trying to reason with me. I wasn't used to being the sensible one.

"I'm not Charlotte, Adam. I never was. I'm Charli Blake, scattered and a little bit crazy most of the time. "

He didn't hesitate. "And I am Adam Décarie, the guy who never took a chance on anything before you. I never even *believed* in anything before you. And somehow we found each other. You're telling me that means nothing. What are you suggesting we do, exactly?"

"You will go. And this will end. That's what I want." I sounded remarkably strong considering I was dying inside.

"You can't even look at me when you say that," he pointed out.

I had spent the entire night wrestling with myself, searching for solutions to problems we hadn't even faced yet. I could justify everything by telling myself that I was saving us both a lot of heartache in the future. Punching holes in his chest and tearing out his heart was harder to defend – and impossible to watch.

Adam stood, digging his hands into his pockets as he looked at the grey sky.

"Please understand," I begged.

He closed his eyes. "I can't understand. And I don't believe you. The only way there could be an ounce of truth in what you're saying is if you don't love me."

Whether he meant to or not, he'd given me a way out. I had never once told him I loved him. I'd never figured out how to say it in way that gave it the merit it deserved. That omission might be the only chance I had to make him give up on me.

"You were a great distraction for me, that's all." It was one of Alex's descriptions of him. "For a while, you saved me from this place. I used you and now it's over. You go back to your life and I'll go back to mine."

The mean girl from fifty-three days ago was back with a vengeance. I hated her.

He stood staring at me for far too long. "You think I saved you? That's rich, Charli. I thought you would have realised by now that you're the one who saved me. You gave me everything."

What could I have possibly given him? He was the boy who had everything to begin with. He was whole before he met me. So why couldn't I just shut up and leave him unbroken?

"What did I give you?"

"La La Land."

I blinked in disbelief. "You don't belong in La La Land, Adam. Trust me, when you get back to New York you're going to wake up every morning feeling relieved because I'm not there."

He didn't move. "Tell me you don't love me."

I hesitated, studying his devastated face.

"I don't love you. I never loved you." I said slowly, leaving no room for misinterpretation.

Turning his back he puffed out a hard breath, standing motionless for a long time. I waited for him to speak, or for lightning to strike me down for telling the blackest lie in the history of all lies.

"Well, I guess that's it then," he said, finally.

"I'll make sure Norm forwards you the cheque for the boat," I said unsteadily, making sure all loose ends were tied.

An angry noise escaped him. "I don't want the damned money, Charlotte. I want you to keep it, and use it well. Use it to figure out who you are and what you're looking for."

"And what will you do?"

He didn't hesitate "I love you with my whole heart. The best I can hope for is that I can find a way to change that."

I'd given him every reason not to love me. I was wretched and cruel. I kept being wretched and cruel. "Soon I'll just be a girl you used to know."

The look he gave me wasn't kind. "And what will I mean to you?"

"You'll be the boy who once saved me from myself," I said bleakly.

I was truly a hateful person. Calling it quits and walking away wasn't enough. I had to keep chipping at him until the only thing he could possibly feel was loathing. Then I'd know it was truly over.

He walked over, reached for my hands and pulled me to my feet. His lips pressed gently to mine and my body betrayed me by trembling, just as it had a million times before. Only this was different. This would be the last time.

***

There were a few noticeable absentees at school that day. Nicole, Gabrielle and my brain were missing. I couldn't concentrate on anything and scored detention from two different teachers.

I didn't care that Nicole wasn't there. Ethan's stranglehold on her was making her unreliable. I'd resigned myself to the fact that as long as he was around she was unavailable.

Gabrielle's absence did concern me. I tried hard not to find reason for it. Every scenario I came up with pointed back to me and how vile I was.

It was almost dark by the time I arrived home. Alex was angry, and made no secret of it.

"Where's your phone?" he barked the second I walked in.

"I turned it off."

"Why?" he demanded

I didn't need him yelling at me. I deserved it, but I didn't need it. The flood of tears I'd been holding back since that morning couldn't be blinked away.

"Because I don't want to talk to anyone," I blubbered.

Alex stopped dead in his tracks. Two things he never coped well with were crazy or crying. I was doing both.

"Don't cry. Please, don't cry," he pleaded. I put my hands up, motioning for him to stay put. I didn't feel worthy of comfort. I'd earned every bit of the hurt I was feeling.

"It's going to be okay, Charli," he promised, ignoring me and wrapping his arms around me.

I think he was relieved when I went to bed early. Everything he said was wrong, and nothing I said made any sense. I flitted from insisting that letting Adam go was the best thing for both of us, to sobbing that I'd made a huge mistake.

Sleep came, but it didn't last long. I woke shortly after midnight feeling nothing less than grief-stricken – and finally, I understood why. Adam was about to leave my life thinking I didn't love him. And that was a tragedy.

Annihilating him was the only sure-fire way I knew to end it. If I smashed the road up, there could be no going back. I just wished I had been able to do it without destroying everything we'd shared in the process.

I was left with brilliant memories that a hundred years would never dim. Selfishly, I'd cut Adam loose so brutally that forgetting he'd ever met me was probably preferable to remembering anything.

Throwing back the covers, I jumped out of bed, reaching for my coat that was draped over the back of the chair. I slipped out into the cold night.

My car tried to start. Every time I turned the key it groaned, but wouldn't fire up. After a minute or two, the porch light came on, and my heart sank. I put my seatbelt on, as if that was all it would take to stop Alex dragging me out of the car. I tried to gauge his mood, but the darkness made it impossible to see his face.

Absurdly, I nearly jumped out of my skin when he tapped on the window. It was like a poorly acted B-grade horror movie.

"You used to be so much better at sneaking out," he said through the gap in the window.

I struggled to look at him. "No, you just used to be better at turning a blind eye."

"Here," Alex said, pushing his keys through the window. "Take the Ute."

I finally looked his way. "No catch?"

"There's always a catch, Charli. You jump and then I catch. That's always been the rule."

***

I parked the Ute on Gabrielle's street, worried that the sound of the engine would wake her. The porch light cast a dull but helpful glow as I tiptoed down the veranda to his window, rehearsing what I was going to say – if he let me speak. Adam didn't owe me one second of his time.

I swept the curtains aside as I climbed through. Something was amiss. My eyes adjusted quickly to the darkness of the room. My mind took longer.

He was gone.

I sat on the edge of the bed, concerned that the sound of my body crashing to the floor would wake Gabrielle, but the hallway light came on, telling me that she was already up.

"He's gone, Charli," she said, rounding the doorway.

I lifted my head. She looked nothing like someone who'd just been woken by an intruder. She looked like she'd been expecting me.

"Not for a few days," I insisted.

"He changed his flight. He left this morning."

I frowned, trying to work out the timeline in my head. Adam must have left town the minute I got through obliterating him. And Gabrielle's absence from school made sense. She must have driven him to the city.

"You let him go?" My tone was unfairly angry. I had no one to blame but myself.

She ventured into the room and sat beside me on the bed. "No," she corrected. "*You* let him go."

Gabrielle Décarie was harsh but honest, painfully so sometimes.

"I had to," I told her.

"He left something for you." She handed me a small white envelope. "I'll be in my room if you need me," she said, exiting as quickly as she'd appeared.

Maybe she anticipated a meltdown, or an hysterical woe-is-me tantrum. Truthfully, I was capable of both at that point – simultaneously if the need presented itself.

I tore open the envelope and the opal pendant fell into my lap. I picked it up, dangling it in the air, pondering whether it meant anything anymore. I turned my attention back to the envelope. I'd torn the note inside. Piecing it together, I read quickly.

Charlotte,

I know you love me. I've never doubted it. That makes the end OK.

Adam

Air flooded my lungs. I no longer felt like I was barely alive. Adam had seen through me. I loved him and he knew it. It wasn't a happy ending, but it was one I could live with. I was bruised but not wrecked. Better still, I hadn't broken him.

27. Escape

Keeping busy made time pass faster. Life after Adam would have been unbearably slow otherwise. Even after four weeks, I caught myself thinking of him every time I sat still – so I made a point of never sitting still.

Weekends were easier. Occupying myself was easier.

The Parisienne was spending more and more time at our house. It was nowhere near as insufferable as I expected it to be. She clearly loved Alex and we rarely ate sandwiches for dinner any more. On the downside, sharing a bathroom with her was a nightmare. Gabrielle's assortment of beauty products was mystifying to say the least.

The minute I stepped out the front door I knew that Saturday was perfect. The morning was cold and dewy and bright. Inspired, I balanced precariously on a stepladder, taking pictures from the veranda.

"Charli, what the heck is this?" asked Alex, stepping outside and waving something at me.

Every now and then Gabrielle left something behind. Today it was an eyelash curler. Even after I'd told him what it was, Alex looked baffled.

"So what's it for?" he asked.

"Does the name not give you a hint?" I asked.

"Clearly not. What are you doing?"

"Come and see," I said. I pointed to the eave. Alex looked up and I saw his expression transition from interest to wonder. A huge spider had made its home under the eave, weaving the most intricate web I had ever seen. Drops of dew beaded through it, glistening in the morning light.

"I told you spiders were gifted," he said exultantly. "I'll bet her name is Charlotte."

"Of course it is," I drawled, laughing.

It felt good to laugh. It occurred to me that I hadn't done it in a while. There were too many things I hadn't done since Adam left, and I was beginning to realise that was a mistake. No one had died. I'd spent weeks trying to convince myself that no one had even been hurt.

"Alex, can we surf today?"

"Are you serious?" he asked, taken aback by my request.

"Deadly." He'd been working seven days a week, so a morning in the surf would be good for him. He'd advertised Nicole's position, but the only person to apply was Lily Tate. He wasn't that desperate yet.

I assumed he'd keep the café closed that day, so I was surprised when he told me that we had to stop in on the way to the beach to open up.

"Who's working?"

"Nicole, just for the day," he said, wryly. "I offered her double pay."

There was a time that Nicole would have done it for free. "That was so nice of her," I said.

"Don't be cynical, Charli," he admonished. "It's a small price to pay for a day at the beach with my kid."

If I had been jealous of the time Alex spent with Gabrielle, which I wasn't, spending time at the beach with him would have placated me. It was our thing. The Parisienne never went to the beach, probably worried about getting sand in her Manolo shoes.

I wasn't a winter surfer by choice, and surfing in warm water, wearing as little as possible, ranked high on the list of things I'd never done. Every time I dragged on my restrictive thick wetsuit I thought about it.

The presence of Adam in my life had sometimes clouded the importance of my never-done list. Those tiny dreams were creeping back in. I felt nothing like I had when Mitchell skipped town. Adam Décarie had left me intact. I missed him terribly, but it wasn't paralysing. I would love him forever, but refused to be consumed by it. I was coping; and that was the best I could hope for.

I could have spent the entire day at the beach, but this was a rare day off, and Alex had made lunch plans with Gabrielle.

"Why don't you come?" he asked, trying to include me.

I shook my head. "No. Nic's probably bored out of her mind at the shop. I'll hang out there and you can pick me up later."

Alex didn't press the issue, dropping me at the café as requested. He'd hardly left my side in the first few weeks post-Adam. It was beyond irritating, and things finally came to a head in the form of a huge blow-up one afternoon. My ranting finally convinced him that the only reason I was in despair was because he was following me around like the misery police.

Nicole wasn't alone at the café. I should have known. I hadn't managed to catch a moment alone with her in weeks. Ethan sat at the end of the counter drinking a bottle of water and reading a magazine – neither of which were probably paid for.

"Quiet day?" I asked, ambling towards the counter.

Nicole smiled. Ethan barely glanced at me. "If you're here, can she go?" His flat tone made me want to slap him, and the way he referred to Nicole as *she* made me want to punch him in the head.

"No. *She* can't. But you can." I didn't care that I was rude to him. We were past all niceties when I found out he'd been mentally spending the proceeds of *La Coccinelle*.

He sneered, and Nicole worked quickly to smooth things over. "I'm happy to stay," she insisted.

Ignoring the fact that Ethan was still there, I mentioned the travel brochures Alex had collected for me a few days earlier.

"They're out the back. I'll show you, if you're interested." I wasn't sure if she was. She hadn't mentioned the trip in a long time.

"Great. Go get them," she urged, too enthusiastically to be believable.

I could hear muffled whispers while I was out the back, and when I returned the tension between them was palpable. Nicole joined me at one of the tables and I tried my best to make-believe Ethan wasn't there.

"I thought we could start in Fiji or New Caledonia," I said, pushing the brochures across the table.

"Yeah, whatever you think."

"Or if you want to go the other way, we could start in Bali," I suggested, trying to engage her.

"I really don't mind. Whatever you want to do."

I heard Ethan's condescending chuckle but didn't bother turning around. My eyes were locked on Nicole who was looking past me, towards him.

"Do you have a problem, Ethan?" I snapped.

"I just think you could do better than that. If you want resort beaches, go to Queensland."

"Where do you think we should go?" asked Nicole, showing more interest in his ideas than she had mine.

"Somewhere like Dungeons in Cape Town. Waves are huge there."

"What do you think, Charli?" asked Nicole.

I laughed at the absurdity. A million lifetimes wouldn't provide us with the skills to surf monster waves. "I think he's an idiot for even suggesting it," I scoffed.

"Who's an idiot?" asked Mitchell, barrelling through the door. Obviously supersonic hearing was a Tate family trait.

"Ethan," I replied. "He thinks Nicole and I should give Dungeons a crack."

Mitchell pulled a chair across and straddled it, resting his forearms on the back. "Yeah, if you want to get your pretty heads mashed," he teased, shooting a quizzical look past me in the direction of Ethan.

My friendship with Nicole had suffered because of her relationship with the twit at the counter. I wondered if Mitchell was feeling the sting too – he and Ethan were lifelong friends.

"Are you here for Ethan?" I asked hopefully.

"No. I came to see you, and I've got about ten seconds to explain why."

He didn't get a chance to explain, nor did he need to. A second later, the complete trinity of Beautifuls filed in.

"Charli, you're out of hibernation. How nice for you," purred Jasmine, dumping her massive handbag on the table next to ours. Perhaps she carried her witchy tools in it. It seemed plenty big enough to hold a cauldron and small broomstick.

The junior Beautifuls sat, and Mitchell shifted his chair closer to Nicole, to avoid Lisa who had edged ridiculously close to him.

"I've been here all along," I pointed out.

"Oh, that's right," she said, putting her forefinger to her cheek and tilting her head as if she was thinking hard. "It's your boyfriend who left. I should have known you wouldn't be able to hang on to him for long."

Her words were like a blunt knife through cold butter.

"I did alright, thank you," I said dryly.

"So did we. We got his beautiful car," she said.

"Really? All I got was an expensive boat and his body…for free."

Nicole covered her mouth to stifle her giggle. Mitchell laughed out loud. Lisa started cackling because he did. And Jasmine told them all to shut up before turning her attention back to me.

"I'm glad you're here actually. I've been hearing a story about you and I'm dying to know if it's true."

I tried to anticipate where she was headed but there were too many possibilities.

"I heard a rumour that Alex isn't actually your brother. I heard that's he's your daddy. Is it true?"

Even if she'd been capable of showing any tact, there just wasn't a nice way of wording the question. I was suddenly the sole focus of everyone in the room.

My eyes drifted to Nicole and she half smiled before quickly looking away. It was a gesture that didn't sit well with me. I suspected she'd let the cat out of the bag.

Speaking to Alex before verifying the rumour was probably the right thing to do, but as usual, my mouth got the better of me. "Yeah," I confirmed.

Lisa's gasp broke the silence. My eyes darted across to Jasmine who stood grinning like she'd just fired off a successful headshot.

"Wow, Charli," spluttered Mitchell, drawing my attention back to him. He looked positively green.

Ethan – incapable of anything more intellectual – laughed.

"It's not a big deal," I told them.

"It's a very big deal," insisted Jasmine. "He's totally off my to-do list."

Apparently I wasn't the only one who kept a list.

"Mine too," said Nicole, giggling.

"He'll be thrilled that parenthood has made him less appealing," I snapped.

"Who's your mum?" asked Lisa.

"Maybe Alex slept around," suggested Lily, brainstorming. "Maybe he doesn't know who her mum is."

There was a longer silence than before. "Lily, did someone drop you on your head when you were a kid?" asked Nicole at last.

"Me," admitted Mitchell. "A couple of times."

Everyone except Lily erupted in laughter.

"So is that it then?" I asked. "Do you have anything else to torture me with today?"

"No. That'll do for now," Jasmine said, reaching for her witchy bag.

"Is that all you came in for?" asked Nicole, frowning at her.

"No. I came to tell Mitchell to hurry up. We're supposed to be going to Sorell to pick out a birthday cake. We're not going to wait in the car all day."

"Just go," ordered Mitchell, pointing towards the door. "I'll be out in a second."

I waited until I was sure all of the Beautifuls had vacated the building before speaking. Even then, I couldn't be sure Nicole wouldn't relay the conversation later. I hated the new uncertainty I felt for her.

"So. What do you want to talk to me about?" I asked, leaning back in my chair and folding my arms, staring him down from across the table.

"I need you to do me a favour, Charli. If you do, I'll never ask you for anything else, ever again," he promised.

Nicole leaned forward, hanging on every word.

"What?" I asked, already worried.

"I need you to come to this stupid birthday party with me on Saturday," he said desperately.

"What? Like a date?" asked Nicole, looking strangely at him.

"No chance," I declared.

"Everyone in town is going except you," Ethan chimed in from across the room. "It's the only way you'll score an invitation."

"Please, Charli," begged Mitchell.

"Why? I've never wanted to go."

"Because if you don't come with me, I'm going to be lumped with loopy Lisa and my sisters. I can't handle that by myself."

The grin that crossed my face must have looked positively evil because he retreated.

"Come, Charli. It might be fun. You need to get out," encouraged Nicole.

I failed to understand why everyone was accusing me of hiding away. I'd done far more hiding when I had Adam around.

"Oh, fine," I muttered.

"Good girl," beamed Mitchell, jumping across the table to kiss my cheek. "It's black tie, don't forget."

"I don't own a tie," I teased.

"So wear a dress then. Wear nothing, for all I care." He was already heading for the door.

Nicole and Ethan left soon after Mitchell and the Beautifuls. There wasn't any point keeping Nicole there as long as he was around. I suffered through the last few hours of the working day, then sat on the steps waiting for Alex. I wasn't nervous about telling him that I'd let the whole town know he was my dad – until he arrived to pick me up.

"Do I need to close up?" he asked, leaning across to open the passenger door for me.

"No, I've done it already."

"Did Nic stay all day?" His tone suggested he didn't think she had.

"She left at three. Everyone was gone by three," I babbled, struggling with my seatbelt.

Alex clicked it into place instantly.

"What do you mean, everyone?"

"The Beautifuls, Mitchell, Ethan…everyone."

He kept his eyes on the road while he deliberated. "Are you okay?" he asked finally.

I looked out the window at the trees whizzing past. He was playing misery police again, questioning my emotional state, knowing that Jasmine would have taken her best shot at me.

"I told them you're my dad," I confessed.

From the corner of my eye I could see his knuckles whiten.

"How do you feel about that?"

"Relieved. How do you feel about that?" I asked, turning it back on him.

Relaxing his pose, he glanced across at me. "Lucky," he replied.

***

The next week at school was brutal. Hallway conversations about the Tate twin's upcoming party were loud and inescapable. Everywhere I turned, girls were discussing dresses and dates. Boys were discussing booze availability and dates. The other topic dominating conversation was Blake genealogy. Those conversations weren't loud. They were whispered and muted the instant the gossipers realised I was within earshot. It made no difference. I heard *everything*.

Out of the hundreds of opportunities I had to set the record straight, I never took one. I was definitely off my game.

Gabrielle graciously offered to lend me a dress for the party. Totally unenthused, I left choosing an outfit until the very last minute. I hadn't been to the cottage in weeks. There was no need. Being there wasn't uncomfortable, just different, and I walked out of there with a cute black satin dress, matching shoes and a weird empty feeling.

Mitchell picked me up right on time. Alex laid down the law about having me home at a reasonable hour, taking far too much pleasure in intimidating him. Boy-wonder-with-the-mad-translating-skills never copped the same lecture. Adam wasn't scared of him like Mitchell was.

I doubt Alex was remotely concerned about me attending the party with Mitchell. To him, it would have been a sure-fire sign that I was moving on. I was fine. Adam was gone and I was fine. That was the façade I'd worked hard to maintain. It was one of my most convincing lies ever.

It turned out that Alex wasn't the only one with rules for the night. I had a few of my own, and most of the ride to the Tate vineyard was spent spelling them out.

"Don't leave me alone with your sisters," I warned.

"Don't leave *me* alone with my sisters – or Lisa," he retorted.

"Can't you just tell her you're not interested?"

"I have. At first I was nice about it, and then I was mean about it. She's convinced she can change my mind."

"Jasmine is spurring her on."

"Yes she is," he despairingly agreed.

I had only ever been able to deal with Jasmine in short bursts. I couldn't imagine how Mitchell coped with being her twin. Perhaps that was his motivation for traveling.

The Tate estate was arguably the grandest property in town. I'd never been inside the huge main house, and that wasn't about to change. The party was to be held in one of the cedar outbuildings set among the lines of vines. By day it was a wine tasting centre and barrel room open to the public. Tonight it was by invitation only. As we walked across the car park I could see they were actually checking invitations at the door.

"Who's that?" I whispered, watching a tuxedoed man practically frisking guests as they entered.

"Ugh! Jasmine's idea. Everyone's been hired. Caterers, bar staff, a band…"

"Friends?"

Mitchell laughed. "Some friends have probably been rented…or coerced." He quickly glanced across at me, smiling sheepishly.

"Not me," I told him, letting him off the hook.

"No?" He sounded surprised.

"No. I'm here of my own free will."

Mitchell sighed despondently. "I wish I could say the same, Charli."

I could tell he was dreading it. If I'd suggested leaving, he wouldn't have argued. But I didn't. A few hours at a party hosted by the Beautifuls weren't likely to kill me. I'd endured far worse where they were concerned.

At first I'd wondered if the strapless dress with the full skirt Gabrielle had lent me was too dressy. I needn't have worried. Everyone was dressed to the nines, including Nancy. The ugly little dog wore a big silver bow around her balding neck. The Beautifuls were overloaded with ruffled taffeta. Jasmine wore hot pink while Lily epitomised bad taste in aqua and sea green. Lisa fared much better. Her maroon satin gown with low neckline and three quarter sleeves would have looked perfect if only she'd ditched the silver bangles.

Nicole had borrowed the pseudo-vintage dress I'd worn to her sister's wedding a few months earlier. I had to admit it suited her much better. It fitted her better too. From across the room I watched her for a while. She never once fussed with the plunging neckline. She caught me looking and waved me over with her free hand. I pretended not to see her, mainly because her other hand was gripped firmly around Ethan's. I stuck with Mitchell instead, much to his mother's disgust. There was no chance of ever making a good impression on Meredith Tate. She was a grownup version of Jasmine who believed every word her daughters told her. One of her daughters was traipsing around looking like a dolphin had vomited her dress, and yet to her I made questionable life choices – a brief liaison with her son being one of them.

Seeing Nicole sneaking out of the party after just a few hours came as no surprise. What did surprise me was that she'd changed into jeans and her thick winter coat. Something was going on.

313

Slipping away from the party was easy. Finding her in the dimly lit car park wasn't as simple. She spotted me first, and called my name. I walked over, annoyed to see that Ethan was with her, standing beside her car.

"Here, take this. We've got plenty," she said, handing me a bottle of vodka as soon as I was within reach. "And this," she added, hooking my green dress over my shoulder.

"Did you swipe this from inside?" I asked disapprovingly, waving the bottle at her.

"It's free, Charli. It's a party," said Ethan.

I ignored him, keeping my focus on Nicole.

"It was one for the road," she beamed, excited. "We're out of here, Charli."

"Take me with you. I want to go home too," I told her.

"No, I meant we're leaving town. Tonight," she clarified.

"With him?" I asked, pointing to her loser boyfriend.

Even in the dark I could see Ethan smirk. At least he kept quiet.

"Yeah. We've been planning it for a while."

Deep down inside I had known something was in the works. Nicole had left me long ago. We'd hardly spoken in weeks.

"Nic, you can't. Just wait a few more months. We're leaving then anyway."

She shook her head. "I'm not waiting. Ethan wants to go now."

"And what do you want?" I asked.

Nicole shrugged. The weak gesture infuriated me.

"Stand for something, Nicole," I growled. "Or you'll fall for anything."

Ethan sniggered, and I knew he'd received my insult loud and clear.

"I'm going," she insisted.

"And what about me?" I asked.

"What about you?" Ethan jibed. "It's not her fault your boyfriend shot through."

No one except Gabrielle and Alex really knew why things had ended between Adam and me, not even Nicole – my so-called best friend. We'd spent so little time together that I'd never had the chance to tell her. Evidently, just like the Beautifuls, she thought he'd dumped me.

"Adam went home, just as he'd always planned to do," I hissed.

"But you would have gone with him if he'd asked," reminded Nicole, speaking slower than usual.

I hated being reminded of how close I'd come to bailing on her. I wondered if that had made it easy for her to leave me.

"But he didn't ask her. Strike two for Charli," said Ethan, leering at me in a way that made my skin crawl. "That's why she's begging you to stay."

Shooting him a baleful glare, I reached for Nicole's hand and pulled her aside, to get her away from him while we talked.

"If you're leaving town in the middle of the night, you're obviously running away. Your mum will be beside herself by morning." I was sure I could make her see reason.

"I really don't care. I'm eighteen, she can't stop me."

Her attitude was outrageous. Nicole was the good one. The wrath of Carol Lawson scared me, but it usually terrified her. Nothing I was saying was getting through. I wasn't sure if she couldn't see the knock-on effect that skipping town would have or if she simply didn't care.

"What about our plans? You know I can't travel without you. Are you just going to leave me here?" My tone became more desperate as I pleaded my case.

Still she remained unaffected.

Ethan got into her car and started the engine, revving it to hurry her along. She glanced over her shoulder like she was gearing up to run from me. I gripped the sleeve of her coat futilely.

"Look," she said, marginally sympathetically. "You'll be fine. You're always fine. You'll work out how to leave. Try patching things up with Adam."

"Adam has nothing to do with this, Nic," I spat. "This is about you and me. We've been planning this for ten years. Don't you care about that?"

Her body seemed to relax and I loosened my grip. Her expression was completely blank. "I really don't, Charli," she said wearily. "I have Ethan."

"You don't love him!" The words raged out of me. I couldn't have toned it down if I'd tried.

"I don't need to love him. I've learned from your mistakes. Where did falling in love get you?"

"Are you trying to hurt me, Nicole?"

"I'm pretty sure not everything is about you."

Shrugging free, she marched to the car. Ethan wasted no time, peeling down the driveway as soon as she closed the door. I thought I saw her look back at me as they drove away, but my tears were clouding my vision.

I was wandering aimlessly around the car park, kicking stones with Gabrielle's hellishly expensive shoes when Mitchell finally found me.

"What are you doing out here?" he asked, taking off his jacket and draping it around my shoulders. I couldn't find the coordination I needed to put my arms through the sleeves.

"This." I thrust the half empty bottle of vodka at him and he jumped back, trying to avoid the splash of liquor heading his way.

He looked perplexed. "Are you drunk?"

I pinched my thumb and forefinger together, confirming his suspicions. "Li'l bit," I slurred.

"Do you want me to take you home?" he asked as he took the bottle and emptied it onto the ground.

"No, I want you to take me to the beach."

He tossed the bottle into a nearby garden. "Charli, I don't think that's a great idea."

Inexplicably, I burst into tears. I couldn't explain why. Perhaps the half bottle of vodka I'd guzzled in less than half an hour had something to do with it. Mitchell pulled his jacket tighter around me, buttoning it up like that would contain me. How dismal I must have looked, in a cocktail dress and ill-fitting dinner jacket, empty sleeves flapping in the breeze, blubbering like a child.

"Alright, alright. We'll compromise," he offered, bringing his finger to his lips to shush me. "We'll go for a walk down to the grapes, okay?"

"There should be no compromise at seventeen," I recited in a voice that sounded nothing like Alex.

"You're a certifiable nutcase, Charli Blake," he said. Grabbing my shoulders, he pointed me down the track to the vineyard. We seemed to walk forever.

"Nicole and Ethan have done a runner," I told him out of the blue.

Mitchell stopped dead. "Tell me what happened."

I told him everything I knew, leaving nothing out. "She's been planning it for weeks," I snivelled.

"Nicole couldn't plan a day at the beach," he replied. "Ethan's the ringmaster."

"Are you mad at him?" My brain was starting to fail me. Even I could tell that I was slurring my words.

"He never said a word. I'm shocked."

"Nicole never does anything bad. She's the good one," I rambled. "All the trouble we've ever been in was my fault."

I thought I was confessing to something he didn't know. "You don't say?"

"It's true. I'm the bad one."

"You're not bad, Charli," he said sympathetically, putting one arm around me as he pulled me in close.

I could feel my tears saturating the front of his shirt but made no attempt to move or stop crying.

"First Adam and now Nicole. Everything is a mess," I wailed.

"It's not your fault. Nicole's just a sheep following a wolf, and Adam's a fool for – "

"Shut up!" If my arms had been free of my makeshift straightjacket, I would have hit him. "Adam never dumped me. I ended it."

He stared. "Why would you do that? I thought you were looking forward to going to New York."

"I was looking forward to being with *him*. There's a difference, a big difference as it turns out. Even in my head, I couldn't make a fairy-tale ending."

"I'm sorry, Charli."

"So am I." My voice was barely louder than a whisper. "I'm not going to New York. I'm not going anywhere anymore."

My impromptu decision to get blind rotten drunk was purely to drown my sorrows. For a while it had worked. But now I was starting to feel sick, and my sorrows were magnifying at a rate of knots.

"You can still travel," Mitchell insisted.

"Sure I can," I replied sarcastically. "My father will love the idea of me heading off into the big unknown by myself."

His pained expression made me laugh.

"What's funny?"

"You were scared of him when you thought he was my brother. You must be scared stiff now you know he's my dad." I giggled through my tears.

He looked at the ground. "Especially tonight," he muttered. "I have to take his daughter home, and she's smashed."

I hadn't put much thought into what Alex's reaction would be. The second I did, I regretted ever taking a sip. Given my grandmother's history and his tendency to overreact, he'd be signing me up for Alcoholics Anonymous meetings.

"Mitch, can you take me home?" I asked, sounding downtrodden even to myself.

"Absolutely." He pointed me back towards the car park.

Sleep was the only thing I was looking forward to about getting home. Mitchell did his best to prop me up as we walked into the house, but it took Alex two seconds to figure out I was drunk. He grabbed my chin, tilting my head up to look at my eyes. The bright light made it impossible not to squint.

"Oh, Charlotte, you are in a whole world of trouble." He was remarkably calm, all things considered.

"Don't be too hard on her," said Mitchell, bravely pleading my case. "She's had a rough night."

Alex turned his vexation to Mitchell. "You don't need to speak," he growled.

Mitchell helped me across the room and lowered me on to the couch.

"I do need to speak. There's a problem. I think Nicole's mum thinks she's staying here tonight."

Alex swiped both hands down his face. "Nicole is Carol's problem. Where is she? With Ethan?" he asked, furious.

"Technically," mumbled Mitchell.

I tried to stay awake while Mitchell explained the whole sorry saga, but I couldn't. My eyes started closing the second my head hit the cushion.

***

Waking up the next morning with a thumping headache and very queasy stomach should have been punishment enough. Alex didn't see it that way. I was jolted awake by the sound of him smashing the lid down on a saucepan as he circled the couch.

"Stop!" I pleaded, covering my head with a cushion.

He ripped the cushion away. "I'm sorry, Charli." His voice was sweet. "I didn't mean to wake you."

"Just stop," I begged.

I closed my eyes because I needed to. The morning was much too bright. Alex was much too bright. He chuckled maniacally as he walked away. I heard the tap running and a few seconds later he returned, presenting me with a huge glass of water.

"Here, drink this. You'll feel better." I sat up and took it from him, gratefully.

"How much trouble am I in?" I asked, preparing for the worst. The worst didn't bother me. I didn't feel as though I had much left to lose.

Alex sat on the edge of the coffee table. "Not as much as Nicole. I've been to see her mother."

"Why did you tell Carol?" I asked, horror-struck.

"Someone had to. Nicole didn't even leave a note. Carol's a mess. Did you know she was planning this?"

I instantly regretted shaking my head so fervently. I had to swallow hard to stop myself throwing up in his lap. "No. Not a thing. I still wouldn't know if I hadn't noticed her sneaking out of the party."

His hard expression softened. "Are you upset with her?"

Alex wasn't stupid. He knew the repercussions of Nicole leaving town were huge. Without her, my travel plans were sunk.

I shrugged, faking indifference. "I forgive her. I'll work something out."

"You can come to Marseille with me and Gabs." He said it like he'd just solved all my problems.

Never, I promised myself, determined to resort to plan B. I shuddered, wondering how long it would take to come up with a plan B.

It took a long time to pull myself together that morning, but I did it. Wallowing in self-pity wasn't an option. Neither was tagging along to Marseille with Gabrielle and Alex, so I was determined to figure out a way around it. The best way to start was to work out my finances.

Nicole and I had been saving for years. Realistically, the proceeds of my tiny postcard business would have added up to little more than a few thousand dollars. She'd probably fared much better, working every shift Alex had offered her since she was fourteen. My saving grace was the unbelievable bonus of receiving the proceeds of Adam's boat – only I hadn't received it yet. I wasn't worried. Norm was hardly the type to rip anyone off. Needing an excuse to leave the house, I made the short drive into town to visit Norm and Floss.

Floss seemed to have a sixth sense. I couldn't remember a time that I'd ever visited and got as far as knocking. She was always waiting for me on the front step.

"How's the head, Charli?"

"Is there anything you don't know?" I asked, hugging her tightly so she wouldn't see me blush.

"I saw your dad at the café this morning. He mentioned that you were feeling under the weather."

It was amazing how quickly Floss dropped the façade and began referring to Alex as my father. I was astounded that she'd managed to keep the secret going for seventeen years.

I released her and stepped back. "Is that what he called it?"

Floss's trademark roar of laughter filled the air and I couldn't help laughing with her.

"No. He told me you had a skinful last night and were paying for it this morning."

"Is he worried?" It was a question I was too fearful to ask Alex.

She shook her head telling me no, and I huffed out a long breath. He wasn't about to ship me off to rehab.

"He's very worried about Nicole running away, though, and how that will affect your plans."

Everyone around me had jumped to the same conclusion. My plans were dead in the water the minute she left.

"I'll be fine," I insisted.

"So what brings you here today?" she asked, pulling the screen door open and ushering me inside.

"I came to see Norm, actually." I scanned the front room as I walked in ahead of her.

Floss's house was cluttered to say the least. Figurines and ornaments decorated every surface. Heavy lace curtains hung on the windows and everywhere I looked, there seemed to be a sleeping cat. Floss claimed to have three cats. I'd seen at least four in the minute and a half that I'd been there.

"He's not here, love. He has a new mistress these days." My expression as I turned to face her must have been strange because immediately, she explained. "The boat, Charli. He's gone fishing."

"Oh," I mumbled. "That's what I wanted to see him about. I was hoping he'd have my cheque for me."

I felt embarrassed even asking. Floss stood motionless, frowning at me for so long that I had to look away.

"Adam asked Norm to make out a cash cheque and give it to you," she said slowly, replaying the scenario out loud.

I nodded in agreement, prompting her to continue.

"He went to the café last weekend to give to Alex but he wasn't there. Nicole was working. She offered to pass it on to you, so he gave it to her."

"Has the cheque been cashed, Floss?" I asked shakily.

Floss staggered back a few steps and flopped down on the red velvet recliner behind her. "I'm so sorry, love."

Her apology instantly confirmed my worst fears. My heart was screaming at me to come up with a plausible explanation for the picture coming together in my head. But I couldn't. There was no denying it. My so-called best friend had betrayed me in the worst way imaginable. The Pipers Cove version of Bonnie and Clyde were hobnobbing around the world, living my dream – on Adam's money.

I reached for her hand, like she'd done for me a million times.

"It's not your fault, Floss," I insisted. "Don't waste another second thinking about it."

The hooligan half of me was plotting revenge. The sweeter, less well-known part of me spent the next half hour trying to console Floss. It took a long time and a gallon of tea to calm her down.

Before I left, I swore her to secrecy. Until I could figure out a way around it, no one needed to know. The only person in town that I trusted with the news was Mitchell. And I suddenly became desperate to see him.

To get to Mitchell's shack, I had no choice but to drive past the main house. Thankfully the Audi was nowhere to be seen. I wasn't in the mood for fending off Beautifuls.

Everything about the Tate property was impressive except Mitchell's shack. It was originally the main house and probably once quite charming, but now it was ramshackle. If I didn't know for sure that he lived there, I would have sworn it had been abandoned.

I pounded on the front door, fighting to be heard over the loud, angry music coming from inside. The door flew open and I took a quick step back, shocked by his fierce expression.

"Oh, it's you." The choler disappeared instantly.

"Who were you expecting?"

He poked his head out, looking from left to right as if he expected to spot someone in the bushes.

"Lisa," he uttered, motioning me inside. I didn't ask why. I could handle no more drama that day.

He walked across the cluttered room to the stereo, turning it down. I stood, too scared to sit on the manky couch.

"You're a pig," I told him, making no secret of my disgust.

"Is that what you came here to tell me?" He didn't stop moving, sifting through piles of clothes like he was searching for something.

"No. What are you doing?"

"I'm trying to figure out what else he's taken."

"Who?" My question was superfluous. I already knew the answer.

"Ethan. He's taken two of my boards and my camera. And those are the things I know about," he growled, understandably furious.

"That's not all they took," I told him.

He looked at me for the first time since I'd walked in. "Tell me everything," he demanded.

I launched into my woeful tale. Mitchell said nothing for a long time, probably trying to make sense of it, just as I had tried to do. "So, what are you going to do?" he asked finally.

"Nothing. There's nothing I can do."

Mitchell swept a pile of clothes off the couch and sat. We both stared straight ahead, lost in our thoughts. The two people we never thought would, had betrayed us.

"We were talking about South America just a few nights ago. That was the plan," he mused. "My dad gave us work in the vineyard. Three months of saving and we were to be out of here."

Apologising seemed absurd but I found myself doing it anyway. He shuddered like he was warding off ugly thoughts.

I heard tyres screeching on the gravel driveway. I hadn't heard the engine, which meant only one thing. It was the Audi. The beautiful, sleek, quiet Audi…with the hot pink seat covers and butterfly decals.

Mitchell groaned, and buried his head in his hands. I didn't need to ask why.

The wooden front door flew open and Jasmine appeared, looking every bit the fiend she was. Even without the hangover, she would have been hard to take. Lisa stood behind her, looking past the chief Beautiful at Mitchell.

"Do you ever knock?" he asked irately.

"No. What's she doing here?" Jasmine pointed at me.

"None of your business," he told her.

Jasmine thrust Lisa forward.

"It is my business. You need to make up your mind who you want."

The closest I'd come to throwing up that day came at that moment. "I was just leaving," I said, suddenly keen to escape.

Mitchell grabbed my sleeve to stop me. "No, you weren't." He marched to the door and pushed his sister and Lisa out, slamming it behind them and locking it.

Jasmine was unrelenting, pounding on the door and screeching something about us both having the morals of alley cats. Mitchell ignored her.

"Charli, how much money do you have?" he asked, leaning on the door like there was a chance she'd kick it in. I wondered if he was going to pay her to go away.

"About twenty bucks," I replied, reaching into my pocket.

"No, no. I mean in the bank."

"Not much."

"Enough for a plane ticket?"

I nodded, unsure where he was headed.

"I can probably cover a plane ticket too. Let's just get out of here. Right, now. Let's go," He almost sounded desperate.

"I'm not – "

"What's the point in staying? Nicole's gone. Adam's gone. You want to get out of town. You're looking for a travel buddy. I'm right here." He pointed at himself.

He made it sound so easy. In reality there was nothing simple about it. I hadn't finished school, I had far less money than I should have…and I had Alex.

"When?" I asked.

"Today, tomorrow, as soon as we can."

"I need more time."

"Charli, The more time you take, the more likely you'll talk yourself out of it."

He was right. That's exactly what would happen.

Finally the pounding on the door stopped and we heard tyres spinning on gravel. I could only imagine where the Beautifuls were going. I didn't want to know.

"Can I think about it?"

"No," he replied quickly.

I walked towards the door, which he was still blocking. "Fine," I said vaguely.

Mitchell unlocked the door, stepping aside to let me pass. "Fine, what?"

"Fine. I'll go. Book the tickets. I don't care where to." The words tumbled out quickly, but I was telling the truth. I really didn't care. Travelling with Mitchell meant my horizons broadened considerably. Almost nowhere was out of bounds. "We'll leave the day after tomorrow."

He lunged forward, squeezing the life out of me as he hugged me much too hard. "Good girl."

"Ugh! Get off," I demanded, trying to wriggle free.

Mitchell released me, grinning like he'd won something huge. "Stay a while. We should decide where we're going to go."

I shook my head. "No. I have to tell Alex."

"Shouldn't you wait until we at least have a plan?" he asked, sounding unsure for the first time.

"I'm leaving town the day after tomorrow. That is a plan," I replied.

28. Three Options

I had no idea how Alex would take the news of me leaving town with Mitchell. What I did know was that I'd only have one chance to convince him that I hadn't lost my mind. I figured the best place to corner him was at home. It also gave me an hour to work on my speech.

The weather that afternoon was glorious. The miserable winter had given way to spring. Tulip blooms had popped from every spot in the garden. It was a happy sight that I looked forward to every year, secretly still hopeful that one day I'd find a sleeping baby fairy. Curiously, for the first time ever, we had a sea of orange tulips amongst the traditional red and yellow blooms. Alex thought they'd mutated over the years. It made sense. Some of the bulbs had been flowering since I was a kid.

Adam had once told me that the fairy garden would be my legacy. The thought of leaving town made me hopeful that the mark I left on the world would be much bigger.

I sat on the steps of the veranda, soaking up the last minutes of the day's sunshine. Gabrielle arrived home first. That changed my game plan a little bit. It was definitely favourable to have her there because her influence on Alex was generally calming. The Décarie effect. I'd fallen under that spell myself.

"What are you doing sitting out here?" she asked, walking towards me with a bag of groceries.

"Waiting for Alex. What are you doing here?"

I shuffled over to make room for her to pass but instead she sat beside me, resting the groceries on her lap. "I thought I'd surprise him with dinner. What are you planning to surprise him with?"

Lying in wait to ambush him the minute he got home made it pretty obvious that something was going on. I told her my plan in its entirety, which took about five seconds, highlighting just how harebrained it was going to sound to him.

"I have to go. It's come down to a case of now or never," I told her.

Gabrielle deliberated for a long time, making me nervous.

"Then go, Charli. I will support you all the way," she said finally, shielding her eyes from the sun with her hand.

"Really?"

"Did you think I wouldn't?"

"I had my doubts," I admitted.

She laughed lightly, repositioning the bag on her lap.

I hadn't treated Gabrielle well in the past. I'd wasted a lot of energy making her life difficult, which was stupid. She'd turned out to be my greatest ally. One day, when I was braver, I'd tell her so.

"You seem to have a lot of doubts," she said, hinting towards a different subject matter.

"Not about this. Getting out of here has always felt right," I insisted.

"What about other decisions you've made lately?"

Her question was as subtle as an avalanche. Gabrielle had never once questioned me about my reasons for ending things with Adam. I was miffed that she'd chosen that moment to raise the subject.

"Have you spoken to him lately?" I asked.

"Who? Adam?"

"Of course, Adam," I grumbled. "Who else?"

"Well!" she said theatrically. "It's funny you should mention him. I got a letter this morning. He usually sends me emails so it was a wonderful surprise to see that he'd put pen to paper."

She reached into her pocket and pulled out a crisp white envelope.

"Did he mention me?" I asked, trying to ignore the fact that she was waving the envelope in my face.

"Of course he did. You may read it," she permitted.

I pushed her hand away, unable to imagine being desperate enough to read a letter he'd written to someone else. "No," I griped.

"Charli, it might be good for you." She sang her words, trying to tempt me.

"No, vitamins are good for you. Reading someone else's mail is not good for you, it's creepy," I retorted.

Gabrielle squared her shoulders and huffed loudly. Emotional restraint wasn't her strong point. When she was cross, the whole world knew about it. Huffing, I could handle.

"How many classes are you failing at school?" Conversations with the Parisienne were often confusing. I'd given up trying to conquer that problem.

"One. French," I replied, pulling a face at her.

"That's right. You owe me one more assignment before the end of your school career." She held one finger in the air, emphasising her point.

"I'm leaving the day after tomorrow. You'll just have to fail me."

"No, I'll give you a chance. Take this letter and translate it in its entirety. If you do it well – without cheating – I'll pass you." She smiled like she'd offered me the chance of a lifetime.

It was a futile exercise. Leaving school early meant there was no chance of graduating anyway.

I pointed to the letter in her hand. "Those words weren't meant for me."

"Charli, the French language wasn't meant for you."

I couldn't help laughing. "Why would I want to read it?"

"Because you love Adam. And when you love someone, you do all sorts of dreadful things."

She'd made that statement many times and it made no more sense now than it had the first time. I was about to demand an explanation when she jumped to her feet. The grumbling V8 engine in the distance explained why.

The letter fluttered onto my lap as she dropped it. "I'll give you one week to translate," she said in her best schoolteacher voice. "No extensions, no excuses."

"I'll think about it," I mumbled, stuffing the envelope into my pocket.

It took forever for Alex to mosey up to the veranda. He seemed more interested in the apple he was eating than in making it to the house.

"Hey," he said, sitting in the spot Gabrielle had vacated seconds earlier.

"Alex, I've got to tell you something really important." I didn't mean to sound as bleak as I did but my tone didn't seem to affect him.

He took another bite of his apple. "When are you leaving town, Charli? Jasmine came in as I was closing up, busting to tell me that you and Mitchell are flying the coop."

Damn Jasmine Tate and her bionic hearing!

I'd anticipated a ferocious argument, but he was as calm as I'd ever heard him. I was supposed to ease into it, explaining my reasons before sitting back and watching him explode.

"The day after tomorrow."

He didn't react, unless munching an apple could be considered a reaction. Finally he glanced at me, still looking nothing like a man in danger of detonating. Pegging it as hard as he could, Alex threw the core into the garden.

"Fairy food," he told me.

I said nothing, waiting for the diatribe to begin.

"Carol came into the shop today too," he told me, completely off subject. "She's aged a hundred years overnight."

"Has she heard from Nicole?"

"Not a peep. She's absolutely devastated because she doesn't think Nicole is going to handle the big bad world on her own. And I think she's right."

"Why do you think that?"

"Because her kid believed every cockamamie story my kid ever told her. That makes her a few feathers short of a whole duck. Remember that year her mum made angel cake for her birthday party?" He smiled at the ancient memory. "Carol sent you home early because you told Nicole that angel cake was made with real angels."

I did remember. It was her sixth birthday party. Nicole freaked out, bawling like the world was ending when her mother tried to cut the cake. She refused to eat it and screamed at anyone else who dared to take a bite. Carol was so furious that she left the party to drive me home.

"She told me I was a monster."

Alex chuckled, exactly the way the father of a monster should. "I can still remember watching her march you up to the house," he mused. I wondered if it was something I was supposed to apologise for. Realistically it would take years to say sorry for all of my past misdeeds. I had no idea why he was mentioning it now. "Carol took great delight in telling me how naughty you were. You strutted up that path with your lopsided pigtails like you owned the world." He stared at the path, almost as if he could see it all over again. His eyes drifted back to mine. "The point is, she told me today that she wished you had gone too. She would have felt a lot better knowing that you were with her."

"Because I'm a monster?"

"No, because *you* are ready for this. I've spent your entire lifetime trying to rein you in. Maybe it's time to stop doing that."

"I am ready for this, Alex. I've wanted this forever." I hoped I spoke seriously enough for him to believe me.

"The timing sucks, Charli."

"I know it's not perfect but I can finish school later," I reasoned.

He frowned like he didn't believe a word I'd just said. I wasn't sure I did either.

"Please tell me you have a plan. Mitchell can be the brawn but I'm relying on you to be the brain. Your money won't last long unless you're careful with it."

I knew Alex was taking comfort in the knowledge that I had the proceeds of *La Coccinelle*. It was a bubble I had no intention of bursting.

"Tomorrow, I'll have a plan. I've left it up to Mitch to book the tickets."

Alex tutted. Perhaps I shouldn't have been quite so honest. "Oh, great," he grumbled. "You're going to end up in a jungle somewhere."

I was slightly irked by his lack of faith. "He'll look after me. You know that."

"I actually wish Boy Wonder was around."

Cue the unintentional dagger through my heart.

The habit of saying what you're really thinking when not concentrating was obviously hereditary. Alex grimaced. "Sorry, Charli. I didn't mean – "

"It's okay." I cut his bumbling apology short. "I miss him too, but it doesn't change anything."

Alex looked stunned, suddenly awakened to the growing regret I'd been feeling for the past month. Sometimes being such an accomplished liar bothered me.

"Do you think you made a mistake?"

I nodded. "I'm certain of it. I think I lost more than I'm ever going to have again. I love him even more now that he's gone, and that wasn't even supposed to be possible."

It was a strange confession to make, but not an uncomfortable one.

"Are you going to go to him, Charli?" he asked, narrowing his eyes.

"No. I promised him he'd get his old life back. No drama, no crazy. Staying away is the least I can do," I said, smiling artificially. Even talking about him was crushing. I could accept that Adam was gone forever a whole lot better if I could find a way of getting over him.

"Adam always liked your drama. That bothered me. And there was enough crazy to destroy a small village, but he liked that too."

"Yeah, well, you told me to take intensity over longevity, remember?" My voice took on a defensive edge and he was instantly remorseful, flinching as if I'd reminded him of something terrible.

"I'm going to tell you something. I want you to remember it always, okay?" I nodded. He continued without pausing. "On your travels you're always going to have three choices."

"Only three?"

"There's only three that I'm comfortable with."

"Okay."

"If you're ever unsure, you can always come home to me. You can revisit a safe place you've been to, or you can find your way to Adam." He ticked off my options on his fingers as he spoke.

"That's it?" I asked.

"They're the only three I'm comfortable with, Charli," he repeated. "If you remember those options, I'll feel much better about taking a step back from the tree."

"You're not going to try catching me this time?" I teased.

"I don't think you're going to need me when you jump this time." Alex looked straight at me. "This time, I think you're going to fly."

29. Magic

It's amazing how quickly a plan can come together when there isn't actually a plan.

We were bound for Mauritius. Mitchell and Ethan had been there the year before, and after hearing Mitchell's stories of white beaches and endless sunshine, I was getting excited.

Saying goodbye to Alex was every bit as hard as I expected. We stood in the front yard and hugged each other harder and longer than we ever had before.

"You're the very best part of me, Charli. I love you," he whispered, choking on the words.

I searched my heart for something I had never said before, wondering if the words would sound wrong. "I love you, Dad," I whispered.

I felt Alex buckle. He held me tighter and I knew that to him, those four words sounded perfect. I wrestled free, unwilling to prolong the agony.

Big things awaited him too. By Christmas, Gabrielle and Alex planned to be in the south of France. I'd pulled her aside the night before and made her promise to make sure he went through with it.

"I will give him no choice," she said, looking ferocious. I believed her. Alex's no-compromise policy didn't seem to apply to Gabrielle. He was capable of moving heaven and earth for her, and with me gone he'd be more likely to do it.

I refused to let Alex drive us to Hobart. There was no point dragging out a long farewell. We took my car instead, which turned out to be a coup. Next to the airport, amongst the car rental companies, was the junkiest car yard in existence. The shifty-looking salesman handed me two hundred bucks and a stomach-churning wink in return for my little car. It was another goodbye I was sad to make.

My old life was fading very quickly.

After a quick flight, we were in Melbourne. We made our way to the international airport terminal. That was where my naivety began to get the better of me and I had to ask Mitchell for help. I had no idea about filling out a departure card or clearing customs, but he was an old pro. After helping me with mine, he completed his card in seconds, including his passport number, which he knew by heart.

Once we were on the plane I began to relax a little. Sleep on the long flight was impossible, for me anyway. Mitchell was dozing before we'd even taken off. I passed the time reading for a while, confident that in case of an emergency I'd read the passenger safety card enough times to be able to save my own life – ignoring the thirty thousand foot nosedive into the sea, that is.

The elderly lady to my right was chatty, and I appreciated the company. Her English was fractured and I recognised her accent instantly.

"Are you French?" I asked, accusingly.

The lines on her aged face crinkled as she smiled. "Mauritian Creole. My name is Heloise."

I frowned as I shook her hand, convinced that the French language was taking over the world. "My name is Charli."

Heloise snickered in a way that made her frail body shake. "You have a boy's name," she said.

I took no offence. "My father named me after a spider," I told her, making her cackle again.

We were quiet for a while. It was Heloise who spoke again, to ask my reason for travelling to Mauritius. I hadn't taken me long to work out she was hard of hearing. Explaining my lifelong dreams of travel would have been an ordeal, so I summed it up in one word. Surfing.

"I will draw you a map, for the big waves," she told me, pinching her thumb and forefinger together, pretending to write in the air.

Thrilled at the prospect of finding a surf beach that Mitchell didn't know about, I reached under my seat for my bag, fossicking around in it for pen and paper. The only paper I could find was the envelope Gabrielle had given me. Inside it was Adam's letter.

She'd promised me a passing grade if I translated without cheating. Was asking Heloise to translate cheating? Perhaps it was bending the rules – but I did it anyway.

"It will be broken," she told me, referring to the difference in dialect.

"No worries," I assured her, unfolding the letter.

Heloise reluctantly took it and began to read.

At first, I couldn't understand Gabrielle's eagerness for me to read it. Adam wrote about his first few weeks in law school, his family and his friends. It was lovely to hear – but not meant for me. None of it was meant for me; but there had to be a reason the pushy Parisienne insisted that I read it.

Heloise got to the last paragraph. I could tell by the way she touched each word with her finger as she read. Slowly, she translated and I pieced together the grammatical gaps.

"How is Charlotte? It seems strange to ask. I think of her every day and the strangest things remind me of her. I arrived home to find a new painting hanging in the foyer of our building. It's huge, Gabi. Most would see a vase of orange tulips. I stare at it like an idiot, seeing a hotel for fairies."

Heloise frowned perhaps doubting her translation. I tried to gather my thoughts, but it defied logic. Our garden had never been home to orange tulips before, yet for the past few weeks I'd seen them every time I left the house. Whenever Adam left his house, half a world away, he saw them too.

Pointing to the letter, I prompted her to continue.

"Please tell her I love her. It's purely for my benefit, not hers. Wait until she's sleeping. She won't argue the point with you then."

My chest felt tight. I glanced around to see if anyone else looked like they were about to implode. I expected little yellow oxygen masks to start dropping down. Nothing. I was the only one experiencing bone-crushing air deprivation.

"You are Charlotte?" asked Heloise, tapping the page.

I nodded, unable to speak. "The boy loves you." She spoke gently, perhaps sensing my distress.

"He does," I agreed, shakily.

"Do you love him?"

"Yes."

She leaned back in her seat, brought her hand to her chest and patted her heart. "A girl of courage would fight for him," she said.

By the time we landed I was exhausted, physically and mentally. Mitchell, having slept for hours, was raring to go. We cleared customs, grabbed our luggage and stumbled out into the sunshine.

"Hurry up, Charli. You're a long way from where you need to be," griped Mitchell, realising I was lagging behind. He meant the long walk to the cab rank but I interpreted it differently.

I was nine thousand miles from where I needed to be. Trekking to New York was always going to be wrong. It was crazy. But everything I'd ever shared with Adam was magic.

There was an unwritten rule in La La Land. Magic trumps crazy every time.

The End.

Please turn the page to read an excerpt of Second Hearts, Book II of The Wishes Series.

Second Hearts

By GJ Walker-Smith

1. Sober Words

It was shaping up to be a bad day.

We'd been in the tiny southwestern African town of Kaimte for almost three months, the longest we'd stayed anywhere since leaving Australia over a year earlier.

Kaimte was a haven for backpackers over the summer months. Constant sunny weather and brilliant surf were a huge drawcard. Casual work was easy to find and short-term rental properties were in abundance, thanks mainly to a local landlord called Leroy Van Der Walt.

He owned a long row of decrepit old shacks along the beach, affectionately known as the cardboard village. The miniscule rent he charged made them perfect abodes for non-discerning tenants like us.

Mitchell maintained that one big winter storm would be all it would take to send the huts toppling like a deck of cards. On days when the wind shifted the loose roof tiles, and we could see sunlight bleeding through the cracks in the ceiling, I believed him. Not surprisingly, our plan was to be long gone before winter.

Leroy was a great landlord – unless you owed him money or needed something repaired. It wasn't unusual for residents to pack up and skip town in the middle of the night rather than face him over a couple of hundred dollars in owed rent. Defaulters often came home to find all of their possessions scattered along the beach in front of their house. He was by far the most intimidating man I'd ever met. And that was partly the reason it was shaping up to be a very bad day.

Our rent was due.

Mitchell and I had secured jobs within days of hitting town. I waitressed at a local café and Mitchell laboured for a local building company. The money wasn't great but we were managing.

Every Friday afternoon Mitchell would walk to Leroy's office in town to deliver the rent. It was a routine that had gone off without a hitch for weeks – until today.

Taking a short cut through an industrial estate didn't work out so well. Mitchell was a big guy, over six foot tall and brawny, but he was powerless against the three men that knocked him to the ground and emptied his pockets.

Sore and shaken, he made his way home sporting a nasty cut above his eye.

"I think it needs stitching," I said, working hard to keep the worry out of my voice.

"We don't have money for rent, Charli. We definitely don't have money for a doctor," he grumbled.

Gingerly removing the cloth from his forehead, I held it out to him. I didn't need to speak. Mitchell grabbed my wrist and pulled it back to his face, catching the trickle of blood as it ran down his cheek. "I'll go to Zoe," he said shakily.

We'd met a lot of travellers during our time in Kaimte. Mitchell had fallen head over heels for an English nurse called Zoe. I don't think it was quite love – just major like. She was a female version of him. Blonde, tanned and good looking.

Twenty-four year old Zoe and her best friend Rose lived a few houses down from ours, at number sixty-three – a curious number considering the amount of shacks totalled eighteen. Maybe the other forty-five had succumbed to the weather – or a rampaging Leroy.

By the time we'd made the short trek down the beach to their house, I was exhausted. Mitchell's arm was slung over my shoulder and I did my best to prop him up but it was hopeless. Woozy and weak, he was dead weight.

Zoe appeared on the balcony as soon as I called her name. "What on earth happened?"

"He was mugged," I explained, staggering to the side as Mitchell did. "I think he needs stitches."

"Oh, dear. I'd better take a look then."

Zoe walked out the front door a minute later, armed with a small toiletry bag filled with medical supplies. Mitchell sat down on the edge of the veranda and she knelt in front of him, humming a tune as she stitched him back together.

"It could have happened anywhere," she reasoned. "I once had my handbag snatched in Knightsbridge. Any place can be rough."

I wasn't used to rough. I was used to Pipers Cove. The only crimes to happen there were crimes against fashion. And as strong and tough as Mitchell was, he was clearly traumatised by the whole ordeal too. His hands were uncontrollably shaking.

"There. All done," Zoe announced, quickly kissing his lips before leaning back to admire her work.

Mitchell snaked his arm around her waist and pulled her in close again. That was my cue to leave. He could thank her in private. I needed time alone to think.

Hanging out at our shack wasn't exactly inspiring so it wasn't something I did often. It was tiny and tragically under furnished. Our beds, two beanbags and an old tea chest were just about all we had, and unless I could come up with a way of paying the rent, we were about to lose it all.

***

Daylight had long since faced by the time Mitchell arrived home. He looked a mess. A jagged line of sharp black sutures ran horizontally across his brow and in the few hours since I'd seen him, his eye had blackened.

He smiled. "No real harm done, Charli."

"It doesn't look that way."

He flopped down beside me on the beanbag, pushing me aside. "What are you doing?"

Irate, I shoved him with all my might, and didn't shift him an inch. "Trying to work out how we're going to make up the rent."

"What did you come up with?"

342

"I think we should move on," I suggested. "We can fly north to Dakar and go just about anywhere from there."

Half frowning, he brought his hand to his head. It must have been an expression that hurt. "I like it here. I thought you did too. What happened to our plan of staying until the end of summer?"

"I want to leave, Mitch."

"Look, if it's about the rent – "

"It's not about the rent. Didn't today frighten you?"

Mitchell drew in a deep breath, exhaling slowly. "I'm sure it was a one-off. I shouldn't have been anywhere near that area."

"What if I had been with you?"

"I would never have taken you down there," he scoffed.

I changed tack, still trying to talk him around. "We've been here a long time. There are other places to see."

Levering himself off the beanbag, he reached for my hand, pulling me to my feet. "I like it here, Charli."

I had no right to argue with him. Mitchell had made so many concessions for me over the past year that pushing the issue would have been criminal.

Whether I liked it or not, our partnership was never going to be equal. Throughout our trip he had protected me, watched out for me and sometimes carried me, never once complaining. I don't know what I did for him, other than provide company. And judging by the string of broken romances he'd left along the way, companionship was not something Mitchell Tate ever lacked in the first place.

We never argued. It wasn't something he was good at. When we disagreed, he'd walk away before I had a chance to kick up. He didn't respond the being given the silent treatment either. If anything, he seemed to enjoy it. That meant I had no choice but to let the subject drop – for now.

***

It took three days for Kaimte's very own dictator to catch up with us. Leroy was sitting on our porch when we arrived home from our morning surf. We'd had fair warning that he was there. His loud paisley shirt could be seen from half a mile down the beach.

The aging man with wiry long grey hair walked with a wooden cane. It was an unnecessary prop. There was nothing frail about him. It was more likely a big walloping stick for his delinquent tenants.

I approached the shack with my arm hooked tightly around Mitchell's.

"I'll deal with it," he promised, leaning down to whisper the words.

I nodded stiffly.

"I've been waiting for you two," roared Leroy, levering himself off the deckchair with his cane.

"We just need a few more days," explained Mitchell.

"Impossible!" he boomed, smashing the cane down on the concrete floor. "You're out!"

"We just need a couple more days, Leroy," pleaded Mitchell.

Pointing his cane, Leroy stared straight at me, narrowing his already beady eyes.

My grip on Mitchell's hand tightened.

"I've been more than patient with you two. You have twenty-four hours." It didn't sound like much but coming from Leroy, it was a remarkably generous gesture.

"We'll have it for you tomorrow," promised Mitchell, relieved.

I said absolutely nothing during the whole exchange. Leroy hung around much longer than necessary, ranting and raving about how irresponsible we were, occasionally whacking his cane on the floor for effect. By the time he finally left, I was a nervous wreck.

I followed Mitchell into the house and paced around the small room, trying to calm myself down. Mitchell didn't look anxious at all. He flopped down on the beanbag, leaned back and closed his eyes. I hoped he was hatching a plan and not sleeping.

"What are we going to do?"

"We're going to pay him," he replied flatly.

"With what? Good intentions?"

He opened his eyes, tilted his head, grinning craftily at me. "Since when have I been full of good intentions? We'll just have to dip into the travel money."

His lax solution infuriated me. Keeping money aside for plane tickets was the most sensible thing we'd done. Neither of us had saved a cent during our time in Kaimte so our travel kitty was the only hope we had of being able to move on.

"If we use that money, we'll never save it up again. We're never going to get out of here."

"Charli, have I ever let you down?" I glared at him and he laughed. "Okay, let me rephrase my question. Have I ever let you down since we left home?"

"No," I mumbled.

"So trust me."

I trusted Mitchell implicitly but that was beside the point. My desire to leave was growing stronger. Unfortunately, he didn't feel the same way.

"I'm not going to be able to talk you around, am I?"

"I like it here, Charli," he repeated for the umpteenth time. "I just want to see the summer out."

I shook my head, defeated. I walked out of the room giving him the false impression that the matter was closed.

***

I was less than thrilled with the idea of using our travel money to pay the back rent but we had no choice. Mitchell retrieved it from our hiding spot under the loose floorboards in my bedroom and took it to Leroy the next day. We were square. The monkey was off our back.

I took every extra shift at work that was going over the next week, desperate to build up our savings again. Being a grown up was beginning to suck.

Free time was usually spent at the beach or hanging out with our friends. Any precious free time I had lately was spent sleeping, which is why seeing a group of people partying on the beach in front of our shack when I got home made me groan out loud.

"Charli!" Mitchell called, rushing toward me. He lifted me entirely off my feet as he hugged me much too tightly. "I'm glad you're home."

I wondered if that was because his party was already out of hand and he needed me to tell them all off and send them home. It had happened before.

"Why are we having a party, Mitch?"

He slung his arm around my shoulder as we walked. "I only invited Zoe and Rose for a few drinks, but you know how word travels."

I looked ahead to the house. He wasn't kidding. All of our fellow cardboard villagers seemed to be there. A huge bonfire roared. The sun was setting, slipping behind the line where the ocean met the sky. The air was still and warm. It was the perfect night for a party.

Rose and Zoe sat on the front step talking to Melito and Vincent. Mitchell had nicknamed them the sleek Greeks because of their Casanova type personalities. They lived in the shack next to ours and were forever bringing us trays of pastries and other homemade treats.

"From our motherland," Melito would proudly announce.

Mitchell would tease me, insisting that it was their way of trying to woo me. Mitchell missed the bigger picture. I was certain that middle-aged sleek Greeks had eyes only for each other.

The residents of number four were a Lebanese couple, Rashid and Sabah. Their English was poor so conversing with them was very difficult. Our friendship was based purely on smiles and hand gestures.

Bernie and William, two twenty-something Brits taking a year long sabbatical from their jobs in advertising found their way to Kaimte after reading a travel brochure at a bus stop in Tanzania.

Our new friends were the most eclectic bunch of people imaginable.

It was Vincent who called out to me first, raising his glass in my direction and speaking loudly. "Welcome, Charli!"

Before I'd even stepped up on to the porch, I had a glass of cheap wine in one hand and a plate of food in the other.

The last of our guests finally left at three in the morning, relocating next door to Melito and Vincent's shack. Rose, Zoe, Bernie and William were lured over there by the promise of ouzo and Greek pastries.

I collared Mitchell at the door. The last thing he needed was more alcohol. "Stay here with me."

I tugged on his shirt and he staggered back as if I'd tripped him. It was impossible to think I could save him if he'd fallen. All I could do was step aside to stop him squashing me on the way down. Somehow he remained upright by leaning his back against the wall for support. "You're my best friend," he slurred.

I smiled at him. "You're my best friend too."

"Leaving the Cove was a good decision. We have fun don't we?"

Mitchell was very reflective when soused. It made a nice change. He wasn't exactly renowned for deep conversation when sober.

"We do. Are you ready for bed?"

"That wouldn't be a good idea for three reasons," he said, holding four fingers in the air.

"What reasons?"

"One, I'm scared of your dad." He took a heavy step toward me. "And two, I'm very afraid of your dad."

I had to laugh. Alex was scary where Mitchell was concerned, even from half a world away.

Alex and Gabrielle packed up and left Pipers Cove a couple of months after us, arriving in Marseille in time to spend Christmas with her family. That was supposed to be their happy ever after. But through no fault of Alex's, they ended up back in Piper's Cove six weeks later, just in time for Gabrielle to resume her teaching position at beginning of the school term. *She* got homesick.

It turned out that small town gossip and her little cottage on the cliff trumped Marseillaise castles and baguettes. I doubt Alex tried too hard to talk her out of returning to the Cove, nor would he have needed to. He was never thrilled about leaving in the first place. He was, however, still thrilled by anything to do with the Parisienne.

Mitchell took another step forward; so unsteadily that it couldn't possibly have been intentional. Both of my arms shot out in front of me. Luckily, he managed to steady himself.

"What's the third reason?" I asked.

Mitchell turned around and staggered toward the beanbag. He fell into it so hard that I was worried it might explode. "The third reason doesn't matter. Reasons one and two cancel out the need for reason three."

"Tell me reason three," I demanded.

He looked at me through lazy eyes, probably seeing little more than a blurred form in front of him. "Reason number three. Never sleep with a girl who's in love with someone else."

"Yeah, okay. You got me. I'm madly in love with Vincent."

He groaned. "I'm not an idiot, Charli. It's written all over your face.... and your diary. You still love Adam and no matter how far away you go, it's not far enough."

"You read my journal?" I was appalled and embarrassed.

It was the first diary I'd ever kept. I'd always maintained that pouring your heart out via pen and paper was asking for trouble and Mitchell's snooping confirmed it. My journal had nothing to do with documenting our trip or my day-to-day life. Our trip was well documented by the thousands of pictures I'd taken. I wrote about things that were too hard to explain, and too private to tell anyone. Mainly, I wrote about *him*.

Even in my head, I referred to Adam as *him*.

I had travelled many thousands of miles from home but hadn't moved an inch. A year apart had changed nothing. I loved him. I had always loved him. And my decision to end our relationship had grown in to the most painful regret of my life.

"I didn't mean to read it," he said, unconvincingly. "I didn't even know you kept a diary."

"You weren't supposed to know," I barked. "It was private."

"I read the whole thing. Every word."

"Ugh! Shut up!"

"It was actually pretty good. March was pretty dull but it picked up again in April."

"Shut up, Mitchell!"

I wanted to clout him but it wouldn't have been a fair fight. He was clearly disadvantaged by the alcohol he'd consumed. It was acting as a truth serum and for some reason he just couldn't stop talking. "You should find a better hiding spot if you don't want me to read it." He shifted to the side, producing my journal from my not-so-great hiding spot under the beanbag. "Ta-daa!"

I snatched it from him. "There's something seriously wrong with you."

"I know," he agreed. "But there's nothing wrong with you."

I shook my head, scowling at him. "What are you talking about?"

He made a half-hearted swipe for the book in my hands but was too uncoordinated to take it from me. "I read it. Have you ever read what you've written? If you did, you'd see that there's nothing wrong with you. You're just scared. You were scared when we left home and you're scared now."

He'd hit my rawest nerve, dead on. "And you're drunk."

"Of course I'm drunk. Do you think we'd be having this conversation otherwise? Get brave, Charli. Toughen up and go after what you want."

Within days of leaving Australia I'd made my decision. I planned to spend a few weeks travelling with Mitchell before jumping on a plane to New York.

But time was my enemy.

After three amazing weeks of surfing in Mauritius we found our way to Madagascar. By the time we arrived in Johannesburg six weeks after that I was second-guessing my decision.

What if he'd moved on? What if he'd met someone else? Or worse, what if he'd forgotten all about me? The longer I spent without him, the more I'd convinced myself that Adam Décarie was doing just fine without me.

Writing down my fears had preserved my sanity. I was on the trip of a lifetime, visiting some of the most beautiful places on earth and yet I couldn't shake the hopelessness of being completely in love with a boy I'd known for only two months – a very long time ago.

"It's not that simple," I mumbled.

The beans crunched beneath him as he struggled to lean forward. Grabbing his hand, I tried to help him to his feet. Once upright, he fell forward, pushing me backwards. I laid flat on the floor, struggling under his weight.

"It's totally simple," he said, ignoring the fact that I was gasping for breath beneath him. "What's the worst that could happen?"

Answering him required air in my lungs. With both hands on his chest, I managed to heave him off me. "What if I go all the way to New York and he doesn't want me?"

"Then you put it to bed. But at least you'll know you've given it your best shot."

I turned my head to look at him, marvelling at the fact that Mitchell Tate somehow managed to become smarter when intoxicated. "What would you do without me?"

He sighed. "I'd manage. I've matured a lot lately." A huge burst of laughter escaped me but his tone remained serious. "It's been a long time since I did anything dumb like try to cook popcorn in a frying pan."

"Mitch, that happened a week ago," I reminded, in between giggles.

He reached across for my hand. "I'd be fine, Charli. And you would be too."

***

I dragged myself out of bed at ten the next morning. Mitchell was already up, sitting on the front veranda soaking up the morning sun, eating something that looked remarkably like one of Melito's filo pastry creations from the night before.

"Is your stomach made of cast iron?" I asked, appalled.

He turned around to face me, grinned and stuffed the whole thing into his mouth.

We sat on the raised veranda, dangling our legs over the edge, gazing at the uninterrupted view of the ocean ahead. The veranda was the only redeeming feature of the shack. Some days, when the ocean was a millpond and we weren't working, we'd waste the entire morning out there.

"You just missed Bernie and Will," he said, grinning. "They were on their way home from the sleek Greeks. It turns out that the party got a whole lot rowdier once we left."

"What did they have to say for themselves?"

He shrugged his shoulders. "Not much. They did mention that they're thinking of heading up the coast next weekend. I wouldn't mind a weekend up north. Too bad we're broke and trapped like rats."

He bumped my shoulder and I looked across at him. I couldn't help smiling at his goofy expression. Mitchell was back to being carefree, content and sober. Nothing fazed him – even the prospect of being a broke, trapped, rat.

That's where we differed. I was beginning to feel as though I was failing and it was starting to weigh me down. The whole purpose of this journey was to find my place in the world. We'd travelled thousands of miles. How far was I supposed to go for crying out loud?

I had to consider that I'd been wrong all along. What if happiness wasn't a place? What if it was enough just to be with the person who made you happy? Surely then I'd be content wherever I was – even if it was New York City.

I looked at the bigger picture. There was a possibility that I had thrown away the best love I would ever know. And going through the daily grind of surfing, working and sleeping was doing nothing to get it back.

"Mitch, do you remember our conversation last night?" I quizzed.

A slow smile crept across his face. "Refresh my memory."

I rolled my eyes. "We talked about me going to New York. I think I'm going to do it."

"It's about time," he teased. "I was beginning to think I'd be stuck with you forever."

I nudged his shoulder with mine, faking annoyance. "Don't get too excited. It's going to take months to save up."

"Why don't you just call Alex? He'd send you money if you needed it."

The mere suggestion bordered on lunacy. As far as Alex knew, I was comfortably living on the proceeds from the sale of Adam's boat. If he ever got wind that we were broke he'd have a coronary.

"I'm going to work it out for myself."

"I'll find extra work, Charli. I'll do what I can."

"You don't need to do that. I only need one thing from you."

"Name it."

"Don't let me talk myself out of going. No matter how long it takes."

Mitchell reached out to me, slinging his arm around my shoulders. "You got it, sister."

2. Crazy Brave

The midweek markets in Kaimte had to be seen to be believed. Vendors selling everything from local crafts to fresh fish and vegetables crowded in to a row of tin humpies lining the main street. I loved the atmosphere.

I roped Zoe and Rose into coming with me. I usually went with Mitchell but true to his word, he'd found extra work that week, labouring for a landscaper.

"It's so grotty," whispered Zoe, much too loudly.

Rose shushed her, grabbed her elbow and quickened her pace.

"It's all really fresh," I told her.

"Of course it is," she scoffed. "It's all still covered in dirt."

Zoe was a mixed bag. I'd always suspected that backpacking was more Rose's bliss than hers. She was a girly girl who liked her creature comforts far too much to be completely content living in the cardboard village.

On the other hand, carrying out a torrid affair with a beach bum surfer like Mitchell showed that she wasn't totally averse to slumming it once in a while.

Mitchell's attraction to Zoe was much easier to define. She was part Beautiful, just like his sisters. She was prissy and her penchant for tiny bikinis and matching sarongs bordered on trashy. But Zoe would never graduate to full Beautiful status. She was far too smart and too kind-hearted, even if scrubbing dirt off vegetables was beneath her.

"Can we sit for a while? It's hot," she complained.

I looked around, trying to see somewhere suitable to dump her for a few minutes while I finished browsing.

"There," suggested Rose, pointing to a small shed over the road.

The makeshift café only traded on market days. Thirsty patrons sat outside on dirty plastic chairs, drinking lukewarm cans of Coke.

"Will you be okay here for a minute?" I asked hopefully. "I just want to check out the stalls over there." I pointed further down the street, but she paid no attention.

"We'll wait here for you," promised Rose.

I had walked only a few metres away from them before the crowd swamped me. I couldn't even see the café when I turned around. All I could do was keep pace with the flow of traffic.

Some days I hated being short. I walked for a few minutes, seeing nothing but people's backs before finally breaking off to the side. I had no idea where I was. I didn't seem to be in the markets anymore. The buildings were permanent structures but still ramshackle and dilapidated.

To my left was a fabric store, overflowing with bolts of brightly coloured cloth. A heavyset African woman stood in the doorway calling me inside with a flick of her head. "Come and see, little girl," she coaxed.

My reply was forceful but polite. "No, thank you."

I began walking again but got no further than the shop next door to hers. A man tugged at my backpack as I passed his doorway, yanking me inside. "Little girl," he purred. "Come inside."

It was hardly an invitation. I was already inside. The relative safety of the road might as well have been miles away.

Desperate to regain some control, I turned around, pretending to browse the shelves. Crooked wooden shelves lined the corrugated tin walls, displaying dodgy looking electrical items and bric-a-brac.

The man followed very closely behind me as I walked, but he wasn't the scariest one in the shop. Another two men sat near the back wall, leering at me.

Playing it cool was not an option. I was utterly terrified. No one knew where I was. *I* didn't even know where I was.

"You have a nice shop," I complimented shakily.

He looked past me to the other men, speaking in a language I didn't understand. More unnervingly, they all laughed.

I didn't dare look at the thugs behind me. All of my attention was on the one blocking my exit.

"Find what you like," he instructed. "We buy and we sell."

I nodded, unable to swallow away the lump in my throat so I could speak.

They weren't typical villagers. Their clothes were western style. The ringleader wore jeans and a long-sleeved shirt – totally inappropriate considering the hot weather. Around his neck was the thickest gold chain I'd ever seen. The necklace looked authentic but the huge kitschy gold Rolex watch he wore looked like a prize out of a gumball machine.

"We have phones. Do you need a phone?" he asked.

His question reminded me that my phone was in my bag – albeit useless. Who was I going to call? Mitchell's phone had been stolen during the mugging. I could call Alex. If he hurried, he could catch the next flight out and come to my rescue in about three days.

Quickly, I hatched a plan. Mitchell needed a phone. I'd buy one, thank the scary men and hopefully be on my way in one piece.

"I will buy a phone," I told him, trying to sound strong.

Rolex man clicked his fingers twice. "Get the box," he ordered.

I heard the goons behind me shuffle to their feet.

Please don't let it be a Charli size box, I prayed.

I contemplated making a run for the bright light of the outside street but wasn't sure I'd make it out before he grabbed me again. When he called me over to the counter, I did as he asked.

The smaller of the henchmen upended a cardboard box on the counter sending at least fifty phones tumbling in all directions.

"I'll give you a good price," he assured. "Choose one."

They all looked the same to me – with one exception. Mitchell's phone had a distinctive bright orange cover, just like one of the phones in front of me.

I picked it up, moving quickly to hide the fact that my hand was shaking.

"I like this one."

"A very good choice," praised Rolex man. "It's only just come in."

I was certain it was Mitchell's phone. My potential murderers were also vicious thieves. Fear quickly gave way to anger. Standing in front of me were the men who'd knocked the stuffing out of Mitchell and left him bleeding in an alley. Convinced that my fate would soon be the same (or worse) I realised I had nothing to lose. "I have something to sell," I announced, shrugging my off my backpack.

The men watched silently as I took out my camera and unscrewed the lens. If there was a chance I might live to continue my trip, I didn't want to do it without my beloved camera. Parting with one lens was bearable.

Rolex man studied it closely. "This is no good without the camera. I will take both."

I shook my head. "No. Just the lens."

"No." He handed it back to me.

I actually felt deflated. For a second, I'd been hopeful of solving all of our money problems. I saw no point in haggling with him. He was calling the shots and I'd just revealed all of my cards. The thieving would-be murderers now knew I had a valuable camera in my possession.

"What else do you have?"

I tried to think quickly but came up blank.

"The stone," he said, pointing to my necklace.

I brought my hand to my throat, clutching my black opal pendant.

"No." My rough tone made them laugh.

"Black opal is rare and valuable," said Rolex man, amazing me with his knowledge of gemology. "Give it to me."

I wanted to put up a good fight. He was probably about to rip it off my neck at any second anyway. "I want five thousand for it. U.S. dollars," I declared.

A huge grin swept his face and I could hear the other men snickering. "You are a very funny girl." Funny was good. Funny meant they might not kill me.

"Five thousand," I repeated.

Rolex man paced around, rubbing his chin while he deliberated. "I will give you three thousand."

It was actually a pretty fair offer – much less than what it was worth but not altogether unreasonable. I had to consider it. Three thousand dollars was a ticket to New York and back again if I needed it. I tried to focus more on the bigger picture and less on the heartbreak of parting with the opal Adam had gifted me.

"Fine. Three thousand.... and the orange phone," I agreed. "And I want U.S. dollars."

"I do not keep that amount of money here. There are many thieves around." I almost laughed out loud but thought better of it. "I will have to go and get it."

"I'll wait." I truly was an idiot.

More than an hour and a half passed before Rolex man returned. I had no choice but to wait for him. I got the distinct feeling I wasn't free to leave. He strolled in as if he'd been gone only minutes and dropped a tattered manila envelope down on the counter in front of me. "Count it," he instructed.

I thumbed through the notes, counting silently in my head. I was glad I counted silently. Unbelievably, there was an extra four hundred dollars in the pile.

"Three thousand dollars, right?" I asked, confused.

"That is what we agreed."

I quickly tucked the envelope under my arm, hoping that the smugness wasn't evident in my expression. With a heavy heart, I undid the clasp on my necklace and handed it to Rolex man.

"Come back any time," he said, focusing all of his attention on the necklace in his hand.

I didn't bother answering him. I turned around and walked as fast as I could, straight out into the safety of the crowded street. It had been almost two hours since I'd left Rose and Zoe at the café. Knowing they'd be long gone, I began walking home, totally oblivious to how frantic Mitchell would be.

"Where the hell have you been?" he yelled, running down the beach toward me. "The girls said they lost you. I've been looking everywhere."

I stopped dead in my tracks, bracing myself as he threw his arms around me. It wasn't a tight hug, just badly executed. Perhaps he forgot that he was a foot taller than me and that's why he hugged my head.

He looked me up and down, inspecting for damage.

"I'm fine," I insisted.

"Where have you been?"

I was excited to tell him. Doing business with gangsters wasn't an every day event for me. Mitchell didn't seem to share my enthusiasm but to his credit, he let me finish the tale before berating me. "You sold your necklace to thugs? Are you out of your freaking mind?"

"You're the one who told me to get brave."

He wrinkled his nose at the reminder of his drunken remark. "You weren't meant to take it so literally! What if something had happened to you? Imagine *that* phone call to Alex." He groaned in absolute disgust.

"I'm sorry."

"I'm done. Don't talk to me." he quickened his pace, knowing there was no way I could keep up with his long strides.

Mitchell didn't go home. He trudged through the sand, up to Zoe and Rose's hut, disappearing through the front door as soon as it opened. I didn't really care. I was still flying high, exhilarated by my rare rush of courage. The feeling remained long after I arrived home. I sat on the floor, counting out the hundred dollar bills and stacking them in a neat pile, elated to confirm there was indeed an extra four hundred dollars in my bounty.

I, Charli Blake, had successfully crossed into the big leagues. I'd ripped off my very first gangsters.

The money was safely tucked away under the loose floorboard when Mitchell arrived home.

He walked in and thumped down beside me on the beanbag, throwing me aside like a ragdoll. I waited for him to speak first, unsure if he was still angry.

"I'm sorry I yelled at you. You deserved it but I am sorry. I'm not your keeper. It's not my job to look after you." His speech was obviously well rehearsed. He spoke slowly and precisely.

"But you do look after me. I would never have made it this far without you. Today turned out to be good for me. It's my turn to look after you."

Mitchell tilted his head, staring at me like I was crazy. "How do you figure that?"

I reached into my bra, retrieved his orange phone and held it out to him.

"I think this belongs to you."

He snatched it from me, shaking his head in disbelief. The colour literally drained from his face. He realised what I already knew. I'd spent the afternoon in the company of the men who put six stitches in his forehead.

"Did you see what they did to me to get this phone?" he asked, gritting his teeth. "If they'd cut you up in to tiny little pieces and chucked you in a dumpster, you would have deserved it. And you think today was a good day for you?"

Seeing Mitchell angry was completely foreign territory. I had no idea how to handle him. "The end justified the means, Mitch. I've got enough money to go to New York now."

He wasn't the least bit impressed by my sketchy reasoning. "You're never going to see sense, are you? I can't let you go off on your own, Charli. It's not going to end well."

"You can't stop me." I regretted the childish comment instantly. I'd just made him more furious.

Mitchell quickly stood up. "I don't want to stop you. It's not up to me to stop you. You get yourself in to the worst scrapes purely because you don't think." He tapped his temple with his index finger. "How much thought have you put in to your trip to New York?"

"Enough," I uttered.

"Great. So you've contacted Adam to tell him you're on your way."

"No," I scoffed.

Where was the romance in that?

Mitchell leaned down close to me. "You know why you haven't called him, Charli?" He didn't pause long enough to let me answer. "Because you're winging it, just like you always do. Leaving things up to the universe isn't always going to work in your favour."

I didn't feel as though there was an alternative. If I'd put any real thought into it, I'd talk myself out of going. I desperately wanted Adam back in my life. I craved the happy ending I'd been dreaming of for over a year. But in the back of my mind was one constant thought. He might not want me anymore. No amount of planning would prepare me for that. I had no choice but to throw it out to the universe. Whatever would be would be.

It was that philosophy that got me through my encounter with Rolex man and his henchmen. Explaining it to Mitchell was impossible. I saw no point even trying. "I think we should agree to disagree."

"Fine, crazy weirdo."

I'd heard him call his sisters a mountain of names far worse than that.

Crazy weirdo, I could live with.

3. Lessons

New York in November was not a place I wanted to be
without winter clothing. There wasn't much call for winter
coats in Kaimte – or anywhere else we'd been in the past year.
One phone call to Gabrielle solved that problem, and one I
hadn't even considered.

Within days of speaking to her, Mitchell and I
borrowed Melito's jeep and drove down to the parcel depot at
the small airport. Waiting for me was a huge suitcase filled
with enough winter clothes to see me through several New
York winters.

"She was supposed to just pack up my stuff," I
grumbled, poring through the mass of clothes on the floor in
front of me.

"Beggars can't be choosers, Charli," teased Mitchell,
pulling a very chic grey wool cap on to his head.

I didn't recognise a single item. I couldn't even
consider them to be hand-me-downs. Everything was brand
new, including the shiny brass key that tumbled out of an
envelope I'd just found.

Mitchell waited until I'd read through the
accompanying letter before asking me what it was for.

"This," I said, waving the key in front of him, "is a key
to an apartment Gabrielle owns in Manhattan."

Of course the Parisienne owned real estate in New
York. Nothing about the idea was shocking to me.

"You really do have a way of falling on your feet, don't
you?" he asked, donning the scarf that matched his hat.

"I have connections," I replied, leaning forward to
snatch the hat off his head.

It was almost embarrassing. I was hardly able to claim
independence when I'd been gifted a roof over my head and a
complete new wardrobe to boot.

"Can I ask you a question?" Mitchell's tone matched his suddenly serious expression.

"Sure."

"What are you going to do if it doesn't work out with Adam? A lot can change in a year."

I paused only momentarily. "I'll be sad."

Truthfully, I'd be devastated. I'd probably just curl up and let the despair have me. At least I'd look good, courtesy of my new designer wardrobe. But all Mitchell needed to know was that I had enough smarts about me to be able to survive. Alex had demanded the same reassurance. He'd never understood my need to have Adam in my life. Needing him was never a term he was comfortable with.

"He might not feel the same way, Charli," he'd said gently.

When it came down to it, it didn't matter. I wanted to see his face – even if it was to be for the last time. I had thought of nothing past that point.

***

Once all loose ends had been tied, there was no point in staying in Kaimte any longer. Letting go of Mitchell was going to be hard so I drew it out as long as I could. We made a weekend of it, borrowing Melito's jeep again and driving south to Cape Town. Two days passed quickly and before I knew it, we were saying our goodbyes at the airport.

"If it doesn't work out, you come back," he instructed.

"I will."

Excitement bubbled within me, which prevented me from standing still. Mitchell grabbed my hand to keep me stationary while he rattled off his list of rules. "Don't let anyone near your bag, make sure you keep some money in your pocket, call me as soon as you get there and don't forget to wind your watch back."

"Anything else?"

"Yes." He released my hand and slung his arm around my shoulder. "Don't talk to strangers."

I smirked at him. "Mitch, everyone will be a stranger."

"Okay, don't talk to strange looking strangers," he amended.

There were a million things I wanted to tell him, none of which I could articulate into a sentence that would be true enough.

Mitchell Tate had saved me. At the lowest of the low, after my best friend Nicole had betrayed and deserted me, he'd picked me up and dusted me off. We hadn't spent longer than a few hours apart in over a year. Mitchell had never needed me. I however, wouldn't have survived the first week away from home without him.

There was something very cathartic about leaving him behind. Mitchell was free to make his own way without having to worry about me.

He wouldn't have to worry about the rent for a while either. I'd used some of my gangster loot to pay his rent up until the end of summer. It's not something he would have approved of so I held off telling him until the very last minute.

"You're going to need that money," he scolded.

"You can't miss what you don't have."

"I know for a fact that's not true. I'm going to miss you, crazy weirdo." He grabbed my face in his hands and kissed me hard on the lips. "Now go. You've got a plane to catch."

I fought against turning back to look at him as I made my way through to the departure lounge. The only way from there was forward.

27308149R00197

Made in the USA
Lexington, KY
05 November 2013